OSBORNE'S ARMY

By the same author

CALL OUT THE MALICIA

John Anthony West

OSBORNE'S ARMY

NEW YORK
WILLIAM MORROW & COMPANY, INC.
1967

OSBORNE'S ARMY

Gradually the word spread. A deserted island: full of
women: with free drinks. Amos Osborne had rediscovered
the island of Escondite (*see page* 11).

His friends came (*page* 108).
And the friends of his friends (*page* 128).
And those who were not so friendly (*page* 194).
And those who were not friendly at all (*page* 216).
And ultimately:—Grockles (*page* 224).

Osborne decided that action was called for (*page* 273).
Action which shocked the world (*page* 280).

¿No oyes el relinchar de los caballos, el tocar de los clarines, el ruido de los atambores?

No oigo otra cosa—respondio Sancho—sino muchos balidos de ovejas y carneros . . .

Dost thou not hear the neighing of the steeds, the clarions's call and the sound of the drums?

I hear nothing—answered Sancho—but the bleating of many sheep . . .

EXORDIUM

(OSBORNE IS WRONG AND GRIMES IS RIGHT.)

The *Sailing Moon* pushes her blunt prow through the Caribbean her course NE out of Campeche: an island rises before her.

Osborne has checked and rechecked the charts, and nothing short of a hoax (such as forging a chart) explains the island; green and imminent, looming: from what ought to be wide, blue sea.   𝖂

"Yep," Grimes had said, "I been all over the Carib; Tobago, Saba, Désirade, Tortola, all them places; hell, I been to a island that ain't on the map."

Osborne had yawned lazily. And the yawn was lost in the drone of lazy flies. He had ordered another bottle of tequila.

"Come off it, Grimes."

"I tell you I been to an island that ain't on the map."

(So the long afternoon had been a lie; tales of rum-running, gun-running, refugee-running . . .)

"An undiscovered island in the Caribbean?"

"Nope, not undiscovered, forgot. There's a town there, all fallin' apart."

"And no one lives there?"

"Niggers."

"No one knows about the island?"

"Couple people, supposed to be treasure there."

"Then why isn't it on the map?"

"Them's the people don't know about it."

"Hell, Grimes, you're drunk."

"Sure I'm drunk. But I know a secret island."

Osborne poured another drink . . . and smiled.

"Wanna bet? Betcha hunnerd dollars!"   𝖂

At first a humped shape on the horizon, a surfaced but nebulous whale, the island arrays itself in form . . .

The back of a crescent bends toward Mexico; great inland

11

mountains swoop to the sea in valleys, ridges; valleys, ridges; valleys, ridges; and halt, startled, at cliffs plunging sheer; huge broken jugs and pitchers with astonishing glazed blue bottoms, tawny sides shot through with black and ruddy rose; and behind, the mountain peaks, thrusting through collars of trees, reflect and refract sunlight; so fiercely their stone summits shine black: otherwise the island is green.

Osborne is a shaggy figurehead at the prow; a big man in baggy khakis, flat black thatch of hair unruffled by the breeze, a generous roll of middle bulges over his belt, quaking to the arhythmic but soothing percussive line of the 1924 Buick engine:

concentration is impossible in this sunlit world of wind and wave, his eyes slivered against the glare, focused on –but not seeing– the island that shouldn't be (a vague guilt:—for not feeling guilty, conscience in reverse, he is supposed to think these three weeks, sort things out . . .

Returning?

Returning to what? Without a plan, without a solution? He needs concreteness, definity; he doesn't anticipate an ideal; a direction then.

Or an obstacle!

Any obstacle will do.

The future is a stroll into fog on a plain, nothing to stub his toe against, nothing to trip him up, a long meander into anonymity; he needs a stone wall to bash his head against . . .

no, not true either; were that the case he could have stayed in Benghazi; but that hadn't been *his* stone wall . . .)

The *Sailing Moon* nudges closer, cliffs beetle above; now the rain forest, the satin green kimono of the island is bedizened, embroidered, with violent tropical flowers.

But for the chugging of the motor; and idle rumor of water against the hull; there is silence. Osborne searches the jungle for signs of human life and sees: only jungle.

The gentle crescent hooks sharply at the northern tip of the island; the sierra forming its spine ends in a cape of rock, a jutting tawny wedge three hundred feet high; stone bastions, cliff-colored, terrace the top, and above these bastions, rising from patchwork greenery, stands the fortress.

Slowly, the boat wallows around . . .

White, faded pink, faded ocher, mullioned with green, the town tumbles down the hollow of a hill; its apex, a ruined cathedral: its base, mansions gracing the broad beach: as though some giant hand –in anger– had hurled a huge varicolored vessel at the peak of the hill, shattered it, and touched off an avalanche of gay debris; whose force had sent glittering shards and splinters flying far out of the pattern; to find a bright place amid ceiba and acanthus trees.

Osborne goes aft the cabin.

"But Grimes, it's magnificent."

"Nah, when you get up close it's all fallin' apart."

No movement, no vehicle, no smoke; Grimes at the wheel skirting a chain of reefs, gliding through the shadow of the fortress. And Osborne sees turrets and bartizans in ruins; parapets, quoins, all geometric planes humbled by hurricane, sun, and centuries . . . still strong, the fortress no longer stands proud.

Muffled explosions of the engine echo from the rocks, Grimes eases off the throttle. The *Sailing Moon* cleaves, gently, the lagoon's improbably blue, and dawdles in, tantalizing!

Now a gaudy cheering mob throngs the beach. And the clamor is overruled . . .

(Once again Grimes is right.)

Huge houses are shrouded in foliage but this camouflage cannot conceal whole corners gone; great cracks fork through militant façades, stucco facing has fallen away, and the noise of the native crowd at the sea is voided, by the town's silent edict of decay: the sun, beating for the Pacific, balances briefly on the bell tower of the Cathedral.

"You mean no one knows about this place?"

Grimes spins the wheel neatly, corrects, and noses the boat up to a tilting jetty: "Sorta looks that way."

The crowd, a one-celled creature about to burst, surges and writhes; the men, running a color gamut from high yaller to

13

Senegalese indigo are tall and lithe, dressed in crude adaptations of trousers and shirts; the women grin beneath flaming bandannas; spectacular in outrageous sarongs; ear lobes, breasts and bandannas sparkling with baubles and trinkets.

One man steps forward, threads down the blanched broken-keyboard planking of the jetty: onyx black, mummy dry –as though sun had rendered away all flesh and left thin bones, knotted fast with thin sinew– a man definitely past forty, but perhaps seventy, his leather face crinkled as a crone's palm.

Grimes tosses him the frayed hawser and he snubs it to a dubious post. Osborne waits to see what protocol demands; the crowd stands motionless, watching, grinning. Grimes hoists himself to the jetty, the native takes his hand, pumps it gravely, a hundred wrinkles unscramble into a gapped picket-fence smile; "Greem!" he says, and launches into a mellifluous babble vaguely reminiscent of French.

Osborne shifts from foot to foot, gazing.

For the sun has slipped back of the Cathedral, silhouetting it in a blaze of light, long tomcat shadows prowl over the rooftops and walls of the steep town, cabbage palms along the esplanade cast purple simulacra upon the sand; and Osborne feels the languor, the soul, of the sun-mottled reliquary: seeping into his bones. He waves to the waiting crowd and, gaily, they wave back. His name is mentioned, and he climbs to the jetty, to be introduced to Theodore, who pumps his hand, smiles his smile; and singsongs awhile at Grimes.

"He says," says Grimes, "welcome to the island, he likes your size, and let's go have a drink."

"But we finished all the tequila."

"Rum," says Grimes, "make it themselves; oldest still in the Carib, best rum. Hang on . . ." He clambers back aboard, returns in several minutes with a small packing crate. "Fishhooks and crap, bring us back a barrel, trade with the natives."

Along the jetty Theodore moves easily, Grimes with surprising agility, Osborne with difficulty, ungainly, determined not to plunge through one of the laughter-provoking holes. Grinning faces jabber at him, hands reach out for his, and Theodore calls a roll of puckish names –Octavius, Horace, another Horace, Legrand, Bonsoir, Mardi, Cavendish, Pemberton– too quickly for Osborne to associate them with their owners.　🦋

On the beach side of the esplanade, here and there, the bleached shinbones of old sheds and warehouses stand awry; and Theodore's bar –as chieftain it is his privilege to run the bar– is the only building intact; a solid stone structure, with tapered walls, black socket windows, creneled parapet and a single square tower – but lush garlands of bougainvillea festoon encircling trellises, espaliered vines teem up stern walls, and, shaded by palms, potted mangoes, and jacarandas, a gay hodgepodge of tables is spread: wrought iron and marble-topped, rough refectories adzed out of teak, sawed-off battered oil drums; flanked by mahogany chairs intricately carved by long-dead artisans, chairs in looped wickerwork for long lentissimo afternoons, rickety cane chairs strung with hemp, simple chunks of palm stump . . .

The crowd splits, some take seats outside, the rest pour through the arched portal, down three stairs scooped shallow by the feet of the endless thirsty. There is a scrimmage for seats and Osborne, Grimes and Theodore are left standing in the bar; a single great room trisected by columns supporting groined vaults; deep and still deeper shadows play; amid a tangle of arches freedom in successive enclosure. Flintlocks and muskets in rust and verdigris decorate the walls, and moldering paintings of distant sea battles. A bar runs the length of the building and behind it hang mirrors in rococo frames, the gilding gone, the tain flaked away; returning the echo of an image, disconcerting, incomplete; and the air, limestone cool, is pungent with centuries of rum.

At fat casks swollen into their bays, the natives queue; and stand aside for Theodore who fills three brimful noggins.

Osborne sips, then quaffs; his weight eases onto his elbows, the heady rum slides through his system, he basks in visceral sunlight, and when he produces his wallet to pay for the round Grimes grins it away, money is unknown on the island.

15

"Christ! Grimes, what do they call this place?"

"Dunno."

Grimes translates. He had never thought to ask. Then retranslates the answer.

"Home."

It is dusk when they leave: down the broad esplanade; tall weeds sprout between the cobbles; the promenade, once lovingly clipped and plucked, is a shaggy palisade of palm and palmetto; an armadillo scuttles into the brush before them. Unhurried, they climb the winding road to the cane and thatch huts of the natives; night drops, star-shot, and fires burn; earthenware pots and casseroles bubble; the steam is sopped up by a gourmand breeze; and at Theodore's his daughters have prepared a feast: shrimp bisque followed by pompano; doves in mango rind sauce, roast wild pig, and bananas aflame. In a tarnished jorum of cool rum half lemons and oranges bob, and slices of melon smile. Before the meal is over, the music has begun.

(Vacation extended. Why not?

Fishing, loafing, treasure hunting perhaps.

And the tantalizing—why?) It is midmorning, the sun sets the town shimmering; steam ghosts rise from glinting ruins, and hover over jungle-stuffed courtyards.

"Whut if you get sick?"

"I never get sick."

"O.K., it's your funeral. See you nex' month."

And Grimes is off with a scribbled note to Osborne's mother.

Osborne watches the *Sailing Moon* sidle into the swell, yaw round the cliff and disappear. Theodore is with him, and Delia, Theodore's third daughter, and a troop of natives; he listens intently; thinks he hears the senile gasp of the old Buick engine –but he doesn't. In the thicket that once was a promenade birds shriek endless heat-addled insincerities.

(Or is the purloined month cowardly procrastination?)

But he checks his watch; and stretches mightily, his thick joints crackle . . .

16

8:35 A.M. Rush hour in New York.

Theodore says something to him –incomprehensible; and Delia smiles; *café crème*, oriental nuance to her eyes and cheek-bones, almost nothing of her father about her –that abrupt smile. Osborne smiles back. He waves toward the town hoping to convey his intention of exploring, jams his hands into his pockets and sets off at an amble. A number of natives follow. 🐾

The mansions' austere walls hide the wrecked splendor of their interiors; hibiscus, convolvulus and bougainvillea trail over arched entrances; but peering through, spacious plazas and fine marble fountains are unveiled; and palimpsests of formal gardens, still decipherable beneath the tropical scrawling; trees and green-ery obscure delicate two-tiered and three-tiered arcades, with their elaborate balustrades. Behind them, wooden shutters have mold-ered away, or fallen off, or hang askew, and open doors and windows gape.

At one of the hulks, Osborne borrows a machete and hacks into the gloom. Hummingbirds rise to his footfall, explode; red, green, royal blue, purple, the birds spark off into nothing; and from the highest arcade, in a shock of light, bright against black doorways, hilarious parrots scream. Osborne fights through vines and brush to an iron-bound brass-studded door, which groans, then gives before his two hundred and thirty pounds; and he is in a dim room rank with desuetude. The crystal chandelier has fallen; the floor glitters faintly with splintered prisms, thin grass grows from hair-line cracks in the intricate mosaic; but despite flaking walls and furniture sheathed in velvet mold, the room is intact. A marble staircase sweeps upward and he ascends.

Inlaid and carved mahogany doors open upon room after airy room; each with access to a porch that runs the three sides of the courtyard, shaded by arcades: but green tendrils pry through the balusters, the polished volutes of veined columns are pitted and worn, and marble tesserae have worked loose from the floor.

Osborne wanders; in bedrooms, suites and salons; though he must pick his way over fallen stone and plaster, and above him,

17

from those beams still fast, bats hang like dirty socks. In frames, old masters of the manor peel from canvas in fat scrolls of oil paint (Conde? Vicomte? Lord?). He moves slowly, through portieres worn cobweb thin; the sour smell of decay pervades, yet where the roof has held –and it has here and there– he finds a room, a suite in habitable condition.

His escort has dwindled to Delia and Theodore as they reach the end of the esplanade, where the divided avenues join, hook acutely right, and merge into the road to the fortress. At the junction stands a statue, a Spanish girl in her bridal gown; bice green and mournful. Bending over the baroque but weather-beaten pedestal Osborne can follow: Francesca Altamire y Torres de la Fé and beneath is a carved legend. (Why a girl in her bridal gown? Instead of the usual king, Conquistador, or Jesuit? Time. There is time for all that.)

They pass a building, a stone cube with tiny windows incised in the walls, the jail; and a square of rampant jungle, the Plaza Real; behind it looms the Palacio.

At the fortress, on the parapet, they stop; Osborne lights a cigarette, Delia and Theodore smoke rough redolent island cigars; they all gaze down the long quarter-moon beach curving into horizon . . .

The road loops upon itself and runs its second level, past houses more modest than the gala masterpieces below; but whimsically designed; rhomboids, trapeziums, trapezoids, parallelograms –building blocks for daft and giant children. The courtyards are crammed with foliage and in the trees the inevitable birds, feathered brats, are heard but seldom seen. Theodore leaves for his bar, Delia to prepare lunch, and Osborne continues alone, aimlessly up and down the ramps and stairways that slice the town into bewildering barrios, sweating happily, whistling. An ancient woman in volcanic sarong and kerchief grins at him toothlessly under a load of bananas; three naked children singing a joyous off-key jargon provide prancing company for a while; but wherever he stops, at whatever turning, the scene is the same: furniture sadly mildewed, rent roofs, falling walls, yet undisturbed. ☙

In a salon of the Palacio, on a chair of cascading mahogany . . . twilight plays upon the wall in muted shapes; things of light and shadow, deepening.

And that flight from Benghazi? Had it been so urgent? (Was urgent in Theodore's vocabulary?)

And his successor?

What was he doing? That round-bottomed young man? Like most of them. Fresh from the lower third of his class. At Amherst, Williams, Wesleyan.

Divorced from all that. Regally, if briefly. But G. Ritchie and his dog. Policemen shoving passengers into packed cars in the 59th Street I.R.T. station. Once (where?) he had seen pigs being loaded into freight cars. Two men tugged at the ears, a third, behind, grasped the tail, his knuckles in the anus, and pushed. A moment of straining equipoise, one last great! heave, and the pig was sent squealing to baconhood. But the pig, the pig at least: protested.

Vacation. Cuba.

The Larssens, and off in the yacht to Vera Cruz. With a yo-ho-ho and bottles of rum. Storm, and Gunther too drunk to reef in time. Limping into Campeche jury-rigged, with the engine out and the boom broken. Chichen-Itza, Uxmal, and the Larssens off for the States. Minus him.

Drifting about Campeche, wondering what to do next, wondering hours spent hunched over mescals, in one fly-specked bar or another (flea-bitten crummy Campeche. Too hot!).

Sitting in the Barco Verde –though the sign of the green boat had vanished– a few Mexicans slouched at the bar, or supine and alone in deep booths, disheveled white sacks in the sweet heavy murk: flies buzzing soggily over sticky tables.

"You 'Merican?" said a voice into his thoughts, and he turned.

Perched on his stool Grimes was made of globes; haunches and buttocks were a globe; belly, chest and shoulders another; no neck visible and his head was a third globe. Two weeks of stubble beneath a battered gob's hat; in baggy pants and filthy T-shirt, a degenerate little snowman melting under the Mexican sun.

"Yes, I'm American," said Osborne.

"Don't see many 'Mericans round here, dead place," said Grimes, managing to be garrulously laconic.

"No?"   ♥?

Well, it was worth losing the hundred dollars; and there is time for a stroll before climbing to Theodore's for dinner —Delia promised roast iguana. He lolls down the empty esplanade, palm fronds enamel-edged against the rushing dark, listening to night sounds replacing day sounds, very much at ease amid the crumbled aspirations of three empires.

PROLEGOMENA

A THIN SUNKEN WOMAN, OLDER THAN HER FIFTY-SEVEN YEARS, THE thin gray wisps of her thoughts too loose and straggled ever to gather into anything as compact as despair; she fussed and fidgeted through the rooms of the big, sagging house . . . waiting, as she had waited every day of the past eight months. For the postman.

No, it wasn't like that boy, eight months and no word from him and his mother half worried to death, all alone and nothing to do the livelong day but worry. Yes, yes, for the ten thousandth time, he *said* for a while but eight months was a *long* while. And it would be different if Amos was a thoughtless boy; or a careless boy. She smiled wistfully. Imagine! Amos a boy! A grown man – not that he would mind. And she saw him; in knickers, in cap-and-gown at graduation . . . No, other boys might not write their mothers but not Amos. At college if he wasn't coming home for the weekend there was always a card. Or a telephone call. And fighting in Korea and then traipsing all over the world for those government people and the postman always asking for the funny stamps for his son. A month might go by, or six weeks, but always there were letters . . .

She wandered through the empty rooms, besom in hand –Mrs. Osborne always carried a besom which she flicked, hesitantly, at the massive furniture, as though fearful of injuring the feathers– and it occurred to her that the world had lost touch with her. Or she with the world.

How different when Albert was alive! Everything running smooth, everything comfortable.

Then Albert died and her little world; neat, pat, simply fashioned of two equal halves was shorn in two, and the day began to go awry. Unobtrusively, but with a seeming will of its own, the friendly house turned against her. Wind tore shingles from the roof and the plumbing leaked and the window frames warped, letting the rains in and staining the floors in rough semicircles; mildewing the frayed rich old carpets.

She could never cope with all these minor disasters. Eventually she called the plumber, but when he came, weeks after he had promised –tradesmen could always stall Mrs. Osborne while attending to more demanding clients– she would forget to mention the clogged sump pump and the leaky washer in the guest bathroom and he would go off having repaired a fraction of the damage. And then she would be too timid, too embarrassed, to call him again . . .

And so the whole thing was getting out of hand. Eight months! She tried to form a plan, boldly she went into Amos's bedroom to track down a stub of pencil and a bit of paper; but there was his sweater draped over a chair. No, how was she *not* to worry? He wouldn't just forget, he wasn't the sort of boy who forgot. And she was making a nuisance of herself, she knew; why when the postman came with bills and advertisements and saw her and *had* to say; "Oh, cheer up Mrs. Osborne, there'll be one from him tomorrow." But being the postman perhaps he had some special insight into the postal system (she had to believe). And nothing came. Ann Herman next door who read detective stories said to go to the police. The Department of Missing People or something like that. But it wasn't as if Amos had done anything *wrong* and he did say a *while*.

He had quit his job and naturally she wouldn't ask why; whatever Amos's reasons, they were good enough for her. And what are you going to do, Amos? Oh, take it easy for a while and then he'd see. Well, that wasn't like Amos; Amos, like Albert, was a worker, not that there was anything wrong with a vacation. Landsakes, she'd told Albert time and again to take time off from the factory (funny! she always called it the "factory," Albert called it "the shop") but Albert's idea of time off was two weeks traipsing around Canada hunting, no matter what the doctor said. And so, of course . . .

Her watch had stopped; she walked into the living room dusk where the grandfather clock stood sentinel. It, too, had stopped. She thought of calling that number that told the time but didn't remember the number, couldn't find it in the directory; and it was such a small thing to bother the information people about. But it seemed to her that the postman was late this morning, and she kept a hopeful vigil by the leaded window beside the front door, imagining her reaction when, *this* day, at last! he angled down the bluestone drive, crunching, waving a vast letter . . .

A cobweb spanned the upper right hand corner of the window and even she was not impervious . . .

The heyday of the house, Amos in college, every weekend the Fourth of July.

"Orgy at Osborne's!" The call rang through the fraternity, people grabbed girls and toothbrushes, messages relayed to Yale, Amherst, points north, and tipsy carloads come through the night, the driveway jammed. Every bed taken and squabbles for couch rights. The neighbors gossiping but she knowing that they were all "nice" boys and "nice" girls; not that she thought it was *right*.

Albert was host and the whiskey flowed.

Oh yes, there was gossip but nothing a body could do –she rarely thought of herself in the first person– and they *did* have fun. She could no longer think of their names, or what they looked like. Amos's friends.

No, a mother had no right to forget the names of her own son's friends. Imagine! and rummaging through the broom closet of her memories; images blurred, focused briefly, then eluded her; face-less eager boys clutching glasses rush past her as, bewildered, she carries a tray heaped with sandwiches into the party; chattering couples are strewn about the dappled lawn while Albert, mag-nificent in his high chef's hat, officiates over the cauldron of clams —and there is a cheer as Amos flawlessly taps the keg. But who is that one the madras jacket? And that pretty girl who, it seems to her, has been here before? And the funny fat boy everyone picks on? No. There are too many of them. They run, jump, stagger, sing, gesticulate before her – anonymously.

Still she persisted –the least she can do is recall the names of her own son's friends– past those donnybrook days, to the smaller barbecues, corn feasts, turkey roasts, attended only by Amos and his more intimate friends. Haphazard names unattached to their

25

owners float into mind. A boy named Bunny. She smiles. What a silly name for a boy, but she never knew him by any other name, or, for that matter, never knew if he had another name. A boy whose whole name was Bunny! And the quiet handsome boy who Amos said was some sort of genius (mathematics?). And that wild little boy who used to drive all over the lawn; he was Amos's best friend of all, very ugly with his great big nose. Never thought she could forget *his* name. He was very ugly, and very funny, and he had a Jewish name; Amos's best friend . . .

Of course! She could have kicked herself, eight months waiting, waiting. Amos might be in trouble and if Amos was in trouble he might not tell his mother, but he *might* tell his friends.

That little ugly funny boy who drove over the lawn and told jokes at parties with the Jewish name?

What were Jewish names? She was terrible with names. But she remembered those parties with Jonathan telling jokes . . . that was it! Jonathan! But Jonathan what? 〽️

Each time the doctor examined Rosoff he shook his head; twice, slowly, from left to right then from right to left. Freddy Rosoff, the primitive painter, had no right to be alive. Sixty-four years of a roaring life . . .

En route from Pamplona for the fiesta, to Madrid for an exposition, via Zaragoza, he had collapsed over a cognac. Rushed to the nearest clinic, the doctor diagnosed, sterilized neolithic instruments, and cut. He found cancer everywhere, removed what he could, sewed Rosoff together, and waited for him to die. Three days later Rosoff was alive; and gangrene set in. The doctor cut again; watched, awed, a week as Rosoff fought . . .

Once, certain, he summoned the priest. Rosoff woke from his death sleep and threw a glass of water at him. The nurses called it a miracle. And Rosoff, rising out of a coma into short spasms of delirium, cursed and bellowed and called the names of his five wives and Conchita, his favorite whore in Barcelona . . .

Rosoff awoke in perfect health. He was fine. The bandages, the plugs and tubes bristling from his swathed paunch; it was all a ruse: they were after his money. He had passed out, drunk, and

26

they put him in a hospital pretending he was sick since they wanted his money. But the nurse changing his dressing had a bosomy Spanish body beneath all that starch even though she was part of the plan: and he shot a hand up her dress. She screamed and bounded back. Rosoff threw off the covers, said, "Hey, baby, come to Papa," ripped out the plugs and tubes, and ran after her.

She fled down the corridor collecting reinforcements. Two more nurses rushed out, finally the doctor. But Rosoff, his arms flailing, held them all at bay. And then collapsed.

They strapped him into the bed; (though he hadn't a chance) Rosoff refused to die. Let a bunch of Spaniards steal *his* money!

A week later he was sitting up, lucid, complimenting himself upon surviving a serious operation for ulcers. In three weeks he was up and walking. The doctor –suddenly a distinguished surgeon who had saved the life of a rich American artist– presented a bill for $500, and Rosoff gave full vent to the dozen words of Spanish he had learned in four years.

"*Hombre! No es posible! No soy rico. Pobre! Pobre, yo. Pobre Americano, bandidos!*"

"*Pero, Señor . . .*"

"*No es* fair! Robbers! Sons of bitches! Who the hell d'ya think you are!"

The doctor explained, in implacable Spanish, that he had saved his life.

"For thirty thousand goddam pesetas you ought to give me a new one!" but he was unable to translate this complexity.

Operations, nurses, antibiotics –the doctor ticked them off.

Rosoff fumed, collected his Spanish for a new and angrier salvo. A white lash of pain disarmed him. He stood mute, furious, and in agony; for the first time acknowledging that he was a sick man: for a month ago he would easily have outhaggled, out-chiseled, outshouted and outjewed better men than this mustachioed little doctor with his varnished fingernails.

The spasm subsided. He paid. The doctor ordered a month's rest, a strict diet, no alcohol. Rosoff laughed.

"*Yo . . . voy*," he said in his inimitable Spanish. "Madrid.

27

Ahora. Pronto. If you think I'm gonna stay one more day in this clipjoint, you're nuts," he added, and invited the doctor to share a *paella* and a cognac. The doctor demurred: he had no desire to witness a suicide. Rosoff ate alone and tossed down his defiant cognac, which he gagged on.

He loaded his veteran, battle-scarred Austin station wagon, shook a fist at the white and callous façade of the clinic, pressed the starter, and set off non-stop for Madrid.

He had the equivalent of fifty dollars in his wallet –all he had in the world– and the old Austin, registered in England, that could not be sold in Spain.

Delaney Pierce kept to his journal in the fo'c'sle of the *J. J. O'Rourke* plying New York, the Caribbean, Houston, New Orleans.

Three weeks left, he had earned another year of freedom. It was time –he wrote– to write or get off the pot.

Behind drawn curtains he nipped at a pint of bourbon. Where to? Apart from drinking, and his novel, and the United States of America, and the atom bomb, et cetera –a composite malaise he dubbed "worlditis"– was where to spend that freedom. In London, pubs closed at eleven, Paris was full of the French; all cities were expensive, impossible; he was tired of Spain.

As Seley said, pounding the table, "Spain? That's no country! You can't eat their food and you can't fuck their women! You call that a country?"

Still he had a fondness for Spain. Where bootblacks and street sweepers had dignity. Having been raised, as he had been, in a country where presidents had none. But the mainland was too hot, and the Balearics were ruined, and red with Germans everywhere. Prices were soaring. Still nothing was cheaper. Even Greece. And the food there was worse than Spain. Turkey was cheap. Who wanted to live in Turkey?

He wrote slowly, nipping the bourbon.

The day before his four-fifths of a novel was another book about men at sea. It was not enough. To be a poor man's Joseph

Conrad. Yet the day before that it had been better. Crude, but at least there was no bullshit; he wrote what he knew. And he knew that he was condemned, like every man, to the oubliette of his own being.

But four years to finish four-fifths of a novel; he could finish four-fifths of a quart in an evening. He wrote a resolution: go on the wagon as soon as freedom began –then crossed it off. His father was a drunk, as had been his grandfather, and his great-grandfather before him. The family's pickled cross; though –he noted– there was nothing wrong with alcoholism. Liquid suicide; like being in love:– pointless, irresistible, mostly misery, an occasional glow. Except for the guilt. If he could –and he was trying– convey on paper that sense of appalling guilt when, on a binge, he tried to pour that first, utterly necessary, morning drink and his hands trembled so, that even holding the bottle in both hands he could not get but a fraction of the alcohol into the glass . . . if he could put that down, and well, he would have accomplished something: for all that one had to know of degradation, hell and death was contained in that trembling morning minute; a bottle standing in its own puddle on the marble top of a night table.

And was it possible to write drunk? The great alcoholics wrote sober, then binged. Yet it seemed to him, after five morning drinks, that he achieved a certain clarity, an intensification above sobriety. Perhaps not.

Too sophisticated to seek a meaning in life, he still sought something that meant: all was not lost. It was –he wrote, chuckling– a sobering thought, though he knew he had to snap out soon or he would have rolled –deleted rolled, wrote staggered– too far downhill to return. Of course he could always sober up enough to go to sea, he always turned to whatever his condition, hadn't missed yet. As the captain of the *New London* said; "Pierce, it's been a pleasure to have you aboard." And he meant it. "It's been a pleasure to sail with you, Captain," he replied, and meant it. *J. J. O'Rourke* with her sober captain and queer stewards, a fink ship, but just three weeks left. He needed a title for his four-fifths of a novel. DON'T MAKE WAVES was too glib.

He was thinking of his youth; not so long ago: at a brawling boozing twenty, too good-looking, suffering already from worlditis but already aware that he would steal –had, in fact, already stolen– before he would punch a clock again, of a Hollywood offer he had turned down with a derisive leer; he was thinking of the women he had had, of those who loved him for his profile; and the grotesque feminine need to save his drunken soul –Helena who had died.

The pen fell from limp fingers, his head lolled back. He passed out, snoring just audibly.

Someone gave Mal Katona a car.

He had been sitting at the Select, drinking *vin blanc*, pondering dinner, (*boudin avec* mashed potatoes at the student restaurant? –braving the press, the queue, the steamy smell of too many French intellectuals– or a wastrel 450-franc dinner at Pied de Mouton?) when Hank (or was it Jerry?) Millette walked in and asked him if he knew anyone interested in buying a car.

Katona obligingly thought, but those friends who were not penniless already owned cars.

"Sorry, Millette," he said, "I can't think of anyone."

"Hell," said Millette. "I'm going back in three days. The damn thing's got TT plates. Some guy was supposed to take it and reneged . . . It's not a bad car," he added hopefully.

Katona made a sympathetic gesture.

Hank (or Jerry) Millette stood before the table a minute, thinking.

"Hell, Mal," he said, "I don't have time to mess around with the damn thing. I've got a lot of stuff to take care of. I've got to pack my junk. You want the car, you can have it."

Conversation ceased at the small round table. René Bouton, journalist for *L'Express*, who had been saving three years to trade his tired Vespa in for a car, said softly:

"*Merde alors.*"

But Mal Katona eyed Millette. His thick eyebrows vaulted. He stroked his long, sage, clown's face.

30

"I don't know," he said. "Let me take a look at it first."

"*Cochon!*" said Dan Berryman under his breath . . .

since, the previous summer, Katona had been in Warsaw, all expenses paid and a per diem allowance, one of three American delegates to an international conference of welfare workers, a subject about which he knew nothing; and the summer before he had been in Helsinki, delegate to an international Quaker conference; and the summer before that, hitchhiking through the Near East, he had been entertained for a full month at the villa of a Turkish general –bagnio privileges, swimming pool, erotic movies– simply for expressing a hatred toward Greeks. In Greece he hated Turks.

Mal Katona stretched his long, long legs and stood. With Millette and the others he went to examine the car. He inspected the tires, inquired about the mileage, kicked the bumpers.

"It looks O.K.," he said. "I'll take it."

The windfall car augured well. The G.I. Bill (and Ball) expired in June, and now he could sell the car, exist through the summer, and see if something good could be prodded into occurring; or, he could drive around Germany and Spain and perhaps con a teaching job; or, things going well, should an appealing conference develop in Russia –he wanted to see Russia– he could even drive the car there.

"How about a drink, Millette?" he asked. "On me."

They arranged to sign over the papers the following morning. In the afternoon, Katona, trailing René Bouton and Dan Berryman, picked up the car.

They climbed into the soiled but sound 11 CV Citroën. Katona slid the seat back as far as it would go and lit a cigarette.

"Who wants to go for a ride?" he said. "They run the Grand Prix at Rheims tomorrow."

Unanimous assent. Mal Katona switched on the ignition, remarking, without surprise, that Hank (or Jerry) Millette had left him a full tank of gas. ❦

"Will you marry me, Janine?" said Major Timothy Edward Ayreshire, eighth earl of Braxton. "I love you," he implored.

The bright blue eyes of the blond head cradled in his arm closed tight; a man not in love would have known better.

"Ah, no, Tim," she said, saying (charmingly) "Teem."

"I can make you happy, Janine."

"But I am not sad."

"I love you, Janine!"

and she him! or else why would she? . . . on the very first night:— thought Timothy, Lord Ayreshire, discriminating judge of horses and women.

"Because we've only known each other one day? A day is enough, Janine. If we listen to our . . . hrumph . . . hearts and not our heads."

Once upon a time he had read a book, and it said that and he had thought it "rot." It was not. "I love you," he said.

She trilled with desire,

"Marry me, Janine?"

and he talked of love.

"No, Teem."

"Because of that?"

"Because I will not marry."

And because she had been asked by so many men. And because in bed with Major Timothy Edward Ayreshire it was all what-ho! jolly good show, chins up there, lads, and try for the century. And because that morning (damn), the first morning with him, came a letter from Tony, and she liked Tony better than Teem. It was good in bed with Tony, better than with Teem –he was coming in two weeks.

"Don't you like me, Janine? I mean, don't you?"

"Oh, I like you fine, Teem."

"Then come back to England with me. Please. I've never met anyone like you . . . I adore you," he said. As they all had.

"What is this?" she asked, running a finger down the scar on his back.

"That. Oh, the war." In which, of course, he had been a hero. Adding hopefully, "Flak through the fuselage."

And taking his broad square honest earl's hand in hers she directed it down her belly.

"Also I have a . . ."

"I love you, Janine!"

"How do you call that in English?"

"Scar."

". . . scar," she said (with that accent).

He had put into Ibiza instead of sailing for Palma, and had been sipping gin-and-tonic in the sun, on the deck, when Janine, just strolling, strolled by. She paused to admire the salty and proper old schooner.

"Well, hello!" he had called. "Come on aboard! Have a drink! Good English gin!"

"I do not mind if I do," said Janine, (with that accent,) and minced up the gangway.

She stayed for two, then for six, then for ten; gayer and gayer: — while Timothy Lord Ayreshire plunged into love. They were dancing in the paneled cabin, gently rocking, dancing while Timothy Lord Ayreshire, in love, invented courage to kiss her.

He had never been kissed a kiss like Janine's.

"Ah, Teem," she said, "I will make love with you. Come!" A honey voice, murky, slow-flowing. With an urgency no woman had:— at least never for him . . .

"Do you think this . . . how you call it?"

"Scar."

". . . scar makes me ugly?"

He raised the sheet and gazed, in the lovelight of her room, at the narrow cicatrix ridge, pale against her sunny skin, curving down, vanishing in her golden fleece –sought, attained, ineluctably lost by a legion of Jasons.

"Nothing could make you ugly. You are the most beautiful woman I ever met . . ."

A nobleman of archetypal density; he had barely been through the best schools. He stammered and fumbled for words; his accent was just what it should be:

"Janine, come back with me. I . . . I didn't want to mention it before but . . . In England you see, I'm not just anybody. I mean I don't know if it means anything to you but I have a title at home. I mean the earl of Braxton. I have, well, a good deal of: money. I didn't say anything before. Because I don't like to talk about: money." She admired him for that though in bed it was still just what-ho! "I mean you would have a good life with me."

"But I do not want to go to England. It is cold. It rains always. I could not work in England."

"We could take a wing of the house and make a studio," he begged. "You'd see, Janine, you'd like it."

"No, Teem."

"Please, Janine!"

"I do not want to talk more about it," she said, stamping her voice.

"Janine, I would do anything for you, I mean!"

She toyed him erect (again!). He was a far better man than he thought, and his opinion had never been low.

"Ahhh! Tony!" she whispered; guiding him into her.   ✥

"Alain Marsh, you're an idiot!" said Alain Marsh. "What did you come back for?"

In Brussels the rent had been eighteen dollars a month, there were those silly translations, now and then one of his galleries sold *something* . . . he shouldn't have let a single omen sway him; a painting in a group show at the Whitney sold for $1250. And not to a collector, to someone whose name meant nothing to him, someone who simply walked in, liked the painting, bought it. And Alain Marsh, dreaming the seven lean years had come to an apposite end –since the starving-genius-in-garret theory was, and always had been, myth– came back.

At twenty-five he had done the necessary things. He had been as cold in winter as any future biographer could reasonably demand; he had performed his hitchhiking stint through Europe, had dressed badly beyond the call of duty –once, waiting for a bus in Paris, someone slipped him a hundred francs– and he had cooperatively tossed through sleepless nights, faced by that familiar ogre: Next Month's Rent, and his bill at the art supply store.

He had amply and assiduously served that part of his apprenticeship which was poverty. It was time to shed those auxiliary cares, and concentrate upon painting paintings. He abandoned his second wife and his year-old son; he took what remained of his $1250 and came back to New York, ready for a first big show.

The great ramshackle loft turned up almost immediately; he was spared the usual foot-and-soul fatiguing tedium of studio hunting (the seven lean years were over!) and he lunged about with happy scarecrow strides making it fit for only himself to live in.

Flimsy waggling painting walls sprouted everywhere, jerry-built in mosaics of fiberboard, beaverboard and masonite; he tacked oilpaper over missing windowpanes, and, depressed by the gray patchwork effect, painted animals over the oilpaper until the skid-row scene outside was overruled by an illuminated stained-paper circus. A perilous, fire-department-defying string of 150-watt light bulbs was strung for night work.

It was a studio, not yet a home. He foraged the neighborhood for junk.

Three eviscerated armchairs, trundled up the warped stairs, formed the nucleus of the living room; a writhing rusty octopean chandelier replaced the one obscene bulb; followed quickly by an atrophied lawn mower, two gimpy barstools, a fiendish tendril of aluminum floor lamp, and a leather hassock beaten into submission by generations of hippos. Chipped bosomy Victorian glassware took root in the corners, a crumpled model clipper ship with rent parchment sails appeared, and the indispensable molting pheasant, a toy Lionel locomotive demolished by some diminutive John Casey for the mantel, and a stumpy skew-tailed alley kitten named Max.

A kitchen was compiled from a pot, a frying pan, a hobo-type kerosene stove and a drawer full of obscure obsolete utensils, and within three days the empty echoing loft was a stuffed museum of slum flotsam, which, strewn together by Alain Marsh's unerring hand, came to assume a derelict yet rakish –and definite– style of its own, akin to nothing in History, just Marshian.

He bought a secondhand refrigerator, crammed it full of champagne, and since, even solvent, he kept to a strict diet of sand-

wiches –but loved champagne– for several weeks he washed down
sardine sandwiches with champagne, liverwurst sandwiches with
champagne, cheese sandwiches with champagne. (The seven lean
years were over!) He had a party for his old friends, bought a case
of twelve-year-old scotch, and coursed at such flood tide that it
was a week before he knew that the party had been sad; that those
old friends had succumbed –with their jobs and families– all those
painters and writers and musicians; and that back in New York it
was no better than in Brussels. There was no one left for him to
talk to. And in Brussels he could not-talk to people in French.

The studio had a fifteen-foot ceiling, the Brussels studio had
restricted him to twelve. He bought ten rolls of canvas, and a
trunkful of paint, and settled down to work.

Nothing happened.

The few important galleries large enough to show his work were
interested but busy, they had their name painters. Others were
more encouraging. Of course Alain would be expected to pay a
"nominal" rental fee . . . and the brochures and the liquor for the
vernissage and the stretchers and frames and posters and advertisements. "Oh me, oh my," sighed Alain Marsh, "if only I was
queer."

So he slouched in his salvaged armchair, in the looming studio
né loft, at the habitual slum address, stared at a painting stymied
for yellow. Cadmium yellow. Two absent dollars and eighty cents
per tube. The $1250 had vanished, and there was no foreseeable
money.

How could everything go so badly when the painting went so
well?

He had talked himself out of a sale a month ago, sulked himself
out of another a week ago. A cooperative gallery was interested in
his work:— cooperative galleries sold nothing. And made you
help hang other painters' inept shows. And be affably available.
At ten he had jeered at the Boy Scouts.

But for how long could a man live on catsup alone?

The Polish baker down the street liked him; gave him two-day-
old bread gratis; and he had been fond of catsup. A week of

nothing but catsup sandwiches had somewhat blunted his taste. Why had he cached six bottles of catsup anyway? (There had been a sale. He bought four, stole two.) Were it evening he could walk to the Village and perhaps find Sgavicchio who would stand him a beer and lend him a quarter. With the quarter he could buy a dozen eggs – eggs, uncleaned, therefore the quarter, but eggs. It was not, however, evening. It was noon.

If worse came to still worse –as appeared inevitable– he could get a summer job waiting tables in the Catskills.

He thought of telephoning that singular individual, the one who had seen his painting, liked it, bought it. He had the name written on a scrap of paper somewhere . . . ⟡

Jonathan! That was his name. Perhaps that funny Jonathan would know, with the big nose. He had a Jewish name . . . ⟡

Amos Osborne sat, at the edge of the rotting jetty; the blanched mahogany timbers warm under his shredded suntans. His dangling feet footprinted the blue lid of the lagoon and lazily he watched industrious needle-backed fish weave ephemeral wefts through invisible water warps.

It was not that he had not tried.

The first month, of course, he had expected Grimes. Then came the hurricane season and there was nothing to be done. The storms over (and Grimes dead? drunk? drowned?) he had worked hard beneath the work-mocking sun, building a raft to take him to Yucatan. Out of hardwood –not knowing the difference.

A second raft was built of lashed palm trunks, which floated admirably. He set a makeshift sail that Delia wove from grass and fiber. But the trades were averse and saltier skippers than Osborne would have balked at beating into the wind in a Bermuda-rigged raft.

He was not yet desperate enough to paddle fifty miles in a waddling native pirogue, but he was trying to exercise that Yankee ingenuity –which, he felt, should be his by birthright– on a canoe

37

of Osborne design, ribbed in liana and stretched with sewn resined hides, equipped with outriggers and a crude sail: though the impending voyage was as impalpable as tomorrow's dream.

The marrow of his bones was sluggish with the sun; his body now flowed to the mazy rhythm of the Caribbean day.

Not even that he had sought the easy way; just that when trouble loomed, he moved clear of it.

Introspection came unnaturally; despite seven months with his own thoughts he had solved nothing. And each time he tried to be serious there was that (damned!) blue sky and that hot sun. There had always been.

His stomach grumbled amiably and he glanced upward. Were it not for the picture he had of his mother, fussing and fretting through the empty rooms, worrying; he wondered if he would bother to go back at all. Probably. Out of curiosity if nothing else. He had to go back, actually, to try. Though he could think of no reason. His exploration of the island, beginning as a pastime, had become an obsession. His projected history, to be compiled eventually from an inexhaustible supply of yellowed letters and journals, seemed at least as worthwhile as anything he was likely to encounter at home. (Old Mal Katona would revel in his island; laugh at his conscience.)

It was all terribly complex.

He stood. He stretched until his thick joints crackled. That generous roll of middle had disappeared over months of fishing, hunting and swimming. And standing there, at the edge of the jetty, he was a solid hairy column of a man, running a hand over a full-moon face: on which bewilderment etched false and uneasy lines.

He decided upon fish and ambled off in the direction of the Palacio for his spear. It was time to catch lunch. 🌾

She moved cautiously amid attic thoughts; for at a touch that precarious stack of memories shook and swayed . . .

Jonathan, that funny ugly noisy one whose jokes she never understood, and who had always been "The Life of the Party."

Ah! But not always! She remembered.

He changed.

Amos used to talk about it with Albert when they thought she wasn't listening. Something about a girl. 🐾

Should a social register of *The Forest Hills Four Hundred* ever be compiled, the names Ralph and Doris Bonhom would be among those just excluded. For Ralph Bonhom was not, quite, a success. Chief salesman of his lingerie firm, he had never been offered a partnership; he had a Cadillac –the small Cadillac; and Doris had a mink –a natural mink; they belonged to a club –not Old Oaks; and summer vacations were spent –not at Grossinger's or the Concord which were too "showy" for them– but at Kline's In the Pines where the atmosphere was more "relaxed."

Ralph Bonhom was a podgy man, his excess pounds padded about his body in soft swollen dollops. He moved seldom, spoke seldom, but with wide mouth clamped tight, and dull bulging eyes peering out, he endured the world's failure to pay him his due with torpid, batrachian complacency.

It was Doris who dominated the conversation as they awaited "luncheon" at Kline's In the Pines. Ever-so-slightly overrouged, ever-so-slightly overgirdled –looking as though she had spent the entire morning before the vanity table, which was true– she was still an attractive woman. She spoke. Her voice –an affectation for so long it had become natural– a syrupy chirping, the voice a parvenu bird might cultivate to address sparrows. And as she talked she gestured with her little finger, a prim, crimson-tipped pointer, constantly in play, waved indiscriminately about the room, expressive of the etiquette that constituted her way of life: she believed that breast-feeding a baby was "disgusting."

Her daughter, Janice, was beautiful, bitchy, bright, neurotic and flat-chested, and Jonathan Klein, the waiter at their table –no relation to Kline of Kline's In the Pines– had been in love with her from the moment she checked into the hotel.

Though prostitution was a tacit clause in his contract –the staff was supposed to service the clientele when available women out-

39

numbered single male guests– though he had served meals to the Bonhoms for three days, he had not yet had the courage to introduce himself. But his co-workers, suede-shod mambo dancers from deepest Brooklyn, rancid athletes from NYU basketball courts, discussed her in detail:

"D'ya think that one'll fuck?"

"Nah. She ain't the type that fucks."

"They all fuck."

"Her mother's with her."

"She'll fuck too."

(Who cast this pearl before the swine at Kline's?)

He had merely watched her: by the pool, strolling toward the tennis courts; fresh, lovely, infinitely unattainable. He had poured down martinis at the bar and gazed at her on the dance floor; lithe, gay, a shade restrained, nothing sensual about her, the first cool hint of spring. And the wolves converged upon her, baying Brooklynese; he was powerless to help.

He carried a laden tray toward her, with love, and from the table adjacent one of his peroxided charges called "J-O-N-A-T-H-A-N! (yet Janice did not know his name) Marge has three matzah balls in her soup and I only have two. I want three matzah balls."

He turned, tripped over a lump, a ridge where the carpet had bunched together, fought a brief, losing battle against the forces of gravity, almost maintained the tray's equilibrium, but a bowl of borscht slipped to the edge, teetered indecisively, hovered, hovered, and crashed:— into Janice Bonhom's (exquisite) shoulder.

She sat stupefied, sour cream running down her neck, a boiled potato in her lap –clearly the most comic spectacle since martyrs, the audience was wild– and the blood-red borscht turned her summer blue silk an ominous magenta.

Jonathan Klein fluttered about, helpless; but the accident disturbed Ralph Bonhom; he surfaced angrily through the thick chickweed pond of his thoughts.

"Why the hell don't you look where you're going," he croaked.

"You fool, you clumsy fool," hissed Doris Bonhom.

40

"Oh, my God! I'm sorry, I'm terribly sorry. This lump in the carpet . . ." (Come Death!) he pointed a beseeching finger.

"Don't just *stand* there! Get a *nap*kin," said Mrs. Bonhom.

"Yes. Of course. Don't worry. I'll get you a new dress if the stain doesn't come out."

"Young man, do you realize that dress costs one hundred and *fifty* dollars?"

"*Mother!* It was only fifty-five at Loman's."

"That dress, Janice, is an original. It would cost one hundred and fifty dollars to replace that dress."

"It doesn't matter. Please. Just send the bill to me. At the hotel. Jonathan Klein . . ."

And Janice laughed –a quick cool sonata of merriment. With two fingers she plucked the boiled potato from her lap, then a calm hand reached out and touched his trembling one.

"I must look a *scream*," she said and left, walking a sniggering gauntlet with flawless equanimity. Borscht sufficient to dampen her composure was not in existence.

She returned ten minutes later, in another dress that was all summer, and smiled at him.

He smiled back fatuously. 🐾

Delaney Pierce celebrated what should have been his graduation from Western Pacific College, in the Taponville County Jail. A week prior to his diploma he made the mistake of thrashing the local Police Chief's son. Ninety days.

Not that it bothered him. "Best can on the coast!" said enthusiastic hobos and rumbums, temporary colleagues who knew.

The first week, trying to break his spirit, they put him on bread and water and threw him in the drunk tank. There, amid the retching, coughing, stench and delirium he saw the depths to which (free?) men could sink; but he had always known; or, to comprehend heat, was it necessary to experience the Sahara?

Jail was a dose of intellectual castor oil –and left to himself he would not have swallowed it. He would have spent these ninety days like other ninety days. He would have drunk too many drinks, laid too many women, fought too many fights. In jail, he saw now, clearly, that he had outgrown the delights of juvenile delinquency; becoming a professional criminal required too much effort in view of the risk.

"I'm giving you ninety days, Pierce," the Judge had said. Pierce swallowed a smile.

"You realize what that means of course?"

" "

"This goes on your record. Despite your college education you are now ineligible to become an officer in the United States Armed Forces."

His huge guffaw was as spontaneous as it was unsuppressible. But deftly he converted the derisive hoot into a convincing cough, avoiding the consequent contempt charge.

In jail he began his journal, and wrestling with tough tangled sinews of thought he experienced a pleasure/pain that eluded his attempts at definition. Closest was the lingering shock and satisfaction of a perfect left jab into a cheekbone –but more complicated than that. 𝕎

"I'm sorry, Janice, but I *don't* see what you see in that boy."

"He's *funny*, Mother, and besides, he's very intelligent."

"If sneering at everything means he's intelligent then I suppose he is. He isn't even good-looking."

"He's *interesting-looking.*"

"If that's interesting-looking, I'm Clark Gable," said Ralph Bonhom from his lily pad in the corner. "I can't stand these young kids who think they know everything. He's still wet behind the ears and nothing's good enough for him."

"That isn't *true*, Dad. His values are just . . . different."

"Different! He doesn't like television, he doesn't like country clubs, he doesn't like the President of the United States. He doesn't even read the newspapers and he calls the President of the United States a jerk."

"Jonathan has a theory about newspapers."

"Oh, he has a theory. I'd like to hear his theory."

"Well, Jonathan says the newspapers are fooling the public; that nothing actually happens at all; but if the newspapers told the public they'd go out of business. So they make up news. He says if you read the papers once every six months you see that the news is exactly the same and they've just changed the names of the places. Instead of a revolution in Ecuador they make up one in Guatemala. They invent communists in Indochina instead of Afghanistan and have race riots in . . ."

"And I suppose you think that's *funny?*"

"I tested it and it was *true.*"

"*I'll* tell you the trouble with Jonathan," said Mrs. Bonhom. "The trouble with Jonathan is that he's unstable."

The doorbell rang and it was Jonathan, twenty minutes early: he was always twenty minutes early.

"*Jon*athan! I'm not even dressed!"

"Hello," he said, and gazed at her, with love. "You look dressed."

"I can't go like *this.*"

With seconds to spare he remembered, and shook Mr. Bonhom's hand; Doris Bonhom held out five marble fingers, and Janice exited in a flounce of intention.

. . .

"That girl," said Doris, twenty minutes later. "She's *nev*er on time."

"That's O.K., Mrs. Bonhom. I was early."

"*Janice!* Jonathan is *wait*ing!"

"I'll be right *there,* Mother," trilled Janice (so sweetly); appearing in thirty-three minutes; wearing Bermuda shorts of a similar but different plaid and a blue instead of a green blouse.

"Have a good time," warned Mrs. Bonhom at the door. "Don't drive too fast, Jonathan," she called down the corridor, as he (so indecorously) whisked her away.

That portrait of Ronald was Alain Marsh's farewell to his childhood; he was seventeen when he painted it, and a freshman at Barclay.

He had been painting since ten; at fifteen he wanted to become a painter; at seventeen he was one. And could have been nothing else.

But there was Ronald . . .

"Look, Alain, I can see painting as a hobby, hell, lots of guys in the community paint in their spare time. But painters starve to death, you know that. If you wanted to be a commercial artist I'd say O.K.: a fellow down the block pulls down ten, twelve thousand a year, but you've got to be practical. Sure, I know, you think I'm stuffy . . ."

He was seventeen. Outside of school he attended spiritualist sessions; fascinated by telepathy and clairvoyance. They tied in somehow, he knew, with theories of time and space. He was reading a book based on the hypothesis that time is serial but lost himself in the upper reaches of mathematics. Then, too, he wondered how Vermeer made an object come to life with just one dab of light in the exact right place. Did he practice with innumerable dabs of light? Or did he awake one morning possessed with the certain, startling knowledge that he could do something no other painter had done before?

"And you know how tough it is for the folks here, Alain. The least you could do is get a job after school and kick into the kitty. When I was your age . . ."

And he wondered why the stony perfection of Piero della Francesca appealed to him more than the sweet grace of Raphael.

"After school I work," he said.

"What work?"

"I paint."

"I mean some useful work, hell when I was your age . . ."

(Stop painting those bisons on the cave walls. Get out there and hunt!)

His mother, at least, had faith in him; but blind faith.

"Believe me, Alain, painters starve (Ronald was getting fatter.) Oh, I know, everyone wants to rebel, I did myself. But you ought to shave that beard off and put on some clean clothes, (Ronald was balder, too.) you want people to think you're a *character?*"

44

The break had been the scholarship to Barclay. Tuition and some spending money. It was a woman's college, a few men were accepted in the fine arts, yet Alain Marsh was an instant pariah. No one, the professors included, had ever encountered a student with his self-acquired erudition; but he had a beard, and all he owned in the world were two pairs of jeans, two denim shirts, sneakers, a sweater, and a World War I horse-blanket overcoat –too sloppy to be acceptably Bohemian.

In the composition class, Polanyi ignored him for several weeks though he spent time with the girls. One day he approached and said, "You're not making paintings, Marsh." Until then, the girls dabbling away, had been squeamish before his flaring sprawling efforts; confidence was restored.

In mid-December Polanyi approached a second time.

"Now you're making paintings, Marsh," he said . . .

"You know the chances for painters, Alain. Like betting on the daily double."

"Polanyi likes my stuff."

"Who's Polanyi?"

" . . . !"

"All right. We won't talk about the future, we'll talk about right now. You live in the house, you eat the food, you don't contribute and you walk around looking like a bum and coming home drunk . . ." It went on until their mother began to cry.

It was Christmas vacation. Alain awoke very late the next morning with Ronald on his mind like a hangover. Though his semi-logic had some truth in it. He *did* live in the house. He came home drunk. But didn't Ronald *see*? (God! Who's Polanyi?) And just the week before he had been assigned a studio; the first freshman ever to win one.

He ate breakfast in silence. After, he packed his few paint-spattered belongings and left the house. The door clicked shut behind him and he knew what he had to do. Go away and stay away. But stay where? Friends would put him up for a while.

He found himself on the subway that took him to school. It was foolish; Christmas vacation and the place would be locked.

45

The door opened for him. The school was deserted, the corridors empty, and he lurked along on ungainly tiptoe though there was no reason to, he wasn't doing anything wrong. He stopped often, listening for footsteps, heard nothing and took the elevator to the top floor.

He sat on a rickety chair in the middle of his studio and reveled in his solitude. There were street noises sixteen floors below. And the visceral sounds of the building itself, grumbling plumbing and steam gasps and sighs. Thin snow whipped past the window.

The painting finished a week ago was muddy and inept; the next would be better. He was alone, not lonely, but self-sufficient. And for the first time he experienced the surge of power that swept simultaneously through head, heart, and hands.

And as he sat, envisioning the paintings he would one day perform, his breath blowing fume animals into the air, he thought of Ronald. To his surprise, without rancor; a puffy frightened little man with a mortgage and a belly. Overnight the stronger elder brother had become an object of contempt, worse, an object of pity; yet without Ronald he might not have left, who knows? until graduation; and he saw, with glee, that Ronald had been his unwitting benefactor. There, in his studio, he was omniscient. He was, finally, where he belonged.

A battered divan slouched in the corner. Marsh tried it for size. His feet stuck over the edge, an errant spring nudged his rib cage, otherwise it wasn't at all bad. He weighed the consequences of being caught. But briefly. It was superb (it was home!) and all, curiously, Ronald's fault.

There were five days to Christmas. Ronald deserved a present.

Gleefully he cut canvas, chuckling he tacked it to the wall. With charcoal he made preliminary sketches, working rapidly but with precision. The hand had already been trained to follow the inner eye. And the inner eye, this time, saw with (delicious) clarity.

It would be a portrait, and not abstract, exactly the reverse, representational to the nth degree. He wanted Ronald to say, now that's what I call a painting, none of those blots and wiggles, that's real, just like a photograph.

46

Van Eyck with a good dash of Dali.

He stopped only when he had gone as far as he could for the day. A day to dry, a day to complete it, a day to touch it up; it would be finished for Christmas.

He stood back and studied the painting with a critical eye. Precisely what he wanted.

His brother, Ronald, emerged from the oils, balding, a trifle paunchier than reality. Standing stark naked in the middle of his living room; staring dully at the limaciform ashtray next to the fetus-shaped lamp. ♥

Janine walking.

On the Pont she dallied, arched over the edge (harsh stone cool through her chic spring knit, cool through the silken flummery beneath. Delectable.) She paused, she poised, she watched:— the coiling jade-green prase-green April surge of the Seine.

She drew Parisian April through parted red lips, she strolled; stripped naked by every lusting virile eye –and loving it, she lolled: quintessentially feline, lithely aloof, the wake of breeze that followed her eddied with JOY.

Up the Rue de Seine she sailed; she stalked, men gaped. At a gallery she stopped, and frowned. Too fine a day for bad painting.

The tilting houses vie for ambience.

Frowning she zigzagged from gallery to gallery; only a scrawled name distinguishing one canvas from another. And with a tiny jolt she realized that her own paintings were signed J. Lindemann, never J. Lafollette, not even J. Lindemann-Lafollette. Had Etienne noticed, *pauvre Etienne?* She thought of him as Pauvre Etienne, he was a celebrated cuckold. And she made a tiny moue of pity.

Past galleries, bistros, antique shops. Haughtily she threaded through housewives, thronging the Rue de Buci, and stopped, and gazed, with pleasure –as she always did– at the carousel-red Boucherie Chevaline, its three gilded gleaming carousel chargers whinnying above.

She sidled along:

past HUITRES COQUILLAGES: with the rough scale-sequinned hands of his mind the fishmonger handled her roughly. Pivoting neatly she swung by VOLAILLES.

A vegetable hawker named LEGUMES cut short his spiel at "Epinards" and devoured her (raw) with a leer.

Slender, exquisitely proportioned, as delicately and finely muscled as a Siamese cat; her ash-blond hair, cropped close, shone silkily. And her eyes –china-blue like a Siamese cat's– could be bright with gaiety, fierce with passion, tearful with pity: never tender. Her high-cheekboned Finnish face was too strong for beauty; but in a roomful of beautiful women men looked at Janine.

At the Boulevard Saint Germain she paused. She chose her route, one slender finger dimpling a pout of red lips. A pedestrian crossing at PIETONS ATTENDEZ stared; a motorist tooling along in the spring –and abruptly in love with Janine– overlooked the pedestrian. A scream of rubber on asphalt . . . April in Paris ablaze with *Cochon! Salaud!* and *Merde!*

. . . ankles twinkling, a smooth lilt to her sheathed hips, and the brisk staccato of needle-heeled shoes was voided. Down St. Germain she went. Stopped to muse at the *Librairie.* She liked Proust, Virginia Woolf, Colette, Djuna Barnes . . .

She could paint –her lovers would have liked to hate her for that– and when she struck that right elusive note she filled the whole room with brooding fanatic Nordic light: never with warmth.

. . . detours past the Old Navy. Behind glass, fervid young men with pimples or sexual problems debated the quotidian fiction of *L'Humanité* –yet stopped to ogle, indulged in a brief apolitical orgy; and crossed their legs . . .

. . . she stood at the corner of the Boul' Mich' inciting lust, waiting for the light to change. Every man seated in the green and yellow wicker chairs of Le Cluny shifted to observe; each eye trained on the cadenced derrière (alas!) disappearing; on its way, an unhurried hour late, to a rendezvous (Pauvre Etienne!). A single decibel more and her walk would have been strident –it was

48

perfect. Had she not been irrevocably a lady, she would have been a tramp; and, in a blond study, in the spring sunshine, she mouthed, *je voudrais bien être moins seule,* tossing a red smile, like a poison rose, to a gaping student who would never know her name. 🙟

Pierce met someone who knew someone who knew someone in the Union. He bought a few drinks, hung around the hall a few weeks, and shipped out to the Orient. It wasn't a bad life. He stayed sober most of the time. No one cared about the color of his shirt. 🙟

Back at college, his senior year, he waited for her letters. He cut ten o'clock classes to greet the postman, a sadist in blue who invariably lagged behind schedule. First to handle the sheaf of letters, Jonathan would riffle them, in anguish, searching for that rare square blue envelope with Janice Bonhom embossed discreetly on the back; and which contained (always) but a few lines in her neat, backhand, polar script.

He answered her with love.

And Grantlow University –selected because it had the shortest application blank– was symbolized by a fraternity brother named Norm Geistman:—Norm who once had burst through the front door at eight in the morning, with theatrically lipsticked collar, and hand outstretched, shouting, "Boy! Five times! Five times!"

He decided to flunk out of school; the few classes he attended were spent writing letters to Janice; but he recanted before each examination. Two hours with a textbook, underlined by a less gifted comrade, was enough to convince the IBM machines that he merited passing grades. He did not belong in the company of his twisted heroes the poets, composers, and painters; however uncomfortable, he was part of Norm Geistman's world; he wasn't a round peg in a square hole, merely an off-center one; he loathed himself for his ability to function in a society he loathed, and was tormented by the thought that he was not tormented enough. (And Janice did not write.)

During Christmas vacation he saw her twice, and kissed her

49

once:— everyone else slept with the girls they took out, or said they did. Nothing happened the last semester of his last year at college except that he got himself a crew cut. Janice liked crew cuts.

"It makes me look like a paintbrush," he complained.

That trill of laughter. "Jonathan, I *like* it that way," she said, and ran her hand through it. "I like to run my hands through it."

(But so seldom.) ❦

Selective Service Commission
Local Board 17
258 Drake Street
Taponville, California
U.S.A.
Dear Sirs:
Mr. Delaney Pierce has requested this office to inform you that he has applied for, and been accepted into the Reading School of Social Sciences of the University of London, intending to complete the requisite credits toward his Bachelor of Science degree, and preliminary to further graduate studies in the field of Psychology. I am informing you of his plans in the expectation that he may be deferred from active service in the United States Armed Forces for a minimum period of two semesters; the period necessary for him to effectuate the former of his degrees.

> Very Faithfully Yours,
> Winthrop Griffith-Simmons
> Student (. . . ?)

Student what? Pierce tapped his pen on the table. Student Co-ordinator! (What does the Student Coordinator do? Coordinates students.) He was quite pleased with the "Winthrop Griffith-Simmons" and thought "effectuate" was a nicely pedantic touch. The Korean war was on, it was no time to go back to sea.

The first three printers he approached were unimaginatively righteous; a fourth forgot his scruples for five pounds. Pierce selected an impressive and official-looking crest, wrote "LAISSEZ

50

FAIRE" beneath it, and had stationery printed for the Reading School of Social Sciences of the University of London; whose main offices were (happily) located at Letitia's Chelsea address. Waiting for his deferment, he ran into someone who knew someone who knew someone. Three weeks later he was in Zürich. The following week he was on a plane bound for India, all expenses paid:— with sixty pounds of gold strapped to his body. ♥

Marsh lived happily in his studio haven. After school he painted.

But one Blue Monday, he was taking a midnight shower, and forgetting himself, was singing. His arch-enemy, the Polish washerwoman, heard the caterwauling. "I had her schedule figured, she should have been on the *tenth* floor by midnight." A Slavic stubbornness conquered a Slavic superstitious fear: the woman had been ghost-ridden for a year:— those *were* foorsteps she heard slipping down vacant corridors; that was the water running and the toilet flushing in bathrooms occupied by no one. She went to investigate. Gingerly, she opened the door, peered into the steam.

"Who dot dere?"

His only hope was to win the hag to his side. Accordingly he stuck his long, bearded, hook-nosed, soap-streaming face out of the shower and smiled a vulpine smile. She took one look at him, shrieked, knocked over her wash pail –Marsh remembered that it clattered an interminably long time down the marble corridor, and fled.

In vain did Marsh explain to the dean. It hadn't been Alain Marsh taking a shower at midnight but some other student who looked just like him. Marsh had been at an all-night movie on Forty-second Street. There was talk of expulsion, but his record was a neat picket fence of A's, broken only twice by filigree B's. Polanyi and Makropoulous put in a good word. Finally, even his stipend was restored.

It was, however, the end of the only security Marsh ever knew; and the beginning of a nomad existence, from garret to hovel to

51

loft; a life in places where, with few exceptions, no one but Marsh would consent to live. 𝕎

He would have liked to write poetry but he never heard any, and his father's business beckoned. And when Janice realized (as she must) that she loved him, he would have to provide her with all the indispensable luxuries.

She was in Europe for the summer. And returned:— raving about Italian men (had she?).

She managed to see him perhaps once a fortnight. He spent the interim periods hunting for new (expensive) novelty places to please her.

Before each rendezvous he rolled the great stone of his hope up (up, up) the mountain of possibility, only to watch it, upon taking her home early, crash to the bottom.

She was subject to headaches and, during the summer, unable to swim an alarming number of days each month. Other women were unthinkable.

A year went by. 𝕎

In the Merchant Seamen's library he encountered that dust-covered volume of Gogol, understood then: that with luck he could come to the same; conjured up Del Pierce as dust on the unread remains of himself. Not that he had, as yet, approached. And he knew it (how well).

So that night, he and Nikolai went out and got drunk, Pierce furious at History, raging at Today, trying (trying!) to stop, refusing the next one: ordering it. He *would not* submit.

"Cocksuckers!" he bellowed. "Assholes!"

He had not been created to accept the indignities of mere living.

And Nikolai Vasilievich Gogol agreed:— they all did. 𝕎

A student of Philosophy, Katona emerged, the only man in his class equipped with a philosophy. (Ergophobic Epicurean Solipsism.) Therefore, a dedicated man at twenty, his choice of ruse was crucial. (Sociology? Psychology? Political Science? Poli. Sci. by a nose!)

an oxymoron he compared to black whiteness; a field so ill-defined, so consummately inutile, that a man with (His!) intelligence could lounge a life away on grants, fellowships, scholarships, stipends, prizes, remunerations, outright baksheesh; meeds freely bestowed upon purposely pompous goldbricks by a gulled society.

But Katona, intent upon Philosophy –a true philosopher– neglected as so many did, life's smaller sordid details.

He forgot to dodge the draft.

And in Korea, during lulls in the genocide, he complained at length to Osborne.

But Osborne had lived his life sitting in tall thin grass. Drinking cold cans of beer. In the lace shade of high elms, while the ball game squawked on the radio.

In Korean streets, strewn with sewage, flanked by hovels, he walked mortified; unable to meet the beaten gaze of those who had never even been given the chance to struggle.

He told Katona, "There are more important things to worry about."

He said, "It sounds corny, but you know, if I get out of this alive, I'd like to do my bit to leave the world a better place than I found it."

Now Mal Katona knew that every idealist is in some way five feet tall and hunchbacked. Not Osborne. So he disagreed, but liked him.

He said, "Sure, Amos, write me all about it. You know my address after it's over, American Express. Paris. France." ₩

A trim little man minced into his bar –called, with modesty characteristic: FREDDY ROSOFF'S BAR– said:

"What *mar*velous primitives!

"What primitives?" said Rosoff.

who loathed queers,

"Those *paint*ings!"

53

especially wise queers,
"What's wrong with them paintings?"
"They're very *good!*"
who tried to cadge drinks on the house.
"Who did them?"
"Who d'ya think did 'em. I did 'em."
"Really!"
"Really."
"Would you sell them?"
"*Sell* 'em? Sure, I'll sell 'em."
"How much do you want?"
(Five dollars? Ten dollars?)
"Hundred for the big ones, fifty for the little ones."
"Well, then; I'll take those two there," the queer said, pointing.
"And that one there . . . and that one."
He returned the next day with his friend. Arranging a show.

Rosoff sold twenty-four paintings. Three thousand, four hundred and fifty dollars (just for paintings!) less the commission, those bastards! ⟡

. . . and another year. The hours with her were spent telling her he loved her; he didn't care where they were; anywhere; on a crowded bus, in a theater lobby, a Village bar; at galleries, recital halls, sports-car races. Trying to review an evening objectively, he could not understand why she saw him at all. What pleasure could she take in the company of a lovesick bore? He had lost whatever vestige of pride he possessed, yet knew if he debased himself utterly he might achieve that sordid dignity so akin to sainthood – *Notes From Underground*, Leopold Bloom, even Jean Genet– but he lacked the courage to rise to such depths. ⟡

His first wife, Charlyne, he met at a party, "I knew it was a mistake, how could anyone seriously marry a girl named Charlyne?" a Village type with a remote expression, a curiously disconnected manner of speech, and long black hair. Marsh asked her to model for him; she agreed, appeared the next day, and

54

immediately disrobed. Despite that most ancient of painter's ploys, Marsh had honestly intended to sketch her, not necessarily in the nude. "Sure I was serious about painting her, but Christ, not that serious."

She moved into the studio. A month later her mother began making trouble. So Marsh married her.

After a month she bored him; after three months he positively disliked her. "She'd sit there with that way-out expression and when I asked her what she was thinking about, she'd say:

" 'What was I thinking about? oh, I was thinking about . . . the moon.' I thought that was weird but sort of nice. But she was lying damn it. I found out. She wasn't thinking about the moon. She wasn't thinking about anything. She never thought about anything. She was the dumbest goddam girl I ever met." It lasted a year.

"I sold the bar today," he said to his fifth wife.

"You sold the bar? What for?"

"I'm an artist. I'm goin' to Europe."

"To Europe?"

"Yup. I'm goin' to Europe."

"You'll have to go without me, then."

"O.K.," said Rosoff. "You wanna help me pack?"

He had been drunk for so long he had forgotten what sobriety felt like, and he had to be sober to write; he wasn't. Drunk (the hell with it!) dead drunk, he wrote . . .

"In the hotel Paris Contemporain. My room is seven by nine feet. One grimy window looks out on a trash-filled courtyard. The wallpaper, running from the ceiling to a foot above the floor, is an intricate pattern of sad flowers; red, green and blue. The sagging and scratched bed is covered in some sleazy material. More flowers. Different from the wallpaper flowers. A naked forty-watt bulb hangs beneath a scalloped reflector. A pulley runs it up and down. The pulley doesn't work. When it stopped working, it stopped at eye level. On the way to the sink you have to be careful not to get a faceful of broken bulb. There is a wardrobe in the corner, an armchair covered in (he was drinking up his hard-earned year of freedom: Helena died for him) dubonnet velour, another chair covered in white muslin. There is a tottering formica-topped night-table. Above the bed is a dusty twenty-five-watt bulb. To get enough light in the room both bulbs must burn simultaneously. This is impossible. A toggle switch permits only one at a time, to save electricity. Across from the bed is a stained small sink; from which the porcelain has been rinsed away. Pissed away. On the sink lies a slug of rusty metal like a billy. This is the plug. When you remove the plug the water drains off sluggishly. Guck, guck, guck. Next to the sink is the bidet, concealed by a shredding screen. There are flowers on the screen, different from the flowers on the bedspread and wallpaper. A crack like a spider web runs the length of the ceiling. There is, however, only one real cobweb in the room, in this miserable squalid broken-down rotten-ass shithouse of a room; a dirty string hanging from the ceiling. It waves slowly in the draft coming through the ill-fitting door. The cobweb is abandoned; spiders must be intelligent insects. All woodwork in the room is painted battleship gray. There is a rug, a patchwork wonder. Hundreds of small remnants of worn-out rug have been sewn together creating one large worn-out rug. It is brown-gray. There is one ashtray in the room. It says MARTINI VERMOUTH. There is a bent wire trash basket. There are two nonabsorbent towels.

The corridors of the Hotel Contemporain are always dark and smell of vinegar, cabbage and urine. It is the proprietor, I think, who urinates in them at night. A dirty old dwarf of a man. Dirt is creased into his face as into an ancient shoe. His wife is as dirty as he is and as small, but painted bright red. Another woman lives with them, as small, old and dirty, but brown. A leftover mistress from the past perhaps, or a sister. They never leave the office of the hotel, which is an indescribable clutter, heated to 85 degrees Fahrenheit. They never change clothes. The room smells of scorched ironing. It smells like the odds and ends of a thousand rancid years. It smells like a home for old dogs . . ."

just to prove he could, who cared? Helena died, for him.

He was drinking up his hard-earned year of freedom;
as, glistening with alcohol, lurching along with his wooden
drunken lurch, he made it to the street:
(he *would* go on: if only to watch the future parody the past.)
🐾

Each night was the last. Until his rage abated and he lay sleepless.
Then, from the single porcelain kiss she gave him at the door, he
created a caress; and from the caress it was but a short flight to
that fantasy world, all pillows and eiderdown where, as the
Amorous Socerer, he touched her with his wand and she became a
woman, a woman who loved him in return. The morning found
him, inevitably, at the telephone.   🐾

By the age of thirty-five, Stefan G. Verduin had published seven
novels. Praised by the critics, purchased by the public, a success,
he considered himself an artist. And if interest in translating his
work was lacking, restricting his reputation to his native Holland,
still, better to be one of the big frogs in his little frog pond of a
country . . .

But by the age of thirty-seven he was a washout; and knew that
critics, public, and above all, Verduin had been wrong: his seven
books were not good books.

A failure, in no way a suicide, Verduin therefore descended to
the subterfuge practiced by the bulk of humanity: he turned his
life into thoughtless and ceaseless hobby. He wangled a job as a
film director. He generated an active interest in philanthropic and
social-minded organizations. He became president of this. And
vice-president of that.

Tall, erect, balding, diplomatic, and respectable, he was sent by
the government as its "Cultural Representative" to those wise
cities that have learned that by cooking up a big enough casserole
of culture –no matter how *basse-cuisine*– calling it a "festival"
and inviting the world to share, their businessmen made a killing.
And Verduin cultivated a diplomatic and respectable mustache
commensurate to his role. He cultivated diplomatic and respecta-

57

ble acquaintances. He drank too much genever. And he went to see a psychiatrist.

One morning, however, at the age of thirty-nine, he woke up and went to the telephone. He told his ex-wife to expect no further alimony; he told his film studio to look for another director; he told the philanthropic and social-minded organizations that he was resigning his position of president of this and vice-president of that; he told the telephone company to cut off his service; and he sat down and wrote his eighth book.

This book was condemned by the critics and ignored by the public, and Verduin now, at last, understood his early success. For this book, unlike those others, was not the sort of second-rate affair the critics themselves might have written, had they had nerve enough to commit to paper their own second-rate thoughts. As for the public, he bequeathed it to his former fellow croakers in the frog pond; with one bound he was free of it; and from the sidelines, obscured, and in solitude, he proceeded to teach himself to sing.   🐸

On the freighter across, Rosoff won five hundred dollars at poker. When they hit Barcelona he got drunk and went whoring with Pierce.   🐸

But two years' close association with the recondite flimflam and its dragomen taught him his error. They were serious! Incredible as it sounded, the contributors to that steadily accruing fund of hogwash were sincere! And Katona, instead of chortling away four years in the boon company of fellow philosophers, actually had to work. His thesis: *Diplomatic Relations Between France, the United States, and Iceland: 1898–1904* grew slowly.

Still, the experience was not entirely unfruitful. It reassured him that the amusement he had always felt, confronted by the stuffed archives of human idiocy, was scarcely diminished by prolonged inspection of their minutiae. He exulted in the knowledge: that, as long as foundations existed, willing to finance Icelandic study, he,

Katona, was prepared to delve, even delve assiduously into Icelandiana, to secure his due share of the largesse.

It was just that the task had been unnecessarily complicated. For instead of mulcting the public, aided and encouraged by gloating co-cognoscenti, he would now be forced to gudgeon the pseudo-pundits with their own pseudo-science. He was equal to the task, certainly; but the way had become solitary. 🐾

Marsh had moved to Amsterdam, and he was drunk when the Dutch *Time/Life* man came up to look at paintings. He walked in, took one look, and wouldn't buy.

He gazed about adrift; a heavy man, colorless, very friendly.

Yes, he thought he was interested in buying a painting, in his own small way he had been collecting paintings, and he had heard Marsh's paintings were large but hadn't expected *this*. Marsh showed him smaller paintings. The *Time/Life* man thought he saw the "message"; it wasn't going well. Marsh showed him aquarelles and drawings; handling the situation with sullen, consummate unsalesmanship. There was a cold pall at price-quoting time. The *Time/Life* man retreated before Alain's potent breath.

A series of collages hung on the wall, made up of scraps of inane advertisements and blatantly absurd newspaper headlines, and pieces of junk that amused Alain; all held together with suns, splashes, lines, and colors. One was "Cheese," a second "More Cheese," a third "Still More Cheese," a fourth "Further Cheese."

Intently, the *Time/Life* man studied them; then turned to Alain. "Tell me," he said, "I am just a businessman and I don't know much about art, that is modern art, though I know what I like (yes, he said that), and perhaps it is not right to ask this sort of question about art, but you will excuse me, I hope, as I say, I am just a businessman and don't really know much about art, but what I would like to ask is . . . What I would like to ask, if you will excuse me, is: What, exactly, do you mean by 'Cheese'?"

Anecdotes. But Marsh knew better. Once, sitting around the studio, dead broke, half drunk, bored, cold, and too depressed to

59

light the stove, he had said to Stefan Verduin, "You know, if I ever make the grade, and people come up to me and say, 'Boy, you were in Ibiza, and Amsterdam and Europe back in those days, that must have been great.' I'll tell them the truth, you know. I'll tell them, Crap, it was lousy!" ❦

A day came, a day like any other, when it was over. Four years and three days from that inauspicious bowl of borscht. She had broken two successive dates, at the last moment, on her usual jerrybuilt pretexts –generally transformed, by him, into pyramids of Reason. He didn't know why, but it was over.

They met for lunch at a Sixth Avenue seafood restaurant. He ordered two lobsters and a Pouilly Fuissé.

"Jonathan, we're *cele*brating!" she said, with her gayest smile, which it had taken him four years to learn meant nothing whatever.

He raised his glass. "Yes," he said, "our farewell. I won't be seeing you again, Janice. I . . ." but the glazed smile crumbled, and the premeditated salvo of invective fizzled. He stared at his napkin. "It . . . just has to end."

"Well, this is one *hell* of a time to tell me! At *lunch!*" She set down her glass as though it contained nitroglycerin. "At *lunch!*" she repeated, rose, patted her hair, pivoted past the waiter, and sailed from the restaurant in vestal outrage.

He watched her, empty of thought, until the platter of lobster drove home the fact of her departure. He bolted from the chair, flung twenty dollars at the astonished waiter –who gave him a scornful but sympathetic look that said, "That's women for ya, bud"– and dashed after her.

She had disappeared. (How could she disappear?) Myopically, frantically, he searched the street, and spotted her a block away, trailing her unmistakable air-conditioned aura through shimmering July high noon. He caught up to her as she entered a delicatessen.

"Hello, Jonathan," she said.

"Janice, I'm sorry. I guess it wasn't the time or the place . . ."

60

"It certainly wasn't."

The delicatessen was crowded, queues undulated from the counter, lazy fans redistributed a static volume of heat to no effect; Jonathan's jacket was soaked through. Janice disdained the queues, moved to the counter, and became a fresh queue of one. The counterman nearest moved to take care of her immediately.

"What'll it be, ma'am?"

"I guess I'm not very tactful, Janice. But I meant it."

She had assumed her sandwich-deciding face, cheeks sucked in, long slender forefinger placed in the newly formed dimple. Under ideal conditions she could keep a counterman poised and anxious five full minutes. With Jonathan on her mind, almost instantly she chose pastrami, switched to ham and cheese, from a hard roll to rye bread, ordered a pickle –sour but not *too* sour– and a container of milk, no, an orangeade.

"What's yours, Jack?"

"Nothing."

"Aren't you having *any*thing?"

"I just lost my appetite. Look, Janice, darling," he rasped in her ear, hungry customers pressed them against the counter. "It just can't go on this way. It has to end sometime, and this is killing me . . ."

"Mustard or mayonnaise?"

"Mustard please . . ."

(The Cavalier castrated:— *To Janice –Upon buying a Pastrami Sandwich.*)

" . . . maybe it's better this way, Jonathan."

"It's four years now. If you don't love me now, you never will . . . will you?"

"I don't *know*, Jonathan. I don't know my own mind, how do *I* know what I'm going to think . . ."

"Cole slaw?"

(A Seventh Avenue Swann. But he could not ride in sorrow, drawn by matched bays –or whatever they were– beneath the weeping trees of the Bois de Bologne . . .)

Finger placed in the hollow of her cheek, she thought.

"No cole slaw thank you, not today."

"If you would say you thought there was a chance."

"I can't *force* myself to love you . . . people are *watching* us."

"Let them. No, I know. I'm being an idiot, I just don't know how I'll live without you . . ."

"*You're* the one who is saying good-by, Jonathan, not *me*."

"You want that pickle sliced, ma'am?" (Only for Janice do countermen slice pickles.)

"Yes, please."

"It isn't your parents?"

"Well, it isn't *just* because of my parents."

The vast damp woman behind them listened avidly, haltered apparently in chicken wire which cut into Jonathan's back.

"I have to do this. You understand that, don't you. . . ?"

"That to go, lady?"

"Yes, to go."

"If you could just give me one tiny gleam of . . . hope . . ."

"*I* don't know, Jonathan. I want to be fair and maybe this way is better. But," she smiled a sad sweet smile. "I *will* miss you . . . Jonathan, you're *drip*ping wet!"

She paid for her sandwich and, at a smile, a Red Sea of customers was riven. It closed upon Jonathan who fought his way through. Janice was already strolling: slowly down the street. They walked to Macy's in silence and she took his arm –something she never did.

"Good-by, Janice," he said at the door.

"Good-by, Jonathan."

He waited for her kiss but she glanced at the throng about them, and shook his hand. ❦

"Come, Delaney," she said (with that accent), "I will make love with you." ❦

The world had not noticeably become a better place since Osborne set out to improve it –the Assistant Coordinator of Cultural

Relations in Benghazi. He taught Arabs the meaning of democracy: prevented them from pilfering (approved) library books.

Trying to impossibly relate Korea, Benghazi, Chevrolets among the camels, Arabs in rumpled suits amid burnooses –and un-American Osborne liked the latter– to afternoons drinking beer, in the lace shade of high elms, while the ball game squawked on the radio.

What did the big house girdled in orchards mean? compared to "The Gardens" where he lived? that bright warren, with officers and diplomats who drank, and had trouble with their wives, and hated Commies.

"Peace! . . . um . . . er . . . Democracy! We offer . . . um . . . arms. For defense!"

FIFTY THOUSAND JEWS SLAIN BY ARABS IN BORDER CLASH

FIFTY THOUSAND ARABS SLAIN BY JEWS IN BORDER CLASH

BORDER CLASH LAID TO COMMUNIST INFILTRATORS

They all had an answer but Osborne.

"A refrigerator in every . . . um . . . kitchen! A free yoyo for each . . . er . . . anti-Communist child!"

"The Arab nations refuse aid from Capitalist Imperialist America!"

"Israel accepts the generous American offer of yoyos. As long as there are no strings attached!"

In the heat and stench of Benghazi, Amos Osborne pondered, knowing that a standard of living was not a way of life, unable to say so. For his job was to say yes when yes was required. But now thinking perhaps there was no point in becoming –as he certainly would saying yes– Assistant (Ancillary Accessory Adjutant) to the Third Under Undersecretary of State.

Which of those six (sexless) women would old John Adams vote for?

In which friendly community would Henry Thoreau settle down?

For Osborne believed in that great auk: Human Dignity. He believed that each man had the right, and perhaps the duty, to sit beneath the elms on his own lawn and throw green apples for the setters to fetch: and that each man had the right, and perhaps the duty, to run or ruin his life to suit himself: that each man was responsible for the good or damage done: that each man thought his own thoughts.

And handing out (approved) literature to Arabs; examining Government-issued pamphlets —Raising Pigs in Arid Climates, The Truth About Fallout— Liberty, Individuality, Free Will, Moral Responsibility; they trampled through his head: those noble dinosaurs. ✿

Marsh's second wife, Kathryn, was an English girl as tall and as thin as Marsh himself, with the great red hands of a German stonemason; the sort of girl who could hitchhike all over the world, rucksack on her back, and sleep in fields in perfect safety.

He met her through friends in Amsterdam; she made no impression. He met her again; she made no impression. She turned up at his studio one glum November evening and said she was broke, but that if Alain had some food, could she share it, if she cooked it. He had no food except the indispensable can of sardines so he went out and bought some. She cooked it —not well— but she cooked it, and the next day she still had no money. It became a habit. It was a change from sandwiches.

At the end of the month she couldn't pay her rent; Alain was going to London for a week anyhow to see the National Gallery with its Piero's, which he hadn't seen; he let Kathryn stay in the studio until he returned: to find it spotless; scrubbed and polished. She had cleaned all the cat had bequeathed, out from under the painting table, had carted off the rick of accumulated newspapers, cleaned the windows, scraped the crud out of the sink and the crud off the toilet seat,— which was nice. But she still hadn't found a job. And —for reasons too diverse and obscure for him to understand, besides he didn't care— couldn't go back to England.

64

He set up an extra bed for her in the studio since making love to her was inconceivable, until one night he did.

(Oh well,) she was better (though not by much) than nothing, and if she found a decent job it would pay for rent and food and the little money he had could be sensibly spent on paint.

She was, however, incapable of learning Dutch; couldn't type or take steno; she was a photographer.

She spent his money for film and took thousands of human-interest photographs which she developed in a rented darkroom; and then was astonished to learn that Dutch newspapers employed staff photographers; and had ample free-lance material already. She was a painter.

She made little aquarelles and drawings (École de Montmartre) to sell to tourists and after three weeks plying the Rembrant-splein and Leidseplein actually sold two for twenty-five guilders apiece: she was a restauratrice.

She planned to open a restaurant to attract artists and intellectuals –and therefore tourists in the summer. She planned all the menus and priced red-and-white-checkered tablecloths. At The Boul' Mich' everything was to be served on wooden plates; the silverware would be Swedish. She ran about town for wholesale distributors of meat, fish, fruit, and vegetables, discovered just the cellar to convert, and was about to sign the lease when she remembered that she hadn't the requisite three months' advance rent, and of course couldn't raise it. The ephemeral stream of Marsh money dried up; and she was (at last, her métier) a scrub-woman.

The police told Marsh to report to headquarters, his visa had expired six months ago; he hadn't known visas were necessary. Kathryn's had expired as well and she went with him. She gave his address as hers and, it being Holland, living together unmarried was illegal; so, since she was pregnant, he married her.   ❦

"Jonathan? Is there anything wrong?"
"No."

"You don't seem very happy these days."

". . ."

"Is there anything we can do to help?"

Like most Jewish mothers, she was utterly selfless, utterly devoted. To see her son happy she would have gladly sacrificed her life. And she never let him forget it for a minute. ℣

For no known or comprehensible reason, Alain Marsh had moved to Brussels. As he wrote to Stefan Verduin:

"Brussels is a great town. No kidding. It's wild. The Philadelphia of Europe. I'm broke as usual and running up debts impossible to pay. I don't care any more. Or I wouldn't care if the art-supply store would give me credit. They won't. So I'm currently out of paint, canvas, inspiration, energy and food. I know four people here. I don't talk to them. Everyone I meet is a fink. They don't smoke, they don't drink, they don't horse around. All they do is sit around and talk through their asses about ART. I spread the gospel. I tell them that in New York painters would rather get drunk and be millionaires. I don't know why I'm here. I shouldn't have left Amsterdam. The only places to be are Paris and New York. I can't afford either of them. I can't afford Brussels.

"Kathryn is in her eighth month and can't work any more so our only money comes from those stupid translations. Now I'm in the movies though. Last week I was a mob. This week I'm a type in St. Germain. Five bucks an afternoon and carfare. I was depressed as hell about the kid but now I'm used to the idea. There's a foundation helping us. They were founded to give aid to fleeing French aristocrats during the Revolution but they ran out of aristocrats. So now they help escaped convicts, unwed mothers, psychopaths and artists. They came up to the studio the other day. Very sympathetic. Said no one could live like this. We agreed. So there we were expecting tins of ham and caviar and beer and pretzels and you know what they sent? Brooms and mops and soap and window putty and floor wax so we could get the place looking decent for the baby. Also some baby clothes. No whiskey.

"You know what I have? Piles. It doesn't surprise me. I can't

66

afford a doctor so each day I offer a candle to Saint Awdry. I discovered her in a book on medieval magic. She's the patron saint of people suffering from piles. It's the truth. I'm starting a cult.

"THERE IS NOTHING, BUT NOTHING, TO DO IN BRUSSELS. Except get drunk. Also I loused myself up once and for all with Levy. Listen to this letter, he's a bigger fink by the day. About possible show in New York . . .

" 'Alain, let me urge you to try and do good work (what's he think I try to do? Bad work?). Try to scale down your thinking, there is no reason why your painting ideas have to be on so grand a scale, and you must make your small paintings self-contained and self-explanatory, and not fragments of large paintings (blah, blah, blah) . . .

" 'As for a show in New York, I do hope you will not be too disappointed when I tell you that at present the indications are not at all favorable. I have spoken with several galleries but as yet have found none willing to pay the expenses for an unknown painter. As I have told you many times, and I wish you would be reasonable about this, it would be much easier if you would change your mind and agree to finance your first one-man show (NEVER); you honestly can't expect a gallery to take risks until you have established some sort of a reputation for yourself. And you understand certainly that with paintings as large as yours, merely finding a gallery to hang them is difficult, and frankly, Alain, good though your work may be, and you know that I consider you a painter of exceptional promise, I have not dared approach the top galleries for I do not feel that you have as yet achieved your painterly identity . . .'

"My painterly identity! Jesus Christ! What the hell is my painterly identity? You tell me. I wrote him and told him what to do with himself, with Shoat, and with all the ninety paintings they stole from me. If I don't sell anything in this London show I've burned my last bridge. I don't care. And that's from Levy, damn it. He's supposed to be intelligent. He's supposed to know paintings. Sometimes I agree with the New York Junkmen. The question isn't why *should* you build a bidet into your paintings, or why *should* you make a sculpture of old tin cans and inner tubes, but why shouldn't you. Why the hell not? Tomorrow I hope I know why not again.

"Oh yes, Levy did manage to get one of the paintings into some group show at the Whitney. Big deal. Anybody can get into the Whitney. Besides the show is eight months off and who buys paintings at a group show?

"It's a great life, all right. If you feel like coming down for a visit, you're crazy but welcome. We'll split a can of sardines.

I remain,

The Greatest Painter in the World,

Rockhead B. Normalwell

"P.S. The best things in life may be free, but the good things are damned expensive."

Yet that letter, like most of them, scraps of wrapping paper, half drawing, half collage, stuffed into a battered envelope, boasted a scraggy indignant behemoth on ice skates, accurately labeled: "The Shaggy Short-trunked Saber-toothed Ice-skating Elephant." And a page was devoted to four wild-eyed bearded maniacs astride a galloping rhinoceros: "The Four Rhinoceros-men of the Apocalypse."

Yet he stuck it out; not caring to become Assistant (Ancillary Accessory Adjutant) to the Third Under Undersecretary of State; just tenacious:— until Albert died; then he resigned, returned. Flying Benghazi, Rome, New York.

"Well, I don't know," said Mrs. Ella Weinberg, behind him, to Mrs. Bessie Moss, "but there's *nothing* you can buy in Rome that you can't buy *right* in New York City."

"Yes, Rome was nice," said Mrs. Bessie Moss, "but we liked Florence better."

"The only trouble with Florence," said Saul Weinberg, "is that there's no night life there."

"Of course there's no night life in Florence," scoffed Mrs. Ella Weinberg. "The people there are all art lovers."

"Those museums!" sighed Mrs. Bessie Moss.

68

"Aren't they something," said Marcus Moss.

"Of course, at home we're too busy to look at paintings," said Mrs. Ella Weinberg, "but that doesn't mean we're not art lovers. Do you know that Saul spent the *whole day* in the Uffizi Museum."

"Couldn't get me out of there," beamed Saul.

"Marcus likes Michelangelo," said Mrs. Bessie Moss, "but I like Leonardo da Vinci."

Osborne returned. To take over the plant? To live out his life, oblivious, in the big house? Marry and raise a family; breed setters and go hunting in the fall? He couldn't believe it.

His mother met him at the airport: late; she had lost the way, and they drove back to New Jersey in mostly silence. "I'm sorry you couldn't get back in time for the funeral, Amos," she said. And there was not much more that had to be said about Albert. Who had lived his life the way he chose to live it.

Osborne drove, missing the old man, trying to accustom himself (without tears) to the loss; his mother beside him (she had aged) with that quality she had of being simply: there.

They passed Trenton, and Osborne imperceptibly, unconsciously, accelerated; anxious to see the house again; anticipating the curves and bumps of the lazy rural road that led to it.

But the road had been widened.

SLOW
POPULATED AREA
CHILDREN AT PLAY

(What children? What population?)

"Great Christ!" he said.

For the land had been razed; the Victorian houses on their comfortable acres had vanished, the rhomboids and trapeziums of woodland and goldenrod meadow –he used to bag pheasant and rabbit– were gone.

And in their place, like bright fungus, innumerable little boxes had sprung.

"What's all this?" he said.

"Oh, those are the new people, Amos. They built those since you left. A lot of new people have moved in."

The road had been surfaced. Osborne stopped for a traffic light; and studied his new neighbors. At first the little boxes appeared identical. But no. One had red trim, another yellow, another blue; one had the picture window to the right, another to the left; they had been staggered back from the road.

But it was two miles to his house; he drove through a blizzard of boxes; the same children (apparently) played in the same street; the same mothers wheeled the same prams; the same cars peered from the same garages. And the houses, no longer pathetic, ranked and filed as far as he could see, staring out of picture-window eyes like some species of voracious insect:— for they had devoured all the trees.

"My God!" he said, "how can people live like that?"

"Well, Amos, I suppose people have to live somewhere, don't they?"

"I'd live in a tent first."

"It *was* nicer before, wasn't it," sighed Mrs. Osborne.

There was his house! the same as always, leaning on its orchards, the thin cool grass allowed to run wild, the same elms aloft in stately senescence; withering early, blooming late, each year keeping the Osbornes in suspense, wondering if this time, at last, they had died their dignified deaths. Tires crunched gaily on gravel, and from out back sounded the furious joyous carillon belling of the setters.

"Ah," said Osborne, "that sounds good. Where are the beasts?"

"The dogs? Tied up in back."

"Tied up? What did they do?"

"They didn't do anything, Amos. It's a new law. There's a ten-dollar fine if . . ."

Osborne hit the brakes hard, the car left an angry parallel signature on the bluestone.

"What for?" he said. "What in the hell for? Why have a dog then?"

"Well, I know, Amos," she said, "it's not much fun for the

70

poor dogs, but you see the new people complained that the dogs dug up their gardens . . ."

"To hell with their gardens!"

". . . so they passed this new law.

"Anyway, Amos," she said, "there are so many cars now the dogs would just get run over."

He shifted into gear and rolled to the front door.

"Besides, Amos, the dogs are getting old, they don't mind it too much."

He hoped the dogs would remember him; and they did. He broke the new law, and the setters lolloped along beside him, into the house. Where over the course of the evening he drank a bottle and two-thirds of scotch. And remembered how the old man used to come swaggering into the room, rhythmically beating a silver spoon inside a frosty silver shaker; and even the artifact life he (half) planned was no simple matter.

In the morning, Sunday morning, a buzzing sound woke him; an unfamiliar sound; pervasive, grating.

And Sunday-morning sounds were birds, a dog barking in the distance, the paper-boy's bicycle on gravel, the snug thud as the *Times, Tribune* and *Mirror* –for L'il Abner– hit the planks of the veranda.

Model airplanes? Were model airplanes the fad with the new neighboring children? Curious, he arose; his tongue a lump of raw meat stuck in a sandbox. Out of the window he could see only patches of red, green and blue houses; trees blocked the view. He dressed; lumbered off to investigate, the setters illegally at heel, through the mad buzzing.

He reached the edge of his acres; the mystery was solved. On each of the minuscule tonsured lawns that bordered his, and checkered down the street as far as the eye could see, walked a man, clad in shorts and a T-shirt. And each man followed and guided a small, angrily buzzing, green-mist-spewing machine.

(*Voilà!*)

The sons of the pioneers were mowing their lawns.

Osborne watched awhile. Osborne thought: Each lawn was no

more than forty by sixty feet; a power mower must cost a hundred dollars. If a man is too lazy to mow his own lawn, a kid would do it for fifty cents. There are, say, thirty mowing weeks per year. Thirty times fifty cents; fifteen dollars. It would take at least seven years to make up the price of a mower, by that time the mower wouldn't be worth much, and the fifty cents wouldn't hurt the kid any.

But perhaps he was just a stuffed shirt: or had somehow missed the point; and the kid wasn't interested in the fifty cents.

He ambled along the frontier of his land, noticed the picket and split-rail fences erected to keep pat grass from Osborne wilderness, stopped to observe a mowing neighbor. A sign exhibiting Father Mother Daughter Sonny Doggy stylized in wrought iron informed him that he watched G. Ritchie; who spotted Osborne, cut the power, trotted over:— friends.

"Hi!" he said, thrusting a hand over a white and naked wooden fence. "Haven't seen you around before; you a new neighbor?"

Osborne glanced back at his home. "Old neighbor."

"George is the name. George Ritchie."

"Amos Osborne."

"Glad to meet you, Amos," said G. Ritchie. "Listen, I'm just mowing the lawn and washing the car . . ." he gestured to the driveway, where the car stood, pink and white to match the house, and grinning like an airline hostess, ". . . then why don't you come in and have a drink; meet the little woman and the family."

"Thanks," said Osborne, "I'd like to."

They faced each other across the barrier that separated them.

"Damn nice dogs," said G. Ritchie.

That was more like it! Dogs! He could talk about dogs.

"We're great dog lovers ourselves. But those'd be too much dog for us, must eat you out of house and home. Irish setters, aren't they?"

On the other hand he didn't know the make of G. Ritchie's car; or power mower.

"English."

More Cheese from MARSH

1 MARIE-CLAIRE IS KIND
  14' × 11' — 350 guineas
2 RED BUGS IN MY GARDEN
  3' 10" × 3' 10" — 75 guineas
3 JUMPING UP AND DOWN IN FEBRUARY
  10' × 10' — 275 guineas
4 SPANISH MUSHROOMS III
  4' × 4' — 100 guineas
5 BLUE DAYS, HERE AGAIN
  4' × 4' — 100 guineas
6 SPANISH MUSHROOMS II
  4' × 4' — 100 guineas
7 SAD MAX
  3' 3" × 3' 3" — 75 guineas
8 SPANISH MUSHROOMS I
  4' × 4' — 100 guineas
9 I PROMISED R. SOME SUN
  15' × 15' — 400 guineas
10 SERIOUS TITLE I: HOPE (with frog)
  12' × 10" — 300 guineas
11 SERIOUS TITLE II: DESPAIR
  12' × 10" — 300 guineas
12 SERIOUS TITLE III: TRANSFORMATION
  12' × 10" — 300 guineas
13 SERIOUS TITLE IV: MAN'S FATE
  12' × 10" — 300 guineas
14 FOR WILLIAM McGONAGALL: POET AND
 TRAGEDIAN
  6' × 5' — 175 guineas
15 PICTURE PUZZLE: FIND THE BUNNIES
  10" × 8" — 10 guineas
16 SOME OPTIMISTIC SPRING CLOUDS
  15' × 15' — 400 guineas
17 QUACK QUACK QUACK
  10' × 10' — 275 guineas
18 POINTING TO QUACK
  4' × 4' — 100 guineas
19 BLAH
  15' × 15' — 400 guineas

GALERIE STRONDHOMMEL
86 Sloane Avenue, London, S.W. 3

"Wait'll you see our mutt," G. Ritchie turned, and trotted to the house; returned trailing a spasmodically bouncing ball of (could that be a dog!) fluffy black wool.

"Meet Peppy."

Osborne sat on his haunches, inspecting. (That wet nub must be nose; those moist marbles, eyes; there are four legs, a tail, by God! it's a dog!) He pushed his fist through the fence to make friends. With a shrill yip of terror, Peppy bounded three ping-pong ball bounds to the limit of her leash.

"They're all like that, high-strung," said G. Ritchie.

Since, for whatever misguided reason, minuteness was evidently an esteemed characteristic of the breed, Osborne said:

"She sure is small, isn't she?"

"The smaller they are, the more they cost. Paid two hundred bucks for her. Pretty steep by the pound, eh?"

"Really!"

"I'd have been just as happy with a mutt but the little woman wanted a poodle, and what can you do at Christmas?"

"Well, I suppose over a period of time, you must make it up on food . . ."

"Food! Hell no! Ordinary dog food's not good enough for her . . . steak, liver, chicken . . ."

And Peppy, recovered from the first adventure, concealed herself behind G. Ritchie's leg, and yapped at the setters. The setters, placid, on either side of Osborne, waved their tails gently, feigning interest.

"Plucky little devil, isn't she?" said G. Ritchie.

And Osborne, obliged to say something, said: "That's quite a fancy trimming she's got."

"Damn well ought to be. At ten dollars a shot." He rolled his eyes in rue. "And you should see our vet bills, worse than the kids."

"Still, if you sell the pups at two hundred dollars apiece, you come out . . ."

"Pups! Own an unspayed female? Not us. Have every male in the neighborhood yapping around the house every three months? No thanks."

74

Osborne rocked from foot to foot. "Listen, I have some things to do back at the house. I'll take a rain check on that drink. O.K.?" . . . but G. Ritchie's wife had seen him and was approaching, followed by fighting children. Peppy dug up the lawn.

"Peppy! Stop that! Georgie, why do you let him *do* that?"

Introductions were made, amid squalling, and he met Adele; the drink was inescapable.

He told them about Albert's death, Benghazi, his return. Intrigued Adele, who, although scrubbed pink and white, and unremittingly aproned, was an intellectual and a liberal. She was interested in conditions there.

G. Ritchie asked him to try out for the softball team; he invited him to bring his wife and join the Krazy Kupples Klub.

"But I'm single."

"Oh, you see most of us in the community are young marrieds; sorry, I didn't think . . . well, bring a date then. You see, once a month the Krazy Kupples Klub gets together and we all go into New York City to do something crazy. Last month we went to Greenwich Village to look at the characters. We had a ball!"

"Stop that, Jimmy!" said Adele.

G. Ritchie asked about his plans, was he going to stay, or sell the house, since the land, these days, was worth a fortune.

"No, I don't think I'll sell it."

"I see! Sure! Improve the land yourself; cut out the middleman."

"Improve it? What's wrong with it the way it is?"

Peppy peed on the floor.

"Nothing wrong with it, just all that space going to waste, I mean."

"Have another drink," Adele offered.

But Osborne excused himself. And at the door, G. Ritchie said, "By the way, Amos, looks like that lawn of yours could use a haircut. If you don't have a power mower, borrow ours at any time you like, though –G. Ritchie, authority on the subject, assumed a judicious air– actually ours is a bit small. You need a five-horse job at least. Maybe seven and a half."

"Thanks," said Osborne, "but I like the lawn the way it is."

G. Ritchie smiled. "Well, to each his own, I guess . . . but it'll make it pretty rough when hay fever season comes around."

"Oh," said Osborne, "I never thought of that." He rocked from foot to foot. "Well, I'll think about it, O.K.? Thanks for the drinks," and he left.

"He's a snob," said G. Ritchie.

"For someone who's been there, he doesn't know much about conditions in the Near East," said Adele. "That's why everything's in such a mess over there. A decent administration wouldn't hire a man like that."

Osborne walked slowly back to his house, back to a century where dogs were dogs; kicking through the high still-dewy grass; and yet G. Ritchie *had* to have his dreams as well; his ranch-type split-level Cape Cod castles in Spain. ❦

He had drunk away another year of freedom, he had fallen in love:— though he knew better. He had avoided Janine and fallen for Melanie.

Pretty Melanie, she was so damn dumb! he had to have her: she loved another.

He developed Pierces' Law: A loves B and B loves C: Man's eternal E equals Mc^2 of Misery: and longed for Melanie.

And his novel, which *had* to be rewritten, was about six men on a ship –since he wrote what he knew– sailing back and forth across the Atlantic, endlessly carrying coals to Newcastle. ❦

He sold SAD MAX and PICTURE PUZZLE: FIND THE BUNNIES. ❦

Stephen Seley, a success at thirty, a failure at forty, sat down and began to write:— with the knowledge beforehand, that what he planned, would be intelligible, at the most –he hoped– to five hundred people in the world —: a work of art.

Anyone could hunt lions in Africa. ❦

He was tall, flamboyantly slouched, handsome but for his too-wet, too-red mouth. His full beard, red, was grizzled at the temples, and his hair, deeper, auburn, curled and swirled about his collar. His jacket, cut from what had to be the ultimate tweed, was daubed with paint –cerulean blue– and his widest wale olive-drab corduroy pants, daubed here and there with cadmium orange, stopped shy of his ankles, heightening the effect of mahogany boots hand-made from exotic leather. His shirt was raw silk; deep blue, and across his chest was draped, unobtrusively, a necklace of pig's tusks. A beaten but bright-red bandanna, twisted about his throat, said, in the corner that fluttered free, PAMPLONA 1952 – beneath a baleful *toro* head. Although smoking was forbidden in the museum, an empty jade cigarette holder dangled between his lips.

The girl with him was muscular, low slung, bulging in her leotard. She wore Moroccan slippers, no make-up, only emerald eye shadow that lynxed enormous eyes diagonally across a chalk-white face to the temples.

She said something.

He answered, his voice keyed low, deliberate, ripe with supercilious ennui:

"I know, Martha, that this chap takes himself seriously; obviously he tries to impress us with his palette, but when we rip off the façade what do we see? Another academic painter. Look. Over there. Isn't that a *figure*? What is the chap trying to prove to us? That he can draw? Actually, I'm disappointed but not surprised to find this sort of thing here; I've always said that the Whitney is no less and no more commercial than any of the other *brothels*, but when they say they're showing abstract paintings, the least you can expect is abstract paintings. I don't object to eclecticism as long as it's spontaneous. But this? Oh no. I'm afraid not. No, no."

"I didn't say I thought it was good, I said I *liked* it." Her voice, clipped and sibilant, a whisper turned high volume.

"Well, I hope, for your sake, Martha, that you're just talking. Otherwise, and please don't take offense, chickadee, you're owning to bad taste . . . mind you, I've nothing against the man. He's got to make his living, so he's got to pander to the public taste. But to perform this masquerade . . ."

"But you had a figure in one of your paintings. I saw it. Admit it."

"Dearest Martha, of course you saw a figure, and bless you for that. But I don't pretend to be a painter; I'm a poet, and my little daubings are done *purely* for therapy. Come, chickadee, I've had enough of this. I think they've got a Baziotes here and I have this desire to rest my eyes against his green."

"And Kerry Topping," she lisped brightly, as they walked away, "thinks your painting is very phallic."

Jonathan Klein watched them go, smiling his scimitar smile; but the girl next to him, treated also to the gratuitous lecture, clenched and unclenched a fist, in anger. He shrugged. (From whom had he inherited that Jewish shrug?) She was very beautiful.

"You can't fight Greenwich Village," he said, and she turned, and smiled; and then (and after such a smile) continued looking at the painting.

Which was, he judged –and his aesthetic faculty was the only one in which he had confidence– the best, by far, in the show. "Cold Blue Hole, Jump In" it was called for the hell of it –the critics missed the point. Lacking something though. Perhaps that absolute assurance of the mature master's hand? But the card beneath the canvas told him the artist was just twenty-five, and the name was somehow familiar; from where? (Ah well, at least she smiled) he knew that name from *somewhere!* (he didn't want to talk to her anyway).

"Imagine," she said, "a Romantic in this day and age!"

He turned an inner eye heavenward:— "(If you are up there, you Bungler, don't let me talk too much, don't let me push. Make me cool, casual, a sort of literate –if ugly– John Wayne . . .)"

"(And let that one felicitous phrase . . . let that one felicitous phrase: be symbolic and so. Let her talk my language!)"

"Yes," he said, "it's a fine painting, isn't it? He takes chances, and they work. I like that. I don't really care for the paint slingers

78

shouting I Create! I Create! . . . (John Wayne indeed!) I mean, I don't blame them, it can't be very easy to be a painter these days, but the result is a just a spoiled child's yowl (easy, Jonathan.) . . . Anyway, this fellow is terrific."

"Have you ever heard of him? Alain Marsh? I never have."

Her voice was small and cool as rills; she spoke too quickly, nervous (of him? with all that beauty?)

"It's funny. I think I have. But I can't remember where."

"I really love this painting," she said, terribly nervous, terribly excited. "You know it's one of the times, and they don't often happen, when you *wish* you could afford something out of the question . . . well, and where would I hang it?"

"Would you accept it as a gift if I offered it to you? . . . I'm serious. I know it sounds, well, suspicious to say the least. But you want the painting and I can afford it. I wouldn't bother you again, believe me. You don't even have to know my name."

She turned to him, looked at him:— through the brightest darkest eyes he had ever seen. Yet behind the glow? . . .

"I believe you. I do believe you, but I couldn't. I couldn't accept and actually that's silly, isn't it? You wouldn't ask my name, and I *could* walk out with that painting . . . and . . . I suppose I'm being a prude. But thank you."

"You wouldn't mind then, if I bought it for myself."

"Of course not."

And that minute smile transfigured him.

"I can't accept your painting," she said, "but I would like to know your name."

"Jonathan Klein."

"Annette Averil."

"Everyone must tell you it's a very pretty name."

(Words slide smoothly into place; cards shuffled by a shark.)

"I don't mind hearing it again."

"Would you like to meet me for a drink, Annette Averil?"

"Yes I would, Jonathan Klein."

(Delicate, just flawed cameo face; muted and guileless brown dress.)

"After work today, Annette Averil?"

"I can't today but I can tomorrow."

(Elegant body, all contours, no bulges; long, slender, exquisite neck her best feature.)

"Do you work near here?"

"Yes, I work near here."

(She had glorious hands.)

"At the New Weston then?"

"At the New Weston then."

"In the lounge?"

"In the lounge."

"At six?"

"At six."

"Until then, Annette Averil."

"Until then, Jonathan Klein."

(And who would have thought, at winter's end, there could be such, springtime?) ⟲

MERCURY HITS 95 AGAIN! the papers raved. And muggy.

They rushed! Gray hordes, dripping with sweat, pushed past him, jostled him, his pace was all wrong. Osborne had this feeling: fear, inadequacy. He had to stop, to make sure people weren't staring at him. They weren't. They hurried on by, eyes straight ahead, soaking wet. (They were, could that be? mad! Or he was.)

Meet Miss Subways

Peggy O'Hara

This Brooklyn beauty takes the Brighton Express to her secretarial job. Peg likes the theater, ballet, Dixieland jazz and housekeeping. She hopes to become a fashion coordinator. Sorry, fellas, Peg's engaged.

(and who would Miss Sewers be?)

Faces swept by, he choked on the purple air; but he had come to the city to buy a hat and he went to buy a hat. But he wanted a hat with a wide brim and all the hat stores had were arrays of little potties that sat atop his big moon head like party favors; and the suits the salesman said were right, were tight.

It was time for lunch. He waited in line half an hour. Seated finally, he ordered jellied madrilene, soft-shelled crabs, *marron glacé* and light Sancerre. Afterward, he tried to smoke a cigar, but the glaring waiter, manager, queue at the bar spoiled the taste of good Havana.

He left the restaurant, air-conditioned down to Eskimo comfort, and walked into a hot wall of fumes. He had never cared for New York but he remembered a Third Avenue Bar from his college days, where the best hamburger in town was thirty cents, and they had German beer by the stein. He found it jammed. Homosexuals with chic diminutive dogs, and men discussing advertising. Hamburgers were sixty-five cents, the price of German beer had doubled.

Out in the narrow cross-town street, a truck had double-parked to unload a crate, blocking the way. He had to unload that crate. That was his job. Everyone knew it. The drivers of cars stuck behind leaned incessantly on their horns.

Osborne needed fresh air. He had an absolutely urgent need for fresh air. Central Park wouldn't do; he took a taxi, uptown, to the zoo. The meter read three dollars and twenty-five cents. He gave the driver a fifty-cent tip, and wasn't thanked. The full seventy-five cents in change was the going price of courtesy.

But the zoo was green and warm and he had a momentary respite. Then the sight of caged animals depressed him. And those animals roaming in simulated free surroundings, even more so. For he imagined the reaction of spirited zebra or elegant ibex, when, on that first day, after the long voyage in prison, they were set loose in sunlight, and thought they were free:— till they came to the moat.

Osborne stood: before the eagle on his perch, motionless, still as

81

stone, glaring out with his unwavering golden glare of pristine hatred.

And as Osborne watched, the eagle climbed to the ground, very deliberately. And once there he spread his wings, very slowly. Solemnly, the wings unfolded: out, out (Just feather and bone after all; why should they spell what they spelled?) Wing unfurled, until the pinfeathers brushed both sides of the bars of its cage. Then with wings wide he began to turn. Slowly; steadily, the eagle turned, stomping the ground as though tamping it flat. For five full minutes he stomped like that, turning. Then deliberately, carefully, he packed up his wings and climbed back to his perch. Motionless, still as stone, he gazed, out on the world again, his yellow eyes eloquent— with malice.

Osborne took the subway downtown. He had to change at Fifty-ninth Street where the crowd swarmed like fish in nets. He couldn't join; had to watch . . .

The long trains clattered to a halt, doors slid open, a few harried people fought free, hairpins flying, wrestling briefcases loose behind them. A brief moment of truce; and the mob on the platform surged forward. Subway guards and policemen, posted at intervals, held most back, shoved the lucky few mightily, tucked the last struggling rump in, just as the doors would have scissored it (off?)

(And where was that Great Auk now?)

He donated a token to the Transit Authority and walked to where he was going. He called Jonathan, Jonathan wasn't home, so he ate a sandwich, drank some beer, and went to a concert alone. All Vivaldi: it wasn't enough.   🐿

She was never bitchy, never refractory; her caprice was his delight . . .

"Jonathan, let's charter a boat and go deep-sea fishing."

"Let's go to a night ball game."

"The trotters."

"The Cloisters."

"Let's buy a bottle of bourbon and go up to Poundridge, and have a picnic."

She wore outrageous hats successfully.

She bit one, just one, thumbnail to the quick despite her beauty.

They talked: themselves, literature, theater, gossip; in a precious shorthand rare as joy that occurs when words mean the same to a man and a woman.

Hours were a tantivy ride round the face of the clock, and then it was time to take her home.

And back at her apartment; her mouth opened to his, her lissome body tight to his taut embrace.

Until, without his quite knowing how, he was out in the street.

All desire;

trying to convince himself that Yes! was but a kiss away.

And that it didn't matter.

On the nights they were apart, in the velour hours, it was his heart's hand that cupped her small budded breast in love, lingered (briefly) at the hollow beneath the frail rib cage, moved (gently, gently) over the delicate swell of abdomen, giddy descent of mons veneris, to the sweet tabernacle, which would never receive the corban of his love.

On those nights, however, she slept with Kent.

And he knew.

Or suspected with suspicion more gruesome than knowledge. (He dared not ask the truth: she might have –would have– told him.)

There was no Time the Healer. The white smock was disguise, and beneath it pranced that antique jester, Harlequin Time, with his bagful of wrinkles and bad memories, tootling the same old tedious irresistible tune.

(Does she sleep with him?)

(Can she love him?)

(And their own evenings, but for the end, were so . . . fine.)

He met Kent once. He had driven over, on a Saturday morning, and was waiting for her to put the last unnecessary touches to her beauty, when Kent arrived. He had forgotten his watch.

He picked it up from the night table alongside the bed.

"So long. Nice meeting you, Jonathan."

"Good-by."

And he had a day full of seconds to rationalize the watch away.

(He had taken it off when he went to help with the dishes.)

The busy alembics of his soul distilled: pure agony.

(He had taken it off, and left it there, on the way to the john to wash his hands.)

And from that brief encounter, and from the little (she knew: he couldn't, really, bear to hear) she told him, he tried to see objectively, tried to plan strategems (for love's rigged game;) he couldn't. The Kents of his imagination were such easy prototypes, he *had* to win. And wasn't winning.

There was Casanova Kent: roué, Don Juan, the man from *Playboy* magazine; gay seducer, devil-may-care; shock of curls to run her fingers through, a look that promised Paradise in bed –a Goliath of love.

And there was Dull Kent, Pope of Clods; Illiterate the Tenth. (What could she say to him? over the dinner table? over the breakfast table? anytime? There were moments –there *had* to be moments, no matter what– when a man and woman *must* talk.)

Last came Kent the Swine, the Hypocrite; Kent the Deodorant Salesman whose daily cake ($12,000 a year) depended upon the assumption that mankind finds itself so loathsome it can't bear its smell.

"(Annette! my love! Annette!, why Kent?) (If not me, then at *least* a poet. Or a truckdriver!)"

Jonathan Klein! Of course! How could she have forgotten that Jonathan Klein, with his big nose, and he lived in New York City. Or he used to. She didn't know the address which meant she would have to call Long Distance and she hated to bother Long Distance. How many Jonathan Kleins would there be in New York City?

Bravely she went to the telephone, timidly she spoke into it.

Eventually Long Distance said, "Long Distance" in a hostile galvanized Long Distance voice, and Mrs. Osborne circuitously explained.

There were two Jonathan Kleins. The first didn't answer and the second was a business address, Jonathan Klein Overcoats. She smiled. Yes, that would be the Jonathan Klein, Amos's friend, she told Long Distance, and jotted down the number with trembling fingers. For, she remembered, Jewish people always did things like make overcoats. ❦

"Annette, my love! It *can't* be Kent!" Clutching even that last straw.

"Jonathan, please! I don't know,"—she said, knowing. "Please, don't ask me why. I can't see you any more. But, believe me, you own a part of me."

"Yes," he said, "the wrong part."

"(Oh, do be cruel, Jonathan!)"

She covered him with kisses, frenzied and soft as moths, crushed his body to her body,

(which could mean: nothing: if not love . . .)

His hand found her breasts, her lips caressed his.

"(Now Annette!)"

For certainly, at a touch, the bud frozen fast in this undecipherable and impalpable winter must flower: when, with his teeth, he prints the rubric sign of his passion on the pale ivory skin of the long, slender, exquisite neck, her best feature: beyond the roistering act, and moan of ecstasy: during the languid sighing cernuous afterglow, she *must* say:

Jonathan, I love you.

He prowled past the curve of her hip, slipped through parted knees, to her thighs on fire.

And she was up from the couch, weeping: furious, wanton, entreating.

"Jonathan, I . . . can't! You must leave, please, you must!"

And he did. ❦

The GI Bill (and Ball) was over; he was pressed for time and money. He needed a year, at least a year of pretending to work: before he could present the wary duennas of foundation treasure with the required detailed plan for projected further research –into

85

whatever facet of academic flapdoodle it was that would serve the purpose.

A year. It wasn't much. But he had to weather that year; and the possibilities for stop-gap finance were limited, uninviting and humiliating.

Return to the United States?

And stand before the lectern at some Midwestern Pepsi-Cola plant, or simpering Eastern girls' school, or Ivy League snob hive, talking recondite gibberish at rightfully uninterested students? He? Katona?

Or stay in Europe?

Talk similar gibberish at slack-jawed GI's bent upon improving their minds at one of the University branches wistfully established toward this purpose? *Merde alors*.

He chose Charybdis, since, with luck, he might land Seville or Madrid –for the sunshine– and, accordingly, composed a letter recommending himself; couched in jargon so impenetrable that, he was confident, the coming month would find him deluged with offers and money.   🌾

He sat in his office, waited for Bernkopf, the button man (Annette!) who would tell him the same joke he had just heard from Halpern, the lining man (my love!) who would ask his advice: (I shall die without you,) pimply Seymour, his son (but much too slowly) had to decide upon a fraternity; wanted to join that one (Or was the blame ancestral?) which promised the most beneficial social contact (Fifty-seven wailing centuries of masochists?) after graduation. Bernkopf who called him Johnny; he detested people who called him Johnny . . .

And yet when cut did not Bernkopf, too, bleed? when the phone rang and a dry timid tiny voice said:

"Excuse me, I hate to be a bother, but I wonder if you could tell me if you are the Jonathan Klein who used to be a friend of my son, Amos Osborne, when he was at college? You see . . ."

"Mrs. O.! Of course I am! My God! What a surprise! How are you!"

86

"Oh, I'm fine, Jonathan. I'm so glad it's you, you see the reason I called is that . . ."

"And how's that big oaf, Amos? I haven't heard from him in an age,"

into a silence that grew.

"Oh dear," at last. "I'm sorry to hear that, Jonathan, because you see that's the reason I called you. I haven't heard from him in eight months now . . ."

"Eight months!"

"and I thought he might be in some sort of trouble and that if he was in trouble he might not want to tell me but he might tell his friends, so I called you hoping that he might have . . ."

"Where is he?"

"That's the trouble, Jonathan. I don't know."

"You don't know? I thought he was out in the Near East somewhere."

"Well, yes, Jonathan, he was, but he quit and came back."

"He was back here? He never even called me."

"I don't think he was very happy, Jonathan. When he got back. Of course he never said anything but I don't think he was very happy. And then he said he was going to go on a vacation and . . ."

"Look, Mrs. O.," he said. "We can't talk about this on the phone. You just sit tight, I'll be right out there."

He hung up, rushed from the office, past the reception desk . . .

"Mr. Bernkopf here to see you, Jonathan," said rosy Rosie, the receptionist, in Bronx through gum.

"Tell him to drop dead."

"But he has an appointment."

"In that case," he flung back, already at the door, "just tell him to stick it up his ass."

Past Trenton he sought the familiar road and had to ask directions; the new housing project confused him. But Osborne's house fanned the ember of memory, and he tramped the pedal to the floor, sent the sleek Alfa flying down the bluestone drive, trod the brakes, swung the wheel, executed a deft glissade that sprayed gray shingles with a gay and noisy hail of gravel –his quondam calling card.

Mrs. Osborne remembered, came smiling to the door (she looked awful) and he slid out from the low seat, took the dry linnet-boned hand she offered him in his. From the bits and pieces of her story he learned nothing at all.

He had quit his job.

He hadn't been sent? He had quit?

Yes, he had quit.

And what did he say he was going to do?

Well, he was thinking about taking over the plant. But he didn't seem to like it.

And then he decided to take a vacation?

Yes, he said he "was going to take life easy for a while." (She was almost certain he said that.)

But he didn't say where?

She couldn't remember.

She had to try to remember. It was very important.

Well, she wasn't *sure*, but she *thought* he might have said down south somewhere . . . or maybe he said Europe.

It couldn't have been a secret mission of some sort. That he had to keep quiet. Since he did work for the government.

No, he had quit.

"My goodness!" said Mrs. Osborne, "Here we've been sitting all this time talking and I haven't even asked how *you* were, Jonathan. How are you doing?"

"Oh, fine, Mrs. O."

"You're working for your father?"

"Yes."

"How nice," she said. "You know, Jonathan," she smiled, "I think it's about high time you found yourself a nice girl and settled down. What do you think?"

Of course!

He would *not* return: to that place he knew so well: the other side of Nirvana, the dark of the moon. He would not resume that zombie round: in streets filled with mementos: buying buttons from Bernkopf.

He didn't know –or care– how he did it.

"I'll find him myself, Mrs. O." he said. 🐾

That canoe of Osborne design was successful; effortlessly the double hand-carved kayak paddle sent it skimming; the fiber sail bellied before the gentlest of breezes; the outriggers provided soft and swaying stability. But during the enormous bon voyage party on predeparture night, it somehow caught fire and burned. He couldn't be angry. He shrugged mental shoulders and, becoming expert now, began a new and identical craft. 🐾

Jonathan Javert, the Bloodhound of Black Plains! as pith-helmeted and intrepid he led a hundred gibbering natives (along the heming-way;)

or anorakked and muklukked he mushed ten trusty frost-rimed huskies over frozen tundra,

and sipped sweet fumes of opium in sinister Macao dens, he . . .

was terrified of the telephone; to have to put questions to hostile strangers took one more hitch in the Gordian knot of his guts (and Alexander was dead, Annette, I adore you) the giant step out of the familiar unassailable (cozy!) horror of a microcosm he knew by rote, the leap that would land him before Torquemada the public, accused guilty condemned: for total social inadequacy and incompetence, the roller-coaster plunge into a macrocosm in which somewhere? someplace? perhaps? he might encounter Amos Osborne, was a step a leap a plunge requiring more courage than he, Jonathan Klein, ever hoped to possess . . .

Books!

There had to be books on the subject.

He couldn't be the first.

Once upon a time there must have been some previous sleuth, who had set forth in fear, in agony, and in ignorance, in search of, say, a lost lover; some flying Dutchman of the spirit who had beat against the winds of fortune to the four corners of the earth, and who at last had found her; had spirited her from the seraglio and, on the Sultan's stolen and priceless albino camel, had fled across the desert sand, pursued by shrieking eunuchs . . .

"Yes?" said the bespectacled white-haired little lady behind the information desk.

In panic,

"Books . . . about people who've disappeared . . ."

(The people in the queue behind looked at him as though he were a freak.)

"Detective fiction. Room . . ."

"No, I mean, would there be books with actual case histories?"

(The people in the queue behind looked at him as though he were Dillinger.)

"Criminology. Room Three fifteen. Next."

Which was the size of the Colosseum and, martyred, he walked amid cabinets, searching for C, but the cards meant to divulge the contents of each drawer appeared to follow, if a known alphabet, then one designed to discourage any potential seeker after knowledge. C, at last!

Five drawers of criminology: criminology by countries, criminology by states –at school he had always shunned the library– and the table he stood at to pore through the files was built to specifications of scientifically tested precise neck-crick height; his fingertips went numb from riffling cards.

Entries in French, entries in German, entries in faded purple ink from the library's primeval pre-typewriter youth.

Jurisprudence in Bolivia.

An hour went by.

And even had an appealing or revealing title appeared, its whereabouts would have been concealed in runic fretwork. He would have to ask questions; bribe the special druid they kept locked in the cellar for the code . . .

Prison Reform in Idaho: 1900–1950.

Prostitution Under the Weimar Republic.

. . . "Excuse me. I'm looking for information on criminology . . ."

"Criminology? Under C. Next."

"I've *been* looking under C. What I want is a book about people who've disappeared, some police department thing, or . . ."

"Police department? Missing Persons Bureau?"

"Yes! That's it!"

"Municipal and Government Room Two Twenty-eight. Next."

"Excuse me. I'm looking for information, or a book about the Police Department of Missing Persons."

"I'm sorry. There is no police department by that name."

"The department that traces people who've disappeared?"

"The Missing Persons Bureau."

"Isn't that what I said?"

"No. You said the Department of Missing Persons. There is no department by that name."

The librarian inclined his attention abruptly to the desk; to a card on which, a moment before, he had been inscribing still-inscrutable but now-familiar runes.

"But what do I look under?"

"I beg your pardon."

"Under 'Missing' or 'Persons'?"

"Under 'Bureau,' " and he resumed writing futhorc on the little file card.

Nervously, he copied the prescribed information from the file cards onto the insufficient space allotted on the request slips, made mistakes, recopied; painstakingly transferred the requisite arcana; eventually had a happy little sheaf of slips which he delivered to the librarian,

who glanced at them and said:

"You'll have to do these over; they're written in script. Request slips must be block-printed."

"But it's perfectly legible script."

And, smiling, he pointed to:

PLEASE PRINT IN BLOCK LETTERS

"Sorry," he said.

Jonathan Klein understood. This was the civil servant's compensation. For his civil servitude. And Jonathan Klein submitted. He recopied the request slips in block printing of glaring clarity, retranscribed the runic coding, and turned the little sheaf in again.

"No seat number," said the librarian.

"Because I haven't sat down yet," quipped Jonathan Klein.

"Seat numbers are required," said the librarian, "since in Room Two twenty-eight, books are delivered to the reader's seat. Therefore the seat number must be registered in advance. Without a seat number the stockboy does not know which reader has asked for which book. If you will step inside Room Two twenty-eight, select a seat, writing this number on your request slip in the area designated 'Seat Number' your books will then be brought to your seat by the stockboy. Seat numbers are printed on the backrest of each seat."

(And one and one makes two.)

Room 228 was large and crowded: with men in shirt sleeves, and just the sort of dumpy rumpled women who probe into federal and municipal archives. Long reading tables were piled high with books; and along the aisles gum-shod gnomes prowled noiselessly, distributing and collecting volumes; snuffles, wheezes, an occasional cough, the barely perceptible susurration of innumerable turning pages, subtly exaggerated a martial and sacrosanct silence; there was a faint stale pervasive incense of old paper, dust, furniture polish, pedantry; and into this atmosphere stole Jonathan; crisis weighing heavy on his solar plexus. He selected a seat, wrote its number in the area designated "Seat Number," handed it in and sat down –between a small man with very dirty fingernails and a squirrel's nest of wiry wild hair, and a nun absorbed in an immense book rife with diagrams– to wait for the gnome assigned to him to bring his books.

Ten minutes passed.

He wanted a cigarette.

NO SMOKING

(Annette!)

And behind his back prowled gnomes on their missions.

Twenty minutes passed.

Where was *his* gnome?

"I am Hungarium," announced the small man with dirty finger-nails, "but now I live America, work as translate. You are imgymyeer, no?"

"I beg your pardon."

"You are imgymyeer."

"Engineer?"

"Sure!"

"No. I'm not an engineeer."

"Hah! Then you are paintner."

"A painter?"

(At last!) *his* gnome sidled up, delivered a modest stack of books:—he went for them with terrier enthusiasm.

"Also my brother is paintner, makes much moneys."

"Please," said Jonathan.

"When I come America I also try to paintner, but could not in uny."

"Could not in what?"

"Paintner uny. Unless got uny card cannot paintner America."

"Oh, the painters' union!"

"Sure!"

"Excuse me . . ."

He plunged into the first book, the adventures and experiences of the Missing Persons Bureau . . . 98 per cent of people reported as missing are recovered! There was hope. Several hundred thousand are reported missing each year –leaving thousands still at large; innumerable specially trained detectives scour the surface of the earth . . . there was no hope.

"Is wonderful country America. Buildings high like so! In Hungary buildings are more low, are nothing. Pah! Buildings in Hungary!"

And the second book was less help; accounts of famed unsolved disappearances, in empurpled journalese.

". . . many automobiles America," raved the Hungarium. "In Hungary few automobiles, no automobiles! Street America fulled with traffic, in Hungary empty streets, Hungary pfui!"

He moved ostentatiously to another seat.

I Find the Missing, by Daniel Eisenberg. The self-told tale of one man's quest for the vanished; and one man: just flesh and blood (like himself!) He read, thrilled to dauntless Eisenberg, alone, following gossamer threads of possibility through mazes of misinformation, into sunlight.

This was it! The method, the manual. Eisenberg checked on passports, called airplane and steamship companies (of course!). He stalked his quarry down the paths of their penchants. A yen for Chinese food and there was Eisenberg, investigating all the Chinatowns of the globe; a case involving a ski enthusiast and Eisenberg combed the Rockies, the Andes, the Alps, the Himalayas . . . Eisenberg thinks nothing of minutely examining the vital statistics of a hundred minute forgotten towns . . . (Annette! Think of me sometimes!)

(Oh Lord,) and Eisenberg is a serendipitist. In an elevator, by chance, he runs into a man he has been looking for; for months. He has an automobile accident; the driver of Car B is the lost heir he has been commissioned to find.

(Worst of all,) Eisenberg is covered in rhino hide, he balks at nothing. To prise information from unwilling lips he transmogrifies: he is friend to the vanished, his partner, his brother, his sister, his mother, his lawyer, the cop on the neighborhood beat (how could he possibly . . .)   ☞

(Say Yes, Annette! let Eisenberg find Amos,) he tried not calling: had to: his watch said three A.M.: the phone rang several times before her small sleeply hello: but she hadn't been sleeping: music played in background: he knew that record: Monteverdi: V*espers of 1610:* he had given it to her . . .

"Hello," she said,

Side three, part ten, Sonata Sopra Sancta Maria; the solo soprano again and again: "*Sancta Maria* . . .

"Hello?" she said.

ora pro nobis!"

94

"hello?" she said, "who's calling?" as:

the volume decreased: to a whisper:

"*Sancta Maria . . .*

ora pro nobis!"

and at last, for whatever it was worth (not much) he knew: what he had always known: for the record player was irrevocably, irremediably, on the other side of the room: "hello?"

He pressed the lever and cut the connection.

"Ah, my Annette," he said, "not very good music: to make love to. Not with him."   ✠

He remembered distinctly that Amos disliked airplanes, preferred boats. Or did he like planes, dislike boats? One or the other . . . He opened the Yellow Pages: to Steamship Companies. There were seven pages of Steamship Companies.

(Annette!)

What was the Adamanthos Steamship Co.? And where did it go?

What could be the function of the Aeolian line?

He would start with outfits whose names were familiar; make a list, go systematically, first call those that went places intelligent deduction told him Amos might go.

(Anywhere!)

He closed his eyes, described three blind circles above the directory, drove one finger into the page, and dialed the number nearest the nail.

"Forslaw frammisbars, Good afternoon," said a woman's voice.

"I'd like some information from your passenger lists, please, would you connect me?"

"Certainly."

And the receiver spoke to him in Switchboard. Until another woman's voice said:

"Passenger lists."

"I'd like some information, please. Could you tell me if a Mr. Amos Osborne sailed on one of your ships around the third week of July last year?"

95

"One moment, sir."

And briefly he shared the private lives of secretaries . . .

"Yes, Mr. Osborne sailed for Havana on our *Qwertyuiop* on the eighteenth of July."

"Thank you," said Jonathan Klein.

"Not at all."

EVERYBODY'S ROSE
PERIOD

DRUNK AGAIN (HELL, STILL) BUT GOOD DRUNK FOR A CHANGE: JUST one more run . . .

and this time he would finish that book; so what if, with luck, it ended covered with dust, on the shelves of the seamen's library?

Dragging Anchors (? . . . no)

One for the Road

(no again, too much bravado, derivative besides.)

It was a good book goddammit as counting idle unhatched chickens he toyed with fame and fortune:— anyone to put pen to paper or paint to canvas who said he didn't, lied.

"(And what, Mr. Pierce, would you consider the rôle –with– of the novel in the twentieth century?)"

"The novel plays no rôle –with– in the twentieth century. It once played a part in a farce called Civilization. But the play flopped and no one's bothered to revive it."

(ho . . . hum)

But fortune; fortune was different. Rich, he could say Fuck You to the world in the only language it understood: the insipid esperanto of money talking, he wouldn't have to go back to sea.

Prudencia (Prudencia! he liked that) pressed soft familiar breasts against him.

"Come, Del, we go now. No?"

"No. We stay."

"Then you get drunk and fight."

"Not tonight."

"Always you say that. Then you get drunk and fight."

"Have 'nuther drunk, baby," he said crookedly, miming what would be his own style several drinks hence. He ordered.

She pouted.

He wrapped one arm about her shoulder: gruff but tender.

She smiled.

It was a pet Pierce theory: For every woman there is one man who can make a whore of her. Its converse worked as well, he saw: For every whore there is one man who can make a woman

99

of her. But why pick on him? She wanted to go with him, cook for him, care for him, and it wasn't, after all, such a very bad idea; only in Valparaiso, not counting Japan, had he had better than Prudencia: he couldn't do it . . .

Pierce's World Guide to Brothels: Illus.: Revised Annually. $4.95; an instant best seller, a reference work of unique value to mankind, a noble (and perpetual) vocation, to hell with literature! He felt (damn near merry!) like celebrating if only his shipmates hadn't been finks or fairies,

when two Negresses, naked, supple as smoke, began a lesbian *exhibition* on the dance floor,

which amused him:— though that fat whore with the donkey in Venezuela had been even sillier, *chacun à son gout*, however.

A nice sordid squalid seamen's bar that made him feel at home. Las Palomas, Prudencia; Prudence of the Doves, indeed! A good mood made the world a laugh.

The *exhibition* writhed to a climax; to wild cheers behind him, and it was unnecessary turning, to know that a group of tourists on vacation, had shaken their wives for the evening and somehow (*Pierce's World Guide to Brothels?* Bribed the taxi driver?) had discovered Las Palomas.

He would *not* have this last evening ruined, he ordered another, refocused his attention upon a fellow barmate whose anomalous presence had already whetted his inquisitive –even when drunk– writer's imagination:— inventing a fictional life that moved (factitiously) from easy A to vicarious B to C . . .

A Jew, drinking, at the forced pace of a man determined to get drunk, therefore staying sober. It had to be severe worlditis: and a woman. Ignoring the *exhibition*, and the tourists now clamoring for more, more, more.

Mr. Charles (Chuck) Muller laughed a gust of gusty Midwestern laughter: for that great card, Duke Dexter, was feeding silver dollars onto the table edge, which his whore snared adroitly with her vagina.

"In Germany! After the war!" said Duke, "We used to heat 'em up! On our Zippos!"

100

So Del Pierce, although his ritual of minding his own business approached fetishism, instructed the bartender to set a round before the young Jew –whose impending suicide was obvious– and when he turned, surprised, to acknowledge the drink, Pierce raised his own glass, and said:

"Forget it. She isn't worth it."

Jonathan Klein drank, then shrugged his Jewish shrug, and said to his friend –since friends occur– "That's the trouble, she is."

And, relieved of the obligation to pick up a woman –he had only come feeling that his standard unrequited love called for the standard antidote, of purchased placebo kisses– Jonathan talked, not about Annette, but about Osborne.

"¡Ah, sí, señor! Señor Osborne," said the desk clerk,–pronouncing the final e–"but I know him well. Señor Osborne who stayed here last summer, who drank much vino, who was muy amigo with the two noruecos, no suecos, los Larssens, who owned a yate. Sí, señor, Señor Osborne!" (pronouncing the final e), "who left the hotel on the same days with the two suecos, therefore perhaps on the yate, you must ask at the club, señor."

"Let's go drink lunch at the yacht club, then," said Pierce when they met, and hailed a cab.

But before installing themselves in the bar –amid peaceful shipyards sounds: the desultory saw, and uneven staccato of a hammer– they admired the sleek yachts rocking in sunlight, and Pierce went: "Heh! Free drinks!" pointing to the big deep-blue ocean-racing yawl.

He cupped his hands and saltily hallooed, "Ahoy, Tony Vale! You Aussie bastard! how about some booze!"

Nimble footsteps up the ladder; a curly head appeared; Pierce coughed.

"Sorry, miss," he said, blushing. "Tony Vale still skipper this boat?"

"Sure does," and she smiled –caught by his blush . . . and his profile. "Come on aboard, have a drink. I'm Pat."

"Didn't expect cunt aboard," said Pierce, *sotto voce*, up the gangplank.

"Tony! Company! . . . Tony's below," she said, smiling.

Tony Vale appeared, unhurried; and unsurprised, said, "Del bloody Pierce! What are you doing here?"

"Getting thirstier."

So they went below: Tony Vale and Del Pierce trading stories, plans, profanities: Jonathan Klein following, down the ladder, into the cabin, into a life so infinitely strikingly superior to his own that he stood dumb. While Pat –at the bar, mixing punch– was admired by Pierce, who found her movement in slacks quite satisfactory, and winked approval at Tony Vale, who signaled back No, not his. Pierce's reply in gesture expressed sympathy, *c'est la vie*, as he eased his solid capable torso back on the cushions (Vale was mad! And she was easy!) but there were other, more important things to think about in life, though –a breeze sailed through open ports, brass fittings flared, struck by shots and darts of sun, and polished walnut woodwork glowed– at present he couldn't think of them.

"Cheers," said Tony Vale, "and I want to warn you in advance. No cracks about Blakey, Pat's his daughter."

(Ah so!) Pierce's grin was wolfish, "cheers!" he said, and (untouchable –for Tony Vale) Pat smiled shamelessly . . .

Blakey was coming in a few days and then they were off for Marseilles; Blakey, Pat, Tony of course, and Mrs. Blakey; and Tony Vale had heard about the Larssens' boat.

"Larssen? Sure," he said. "Got caught in a blow last year and ended up in Campeche, poor bastards." So that part of the problem was solved.

Pat prepared another pitcher of ferocious punch, Tony Vale made sandwiches, "Rough life!" said Pierce, "Cheers," said Tony Vale and they all eased into afternoon.   ❦

"¡Ah, sí señor, Señor Osborne!" said the manager (pronouncing the final e). "Señor Osborne who was here and who did not pay his bill. No, señor, I do not know where Señor Osborne has gone. If I knew where Señor Osborne has gone I will write to him and demand him to pay his bill, for Señor Osborne . . .

Yes, señor, Señor Osborne was here with two other peoples, Señor and Señora Larssen who paid their bill, but Señor Osborne, he did not pay his bill. Señor Osborne, how you call it? skip? without paying his bill. Not even did Señor Osborne take with him his valise, but left those valise in his room, which he may not return until he pay his bill . . .

Nada de que, señor, and señor, I hope you find Señor Osborne, for if you find Señor Osborne, you must demand him to pay his bill . . .

¡Adios, señor!"

"Beer," he said to the bartender.

"*¿Que?*"

"Beer. Beer. You know, beer," he drew an airy tankard.

And that bitch, that whore, that cow, that . . .

Lady Luck had stood him up, stood him up again. And he would return, return to buy buttons from Bernkopf (*Sancta Maria* . . .).

Del Pierce and Tony Vale had already taken on unreal and figmented shapes, phantom yachtsmen sailing (*ora pro nobis!*) private and –to him– forbidden seas.

"You 'Merican?" said a voice into his thoughts, and he turned.

Sunlight. Silver parabolas of flying fish. The cabin of the *Sailing Moon* magically majestically aglow: with emerald, ruby, topaz, diamond:— empty bottles on the deck refracting. Grimes at the wheel pulling on tequila; spitting "To lee'ard, young fellar; to lee'ard!" Pointing out, off the port bow, into bright space;

"Wazzat, young feller?"

Jonathan squinting through spectacles saw nothing whatever.

"Something out there," Grimes concluded, heading for it, and after several minutes Jonathan was able to detect alternate reflecting flashes. Grimes had him hold the wheel on course. Returning with a spyglass.

"Yep," he said, peering through, "guess that's him."

"Who?"

"Yer buddy."

And it was Osborne, all right, paddling steadily along in his canoe of Osborne design.

Jonathan concealed himself in the cabin.

Grimes let the engine idle and lowered a ladder.

"What the hell happened to you?" Osborne demanded.

And Grimes explained. He had been drunk the day he got back. And then he had some "business" to attend to. And then the boat broke down. And then the hurricane season came. And then he "well," forgot.

Jonathan Klein stepped from his hiding place and said; "Hey, Osborne, why don't you write to your mother?"

Which had the expected effect. ▓

Mal Katona's thesis: *Diplomatic Relations Between France, the United States, and Iceland: 1898–1904,* –three hundred pages of fraudulently footnoted, studiously arid prose– was examined minutely by the Sorbonne's Icelandic department, and awarded a well-merited *très honorable,* his sheepskin key to the city of the idle.

Yet the gates creaked and refused to open, and outside the walls Katona seemed in depressing danger of being run over by his own wheel of fortune. For, out of the dozen letters designed to deluge him with jobs, only one offered him the possibility of an opportunity, and even that forlorn maybe entailed a trip to Madrid (interviews, money!). He would have to forego an International Economists conference in Bulgaria.

Of course he could just forget the whole thing and trust to fate to produce a suitably wealthy woman, but if that failed, the consequences were redoubtable. He would have to return to the United States of America.

And once there he could foresee nothing whatever that might relieve him of the necessity to: work.

He could not afford to take that chance. Doctor Mal Katona, Ph.D., to pay his expenses, sold the car that Hank (or Jerry)

Millette had given him; and boarded the train for Madrid, a philosopher feasting on crow. 〰

It was National Marsh Day! a genuine, big, painting-selling, money-making gallery was interested in him; an appointment was set; and Marsh flapped about the studio, tidying. He scraped up after the cat and shut the bedroom door eliminating the unmade bed; he cleaned (he would not fuck up this time) the john just in case:— how many times had good events teetered, right on the brink of occurrence, only to be blown back, into the realm of daydreams, by that ill wind specially assigned to him?

Not this time! He swept up. And Jenny Burrough would see! so what if she looked like an aging giraffe, she was used to American abstracts. He collected all the filthy painting rags and hid them under a chair. A contract! With a clause giving him a percentage of anything sold above his stipend. He threw dirty socks and ruined sneakers into the bedroom and closed the door. Or a no-damn-strings-attached one-man show . . . Refreshments! They had to have something to drink –anyway he did. He checked his wallet, no bills, as though he didn't know already. He searched his pockets, eighty-three cents. He needed whiskey, he bought Dago red wine. He opened his two cans of sardines and cut up the last bit of salami. Glasses! No glasses. Cups! Two, one cracked, but, good enough, one each. He made room amid jars, cans and pots of turps, brushes and pigments on the painting –and only– table; he moved two flagging chairs into social position.

A knock at the door. And Jenny Burrough entered smiling, trailing two . . . "associates."

Not enough cups! Simultaneously he pulled up chairs and ran for the kitchen to wash out jars of turpentine. Jenny Burrough, smiling, planted herself dead center in the studio and gazed at paintings; she noticed the lines Marsh had measured off on the floor (Oh God! He'd forgotten to paint them out!) indicating, for each category of visitor, the proper distance at which one looked at a canvas: FRIENDS –twenty feet, TOURISTS –ten feet, ART COLLECTORS –two feet, MUSEUM DIRECTORS –six inches.

The two associates ignored the paintings. Exchanging busy sibilants, they discussed Marsh's palette and working paraphernalia.

"How did you enjoy your stay in Brussels, Mr. Marsh?"

"(+¿%ç!!!!!) Oh, Brussels was O.K., but you can't sell paintings this size."

"Isn't that so! I feel that's because European houses tend to be smaller than ours."

"Yes. Much smaller."

"And what did you think of Contemporary Belgian painting?"

"(Yarrgh!!) Oh, they're doing some interesting stuff over there."

"I'm so glad you think so! We handle a young Flemish painter,

"(Whew!)"

"Cees Flapdrol. Do you know him?"

"(¡Sale con!) Sure. Flapdrol's really selling these days."

Everyone sat down. Marsh made (un)easy small talk. Soon (please!) everyone would start saying intelligent things.

"Oh, *dear!*" said one of the associates, pointing, in anguish, to a smear of Naples green, formerly upon the arm of the chair, now transferred to his elbow.

Marsh moaned, racing for the turpentine, having to go back again for the clean turpentine.

"No, *no!* That will just *smudge* it! I'll have to give it to the *clean*ers."

"Have some wine?" Marsh implored.

With acute apologies giving the sound cup to Jenny Burrough, the cracked cup to the smudged associate, the more aesthetic jar to the unsmudged associate, and the jar that he hadn't really cleaned out all that well, to himself; and gulped.

"My *goodness!*" said the unsmudged associate, sipping.

"You see, I was expecting this big check," Marsh dreamed, "but it hasn't come yet. This is pretty lousy wine, I guess?"

"Oh, no. Not at all," said Jenny Burrough. "It's quite nice."

Smudged associate constructed a nod of approval . . .

and it was time to look at paintings.

Marsh trundled out the first huge roll, opened it on the floor, rushed up a perilous ladder, tacked one end to the wall frame, rushed down, carried the ladder across the room, rushed up . . .

"Wouldn't it be simpler to keep the paintings on the stretchers?" asked smudged associate.

"Oh, I don't mind," said Marsh, "I like the exercise."

Silence.

"I suppose that's one way of looking at it."

"(Marsh you're an idiot!)" tacked up the other end, rushed down.

Jenny Burrough stood at FRIENDS, unsmudged associate at TOURISTS, smudged associate stepped from ART COLLECTORS to MUSEUM DIRECTORS and ran one sensitive professional finger over the surface of the canvas.

Marsh tacked up another,

Smudged associate moved from MUSEUM DIRECTORS back to FRIENDS; unsmudged replaced him. He, too, ran a finger over the paint surface.

and another,

Jenny Burrough paced back and forth along FRIENDS. "Very interesting," she said.

"Ah, tell me, Mr. Marsh," smudged asked, "do your paintings have titles?"

They had to have titles. He knew that. "Of course! This one is called *Fiesta on July 17, 1743*," he improvised.

"I see. And, ah, does that have any special significance?"

It had to have special significance. He knew that. "Well, it's the day the Turks chased the Egyptians out of Libya (Ho! Abstract History!) I'm sort of an amateur of Turkish history," he explained. "My father comes from there."

No one wanted any more to drink.

Jenny Burrough walked to midway between ART COLLECTORS and MUSEUM DIRECTORS, both associates assembled at FRIENDS. Somehow, Marsh snuck in another jarful of wine.

a fifth painting,

Smudged nodded his head horizontally, unsmudged nodded his head vertically. "Good," he said, "Yes, good."

and a sixth.

"You have a vital palette, Mr. Marsh," said unsmudged. "I must say that."

There was silence.

It was now time for Jenny Burrough to utter crucial words.

Her smile attained a perfect semicircle . . .

(For every dog must have his day . . .)

"You paint thin!" she said. "Most abstract painters today paint thick, but you paint thin. I've never seen an abstract painter who painted so thin!"

(. . . but every day was dog day.)   🐾

Jonathan Klein had wired Mrs. Osborne after meeting Grimes in Campeche; there was no particular reason for Amos to rush, and having met at mid-Caribbean he had to show Jonathan his island: before going back . . .

They talked. As old friends do after long separation. There was too much to tell to make sense those first minutes, they would need old-fashioned endless evenings to fill in the myriad details. Of course, Osborne's first questions were: what made Jonathan decide to go looking for him single-handed in the first place; then: how did he do it?

To the first question, or story of this adulthood –if it could be called that– he said:

"You remember that girl when we were at college?"

Osborne nodded.

"Then there was another one."

The second question, or story of his past week, took a great deal of time: as they sat, outside the cabin, amid crumbling odds and ends of rope, rusting oil drums, the trove of nautical junk that littered the deck of the worst-kept boat still floating.

Then it occurred to Osborne. That he had written to his mother and had given the letter to Grimes to mail, and he asked him about it.

"What letter?" Grimes demanded.

Osborne reminded him, and Grimes went, "Damn!" reaching

into the back pocket of his execrable trousers, extracting the sad wad that had endured certainly five thousand sittings and one washing.

There was no point in getting angry, and the island was visible now. They stood at the railing, Osborne telling about handing out (approved) literature to Arabs, and G. Ritchie mowing his lawn, interrupting himself to point into unbroken jungle, indicating overgrown plantations, stands of undiscernible cinnamon and spice trees, sighting toward the mountains where the women collected thyme and capers, and snared the great frogs that –dressed and exalted by fond gourmand hands– became the "mountain chicken" of island fiestas.

He said nothing about the town however. Let it strike Jonathan as it struck him –set in its vista of green, priceless, chatoyant– and Jonathan Klein experienced a rare tremor of warmth. For he thought that, having lost the capacity for disillusionment, he had lost with it, necessarily, the capacity for wonder . . .

On shore the native crowd laughed and cheered and jumped up and down. They yelled at Osborne. He yelled back in patois.

The hawser tossed, Osborne led Jonathan ashore, to be introduced to Theodore –who pumped his hand gravely and smiled his picket-fence smile– and Delia, gay and quite charming –who spoke to him in flawed lilting English that finished in laughter. There was the usual scramble for the bar.

Later, before dinner –Delia and her sisters preparing a feast– they sat in half-jungle in Osborne's courtyard, as just one bird sang in the breath between day sounds and night sounds . . . and Jonathan asked,

"What's that?"

"Mockingbird."

"Oh," he said, he had never expected to hear one.

"But doesn't it get boring?" Since *something* had to be wrong.

"No," said Osborne. "Why should it?"

"I don't know." He had always thought –hoped– Paradise would be tedious. "Well, what do you do all day?"

Osborne sipped at his gourd full of rum and told his day.

He rose early –birds sounding a rousing sennet for the sun, and morning filtering through ancient shutters, palest blue– and perhaps caressed Delia awake, or, desire dulled by last night's rum, perhaps dressed for a tonic morning walk and swim. The fishermen would be up already and Osborne might lend a hand, helping the simple-minded Cavendish haul in pots and traps seething with shrimp, lobster, all sorts of crabs; or paddle out in a pirogue to let out a long line baited with whelks, smoke a cigarette, and bring it back heavy with gleaming surprises. Delia made elaborate breakfasts. And after, in the still fresh hours, the natives expended that minimum amount of effort –bearing slight relation to work– essential to live their lives. Osborne pitched in and did his share; he helped cut cane at harvest time; he learned the delicate ritual of the primitive still; he anticipated those days when the men set out for the rain forest carrying spears, bows and snares for wild boar and iguana; but if there was no particular work to be done, he ferreted about town, rummaging dilapidated houses systematically, adding to the formidable, if unsorted, pile of yellowed documents, letters and journals which, had he read French and Spanish, would have given him the key to the island's history. And the island's history –that tantalizing why?– had grown from a hobby to a near obsession, though procrustean fingers of a recurrent incubus conscience tried to force handing out (approved) literature to Arabs into the mold of Higher Meaning; by lunch it was hot. He ate fruit. He drank the milk of a coconut, then siesta –a good time for loving, in the cool of the gigantic bedroom, in the proportionately outsize ornate bed that Osborne, a sybarite of sorts, had coaxed back into comfort– and they slept.

He awoke as the afternoon heat subsided, straddled the dappled, perforce sturdy, little burro Theodore had loaned him, and with Delia alongside, went for a trot down the deserted shell-bedizened beach; they took a prolonged swim, for the exercise, and the hell of it –Delia café crème and sleek, gamboling; Osborne ponderous but powerful, capable of immense unhurried distance– or, on the same burro, with Delia filing behind, he might plunge into one of the jungle trails for a session in green; unless it was rainy season: then he watched the great goose-shaped clouds boil out of the west, thunder shook his bones, lightning struck, and the whole world was rain –he had to bail out the house, vowing to do something about all those leaks, at least those affecting his immediate living quarters. He emptied basins, buckets and bowls. And when the rain stopped, the town was too lovely not to wander about it, admiring –even the natives did. Sun invaded, everything was steam, rising; one by one, birds shook themselves dry, began their individual song or noise: cascading water down ramps and stairways dwindled to streams, to trickles, ceased . . .

In the hour before dinner he missed English conversation, he would have liked to have some books; dinners were excellent. And afterward there was nothing at all to do except go to Theodore's bar to drink, and talk –hunting fishing notable hurricanes the weather current flotsam washed up on the beach, local fights– almost inevitably there was music and dancing.

"I keep damn busy," said Osborne: as Delia appeared.

"Dinner is ready," she said, lilting, and laughed. Everyone trooped in, took places around the vast banquet table, candles high in the rusted chandelier cast swinging shadows, the women brought in casseroles, pots and salvers –fiery conch chowder, lobster soft as petals, suckling pig couchant in mango rinds, nameless glorious salads and vegetables, rum punch cooled in the well . . .

"What do you think of it?" asked Osborne.

Chewing, preferring to extort the final flavor from his mouthful rather than rush, Jonathan Klein considered.

"It's sensible," he said.

And later, sated, they sat on the rough timbers of the jetty, the bay bursting with dolphins, girandolas, comets in their wakes; a hump-backed man in the gibbous moon smiled on the sea, and Jonathan Klein said, "Oh well. What the hell."

They enjoyed a tremendous silence.

"(Annette!)"

"Amos?"

"Yes."

"Can you think of one single reason not to stay in this place for the rest of your life?"

"No." His conscience! "Not really."

"Neither can I," said Jonathan, and better to long, if long he must, in Arcady.

But Grimes was bored with sitting around, he needed a drink, the exuberant bastinado of island music had begun blasting out of Theodore's bar.

Where delighting in their decision, they toasted. Osborne made plans. He would go back, sell the house after all, and let whoever cared to improve the land. He would collect his mother, and the dogs, books, whatever few articles progress had created that actually enhanced existence: and return. And looking forward to his new life he thought –as he had often done during his enforced residence– of Mal Katona,—who would understand, and know how to use his island. He remembered what Katona said:

"You know my address for the next four years. American Express. Paris. France."

and decided to write a letter. He told Jonathan about Katona; so Jonathan tried to think of people to whom an island was imperative, but could only come up with his new friend, Pierce, and Pierce, he seemed to recall, said something about going first to Paris. He might try American Express. It would be nice, having company.

Of course he might have applied for a grant; but couldn't face the applications, the prerequisite insincerities, the ignominious interviews. Besides his chances were slim, he knew: he wasn't famous enough for the coveted prizes, he wasn't mediocre enough for the others.

As usual, at the end of his very short, very frayed rope, Alain Marsh did what his pride found repellent. He wrote that letter, a letter of exemplary businesslike calm and persuasion, to the unknown person who had seen his painting, liked it, bought it . . .

But couldn't resist the envelope.

On it, he drew an elephant cheerfully tooting smoke through a stack, mounted on wheels, fixed on rails.

And below the careful businesslike printed address, in Marsh's zany spiky script, ran: Elephant Express – Ship Your Trunks with Confidence. 🐘

Madrid was expensive, his interviewer developed the flu, the final interview was postponed one full financially disastrous week, the wheel of fortune had become a veritable juggernaut, and Katona, genuinely worried now, summoned that agile djin supposed to come to the aid of imperiled philosophers.

"(Eh bien! Katona!)"

It came.

He donned his professorial suit, took his professorial notebook, went to the Prado. And sat in the Velasquez room, pretending to take notes: waiting . . .

Nothing happened.

"*Tu es cretin!* Katona," he muttered to himself, moving to the Goyas: waiting . . .

But it was the wrong season; the museum too full to maneuver: guided tours were everywhere, purveying guided culture:— Germans quaffing statistics at this Oktoberfest of art: "*Ach!*" they said. "*Wie schön!*" Americans listening politely, not really interested, uneasy in the unfamiliar presence of paintings; English women, like milling gardens –their guide's peaked cap proclaimed: ANOTHER JOLLY TOUR FROM BRISTOL ENGLAND– murmuring jollily among themselves. Katona had to sink, for there was no room to swim, while all around him the Common Man bathed in rented polyglot enlightenment . . .

There went one alone!

Blonde (Dutch? Scandinavian?) young, attractive, perhaps intelligent –Katona cocked one bushy eyebrow at her– available, and (*hélas!* disqualifyingly) poor . . .

Time passed.

Something *had* to turn up.

"*Fijn, hoor!*" said a Dutchman.

"So that's the famous Goya," said an American.

Anything at all . . .

And *there* she was, even something familiar about that: face, (Integrity! What indignities are suffered in thy name!) and angling to her side through art lovers, he employed the we-are-both-of-us-too-sensitive-for-all-this approach. Successfully.

They sat at an outdoor café; Katona working with easy expertise, and quickly:— she had to fall by dinner, he couldn't afford to pay. Nudging the conversation –eyebrows under control– from Art to the Artist, to the Artist and the Model, to Man and Woman, to Love, to love-making . . . she fell. 𝕎

Spending money in Paris but still on his good drunk for a change, and feeling his thirty-one years of gin amid kid students crowding cafés of the 6°, still not knowing where to go though it had to be Spain, wondering which of the women who wanted him to call:— Renée? the only one to put up with his rages. He really had to cut down, his stomach was shot. Meeting Seley at the Dôme: rampaging: he augmenting the ruckus. Seley was up to page thirty . . . and so what if he never won the Ignobel Prize, that book *had* to get finished,

(pretty Melanie, where was she? the dumb haybag.)

So. Upon reading Jonathan Klein's long letter there was no hesitation whatsoever.

A deserted island: full of women: with free drinks.

Just that getting there was such a drag. He could just say fuck it and fly but it was roughly three hundred to New York, nearly as much to Mexico however you got to Campeche, or take a chance on the bargain-basement flight to Puerto Rico and hope for a cargo schooner or yacht going somewhere in the vicinity. No matter how you sliced it the trip had to run near a thousand.

Or. He could get to Genoa, wait for a ship, and work his way back –to hell with that! he'd just put in a year.

He decided to look for Seley to show him the letter; found him at the Cupole: rampaging.

Of course Seley wanted to go too –a deserted island: full of

114

women: with free drinks, but he didn't have any money at all, and didn't know how or when he would get some (royalties? from the five hundred people in the world? to whom his book would be intelligible?) so he couldn't afford to borrow. He copied the directions to the island, however, against the advent of future windfalls, and was no help figuring out cheap ways to get there.

She was Rhea Hammacher, six feet two, one hundred and eighty-five pounds –tolerable, had the distribution been Junoesque: but no!– with her custard rump, dimpled boles for legs and huge pendulous breasts like plucked geese (and still, something familiar about that: face.)

She lived –she said for ART– for sex; she had read every book in print upon sexual gratification; she had committed to memory the entire convoluted lexicon of possible coital positions; in bed she toiled like an out-of-condition acrobat; at the climax she bellowed like a rutting moose and she had a private income; and in brief lulls during which she allowed him to recoup his strength she talked about ART and The Meaning of Life: she believed, she said, in Absolute Love, and, she told him, she had taken her previous lovers with Absolute Love and a desire to help them, but if, she admitted, her intentions were noble, her judgment was lacking. They left her. She was soured on Men, though she pitied them . . .

"Until you, Mal."

" "
    .
"You know, I'll never forget Goya for this," she whispered, nor he forgive him;

for it looked as though he was about to be aced out of his job, he had a rival,

Eli Rapp, ex-Associate Professor of Political Science at Wisconsin University, with two unreadable books to his credit . . .

They met at what he thought would be the final interview; Katona leaving, having just been informed of the competition . . . he took one close look at Eli Rapp, and capitulated.

The broad brow, sallow skin, the dull eye –that in the classroom assumed the uncompromising, the pedagogic glare– the slack mobile lips –so adaptable to the sesquipedalian Swahili of the field– the acceptable suit and familiar tie and brown shoes that did not need polish today but would tomorrow . . .

"Hello," he said, "I'm Mal Katona, you must be Rapp."

"That is correct," enunciated Eli Rapp, and Katona knew that voice well, precise, measured, solemn, trained to flow at exactly the speed of the pen of the avidly note-taking student; the prototype of voices that had droned amphigories over the head of a drowsy Katona through countless long-forgotten courses . . .

Could he stand living off Rhea Hammacher for a year?

He summoned his by-now-fatigued and sullen djin.

Nothing.

And meanwhile gnawed at the inside of his cheek: he manufactured a tensile smile. "Well, Rapp," he said, "it looks like the job is yours; you've got the qualifications."

"Thank you, yes, they seem to consider them adequate . . ." yet his conqueror's smile was a crestfallen curve . . .

"(*Eh bien*, Katona!)"

Could Rapp be talked out of taking the thing?

And why was he applying in the first place? for a job fit only for ill-starred philosophers? an ex-associate professor? with two unreadable books to his credit?

He hazarded:

"You don't seem very happy about it?"

"Quite frankly," said Eli Rapp, "I don't expect the position to prove stimulating."

Could Rapp have been sacked? For being a Red? For being a Pink? For having been caught in Political Unscientific position – with one of his young girl students?

Boy students?

But the secretary now called Rapp for his interview.

"How about a drink afterward?" Katona said, countering.

"Thank you very much, but I don't drink," said Eli Rapp.

"A coffee?"

"A coffee would be nice."

"The little café around the corner?"

"That will do,"

Where Rhea Hammacher awaited him, and where – in those brief moments when her eyes were averted –she had read a book about making friends that told her the sincere person always looks you straight in the eye– he eyed a trim blonde, alone! two tables away . . . who was introduced shortly by Eli Rapp. As his wife. 🐾

Sipping his gourd of rum; having reached that point where ennui and anguish become synonymous: beneath the banyan tree, whose aerial tentacles, advance parties in an old campaign to conquer the courtyard, had pried, groped, insinuated into flaws in the marble mosaic, found fingerholds, taken grip, and upended the inert luxurious slabs;

although . . . had it not been said? "Those angels sing sweetest who have been in hell," and he sang no sweet songs:— only that same mocking– (*Sancta Maria!*) bird sang (*ora pro nobis!*) obscured, high up in shadow:—nor, in all fairness, did he aspire to angelcy;

and (how kind of) those tentacles sparing the fountain, having slithered from above, into, out of, and over the scalloped lip, holding it now in tight arboreal embrace;

for the island women, willing, gay, stilled only desire, and desire –he learned: at least, still capable of learning– was irrelevant, though he would never have believed it;

while round and round the brocatella basin "(Annette!)" (perpetual love pennies pitched: into his heart's Trevi Fountain) pockmarked moss-clad cherubim ran, still finding Renaissance high-jinks fun;

when Delia invited him to come along with her to the beach for a swim but he found himself incapable of getting up from the chair, though he was sober, and therefore declined: as a tiny green lizard poised, timorous, in a scrap of sunlight deftly tossed through the foliage;

and, under the circumstances, it was absurd, almost immoral, to feel so. 🐾

"Fucking shit," said Rosoff, scratching his crotch, "you know what I got? Crabs, and they're supposed to inspect these fucking cunts, I'd like to know what the fuck they inspect them for? flat feet or something . . ."

"Hello, Freddy," said Mal Katona. "What brings you to Madrid?"

"I should be dead," bragged Rosoff, pulling a chair over, "I'm driving down for a show here, see, and I just get past Zaga . . . Zara . . . it starts with a Z, when I collapse, so they take me to the clinic and cut me open; and the quack says I ought to be dead five years ago. He sews me up and stuffs me fulla plugs like a fucking pincushion but I don't know about all this crap, see; I'm half unconscious. All I see is a nurse with big teats bending over me, and I say . . . Hey Ober!" he shouted at the waiter "cognac! . . . how about it, baby, I say, and make a grab for her. Next thing I know they got me strapped into that bed . . . Seems I pulled out all them plugs and went chasing the broad down the hall; so now they're sure I'll croak, but I fooled those bastards, here I am, the mother fuckers. Charged me twenty-seven thousand fucking pesetas . . .

"You seen my show?" he demanded, slapping reviews on the table. "Look at them critics; 'estilo muy fuerte' 'colores vivantes y una fantasia original' all this bullshit. Fucking Rembrandt and I sell eleven pictures and by the time the gallery gets done chiseling me I end up with seven hundred fucking dollars . . .

"Where the fuck can you live for seven hundred fucking dollars?" fumed Rosoff, anticipating no answer,

yet Katona had one: for that morning, having finally relinquished the job to Eli Rapp, he had moped off to American Express, trying to reconcile himself to an extended liaison with Rhea Hammacher, who was already subtly hinting toward –three guesses what? –marriage (and still, something familiar about that: face), when the Spanish girl behind the mail counter handed him a letter and asked for the Mexican stamp for her younger brother who collected stamps . . .

Katona knew no one in Mexico: he read the return address:

Well! Old Osborne! a glimmer anyway in this current November.

"(*Eh bien,* Katona!)" ❦

In Palma de Mallorca, at a café on the Borne, paying too much for gin; in one hour he counted four street hawkers with Toledoware souvenirs made in Minorca, two vendors of furry toys that jigged and danced when wound up, one balloon seller; two separate women purveying fancy shawls and fans, a gitano type in torero hat supplying the potential Nordic matador with *estoques, muletas* and *banderillas,* and one International phony Parker Pen man enjoying a busman's holiday in the sun . . .

But he figured, if he went to Palma, he might run into Tony Vale en route to Marseilles; and Tony might know of a yacht going the other way; whatever happened he'd at least be in still-relatively-cheap, and sunny, Spain; he could take another look around the Balearics just to see if anyone was there, then wander over to the peninsula . . .

Sure enough, the big, deep-blue, ocean-racing yawl was moored at the yacht club.

"Vale! Hey, Tony Vale!" he hallooed. Flat hard shoes clattered up a ladder; an ash-blond head appeared;

"Del, *chéri!*"

and a moment later his arms were full of Janine kissing. Hot, gay-he had once promised to give up drinking for her, and meant it!-her relinquishing embrace ended, in trilling fingertips down his arm.

"Del, *chéri!* You look fine! How you are? What you are doing in Palma?"

Coolly he studied her: not a wrinkle, not a sag (how old now? thirty-four? thirty-five?) and nodded approval: she preened.

"You look fine too, kid. How *you* are? What *you* are doing in Palma?" He sniffed obstreperously. "Same old joy."

"I buy this bottle *myself! Cochon!*" She pouted, eyes, china-blue like a Siamese cat's danced. "Damn! It is *good* to see you, Del, *chéri.*"

Tony Vale came out, his face full of shaving cream; and Pat, burgeoning in a bikini;

Vale said, "Just the man I want to see! Can you lend me five hundred quid?"

"Of course, how do you want it, cash, traveler's check or gold?"

"I'm serious."

"I'm not."

"Listen to this!" and Tony Vale, all enthusiasm, elaborated through shaving cream: he knew a boat for sale, not just any old boat, The Boat! the boat he had always dreamed of, the boat he never had money to buy; she was old, 1895, but sound, 45-foot gaff-rigged cutter with a jackyard topsail, oak framed, teak hulled, lead keeled, 24-horse Lister diesel engine, two sets of sails, a jenny, a spinnaker, electricity, butagas stove, shower, six berths. "She's got *everything!*" Vale shouted, "and she's owned by some old maniac Spanish countess. Her old man just died; or something, who cares? She wants to sell for six hundred bloody quid cash, Pierce! The keel's worth that! And I have a bloody hundred to my name."

"If she's so great why hasn't someone else bought her?"

"Because she's in *Formentera!* Nobody has six hundred quid. And she's just been put up for sale last week. Can you imagine? Trying to sell a boat out of Formentera! It can't happen again!"

"We've bought ourselves a boat! Read this," and took Jonathan Klein's letter from his pocket.

. . .

"Can I come?" Pat asked. "I can cook."

Pierce looked to Vale for accord. "Sure." And to Janine, "You too?"

"She can't. She's on her way to bloody England. To get married."

"To get *what?*"

"You heard me. Married. To some bloody earl with a castle. He sent her a plane ticket. When I showed up she wrote him and put it off a couple of weeks."

"You! Getting married?"

"Why not? Why shouldn't I marry again?" she said, "I am with Teem before Tony comes. He is nice and he wants to marry me. He says if I don't like the rain in England I can come every year to Spain for six months to paint."

Pierce scratched his head in incredulity. "He's going to *marry* you? And then let *you* come to Spain for six months every year on your own? He'll have a pair of horns on him that'd frighten Manolete."

"No. He is nice guy!"

"Nice guy! You mean he doesn't jerk off in your gear locker and that makes him a nice guy. He must be an idiot."

"Oh, he's just grand," said Tony. "He writes her letters and tells her he's her doormat . . ."

And she was: furious. "How you read my mail, Tony! Who you are to read my letters! That is personal love letter from Teem . . ."

"Well, if it's a personal letter from Teem you shouldn't leave it lying around on the floor of the john. Because that's where I found it . . ."

She stopped. Thought. And fury became hilarity; red mouth wide in silent glee. "Oh, Tony! You know what happened? I am in john and I find out that there is no paper. I feel terrible, *mais, il n'y a rien à faire*, I must use part of Teem's letter . . ."

Pierce guffawed. "For Christ's sake, you've been stepping on doormats all your life, you don't have to marry 'em."

"I don't tell him for *sure*. I tell him I come to England first. And then maybe."

"Well, make up your mind," Vale said. "You want to marry him, go ahead. Or else come with us."

She considered. Just a moment.

"Oh, I go with you, Tony."

"O.K. Now that that's settled let's go have a drink."

"First I must write Teem."

"Write Teem later. Let's go."

"By the way," Pierce asked, "what's the name of our boat?"

Vale grimaced. "Well . . . *Virgen del Mar*."

Pierce said: "We can't have that!"

"No."

Everyone thought for boat names . . . Pierce snapped his fingers.

"*Messalina!*"

Vale put a thumb up, Janine said, "*Salaud!*" and Pat required an explanation. 🐛

The hadj had begun.

Osborne returned, with his mother, the setters, a trunkful of the (perhaps unapproved) literature he had never before found time to read; Spanish and French grammars and dictionaries, a set of carpenter's tools, enough rough clothing to last several years, and —since two centuries of mindless gadgetry was bound to produce something less silly than striped toothpaste, and something less sinister than hydrogen bombs, if only through the law of averages— he brought a transistor record player and records, fishing tackle, skin-diving equipment, and a barrel of kosher dill pickles –a habit to which Jonathan had addicted him in college.

And from Campeche, he brought two letters for Jonathan.

Perched at the end of the rotting jetty, in the sun, his favorite loafing spot, he opened the first bulky and forecasted one.

Dear Jonathan,

Let me begin by saying that this is a very difficult letter for us to write. We read the letter you gave Amos for us and both Mother and I are very worried about you. We had a long conversation with Amos on the phone. We hoped to see him but as he was very busy and we were about to leave for our vacation in Miami we never managed to get together. This is very difficult for me to express, Jonathan, since neither Mother nor I know what to think about this apparently completely unreasonable idea of yours. And of course we wonder about Amos as well, although he certainly sounded very cheerful on the telephone and we always regarded him as a sound and promising young man as well as a friend of yours. He told us about your island, and from your letter as well it certainly does sound like a wonderful place for a vacation. But neither of us can understand why you insisted that Amos not tell us where it is, and since you do not give us any definite idea of how long you intend staying there, this naturally is what worries us most.

You may not think so but both Mother and I know you better than you believe. For instance, we have been aware for some time that you were not happy with the business but neither of us said anything feeling that you were no longer a child and eventually would work things out for yourself. As you know, no one has ever forced you to do anything you didn't want to do. Of course we both hoped that in time you would come around to a sensible point of view, settle down to a decent life, and enjoy the benefits of your position, but this running off to a desert island is beyond our comprehension. We certainly understand a young man's need for travel and adventure but what you are doing seems to us to be past that point. At any rate, Jonathan, you know that Mother and I want nothing more than for you to be happy. If it is your dissatisfaction with the business that is keeping you away please don't feel that Mother or I will try to keep you in it against your will. You are still young and for all we care if you would be interested in going back to school to take up law or medicine it would be alright with us.

What troubles us most is that we don't know where you are or what you are doing. You say everything is fine, and Amos says you are enjoying yourself and naturally we were happy to hear this; but frankly, since Amos seems to be following the same unreasonable course, we can't help but entertain our own private doubts about him as well. You know that I have never enjoyed lecturing you but I do not think, Jonathan, that you are treating Mother or I with the fairness we deserve. As parents you know that if something is troubing you, we are always ready to help. After all, what are parents for? And if we can't help you ourselves, there are experts we can turn to, and I trust you will not consider it boasting when I say that we can afford the best. In fact, we spoke to Dr. Nebbish about you the other day and it turns out that he is a member of the same club as Dr. Grossputz, of whom you may have heard. He is regarded as one of the very top men in his field in New York; and he says that when you return he will find the time to see you. This is a special favor to Dr. Nebbish as his time is very valuable and most of his patients are top executives, politicians and movie stars; but we feel certain that whatever it is that is disturbing you can certainly be cleared up by a few sensible talks.

You must realize how difficult it is for a father to try and give a son advice, but, Jonathan, in case you are not aware of it, you are not the only one who is dissatisfied with the way things are. Do you think that I enjoy every day I spend at the office? If you do, I can assure you that you are very wrong. But we all live in this world and all of us have to face it. It may sound like sermonizing but I hope you will believe me when I tell you that we do learn with age, and as your elder and your father I can promise you that you can't run away from the realities of life. The sooner you learn that lesson the happier you will be.

Furthermore, you and Amos were both very tactful and said nothing about the conditions on this island of yours and Mother is very worried about this. Neither of us understand how you can be happy without all the comforts you were brought up with, and that you are accustomed to. I still try to maintain confidence in your good sense and I can't believe that you would be willing to stay in some primitive or unhealthy spot, but Mother has all sorts of ideas. She imagines some kind of tropical slum without electricity and sanitation, full of insects, disease, Lord knows what, you know how your mother can be about these things. If only for her sake I think you owe it to us to at least come back and let us discuss this matter more fully.

I am sorry to repeat myself but you cannot imagine how worried both of us are about you. We can't understand your attitude, and we can't help but wonder if we have failed as parents somewhere along the line. Certainly you always had everything you ever wanted and did all the things you wanted to do, and you had the sort of education that I wish I had been able to have. Perhaps this was wrong. Perhaps if you had been forced to go out and learn the value of a dollar as I had to do, you would feel differently about things, though in all honesty I must admit that you always seemed to have a due respect for money and never squandered it.

Well, Jonathan, I could go on, but by now I think you must know how we feel about your behavior. Naturally your life is your own and neither Mother nor I can, or want, to run it for you, but we do feel that the least you can do is look at the situation sensibly and unselfishly and give us a chance to help you. We hope to see you soon and in the meanwhile enjoy yourself and keep well.

Your loving father

P.S. Mother says while you are there to get yourself a good suntan.
🐾

The second envelope featured an elephant, cheerfully tooting smoke through a stack, mounted on wheels, fixed on rails.

And below the careful businesslike printed address, in Marsh's zany spiky script, ran: Elephant Express – Ship Your Trunks with Confidence.
🐾

They set off for Formentera to buy their boat, and on the way Pierce explained how he had happened to come to Palma. Tony Vale said:

"It's lucky you're an idiot, Pierce! You're supposed to be a seaman! For Christ's sake the French and Dutch run boats all over the Caribbean!"

"Never thought of that: But I'll drink to it."

Which they did. And then to the avid hope that within the week no one on Formentera had scraped up six hundred pounds.

No one had. They bought *Messalina*, and spent several weeks preparing for the trip. She could have used paint, her bottom needed scraping, but there was no money for that; money went into lines and halyards, necessities; happily her engine needed no repairing, nor her steering, nor her sails. Pierce was delighted with her; Tony Vale was in love.

He gave patient sailing lessons. Pierce knew splices and some navigation although he had never sailed. He borrowed the saltiest book he could find and was soon expertly bandying cringles, luffs and leeches. Pat mastered the galley. Janine offered to do her share; after one meal Tony fired her so Pierce appointed her official figurehead; and it was impossible to get her to understand the reason for calling port port, starboard starboard, and jib sheet jib sheet . . . "Pass me that rope, *chéri*, please. No! Damn, *chéri, that* one!"

Then they were off; a crowd waving from the quai.

For Mal Katona, it remained merely to convert the spirit of Absolute Love into the fact of corporal cash (still, something familiar about that: face); and he feigned academic interest in solving the riddle of the forgotten island:—she agreed at once to accompany him. But sheltered behind (engouled upon!) Rhea Hammacher's financial aegis, he deployed toward another objective . . .

She had struck up an immediate intellectual friendship with Eli Rapp; and Katona had only to mention politics, economics or sociology –that expensive process of turning the obvious into statistics– and off they went; over the misty babblefields; tilting at windmills that have withstood the onslaughts of centuries of busybodies; but which *they*, conquering, entered; and whiled the evening hours away, endlessly milling wind:—while he talked to Betty . . .

The idea was to bring off the switch. And, accordingly, one night, in one of those lulls during which she allowed him to recoup his strength, he asked her if she though Rapp attractive.

"Oh! Intellectually he's very stimulating! But I'm a woman, Mal; a passionate woman! I need a *man!*" she said, her clutch imperiling his manhood, and she kissed him like raw liver . . .

Not very promising (Good God!). Now he knew! She looked like Samuel Johnson! She was the spitting image of Doctor Samuel Johnson! So he cultivated the friendship of Eli Rapp('s trim wife).

Rapp no more wanted to teach GI's than he did; he invited him to collaborate on his projected and quite spurious twenty-volume analytical, political, sociological, and psychological history of the forgotten island; an offer which brought to Rapp's mouth a flow of scholarly saliva, and which made Rhea Hammacher gush with the magnanimity of it all.

(She really did look like Sam Johnson.)

He arranged for tickets for the four of them, and for Freddy Rosoff; wondering if, on the trip across the opportunity would arise to see Betty alone.

It did not.

Mornings were cruelest to Escondite; mornings the cool rational sun, a no-nonsense attendant, shook the invalid city awake, took perverse pride in allowing her no time to repair her wrinkles: every crack in every façade delineated; the mansions along the esplanade wore tatterdemalion cloaks of stucco; worn merlons of the fort faced the sea –a row of giant rotting teeth; rough wounds in bartizans and turrets gaped; Francesca in her bice-green gown was a decrepit jade; and in the pious procession round the sun-blasted cathedral walked dissipated cherubim and leprosied saints; the pediment, once foaming with ornament, was a blur of stone. Mornings the jungle, always hovering by, converged to collect its inheritance; exulting in early light, infinite shades of green, emblazoned, decked in flowers; its tendrils and tentacles curled through the streets; huge green nosegays spewed from courtyards; rampant down the esplanade, thronging what had been plazas and gardens, the jungle tyrannized: but briefly . . .

For by noon, jungle, town, beach, blue Caribbean were ablaze. Nothing was form, all was fire. A torrential sun rained heat and white light on the stupefied city, bleached its bones, drove the natives into somnolent shade, or the cool moist sanctuary of Theodore's bar, lorded it over the shimmering cane, and boiled the lizards' blood –the only animate creatures– as, reveling in insects, they whisked over cobbles, walls and rooftops, etching thin shadows . . .

Later, as the sun careered west, the beach was extinguished.

Then the fort glared out at a steel-gray sea; blackened twelve pounders on the parapet caught, occasionally, a glint of fighting bronze: the predictable –but always astonishing– sunset filled the sky like a gong; held the cathedral in chrome orange and indigo . . . soon mauve shadows soothed old wounds, Francesca in her bice-green gown poised comely and mournful; the jungle receded to tousled imminence: and the ancient town of Escondite burgeoned and prevailed in perfumed, aphrodisiac dusk.

Slowly, and very cautiously; and into such a sunset, motored *Messalina*, Vale at the helm, Pierce prone on the bowsprit, searching the opaque water for rocks, Pat lashing down sail covers, making fast halyards and sheets; Janine stood forward and gazed.

The entire population swarmed on the beach. Jonathan and Osborne waited on the jetty, with Katona, Eli Rapp, Betty, Rosoff, as Vale nosed the boat neatly alongside.

Jonathan said: "Hello, Del Pierce. Welcome home." They tossed the hawsers and snubbed her to. The crowd surged forward. Janine had not moved; she stood at the bow, still gazing. "*Mon Dieu!*" she said to no one in particular, "but I can work here." ₩

Marsh arrived; with one rucksack, a trunk –full of paints, new brushes, execrable palette knives, indispensable hammer and saw– and twenty rolls of fifteen-foot canvas.

As the boat pulled near the jetty, he saw Jonathan Klein. And grinned his long-toothed vulpine grin. He pointed one long gnarled finger at him. "Heh!" he said. "Kline's In the Pines!"

And they drank at Theodore's: to the merry pointlessness of that. Where they discovered that Pierce knew, anyway recognized, Marsh from Ibiza. He had avoided him, anyone looking so much like a painter couldn't possibly be one. And Marsh had seen Katona in Paris (the *Village?* the *Nuage? Aux Deux Magots?*) ₩

By the age of thirty-seven, Carl Orville had published five novels.

He was one of those writers consistently praised by the critics for chronic promise; and as a serious writer he dealt with serious themes:—he worked at least six hours a day, and believed in "The Writer's Responsibility to Society"; his summers were altruistically given over to tramontane universities where he lectured fledgling Faulkners and Fitzgeralds on "The Role of the Novel in the Twentieth Century" and corrected their punctuation; he was available to women's clubs for an evening of "The Writer in the Modern World," and he subscribed to a number of impenetrable quarterlies.

His first three books lost money for his publishers –though each was hailed as progressively promising– his fourth sold out a modest first edition and was reprinted in paperback; and by his fifth –a bulky project dealing with Good and Evil, generously truffé with symbols– he had finally achieved that felicitous blend of dogged solemnity and pedestrian thinking required by those who disseminate prizes and grants: Orville was awarded a Gherkinstein Fellowship for "Creative Writing."

With this money he took a sabbatical from his post; with his wife and four children he went to Mexico, to Oaxaca, where he planned to write his sixth novel –what might happen should a small, irresponsible dictator get hold of an H-bomb– the book he felt certain critics would (at last!) hail as "significant" . . . "A major contribution to American literature."

Unfortunately, this book refused to grow at a significant, major contributory rate. When Orville heard about Escondite he was nearly out of money, so he went there . . .

With Craig O'Connor and Eddie Davidson, his first two disciples. O'Connor was a slender, blond, confused, conventionally handsome young man, ten years Orville's junior, and still searching for "identity and fulfillment." He had published a first novel –set in the Korean war, concerning a slender, blond, dashingly handsome young man in search of identity and fulfillment– but even the critics had been perceptive enough to call it second-rate. Nevertheless, it was supplied with facile erotica and fashionably latent homosexuality sufficient to sell seven thousand copies, go into paperback, and receive a Hollywood option.

Financially secure, but still seeking identity and fulfillment, he went to Oaxaca, where he became friendly with Carl Orville and Eddie Davidson. With the former by staunchly maintaining that his fifth novel –the one about Good and Evil– had already attained significance and was a major contribution; and with the latter because he hadn't as yet been published.

Eddie Davidson, a heavy friendly young man affecting a grandiose RAF mustache, was a playwright; he had just finished a three-act drama about racial integration (pro) and in Oaxaca he was at work on another about capital punishment (con). Among his acquaintances, his inviolate lack of insight into human nature was construed as possessing a heart of gold; he, too, thought that one day Carl Orville would write a major novel; although when asked for his opinion of Orville's fifth book, he would twist the left extremity of his mustache, cock his head in thought, and then reply in his soft, considerate voice, "Well, I don't think it's a *great* book, but I can't think of a better contemporary novel."

The word spread. A deserted island: full of women: with free drinks. Out over the Mediterranean:— to Palma, Terreno, Genova, Deyá, Porto Pollensa, Porto Andraitx; Fuengirola, Málaga, Torremolinos; to Sardinia, Positano, Corsica, Ischia, Capri; to Rhodes, Corfu, Mikonos, Crete; to Tangier, Casablanca, Marrakesh; to Dieppe, Bonieux, Cagnes-sur-Mer; to Perranporth, Tenby, Brixham, Saint Ives; Anguilla, Barbuda, Cozumel; Amsterdam, Munich, Copenhagen; Chelsea, Hampstead, the Latin Quarter; Greenwich Village, Little Venice, Big Sur, Cuernavaca, Puerta Vallarta, Baja, Oaxaca . . . to all the so-called "art colonies" of the world, where, if few were artists, at least most were "artistic."

The first to arrive, naturally, moved into the most desirable houses.

Osborne, by this time, had transformed a wing of the old Viceroy's palace into quite habitable decrepit splendor.

Jonathan took over a relatively modest mansion, in the row

fronting the beach; Janine and Tony Vale appropriated the most lavish of all, a whipped-stone fantasy built to satisfy the whim of some unknown architectural voluptuary.

Excepting Rosoff and Pierce, everyone chose beachside quarters. Rosoff, despite the heat, the climb, and his sixty-four years, preferred the comfort of a remarkably sound house up the hill, just below the cathedral: and the view did things to him he would never have admitted, outside of a painting: the jumbled ocher geometry of rooftops tumbling to the beach, the white strip of beach curving away into distance, the fort perched on its promontory, and the sea that, seen from such height, jelled to blue obsidian.

Pierce moved his one cheap travel-weary seaman –and Polish refugee– type suitcase, his typewriter, and a perplexed Pat, several times before settling down. The airy expanse of salons and bedrooms in his first regal choice depressed him; then he tried the place next to Carl Orville –Craig O'Connor and Eddie Davidson had picked adjacent houses on the other side– but Orville's progressively reared children continually came over to talk when he was making love, or getting drunk, or sitting at his table under the arcade, with the typewriter before him –he appeared to be working but most of the time he was just killing flies– or when he actually was doing some work; and Orville's youngest child, a spindly two-year-old:—"She may look scrawny," he complained to Osborne, "but she's got the lungs of a marathon bagpipe player!" kept crying into what should have been silence and birds; and watching Orville, O'Connor and Davidson walking back and forth in front of the house, hopelessly discussing literature and the day's work, infuriated him.

Once Craig O'Connor, sociable and uninvited, paid a visit somewhere around midafternoon:— he wasn't sure of the time, his watch had broken. At first he had been angry –it had cost $150 in Amsterdam the year before– then he smiled a private smile, shook it to make certain it was broken, carried it to the beach, and threw it in the sea.

O'Connor initiated the pleasantries . . .

"How's the work going, Del?"

Pierce hunched his shoulders to communicate so-so and none of your damn business.

Craig O'Connor rubbed his hands together; "Man," he mused, "I had a great day today! I put down two thousand good words."

"Hell," said Pierce, "I had a better day than that."

"Yeah? . . . How do you mean?"

"I took out twelve bad ones."

Which to Craig O'Connor seemed a defiant –and unjustifiable– attitude to take, for an unpublished writer.

"And that's not all I did," Pierce continued.

"?"

"I got laid three times."

Finally he listened to Rosoff's advice, and searched up the hill, where he found the house that suited his tastes: a claustral stucco cube, just big enough for two to live in, embedded in a niche at the end of an overgrown cul-de-sac, continually in shadow –only the one window of the upper story facing the sea received direct sunlight– almost invisible behind trees and undergrowth, and set in the core of a maze of narrow ramps and stairways:— all nearly identical, deep between sheer walls of the houses, blocking out all landmarks, intersecting at every possible angle . . . you selected an alley heading in the correct direction, followed it up, down, around for a while, only to watch it, eventually, hook obliquely left or right, and irresolutely peter out at some totally unfamiliar crumbling doorstep – a maze so complex that no one, Pierce included, understood how he managed to stagger accurately back every night, after too many drinks at Theodore's bar. Even Osborne took wrong turnings on his way up; and once Katona, invited for dinner, got so confused in the dusk that, after bellowing in vain for help –the buildings and press of jungle muffled his voice – he had to attempt to retrace his steps, at any rate keep going downhill, until he saw water and knew where he was; and then, so angry and sweaty he refused to try again, he made Rhea prepare an impromptu meal. Pierce himself did not know precisely why: but it was home at last;

perhaps because, in a way –and in a hush, in tropical solitude– it was somehow a cross between fo'c'sle and bar, and, he was the first to confess, most of his adult life had been spent in one or the other. ₩

An enraptured child in history's attic, Marsh went studio-hunting, waltzing: waltzing with long scarecrow strides, from house to house, over the sun-struck cobbles. Passing natives stopped to watch, but Marsh's exuberant wave and bonjour were infectious, they walked away smiling.

Studios everywhere! Whole houses full of them! He wouldn't even have to take the things down, roll them and store them. He'd just paint his way through all the rooms, leave everything hanging, then move next door! And he smirked at the peeling canvases still on the walls; students from schools of Murillo, Zurbarán, Watteau, Reynolds, who had learned everything but the secret –yet decided, one day when he had nothing else to do, to look more carefully, just in case . . .

Across a glinting drill yard, behind the parapet, redoubts and curtain of the outer bastion, he found his studio: a room sixty feet long, thirty feet wide, thirty feet high; with just two small doors at either end detracting from wall space; with just right light flooding through arched ventilators beneath roof beams; and with just one negligible hole in the roof. ₩

Tony Vale and Amos Osborne initiated alternate monthly mail-and-supply runs to Campeche; a P.O. box was rented; the growing little colony had an address; and they picked up those new arrivals who had gathered there.

And awaiting the mailboat became ritual on Escondite. Osborne, motoring smartly, starting early in the morning, could be expected back by dusk; Tony Vale generally stayed overnight and returned around midafternoon of the following day; but everyone gathered at Theodore's bar long before the possible hour of arrival and drank away the interim –most of the natives showed up as well, so newcomers were greeted with a great deal of noise and waving. Even Marsh dropped work (perhaps this boat would bring that one right woman who spoke his language, not that it mattered). ✿

Stefan Verduin showed up, with Jan van Gent and Marja. Van Gent was considered Holland's finest young poet; anthologies beginning at 1300 finished at van Gent. He had been writing advertising copy and television plays. ✿

Kurt Kummer came.

A Czech Jew, he had fled Europe just in time, and had spent the past twenty years script-writing in Hollywood. Where he should have been happy.

But the aging script writer like every aging whore, yearns for respectability: Kummer quit; to write honest stuff; to atone for his past and his bank balance, and his first play –Hollywood Expressionist anti-German comedy– failed in New York but was highly successful in Germany. His second play had not been produced. Wandering from one not-quite-first-rate hotel to another through Europe, he had not found the atmosphere conducive to writing. And he was now volubly at work on a modern version of *Candide* –as Jan van Gent observed: a curious enterprise for a man visited with most of the sins Voltaire had satirized– the first part of which Carl Orville admired.

And the Liberals. Liberal Don and Liberal Con, famous in Greenwich Village for their omni-racial parties where, amid Utrillo and Picasso reproductions, under the approving photographic gaze of Martin Luther King, Norman Thomas, Karl Marx and Ghandi, everyone came to argue and drink cheap wine.

Liberal Don –Pierce bestowed the nicknames– was a big, bulky, awkward man; Liberal Con was dumpy, plain, given to wide skirts and peasant blouses. She maintained an egalitarian, socially conscious, earnestly *engagée* indifference to her quite horrid complexion.

He wrote, she painted.

And Ed Robles, with his wife, two children, and picked library of four thousand books.

An English poet, with a young reputation, Robles had fought fascism wherever he found it, until it was war; refused a commission and fought through the war; and then made the mistake:— Robles stayed red when all his friends turned yellow. And the doors –to literary recognition, to financial security– began to shut, politely but inexorably, in his face. He hacked out some books, wrote children's stories, just scraped along; unhappy and baffled in a world that was not at all the sort of world he had fought eight years and lost an eye for.

It took Robles a long time to understand: that if the Poet had a mission in this age, it was: "Fiddle while Rome burns! But fiddle exquisitely!"

But with that understanding he began writing poetry; real poetry.   **ⓥ**

Janine left Tony Vale.

She awoke one morning, wanting him, "*Oui!* Tony, *chéri!*" she silently acquiesced; she stretched out her hand for him, and he had gone. She let her gaze caress the symmetry of her own lithe body, golden, glowing against the sheets; and ran a wanton hand down over her breasts, clamped it hard between her thighs, and then she saw him,

standing at the huge shuttered window, one foot propped on the sill, staring out at the sea, and silently she sent him her love call.

He stood, naked to the waist, barefoot, in a block of sunlight that heightened the hard muscles of his back and corded sinews of his neck.

(He was a very beautiful man) but he kept staring at the sea – cockatoos shrieking outside, she caught the sound of combers purling up the beach– and quite suddenly, and irrevocably, she no longer wanted him.   **ⓥ**

People settled in, each to his fashion; some spending the first few months hard at work –clearing, cleaning, refitting, buttressing, plastering, painting– rejuvenating this or that ruined house into the sort of home they had always wanted to live in, and had never been able to afford; others merely hacked out a path to the front door, scared the bats away, swept the debris off the floor, patched the roof native style –palm fronds tied over a framework of latticed cane– and moved in.

Naturally, problems arose. Water for instance. The bigger houses had wells, a number even had private sources –in Katona's a pure cool underground stream rose right in his courtyard– but others depended upon communal springs scattered about town, still flowing out of ornate fonts the Spaniards had built in their honor. Jugs were plentiful; two native families practiced pottery; shaping traditional amphorae, ollas, casseroles, tureens, whatever, from white island clay for the asking; but it was a nuisance –and tiring– lugging a day's supply of water several hundred yards in the sun.

Kurt Kummer complained: "A whole island full of *schwartzes* and we must carry our own water!"

Osborne and Tony Vale brought blasting powder, cement and hand pumps from Campeche; they made cisterns; the rainy season would see the end of that problem.

And if there were no taps, or running hot water, there was yet a certain –and consistent– compensation: listening to the mellowest of all known sounds:—a wooden bucket's baritone plunge into a well.

The women unaccustomed to wood and charcoal stoves spoiled some meals, threw some tantrums, and shed some tears before getting used to them –it just took a bit more time, which abounded, and once mastered, the food really did taste better, it wasn't imagination:— then they went about collecting recipes from the islanders . . .

Life took on its own rhythm for each of them; familiar to some . . .

"Come Craig, *chéri!*" she said (with that accent) "I will make love with you!"

less so to others.

Keith Cooper came. A tall, amiable English ex-mechanic, actor, racing driver, cameraman; Cooper possessed a soothing talent for loafing –his father, a famous Soho loafer, had once counseled him; "Anyone who works for a living, as doesn't have to, he's an idiot!" It was the only lesson Cooper ever learned from the old man, but he learned it well– and a genius for gadgetry. His reaction to Escondite was in its own way, akin to Alain Marsh's: three centuries worth of (glorious!) junk to fix. Every imaginable sort of splendid rotting carriage –tilburies, gigs, landaulets, curricles, phaetons, berlins– arsenals of useless muskets, matchlocks, firelock fusils, arquebuses, dueling pistols, cannon; worthless clocks, broken furniture; everything just waiting for leisurely resuscitation.

He had his life's work cut out for him,

and his first oeuvre was a preposterous –but turquoise-and-silver inlaid– blunderbuss. He was soon going hunting with Jonathan, and the natives were so excited that Cooper figured he needed five years at least to furnish everyone who wanted one with a gun – which was all right with him. His next project was a slender spidery trotting sulky; his magic hands were available to anyone in trouble, and, since most were completely devoid of mechanical aptitude, Keith Cooper was a welcome man on Escondite.

Ed Robles acquired a burro, Keith Cooper fixed up a cart for him, and he moved, with his wife, two children, and four thousand books, way out of town, into one of the old French plantation houses.

He spent two months making it habitable; the children foraged for fruits, nuts, spices and gourds; his wife cleared a small garden –after the past two years, self-exiled to Marrakesh, what pleasure it gave her to watch her vegetables bursting from rich tropical loam. Jonathan came out for a few days to teach the children the peculiarities and dangers of the jungle –the poisonous manzanilla tree, scorpions, one species of venomous snake– and to put in a supply of provisions. He killed a wild cow which they spiced, then smoked, very slowly –in the ancient manner handed down from

Carib Indian, to Conquistador, to buccaneer, to colonist, to him—over the grates of the still-usable boucan.

Among his new friends Robles counted Pierce, Katona, Jonathan Klein, Osborne, Rosoff (in small doses), Marsh, Jan van Gent, and especially Stefan Verduin: colleague and compeer; a third surviving member –the other was Stephen Seley, to whom he had written: Come to Escondite! Post haste! and received a hastily scribbled reply: "Can't come now. Everything chaos in Paris. Will write details later." Which he never did– of his generation of broken promises. Just three; perhaps there were more, (there *had* to be!) but he had never heard of them, and didn't know where to find them.

Those he knew, his old wild friends, had long ago committed themselves to –advertising, publishing, teaching, the BBC; busy rest homes for crippled and infirm talents– respectability, and therefore, nothing remained for them to talk about.

By mutual tacit agreement, everyone did his share of that minimum amount of effort, bearing slight relation to work, requisite to live their lives . . .

Pierce elected the still –he had always wondered how they went about actually making the stuff– and when Osborne told him that the island had once been held by the English, he had an idea.

From his travels he had learned that wherever the English had conquered, colonized, then later lost, they habitually left a bad taste in the public mouth, but with it a formula for good gin to dispel it. So he asked the two Horace's. And found to his delight – and downfall– that they knew.

He was tall, flamboyantly slouched; handsome but for his too-wet, too-red mouth. His full beard, red, was grizzled at the temples, and his hair, deeper, auburn, curled and swirled about his collar. His jacket, cut from what had to be the ultimate tweed, was daubed with paint –cerulean blue– and his widest wale olive-drab corduroy pants, daubed here and there with cadmium orange, stopped shy of his ankles, heightening the effect of mahogany

138

boots hand made from exotic leather. His shirt was raw silk; deep blue, and across his chest was draped, unobtrusively, a necklace of pig's tusks. A beaten but bright-red bandanna twisted about his throat, said; in the corner that fluttered free, PAMPLONA 1952 – beneath a baleful *toro* head. As he stepped from *Messalina* onto the jetty –carrying a rucksack, guitar, easel– an empty jade cigarette holder dangled between his lips.

Pierce sitting with Pat and Rosoff, already pretty drunk, took one look, pointed a derisive finger, and guffawed.

"That's not *nice*, Del!"

"What's not nice? He's an asshole! Look at him!"

But no one did; for Tony Vale had the mail from Campeche and was reading off the names:—always a tense few moments; waiting –hoping– for news from family, friends, women, publishers, agents, galleries, accountants: no one really wholly escaped —:so his entrance went unnoticed . . .

He stood at the quai, balancing his easel; he stared long and intently at the people spread out before him; and then, pursing his lips, he exhaled significantly. He straightened his shoulders –as the martyrs must have done, entering the Colosseum– and walked slowly, deliberately, eyes downcast, to an empty table at the edge of the crowd. Where he sat for an hour in absolute silence:— natives rushed up to him, pumped his hand, and jabbered; he smiled back gently, waved a misty greeting, then turned away and continued gazing out at the sea.

He kept it up for several days:— he was seen at high noon, standing motionless in the middle of the esplanade, reading; The Liberals, returning from dinner and a long exhilarating night arguing at Eli Rapp's, spotted him by moonlight on the end of the quai, practicing yoga; and late afternoons he sat at the same peripheral table, with the same two books and a quarterly review before him: occasionally he leafed through one; occasionally he took a leather pocket notebook from his shirt pocket –gone were the tweed jacket, corduroy pants and boots. He now wore bare feet, skin-tight black jeans, black shirt –unbuttoned, tied piratically at the waist– Pamplona bandanna, and pig's tusk necklace– opened it, consulted something, and nodded approval, or disapproval; and occasionally he produced a shiv, flicked it open, and cleaned the nails of his right hand, which had been cultivated half an inch beyond the fingertips . . . and when, finally, he spoke, he spoke to Osborne. He said: "Excuse me, but I don't suppose there's a library around here."

Pierce overtly stifled a snort. Rosoff cast a cool (under) worldly fisheye. Katona smiled, cocked an eyebrow, and sat back to watch the fun. "(Annette!)"

"No," said Osborne, "but there are plenty of books. I've got a few hundred, anytime you want to borrow something . . ."

But a remote look had settled in his face, a look that encompassed horizons. "Thanks . . . thanks. You see, I'm looking for something . . . rather specialized."

The conversation –gossip, sea stories, bootlegging stories– had ceased; there was silence, but silence with a timbre:— which was Pierce getting angry.

Osborne said; "I've seen you about a few days . . . I'm Amos Osborne."

"Victor . . . Victor Veritas."

"Well," despite Pierce's savage under-the-table kick, "have a seat."

"Ah . . . thanks." He pulled up a chair, laid the two books and the quarterly review on the table –Katona and Pierce examined them: Dante's *Inferno* in the original Italian, *The Tropic of Cancer*; the review was called *Abyss*– and said: "What do you do, write or paint?"

"Neither."

"I thought everyone around here did one or the other."

"No. Some just enjoy themselves."

Victor cast a supercilious, inquisitive glance at, of all people, Pierce. "And you?"

"I'm a bank robber."

Rosoff: "I run the mob."

van Gent: "I'm the Dutch ambassador."

140

Jonathan: "Napoleon."

Katona: "God."

"I see, I see," said Victor, "yes . . . that's very funny."

And Osborne, returning Pierce's kick, willing to give anyone a chance, asked; "And you?"

"Oh, I write . . . but I also paint. Primarily I'm a poet," and he handed Osborne *Abyss*. On the cover, under *"Poetry By,"* he pointed with one long yellow fingernail to: Victor Veritas.

(So! He had been right after all! And who, for instance, would look at Rosoff and believe he was a painter? Or Marsh?) Conscience-stricken he opened *Abyss*. On the masthead, under: PUBLISHER, R. Schlock, he read: MANAGING EDITOR, Victor Veritas.

Pierce said: "Hey! Why the long fingernails?"

"Fingernails? . . . Oh, I play the guitar."

"You're a phony!"

Victor Veritas studied his hands. When he spoke, his tone was that St. Francis might have used reproaching a mischievous bird. "I suppose everyone in entitled to his own opinion."

Pierce was standing now. Talk stopped at other tables. Everyone watched.

"I said you're a phony."

"Yes, I heard you say that."

"You're a *fucking* phony."

Seraphic still, Victor regarded him. "Are you trying to pick a fight with me?"

"No," quipped Jonathan, "that's his way of inviting you up for tea."

Victor ignored that. To Pierce he replied; "I'm sorry, but I won't fight you. I don't approve of violence."

"I'll teach you to!" He lunged around the table; Osborne and van Gent were ready for him; both were up; each pinned an arm; Pierce cursed, fumed, and strained between them.

"Come on Del. Forget it. He didn't do anything," oil on troubled alcohol.

Pierce feigned calm, then tried to wrench free by surprise –but Osborne was big and van Gent even burlier– he was so angry tears came to his eyes.

"Let me go! Pricks! You're supposed to be my friends!"

"Del, for Christ's sake, you can't hit a man who won't fight."

"Sure I can. Look at him! Phony bearded *ass*hole! He *deserves* to be hit!"

"He didn't *do* anything."

"He doesn't have to. Look at him!"

"You can't judge a book by its cover," aphorized Jonathan, and laughter spluttered through his rage, gradually he subsided.

"O.K.," he promised. "I won't hit him."

Released, arms akimbo, he stood above Victor. He said: "You're ugly, hairy, queer, phony, you smell bad, and your poetry's shit."

"I'm sorry, but I won't fight you. You see . . . I'm a coward."

"Jesus *Christ!*" Pierce turned, hurled his gin glass far out to sea; a terrific pain forked through his shoulder. "Mother *fucker* . . . cocksuckerbullshit *FUCK*, I threw out my arm!" . . .

Osborne had never laughed that hard, van Gent was rolling around on the ground, everyone else was doubled over, Rosoff got a coughing fit, the whole bar was pandemonium: for minutes . . .

Victor, however, took no part in it. He just sat there, intent, inscrutable, consulting something or other in his little pocket notebook, until Osborne politely told him that it would be more peaceful at the table if he left it.

And a drink later, when the normal buzz of conversation again presided –though punctuated, now and then, with an irrepressible giggle– Pierce, still massaging his tricep, found the incident as funny as everyone else did.   ✌

The rainy season came:— each day great goose-shaped clouds boiled up the sky, icy glittering water fell, rain like shafts of glass – now the grasshoppers hopped about with buckets, basins and mops. Marsh, refusing to let the elements interfere with the fundamentals, slopped around ankle-deep in water for two days; until

Keith Cooper helped him dig a channel to drain the studio–while the smug ants sat home dry. And the rainy season went.

Mark Wallin came, with Minerva, his wife, and three children; and Alice Norman, and Ole Isserstedt. There were over fifty foreigners on the island; enough so that, to the old-timers, some were merely faces. The inevitable covey of homosexuals arrived–in their endless quest for an escape from laws instigated by prigs and perpetuated by dolts; and the equally inevitable English pensioners–in their equally endless quest for bargain sunshine.

After an initial show of general interest and friendliness, the English gradually rejected the other nationalities. They sorted out precisely the pecking order that would have prevailed in England, and prepared to spend their doddering days sitting in the sun, red-faced and white-haired, sipping tea or gin at exclusive tables, civilly detesting one another.

"Come, Eddie, *chéri!*" she said (with that accent) "I will make love with you!"

And Craig O'Connor dropped the novel he was working on. To begin a new one. About the brief tragic love affair between a handsome talented young American painter and a Norwegian *femme fatale.* He remained friendly with Eddie Davidson, however. For he knew that Janine had only left him because (deep down, in her heart of hearts) she loved him, and was jealous of his genius, and had gone to Eddie, his best friend, simply to spite him: and because Eddie Davidson was still unpublished.

It was Jonathan Klein who nicknamed Kurt Kummer "The Bad Czech," and talking about him one day, Osborne asked if anyone at the table had ever heard him say anything nice, ever, about anyone. No one had.

But he was a part of island life:— a wattled, sagging sexagenarian, in long white walking shorts, shuffling along the beach with his old Jew's shuffle, muttering contumelies:— and when he finished his modern version of *Candide* he planned to write a psychological dramatic thriller involving an island, a murder, a Swedish nymphomaniac, an alcoholic American seaman, a disgraced American diplomat, a failed professor, and a great Central European novelist.

One afternoon Marsh came running, in the heat, into Theodore's bar, waving a great fistful of ragged weeds, pointing to it, shouting: "Hey! Look! Growing behind the studio! Free tea!"

Mrs. Osborne received a letter from Edna Cartwright, her former neighbor, with the gossip from back home, and inquiring into Mrs. Osborne's health, how she was faring, and what she did all day long. So she asked Amos's advice, –as she did about everything– about what she ought to tell her, and he said; "I don't see any problem. Just write a letter."

"But what can I tell her that I do?"

"Why, just what you do do."

"I can't do *that*, Amos! I don't do *any*thing!"

"Sure you do!"

"No I don't, Amos. What do I do?"

"You tell me."

She considered: "Well, I help Delia with the housework and the cooking."

"O.K. That's something."

"I sit in the rocking chair and read."

"O.K."

"And I mend the trousers and shirts for all your bachelor friends . . . that doesn't seem like very much to write Edna Cartwright about."

"Sure it is! You're indispensable! Without you everyone would be walking around naked."

"Oh, now stop that, Amos."

"It's true, ask anyone . . . all right, I'll tell you what to write her; write her about the time you got drunk and told all those dirty stories."

"Amos! That isn't funny! Besides, I wasn't drunk, I was just the tiniest bit tipsy. And they certainly *weren't* dirty stories!"

She'd drunk –despite Pierce's warning– two glasses of an island drink called by the natives "Magnifique." Brewed out of yams and cactus pulp it went down like a smooth blend of anis and vanilla, but was, in fact, a sort of milky liquid anathema, with a heavy-weight wallop, and a habit of lingering on in the form of interminable hangover.

At any rate, Mrs. Osborne drank two, suddenly her eyes were twinkling, and she began actually telling a story out of the –and her– twenties. About how Albert had once beaten up someone who had been rude to her in a bar in a strange town, and had been brought to the police station and almost thrown in jail, until she explained everything to the police captain, flattered him, coquetted –"You may not believe it, but I was a pretty young girl then, people used to tell me."– and got Albert off.   🎸

The furniture was canvas-strung wrought iron, and orange crates; there was a formidable stereo set, blatantly no TV, abstract paintings –thick impastos squeezed directly from the tube– hung on the walls, stretched but unframed, and in a corner stood a construction made of wire coat hangers and empty cans of pork and beans.

A hundred people milled about, and the party was already a success –held at the home of Jack Thomas, the Village's leading authority on parties– someone had brought Tchaikowsky's Symphonie "Pathetique," and that was a gas! the drinks were beer and California red wine.

Now a group hovered over the stereo, listening to a recording made of a natural childbirth; a plump girl, standing by the window, said –to an approving audience– "Fuck! If I want to say fuck, I'll say fuck! Fuck, fuck, fuck!" Beards flocculated sullenly; desultory conversations concerned their analysts, the work they planned to do; they all hated *Time* magazine in unison, and among the women, the bourgeois sheen of a nylon stocking was nowhere to be found . . .

Although Jack Thomas drudged for *Time* magazine –forced into it by a plutocratic capitalistic society– in order to pay his analyst's fees and the installments on his Pontiac convertible, he expressed his true feeling in a column puckishly called *The Village Idiot*, in a Greenwich Village newspaper. Into this he poured the real Jack Thomas; and it was reportage of superior caliber: seemingly a genial purée of Village events and characters, yet spiced with serious commentary:— for Jack Thomas possessed the born columnist's inherent talent for flinging unerring darts into the barn doors of racial segregation, advertising abuses, and Communist slave labor camps. Indeed, so firm was his grasp upon a handful of habitual liberalisms, so gaudily propitious were his gimcrack insights, so unstinting was his facility for blending the transitory with the biased, so flawlessly irrelevant were his references to women's breasts and buttocks, that his overt bitterness –at seeing his reputation confined to the intellectual kraal of Greenwich Village– was amply justified.

"Browsing through Kierkegaard at the Eighth Street Bookshop the other day," he might begin, "I couldn't help but wonder at the interest shown annually in the Miss Rheingold Contest." Or: "Sipping an espresso in the Figaro, I was discussing Governor Faubus with Madge, the cute and curvy modern dancer waitress . . ."

A very small man with a perfectly round head; his mouth was typed into his face like a hyphen, his eyes like two periods:— and he knew how to run parties . . .

He let this one take its course, to that point of pot-inspired enervation they called euphoria:— then produced the *coup de grâce*. He had a letter to read to them. Someone turned down the music –erotic folk songs from the Quechua– a sandaled beard in the corner stopped plucking a guitar –he hadn't been playing anything, just plucking notes– and in his clipped, metallic voice, Jack Thomas read aloud the letter he had just received from Victor Veritas on Escondite.

Who extolled the abundance of free marijuana and concomitant dearth of policemen. But his account of Escondite social life made it clear that in his opinion it was irrevocably square; he summed it up succinctly as, "Morgueville, man." Therefore he exhorted all his friends –referring to them affectionately as "swinging saints and sinners"– to hurry on down to make the scene. For it was only the lack of catalytic kindred intellect that stood between him and artistry.

Jack Thomas stood, head bowed, his hands at his sides, in the ensuing consecrated silence.

"He's a *great* poet!" said Sue Pinely, the plump girl who liked to say fuck.

"He's a hero!" said someone else.

"A saint!"

A disheveled beard rocked on his heels, threw his head back, closed his eyes. "Yeah, man," he said, "yeah, yeah, yeah." ❦

"Mal!"

"Mm?"

"Aren't you ever going to start work on your book?"

"Well, mmm, Amos has all the material; I can't very well ask him for it."

"But he's just doing it for *fun*, Mal. He's not serious. Like you!"

"Umm, as a matter of fact, Rhea, I don't think *I'm* quite as serious as I was when we left."

"Mal! I can't believe that!"

"Can't you, Rhea?"

"You mean, you don't want to *do* the book now?"

"No . . . not especially."

"What do you *want* to do then?"

"Stay here."

"Stay *here?*"

"Stay here."

"And just do *no*thing."

"And just do nothing."

"But, *Mal?*"

"Yes, Rhea?"

"Don't you want to *do* anything with your life?"

"Yes, Rhea."

"*What?*"

"Live."

"But, Mal! Do you call just sitting around all day in the sun, *living?*"

"I do, Rhea."

"What about your *ta*lent?"

"(Oh, Boswell! Where art thou?)"

Yet he stayed with her, and behind his back the others gossiped: what incomprehensible and profound quirk prolonged this weird alliance? Rosoff put it down, bluntly, to a severe myopia which Katona otherwise managed to conceal; Jonathan Klein suggested that perhaps he mounted her, because like Everest, she was there. But Pierce had his own ideas: doubtless Katona's was more comfortably furnished, better and more thoughtfully appointed:— still he wouldn't have cared to trade oubliettes . . .   ♠

Osborne, however, plugging away with his dictionaries and grammar books, *Don Quixote* and Quevedo, acquired a sound knowledge of sixteenth- and seventeenth-century Spanish. He arranged and organized the wealth of material he had accumulated, borrowed source books from Ed Robles's amazing library, got down to work, and soon accomplished the first installment of his *History of the Island of Escondite* –condemned by Katona, to whom he first showed it, as unscholarly, unbiased, unfootnoted, and readable– which went:

In the year 1498, on the island of Hispaniola –now divided into Haiti and the Dominican Republic– Francisco Roldán mutinied against his absent leader, Christopher Columbus, and with a number of fellow mutineers, fled across the island, where he intended to found his own colony. Dissatisfied not only with Columbus, but with the military service as well, and therefore with the Crown, it was Roldán's hope to set himself up independently, as chief and king of the newly discovered island empire; calculating as he did, that Columbus, upon returning, would not risk further desertions

148

in a reprisal attack, and would be forced to concede their liberty, at least until he could send to Spain for necessary reinforcements; by which time the mutineers would be strongly enough entrenched to defend themselves.

However, soon after building the new settlement, Roldán and his men began hearing tales from the local Indians, of another island, far to the west, where a fabulous treasure lay; and they considered this news impossible to ignore. A suitable boat was constructed, and Roldán dispatched his own brother, Diego, with eleven trusted men and an Indian navigator, to prove or disprove the rumor.

Fortunately, one of this group, Bartolomeo Gutiérrez, a sailor of some education, kept a journal of the voyage, and of the subsequent events, which still extant, affords a minutely detailed account of the discovery, colonization, and first decades of life on the island of Escondite.

The trip itself was routine and without incident; after twenty days at sea they sailed the *Ave Maria* into the long crescent-shaped harbor of the alleged treasure island and prepared to disembark.

At that time, the Caribbean islands were inhabited either by the fierce warlike Carib Indians or the gentle and peaceful Arawaks; and luckily for Roldán, Escondite was in the hands of the latter, who, as the boat lay at anchor, paddled out in their pirogues to greet them, shouting, smiling, and obviously curious about the white men ranked on the decks in their gleaming breastplates and morions.

On shore, the Spaniards were embraced by the local Cacique; they were given presents of fruits, gems and gold; and were invited to share in a whole pig then being roasted in their honor. After eating, Diego Roldán gave the order and his men fired their arquebuses into the ranks of celebrating natives, killing a number of them. Gutiérrez says, ". . . though we did intend but to teach the savages that we were Christians and to be feared; yet they misunderstood our good faith, the which did occasion a cessation of the friendship that had commenced between us . . ."

149

The following day, after torturing the Cacique and raping his daughters, the Conquistadors forced the Indians to lead them to their treasure, and were soon at a temple . . . "where we did see profusions of idols and lewd images and false things, all curiously fashioned in gold and emeralds and silver, and we were sore afflicted by the sight of these heathen practices."

But now, Diego Roldán, confronted by his prize, remembered a slight delivered to him by his brother years ago, and resolved to revenge it. "Why (Gutiérrez quotes him) should we brave men consent to share this gold with my brother who is a pig and a dog and a Jew; and those others who have sent us out into unknown lands and perils to seek gold to share with them, who sit in peace, while we must do battle for our very lives?"

These sentiments met with the instant and wholehearted approval of his followers, but Diego Roldán was not to live to enjoy the benefits of his capture . . . "then so eager was our captain, the pious Diego Roldán, to turn the savages from their brutish ways, that even thus burdened in his armor, he did endeavor to carry away with him down the mountainside, so many of the false gods and idols that, the noxious heat of the jungle overcoming him, he suffered so great a fit of flatulency, the ague, and fainting that he did not arise and was bereft of life. We buried him with much rejoicing for he was a stern man and huge cruel."

It became necessary to choose a new leader. After two days of incessant dispute, they had reached no accord, tempers were strained and violence near at hand, when one man, Enrique Pilar, disclaimed interest in leadership, said that he would willingly follow whichever of his companions the others chose, and announced that he intended to explore the island in search of further treasure. Hearing this, the diarist, Gutiérrez, determined to accompany him. ". . . for I did know him to be a cunning man and guilesome and perceived those designs which had entered into his head." The two went off, spent several days treasure hunting —they discovered another, smaller horde of gold and jewels in a minor temple at the other end of the island, which they sacked— and returned to find, as they had anticipated, that their nine colleagues had killed each other off ". . . and from the Indians we did hear tales of marvelous battle."

The two now found themselves in a dilemma: they possessed immense wealth, but they were alone amid hostile and unreliable Indians (whom they placated successfully but still distrusted) and they could think of no way, nor any place, to which just two men could transport so much booty and live to spend it. Therefore it was decided, rather than risk the perilous allegiance of Francisco Roldán, to present their prize to Columbus, beg clemency, and hope the court in Spain would reward their loyalty with the vice-regency, or at any rate, some position of authority on the island they had won, which, in fact, it did.

Then it was discovered that the treasure of the new colony was indigenous; and not, as had been thought, imported. Rich quartz lodes yielded nearly pure gold in unprecedented quantities; and, as they noticed that the Indian mines were worked at roughly equal altitudes throughout the mountains, there was every reason to believe that further exploration would disclose still more veins. And there were jewels, topaz abounded; and occasionally, in the winter-dried beds of the innumerable torrents flowing from the mountains, emeralds were uncovered.

Delighted with this first proof of real wealth in the New World (antedating Mexico and Peru by some twenty years) the Crown hastened to exploit the island, now officially christened Isla Alegre (Happy Island). "Our Sovereign sends us Christian Spaniards with which to found a city to his magnificence; and with God's will may it be done!" Convicts, dockside toughs and debtors were dispatched to colonize Isla Alegre. The jail was built, then the fortress, cathedral and viceroy's palace; but under serious stress and portentous circumstances. For the Indians, although enslaved, were apparently constitutionally unfit for work, and their relentless apathy drove the Spaniards to distraction. Gutiérrez complains, "Though they be flogged often and fed little, yet do these barbarians refuse to perform labor in the name of the Lord!"

And the peculiarity of Indian customs not only astonished but appalled their conquerors . . . "They believe not in the sanctity of holy matrimony, and among the savages it is their practice that when a youth fancies a maiden of marriageable nubility, and she is willing, the parents are never consulted in the matter, but that they freely bed together like beasts, and as such are considered as married as they can be; and should in time the two find themselves no longer congenial together, then are they allowed to separate, to live with whichsoever other savage Cupid now directs them to, while the children are equally apportioned off between them and they are taught not to despise the knavish sire and adulterous wife, but to cherish and admire them. Further, these savages believe not in the Devil, and are not beset by fear of him."

Moreover, the colonists were soon resorting to measures of a self-defeating character. Away from their homeland, on a remote island, amid hostile natives, and subject to a number of strange, sometimes lethal diseases, they were plagued by both fear and boredom; and the only scapegoats available had to be recruited from the native population. A game called Cabezas (Heads) flourished for some time and relieved the tedium and anxiety. Any number could play Cabezas, which involved simply lining up a row of Indians against a facing line of Spaniards. Then, at a given signal, the Spaniards swung their swords, and whoever cut off his Indian's head with the cleanest blow was judged the winner. Dousing an Indian in oil, setting him alight, and pushing him, flaming, from the promontory by the fortress, was another popular diversion.

But the quantity of gold shipments back to Spain diminished as the Indian population was decimated; and despite urgent exhortations from Madrid, commanding the colonists to encourage population expansion, the Indians were disinclined to breed.

However, the oppressed Indians were soon to find friends in the persons of the humble friars sent hard on the heels of the Conquistadors by Queen Isabella to spread the Faith. Gutiérrez describes the work of a Brother Chuleta: "Of this morning a savage was encountered walking in the street by Don Fernando and accused of not having removed his hat to him, and although the savage did endeavor to defend his innocence by pleading that he had not been wearing a hat and had never owned a hat, he was sentenced to be hung by the heels and bastinadoed and flogged. Upon hearing news of this, Brother Chuleta declared that he, too, would be hung by the heels and bastinadoed and flogged and suffer the same blows as the Indian, thus would he demonstrate to the heathen the strength of Christian fortitude and the mercy of the Lord; the which was accordingly performed and, verily, many who witnessed this spectacle saw the will of God exercised and did convert to the true Church."

Brother Chuleta makes several similar appearances in the pages of the journal, but he dies prematurely, in 1508, scourging himself to death while hearing midnight Mass at Christmas.

Meanwhile, a solution was on hand for the Indian problem. In 1502, Nicolas de Ovando on Hispaniola gained permission from Queen Isabella to import Negro slaves from Africa, and this was shortly followed by like permission to Enrique Pilar on Isla Alegre. The mines were soon increasing production, as it became evident that the Negroes, unlike the Indians, could be forced to work under the harshest of circumstances. And the fact that the purchase of slaves was an expensive procedure tended to mitigate the Spaniard's enthusiasm for maltreatment. Only the very rich could afford such a luxury; and on Isla Alegre, presenting one's son, upon his reaching maturity, with a Negro to murder, developed into a status symbol. Furthermore, by feeding the Indians to the still-cannibalistic blacks, their resentments and complaints were mollified along with their appetites; and as this staple in the slaves' diet developed by necessity into a treat, and finally an event, the priests were heartened to discover that simply by promising the Negroes roast Indian, they were able to convert a considerable percentage into the Faith.

In 1515, Enrique Pilar was stabbed to death by his half-breed son, and the Crown sent as his replacement, Leonardo de la Fé, a sensitive Castilian nobleman of immense private means, but subject to the caprices of a domineering wife and three equally demanding daughters, under whose direction he built an enormous and extravagant mansion incorporating a wing devoted to a private jail, dungeon, and torture rooms. Gutiérrez comments, "Our viceroy does seem wasted and ill and though many do pray for his decease, I do not count myself among them, for it is everywhere known that the blame for the new and unjust laws and restrictions the which we have been made to suffer, lies with Doña María, and not Don Leonardo who, some say, is only ill due to that delicacy of constitution that forbids his sleeping in his own palace by reason of the screams and shrieks of the prisoners and heathen undergoing torture therein. For it is well known that these screamings convey huge diversion upon Doña María and her daughters; and Pablo Lloret told me just yesterday that he had heard Doña María vow that as long as God grants her life, not one moment shall pass in her palace wherein there are not screams and shrieks emanating from a sinner undergoing his chastisement." So even the colonists were oppressed by measures and taxes imposed by Doña María; but any hope of effective pleas for relief to Madrid were rendered futile by the fact that she was a daughter of Fonseca, the powerful Bishop of Burgos (shortly almost to deprive Hernando Cortez of his conquest of Mexico). Furthermore, she had earned the reputation as the most adept poisoner outside Italy; and even the outspoken Father de las Casas, then visiting the colonies and shocking the homeland with his accounts of the maltreatment of the Indians, restricted his disapproval of Doña María's ways to the mild reproof that it was generally felt she carried her religious zeal to extremes beyond the purely beneficial. Assassination attempts failed so consistently she added a reputation for witchcraft to her others; for years the hapless colonists followed her orders, although behind her back they always referred to the island as "Isla Triste" (Sad Island) and it was not until 1528 that better times were restored. In that year, Doña María, having come to suspect her youngest daughter, Francesca, of designs to poison her (a not unrealistic assumption); on the occasion of her daughter's wedding feast, took the precautionary course of poisoning first. The unlucky bridegroom was accused of perpetrating the crime, convicted and hanged, while Doña María had a statue erected to the memory of her daughter, a statue in

154

existence to this day, and about which Gutiérrez commented after the unveiling, ". . . it is as excessive in beauty in bronze as was Doncella Francesca excessive in ugliness in flesh."

Whether or not it was this deed which finally distracted Doña María can never be ascertained; but shortly thereafter she went mad, and urged by her confessor, retired permanently to a convent.

In 1530, Bartolomeo Gutiérrez died, and in his rapidly degenerating script, gave thanks to God for granting him a natural end, the first Spaniard to arrive on the island thus favored; but now, deprived of the diarist, the story of the ensuing three decades can only be sketchily outlined from a few existing church records, trade documents and letters. It appears that the island flourished; for a number of the vast mansions in ruins today, but still standing, date from this period; and there is no reason to believe the island did otherwise: the English, Dutch and French had not yet gained that supremacy of the seas which was later to help them dismember the Spanish Empire; the age of the buccaneers had not yet dawned –although due to hostilities between France and Spain, a number of French corsairs roamed the seas and harassed Spanish shipping– and in any case, the island was ideally suited for defense: the massive fort ensuring the safety of the fine and deep harbor; a constantly manned chain of batteries overlooking the beach precluded landings and flank attacks; and the sheer cliffs and promontories of the back of the island provided a natural barrier to incursions from that quarter.

In Europe, however, tensions due primarily to the rise of Protestantism, would soon break out in fighting; the aftermaths of which reverberated back to the colonies.

In 1541, Protestants met Catholics for the Treaty of Ratisbon, the last serious attempt to affect a reconciliation between the dissident factions; and although both Martin Luther and Pope Clement III sent ambassadors noted for their tact and moderation, increasingly assertive instructions from both headquarters soon made it apparent that the breach was irreparable. Rome, scandalized by Contarini's concessions to the Protestant point of view, sent this message from Cardinal Moroni (later Pope Hadrian VIII) on behalf of the Pope, "On no account, and under no circumstances, are you (Contarini) to tolerate toleration." (re: the then central issue of the Lutheran heresy.) While Melanchthon's urging Luther to refrain from violence brought the following reply from the German theologian, "No one need think that the world can be ruled without blood; the civil sword shall and must be red and bloody."

Thus both parties reverted to extremes; and on the Catholic side, developments naturally following a new policy of internal refortification, were of the utmost significance to the colonies of the New World. Saint Ignatius Loyola founded the Society of Jesus in 1540; and the Inquisition, especially in Spain, began pursuing heretics with increasing zeal, unsparing even of the rich and influential, a policy which, on Isla Alegre, was instrumental in provoking a civil war.

Although the Inquisition did not attend to the search for heretics in the Indies in person until 1574, instructions from Seville to the bishops of the colonies were detailed and unambiguous enough to let them know precisely the direction in which their duties lay. Thus, in 1552, it so happened that Bishop Juerga was questioning the eight-year-old son of the Viceroy as to whether or not he believed the communion wine to be symbolic of the blood of Christ, and received the answer that it just looked like wine. The boy was therefore accused of heresy and clapped in irons. The Viceroy, Esteban Sagrado, alarmed, asked for leniency due to his extreme youth, but the Bishop's answer, "The Devil, too, had a childhood; only God is eternal!" made it clear that he did not consider youth a sufficient excuse. And when, on the rack, the boy not only doubted the communion wine to be symbolic of the blood of Christ, but also denied the existence of the Trinity, the possibility of the Immaculate Conception, and the infinite mercy of the Lord, he was condemned as an arch-heretic, sentenced to ". . . have the skin flayed from thy foul living body, and thereupon thy bleeding back to have one hundred lashes laid, and thence conveyed to the stake and burned alive to the eternal damnation and abomination of thine accursed soul."

Now Rome had empowered the inquisitors to examine and pass sentence, but clemency or repeal had to be solicited from the Pope himself (Protestant theologians say this was done to prevent the inquisitors from accepting bribes; but Catholic writers claim it was imposed to prevent the priests from falling prey to mercy). Accordingly, Viceroy Sagrado asked for a stay of execution until the case could be put before Hadrian VIII in Rome, which was granted. The Bishop refused the Viceroy interim custody, and even contact with his son: and while waiting for the final decision to arrive from Rome the boy was put in prison in the care of the nuns where he died soon after of maltreatment. When the posthumous verdict finally arrived, it not only upheld Bishop Jurega's sentence, but threatened the Viceroy with excommunication if he did not forthwith do the prescribed public penance to atone for the sin of defending his heretic son, and for the sin of Lust –Hadrian VIII, much influenced by Jesuit teaching, believed, with them, that love of kindred constituted carnal affection and was therefore sinful.

Viceroy Sagrado, dissatisfied with the decision, vowed not repentence but revenge. Although the influential and powerful colonials refused to support him –either out of fear of the church, or desiring the Viceroy's falling into disfavor– he soon bought the sympathy of the army, and by utilizing a problem that was later to cost Spain the entire New World, he gained another necessary ally: the Creole native-born faction.

For the Crown consistently refused to recognize the rights of mestizo or mulatto sons of the Conquistadors to administrative positions, reserving these plums for court favorites or those to whom favors were owed, a line of conduct that won it the permanent hatred of this ever-increasing group. Bernardo Gutiérrez, the mestizo son of the old diarist –unfortunately, much his inferior as a source of information– sums up the Creole attitude in a rare entry: "It is the filth and muck of Spain the King sends to be our masters. Why are not our leaders chosen from brave and meritorious Creole blood? Our Viceroy wears lace and perfume and walks like a woman. He is a whoreson Jew." While the following letter by the *alcalde ordinario* under Viceroy Sagrado may be taken as typical of the opinion the Spaniards held of the Creoles, ". . . yet it is deemed an honor to be torn from the cities of our splendorous Spain and transmigrated to these Indies to rule slaves and savages and worse; for the degenerate sons of the Conquistadors are a sneaking and brutish lot; and I have yet to encounter the one who had not dedicated his wretched existence to debauchery, gaming, rum, whoring, lewdness, avarice, fighting, and blaspheming. They have but little learning and they stink."

This being the prevailing atmosphere, it was but a simple matter for the infuriated Viceroy to interest the Creoles in his plans, which were no less than to take possession of the island, sever his ties with Spain; and, if it became necessary to insure independence, even to seek the protection of the old enemies, France and England –a hope that, bearing in mind the wealth of the island, was not unreasonable.

At any rate, on the eve of the coup, the complete secrecy inperative for success was broken by a turncoat mestizo who, approaching the Bishop, offered to reveal a plot on his life if promised a reward and a blessing. The Bishop replied, "My son, I bless thee; and the Lord shall reward thee in heaven," and at a signal, three burly friars seized the traitor and bound him; and shortly after he confessed all beneath the lash and was speedily beheaded since time was of the essence. The Bishop now called all the clergy to arms; the Spaniards whose loyalty he expected were alerted; and meanwhile, the Viceroy, learning that the plot was out, hastily marshaled his own forces. The two parties met helter-skelter near the beach. At the first shock the seasoned troops and enraged Creoles drove the Bishop's forces into retreat; at a second charge the retreat became a rout, and those of the Bishop's army who could manage, fled to the fortress and besieged themselves inside.

For the victorious soldiers and Creoles this was the signal for an immediate abandonment of discipline and the commencement of mopping-up activities: killing those prisoners they held to be unransomable, sacking the houses of their enemies, and raping the captured nuns.

158

The Viceroy, however, witnessing this spectacle, now began having doubts as to his ability to control his unruly supporters, and although he knew that by simply keeping the enemy besieged, he would eventually starve them into capitulation, he had little confidence in the fidelity of his own men; and just one betrayal in the form of a message to nearby Mexico would mean a counter-attack before he was ready to cope with one. He therefore decided to storm the fortress and gain a total immediate victory.

With great difficulty he persuaded his soldiers and Creoles away from their amusements, and prepared to attack the mighty rear parapets. But a first attempt to place the scaling ladders was re-pelled with heavy losses and the soldiers refused to try again. Realizing that his authority was in serious jeopardy, he then had recourse to the following stratagem: under threat of death, he forced the captive priests, friars and nuns to carry the ladders to the walls, hoping that the Bishop would refrain from firing down upon them and would surrender, rather than endure a siege from which he could never emerge victorious in any case. But as the clergy advanced to the walls, crying for mercy and praying, they were met with a barrage of rocks, small arms and artillery fire, and cauldrons of boiling oil. So there was no choice left to Vice-roy Sagrado but to lay the siege.

After several days, however, it became evident to the Viceroy that even the token authority he appeared to wield over his rioting supporters was on the wane; and convinced that he and his family would soon fall prey to the wrath of the mob, he decided to act before they did. Knowing his besieged enemies could have no idea of his own weakness, he therefore waited for evening, by which time his troops were exhausted from the excesses of the day, and conveyed a message to the fortress claiming that his only feud was with the Bishop, and that if the Spaniards would simply hand him over, they would be granted amnesty and the restoration of posi-tion and property.

This struck the besieged as a provident means of escape; the Bishop was made prisoner; and Esteban Sagrado, duping his drunken guard into believing that the garrison was surrendering, had them hold their fire as the gates were opened and the Spaniards emerged, with the Bishop in chains.

Immediately following his initial victory, Viceroy Sagrado had put the Bishop's acknowledged illegitimate son to such torture as his own son had suffered; a like fate befell two other children rumor had long credited to the Bishop; and all three had been chained to a tree and left to starve to death. Bishop Juerga, after being quickly emasculated, now joined them at this tree to await further punishment, while the Viceroy acquainted the Spaniards with the immediate problem of the rioting soldiery.

However, the Viceroy was not to be given time to plan a counterattack; a troop of reveling drunken men, leaving some orgy in town, happened upon them at this moment, and seeing the enemy in front of them, unprepared, they attacked with remarkable celerity. The Spaniards, overfed and out of condition to begin with, and now enfeebled from scanty food during the siege, were again no match for their opponents who descended upon them, brandishing their swords, and crying *"Mata los perros!"* (Kill the dogs!).

The Spaniards knew the futility of surrender and so had no choice but to fight until, at last, all had been dispatched, and Isla Alegre was in full possession of the rebel soldiers, mestizos and mulattos.

Needless to say, when this disturbing news reached Madrid, King Philip made hasty plans for the recapture of his valuable colony. Troops were mustered in Havana, Campeche and Vera Cruz for the job; yet despite the fact that the rebels were without leadership or discipline, and devoted their days entirely to debauchery, the sight of Spanish sail approaching was enough to inspire temporary cooperation, and the Spaniards found themselves assaulting seemingly impregnable defenses raised by themselves in expectation of the French and English.

A year passed, during which a number of unsuccessful attacks were made; and the King, enraged at seeing his army and navy unable to wrest the island from a handful of half-breed rebels, finally took the advice of his confessor and sent Jesuits.

In Cuba, Fathers Cuchara, Cuchillo and Tenedor, three superiors noted for their military knowledge and ardor, were chosen to raise an army of slaves and train them. This being done, ships were provided, and they were directed toward Isla Alegre.

Whipped on and singing hymns, led by the fierce priests, the disciplined blacks rowed their launches through the hail of artillery fire from the shore batteries, successfully landed despite heavy losses, and easily conquered the debauched and terrified rebels; securing the island, once again, for the Crown of Spain.

But the Spaniards returned to a changed island; the houses were in disrepair and their interiors had been ruined; the farms had been allowed to run fallow; those slaves who had not been murdered in feuds and reprisal attacks had fled to the hills; and until conditions could be restored to normal, the Spaniards had a thin time –although often due more to their excessive pride than to actual want; as witnessed by a record of one Spaniard who willingly starved to death rather than perform a slave's labor and collect food with his own hands.

Nevertheless, administrative instructions from Madrid were designed both to get gold flowing quickly into the Spanish treasury, and to prevent the possibility of further insurrection. Those slaves who refused to return from the hills upon being promised all the mestizo and mulatto they could eat, were hunted down by dogs; and work began in repairing the damage.

While Hadrian VIII, ever zealous in the pursuit of heretics, and ever-watchful of the behavior of his clerics, laid down the following laws to the Jesuit missionaries: "At all times set an example befitting a Christian; comport yourselves with meekness and humility; pay for your wine and lodgings at the inns whereunto you repair on your journeys; be unsparing in the use of God's sword upon the heretic neck; do not drink wine immoderately in public places; never permit a woman to accompany you into Church; strike swiftly at anything, be it man, word, or deed, that does not conform in the slightest to the true and only Word of God unto which you have sworn."

Thus, Isla Alegre was soon recolonized; the Viceroy wielded his secular power with imperial authority; while the Jesuits hunted for heretics, set up rigid schools for the sons of the colonists, and even found time to educate the slaves, who were brought before the priests, after their day in the mines and fields, and given lectures on theology and Latin lessons.

Economically flourishing, the Spaniards competed in expenditure and show. Architecture thrived, and during this period many of the finest houses, monuments and public buildings were constructed –in the prevailing Plateresque and Mexican-developed Mudejar styles, retaining much Moorish influence but adapted to the needs of this particular tropical climate. Caravels laden with bullion sailed for Spain and returned with cargoes of furniture, Flemish tapestries, bronze-wrought Chinese balconies, cloisonné enamels, flagons, chalices, silver and gold cutlery, tableware, lamps and ornaments fashioned by the best smiths of Europe, and paintings by the finest painters –a 1586 inventory of one of the largest houses lists a Titian, a Moro and a Bosch.

But if the island appeared to enjoy external calm (in 1576 there were no fatal duels or murders among the colonists; 1578 and 1581 were years in which no Jesuits were eaten) a complexity of internal pressures was in the process of developing which again brought strife to Isla Alegre. To begin with, there were the animosities inherent to the social system: the slaves hated the mulattos, who hated the mestizos, who hated the Spaniards, who hated the Jesuits, who hated the Crown; but added to this progression, there were now the increasing regional hostilities between the Spaniards themselves. If a new Crown appointee of authority happened to be a Castilian, he automatically had to face the jealousy and lack of cooperation of Andalusians, Catalans, Basques, Murcians, and Galicians; if a Galician, a like array, minus, of course, the Galicians, but plus Castilians. And in the face of State and Church disapproval, feuding, dueling and poisoning began to enjoy a hitherto unmatched popularity; all of which reached a climax when, in 1583, the Crown sent as Viceroy, Don Gomzalo Listo, a nephew of his mistress.

Don Gomzalos' method of performing his duties was as follows: each morning his ministers would come to fetch him, and accompanying him to his chambers, they would strap him into his ornate throne. Then, the business of the day –petitions, various legal and judicial matters– would be presented to him. The Viceroy would stare at the papers for a time, finally his misshapen head would loll to the right or the left; which was construed by his ministers as signifying yes, or no; and they would proceed to act accordingly.

Don Gomzalo Listo was an Andalusian, and therefore, his conduct caused mounting resentment to all but Andalusians, who replied to complaints of the Viceroy's incompetence, by pointing out that if Don Gomzalo was not the most intellectual Viceroy the island had seen, he was certainly the only honest one. Nevertheless, tension increased, and in 1584, a minor slave revolt touched off open violence.

It appears that the beautiful spouse of an as-yet-unsubdued black was violated by his master, Matteo Rosario, the mayor of the city, and carried off by him to live permanently in his home as one of his concubines. The slave, Urumguru, however, ignoring all precedents and disregarding the certainty of punishment, sued for her return –with such persistence and such eloquence that at last the mayor agreed to her restitution upon the payment of 500 pieces of gold. The manner in which the slave accumulated so vast an amount remains a mystery, but at the end of the year he presented himself to Don Matteo, handed over the required sum, and demanded his queen, who was presently returned to him, with her nose split and her ears notched. Apparently the bodyguard which the mayor had had the foresight to summon, was completely overwhelmed by the fury of the gigantic slave, who fought through them, strangled the mayor, wrenched his head from his shoulders –according to the record, Urumguru stood seven feet tall and was proportionately strong– and went racing through the town, carrying the dripping head, and calling for his fellow slaves to rise against their masters. A dozen or so heeded his call and they fled into the hills.

This revolt was short lived. Within several days dogs had

hunted down the runaways. Urumguru was sentenced to be flayed and impaled; but on the intercession of Father Cuchara –who realized that the man, although black and a slave, had been wronged– it was agreed to mitigate the sentence if Urumguru accepted baptismal rites. The slave consented and was baptized; he received extreme unction and was then doused with oil, set aflame, and hurled from the parapet. The other runaways were bastinadoed and flogged, and the first slave revolt had come to an end.

But the following morning, in the name of Viceroy Gomzalo Listo, an order appeared: to discourage future rebellion, ten slaves were to be selected at random, and drawn and quartered as a lesson to the others. This was punctually performed, but it was not long before the Murcian faction realized that of the ten slaves selected at random, nine had belonged to Murcians; and when it was recalled that a month earlier, Matteo Rosario's brother, the Jesuit, had been killed by a Murcian in a duel over a woman, the Murcians decided that they were not the victims of mere probability and chance, and they were moved to action. Upon leaving his palace, the Viceroy was stoned to death, as was the Castilian minister of trade –thereby uniting the Castilians with the Andalusians. All other factions quickly joined the fracas; once again there was civil war on Isla Alegre. For six months battles raged, no gold was mined, and the cobbles were red with Spanish blood. Finally, the distraught King, finding his orders for peace ignored, threatened to present the island as a personal gift to Francis Drake; and the possibility of his being in earnest was sufficient to impose reason on the Spaniards and effect a cease-fire.

Drake, however, required no such royal invitation. On previous voyages only the seeming invulnerabiliy of the defenses had dissuaded him from paying a call. But when, in 1585, angered at the flagrant disregard shown by the English and French for Spanish trade restrictions, Philip II issued his embargo forbidding their ships the use of all Spanish ports, Francis Drake put Isla Alegre on his itinerary.

Contriving a perilous landing on the unguarded rear of the island, he and his men marched overland, and fell on the town, utterly unheralded, near dusk. The Spaniards, learning the identity of their assailant, offered no resistance; those who were able fled to the hills; the others surrendered, and the English pillaged at their will.

Drake agreed to spare the lives of the captive civilians but destroyed the Cathedral and ordered all captive priests and friars slain; he then offered clemency to any nun who could claim virginity; but when investigation proved them all to be liars, they were condemned along with the others. Only the Mother Superior was spared, since none of the men had the courage to examine her; and Drake is reported to have laughed and said: "Surely, Mother, it is only thy face that hath forbade thy will's way; but Fortune hath put thee in the hands of a gentleman; and thou'rt free to enjoy thy life and thy looks –if thou can'st. Thank me not, Mother! It will be the Devil himself who thanks me; for when he encounters thee, as he most assuredly shall, surely he will say: 'God bless thee, Francis Drake! For by sparing yon beast thou hast granted me stay of the most fearsome fright I have known since the day of my Fall: as Sin is my trade, yet she doth it surpass in uncomeliness. And I say that if God in his Heaven must have recourse to such as she, then upon the Day of Judgment it will be Satan who emerges victorious.' "

Finishing his speech, Drake gave the signal, and his men slew captive priests and nuns before an audience of cheering slaves, to whom, when the job was done, Drake, with a cavalier gesture, presented the bodies for disposal; and when reports of his departure reached the Spaniards in the hills, they returned to find nothing remaining of their clergy but gnawed bones, and glutted blacks snored, sprawled about the embers of a bonfire. Only the mutilated body of the Bishop was recognizable. Wasted away with the pox, the slaves had deemed him inedible.

The Dragon of the Sea had come and gone; away on the round-the-world voyage that conferred knighthood upon him; and of his visit, the Mother Superior, left alone to keep the church records, writes: "Fifty Christians were martyred yesterday by Calvinist pirates."

The seventeenth century was approaching; the rising English and Dutch were allied against Spain; and sea battles raged throughout the Caribbean as the powers contended for the treasure of the Main; but if laden caravels out of Isla Alegre often had their gold transferred to hostile holds, a number of attacks on the island itself were successfully repulsed; and two Dutch privateers were dashed against the rocks in an attempt to emulate Drake.

In 1598, Clement VIII succeeded in securing the Peace of Vervin; France ceased actions against Spain and Henry IV broke his alliances with England and Holland; but unofficial infractions became so frequent on all sides that, by 1604 all-out war seemed inevitable; until James I, Albert and Isabella of Brabant, and Philip III met and concluded the Treaty of Perpetual Peace.

Although this agreement was observed in the Caribbean for only three weeks –when *guarda costas* out of Portobello apprehended the English brigantine of Captain Oliph Blossome (he was charged with trading illegally and sentenced to be hacked to death)– it remained unbroken in theory, thereby limiting violence in the Caribbean to the status of guerrilla warfare, and maintaining a precarious truce on the continent, keeping various ambassadors, ministers and courtiers in constant doubt as to whether their reception in court would prove to be courtesy or irons.

Eventually, an incident originating on Isla Alegre solved the problem of peace. A Scottish traveler and soldier of fortune named Thomas Pud, visiting the island, was seized by the Viceroy on suspicion of spying –there being rumors, later proven false, of a fleet of English privateers massing for a sortie. Pud, claiming to know nothing of the rumor, refused under torture to admit his guilt, and was therefore handed over to the Inquisition to be tried for heresy; despite an old agreement made by Charles V that Protestants living in, or visiting Spain and Spanish possessions, were not to be subject to the scrutiny of the Inquisition as long as they committed no scandal.

Nevertheless, he was put to the full rigor of Inquisitional methods: broken on the rack, flayed with the lash, starved, tortured with thirst, then bloated with forced gallons of water, hung by the thumbs, then by the heels, etc. Withal, he refused both to admit to heresy or to recant from it; and in his journal –which was soon to inflame the Protestant nations into even more ardent persecution of Catholics, Pud recounts a conversation held, while on the rack, with the Jesuit attempting his conversion: ". . . and then this mad and Maniakall Demon did try to convince me of the Truth of his Diabolikall Faith by vain and superficiall and absurde arguments of their seaven Sacraments, such as Intercession, Transubstantiation, Images, Purgatory, Miracles, Etc.; and I replied: Not Fire, Death or Torment shall made me shrinke from the true Word of God; and I said that I cared not for the hissing of snakish Papists, a tush on all that snarling crew; and especially I told him that the base Mungrells of his Societie were everywhere regarded as the worst and baddest Creatures of the Christian Name, and theyre Order was hated and vilipended to Death upon the Face of the Earth . . ."

Unrepentant, Pud's tortures were continued, and even he, faithful Calvinist that he was, was forced to admire the sincerity of his torturers who, when he appeared to be at the point of death, began to rend their clothes, tear their hair, and weep aloud as they exhorted him to consider the tortures, infinitely worse than those he was presently undergoing, and eternal, that his unconverted soul would be forced to endure in Hell. Nevertheless, he remained adamant, and finally pronounced too intractable for so provincial a chamber, he was permitted to recuperate as far as his meager rations and vermin-infested cell would permit, and was shipped off on the first caravel to Inquisitional headquarters in Seville for further questioning.

The caravel, however, was taken en route by the English privateer, Jonas Sweetly, and Pud, with his tale of torture was returned to England, where at the close of his convalescence, it was found that he had permanently lost the use of his left leg, left arm, and right eye. Indignation rose in England, and James demanded a pension as indemnity. But the Spanish ambassador at first denied that Pud's infirmities were the result of Inquisitional examination; he is quoted as arguing: "What court of men is fit to judge which injuries are liable to the hands of man, and which to the will of God?" Finding this unsatisfactory, he then tried to avoid the issue on the grounds that the English seizure of a Spanish ship and subsequent murder of its crew made England equally culpable. But eventually he was forced into admitting the precedence of guilt, and Pud was offered an annual pension of one pound. Insulted, James I demanded two pounds, which being angrily refused by Philip, was the signal for the outbreak of the War of Pud's Pound.

It was not a popular war, however. Spain was still recuperating from recent Continental reverses, and suffering from increasing internal difficulties; in France, Henri IV was busy pacifying the Huguenots and, with Sully's aid, trying to put through agrarian reform and arrange the habitually scrambled finances of his kingdom; while in England, Thomas Pud was not a character to remain an admired public figure, and furthermore, he was a Scot.

In the Caribbean, the war meant simply a stepped-up pace for constantly occurring hostilities; English and Dutch freebooters now attacked legally, furnished with letters of marque; and occasionally enough troops were mustered to make landings feasible: San Cyriaco was captured and plundered by the Dutch, and Polombo razed by the English.

At the end of a year, no side had gained important advantage, hostilities were terminated by the Peace of Calais and those territories that had changed hands during the course of the war were returned; although news of the cease-fire, either by design or natural delay, not reaching the Ottoman Turks in time –marching to the aid of England and Holland against their old enemy, the Hapsburgs– they laid waste to much of southwestern Hungary; and in the Caribbean, due to a similar delay in the news, Copaverde was sacked by the Dutch.

In England, James, at Philip's urging, had Thomas Pud tried for treason and beheaded; peace again reigned in Europe; guerrilla warfare in the Caribbean.

But relative calm prevailed on Isla Alegre, as attempts to follow Drake's example consistently proved abortive; under Viceroy José

Miraglo, sporadic slave insurrections, racial disturbances, and colonial disputes were quelled with an iron hand; although prosperity was such that men of property had little reason for actual feuding and jealousy and hatreds tended to find their outlets in competitions of extravagance and display.

During Miraglo's tenure there were but few incidents to relieve the routine of island life.

In 1617, a newly converted slave entered the Cathedral; and thinking, in his ignorance, that the stoup of holy water was meant for ablutions, he proceeded to wash his hands and face. Bishop Zarzuela, happening by, noticed this, and to instruct the slave in his error, struck him on the head with his crucifix. But one of the golden thorns in Christ's crown pierced the brain; the man died; and despite the singing of the Te Deum, the Bishop's voluntary fasting for a day, assurances that the slave's soul would fly to Slave's Paradise, and rigorous temporal previews of what Slave's Hell promised: it took a discouraging time before religious fervor was reinstilled in the mass of the slave population.

Then, in 1629, the island was beset by a plague of ants. For no apparent reason, huge armies of the voracious little insects swarmed out of the jungle and into the town, in such numbers as to form a seething carpet over streets and gardens, and even, despite every effort, over the floors and furniture of the houses. It is difficult to be precise to the extent of the plague, various journals fixing the depth somewhere between two inches and two yards.

When prayer and fasting proved futile, the Church assigned its cause to God's wrath at the ungodliness of the laity, while the latter contended that it was just this vice in the Clergy that had inspired divine vengeance; while within the Church itself, recriminations were mutual, the Augustinians blaming the Dominicans for their intemperance, the Dominicans blaming the Augustinians for their pederasty, both blamed the nuns for their incontinence, and all three in one accord blamed the Jesuits for a combination of these sins, adding avarice, gluttony and pride to the list.

Meanwhile, Viceroy Miraglo opened the port to foreigners, promising a rich reward to anyone who succeeded in clearing the plague. Several Frenchmen arrived from the French settlement in Hispaniola, but their methods proving ineffective, and war having broken out between France and Spain, they were seized, accused of espionage and executed.

Of the number of quacks and charlatans who came to try their luck, perhaps the most colorful was the German alchemist and occultist, Gottfried Pflaume. Pflaume maintained that the ant, since it blindly and devotedly adhered to an assigned line of duty, was necessarily a rational creature, and therefore endowed with a language of its own, or at any rate, a means of communication, the secret of which he claimed to know.

Accordingly, Pflaume developed the following plan: to first clear the houses, he intended to hang signs on all the doors, printed in German and ant-cipher, saying AMEISE NICHT GEWUNSCHT (Ants not wanted); secondly, he proposed to meet with leaders of the ants, and by dint of reasoning, convince them that their presence irritated the Christians, creatures superior to themselves since placed on earth to represent God's image. In the event of the failure of logic, Pflaume planned to crush the leaders, assume command himself, and order his unquestioning followers into ovens specially constructed for their cremation.

But the Church, fearing the possible success of science, refused to allow the German to carry out his scheme, and, disappointed, he was banished from the island. Once in Germany, however, his treatise in five volumes, *Die Totale Ameise* (The Complete Ant) much of it based on notes taken on Isla Alegre was immediately hailed as the authority on the subject, and Gottfried Pflaume went down in history as one of the founders of German science.

Finally, Jaap Katz, a Dutch Jew, arrived from Brazil with two cargo schooners laden with anteaters. Within a month, the animals had cheerfully devoured the plague; but upon receiving his reward, Katz was seized by the Inquisition and accused of heresy.

Prepared for this eventuality, Katz had taken the trouble to school himself in the catechism, and under questioning, he confessed the error of his former religion, claimed to have been converted long before, and offered his theological knowledge as proof. On the rack, he consistently provided the proper answers; and, perplexed, there seemed no alternative left to the Inquisitors but to free him. Finally, he was accused of neglecting one of the first principles of Christian virtue: poverty. Katz explained that so deeply did he repent of his former error, that he did not consider himself perfect enough in his new faith to seek poverty, but promised he would begin his search upon his return to Holland. This argument failed to impress the Inquisitors. Katz relinquished his reward and was permitted to leave the island.

Normal life resumed, but Viceroy Miraglo, a severe disciplinarian and a stickler for the letter of the law, was growing in unpopularity for refusing to allow his subects to trade illegally with the English and Dutch for linen, slaves, and trade goods, essential items supplied only intermittently by Spanish ships, and then at unjust and monopolistic prices. But before the disgruntled colonists could work themselves up to violence, Viceroy Miraglo, while beating his greyhound for failing to catch a hare, suffered a stroke and died, and the Crown sent as his replacement, Don Antonio Torres.

Perhaps the best portrait of this Viceroy is that written by Sir Kenelm Burton, a busy and inquisitive English traveler, in his, *Fair Isles of the Caribes: Being an Account and Description of the Said Isle upon Severall Yeares Spent Therein*, a fragmentary and unfinished journal, unpublished in Burton's lifetime, but finally printed in London in 1773.

"Isla Alegre, or Isles of Joyes, as it is named by the Spaniards, is the richest and best favoured of all their Isles; at least eleven percent or twelve moreso than the Isle of Hispaniola which is second richliest. This Isle is, to this day (I think) governed by a most remarkable Spaniarde, Don Antonio Torres. This Don Antonio is of so amicable, learned and gentle a Caractker, and withal so judiciall and firm a Governor, that I say that if hee did not believe in the fantastikall Chimaeras of his Church hee would be a perfect Englishman.

"In stature middling, yet very quicke (the best swordsman of this Isle) head long and oval, eie grey, piercing, but can be merrye, features comely but somewhat hawkish in the Spanish fashion, hair black and plenteous.

"Don Torres is very quiet in his Dress and Bearing, as no other Spaniarde on this Isle is; their fashion beeing to outdo each other in every manner of foppery, and therefore Don Torres appears to great Advantage therein.

"Hee is conversant in the English tongue and in French, and in both haz much reading. Don Torres says that Wm Shakespere is the best writer that haz ever written and next best is the Spaniarde Miguel or Michael Cervantes, and this is a rare thing for a Spaniarde to admit. We talked at great length of the Puritan Calvinists in England. Don Torres called them fanatikall Freeks and Shitt-Breeches. He said they are destinated to cause more Griefe to Englishmen than all the Papists put together, but I see not how this can bee.

"When Don Torres first came to this Isle the young gentlemen of good Familie were much inflamed with the French passion for Duelling and as in that Countrie were killing each other prodigiously. Don Torres declared Duelling was honorable but killing not, and when any two young Coxcombs had a Grievaunce he proposed they were to appear before him, and hee would decide what Weapons and Place whereof to satisfie their Honour. The first approaching, Don Torres bade them follow him, and led them to an Hogges Stye, and providing common spades, bade them fling Hogges Turdes at one another until one should drop of Fatigation, hee who remained standing to be declared the Victor; and thus Don Torres put an end to the Duelling.

"Don Torres despises and disdaigns the King's Cedula, anno 1586, wherein the Colonizers are enjoined to feed their Slaves no Nourishment other than the yam. Hee permits his Slaves the Sabbath to themselves, and they are flogged only when they have done malicious Mischiefe, and they may keepe to themselves any moneyes earned after they have finished their own Travaile; and therefore his Slaves work willingly, and more strenuouslie, and are more zealous of their Religion, and love Don Torres. Don Torres entreates others to followe him in these Methods of proven Excogitancy, but they do not do so, and they hate and envy Don Torres.

"Don Torres enforces severly Cleanliness of the Citie, for hee says in this way are the Plague and the Fever forefended, and verily this Isle is the most Healthfull and Perfumous of all I have seen; but thereby is Don Torres detested by the Priests who abominate him a Calvinist and a Hereticke, for they teach that the Plague and the Fever are Signes of God's Wrath; and also hee is the enemie of the Physicians and the Chirugiens for hee haz deprived them of their patients.

"Don Torres trades with ourselves, the Hollanders and the French freely and does not charge great Excises or Harbour fees, therefore the Merchants gladly bring their finest slaves and wares firstly to this Isle, and so it enjoies great Advantage therein over the other Isles of Spaine. Don Torres extracts more Gold from the mines than any other haz done before him."

Sir Kenelm describes at some length the elegant court and theater life of the island under Don Antonio Torres and then sets off for Havana, leaving the Viceroy to his good works.

In the years following, Don Antonio foiled several plots to assassinate him, but it was in this period (1647–1650) that the gold mines began to peter out; by 1651 they were no longer worth working, all attempts to find fresh mines were unsuccessful, and deprived of gold, the colonists were plunged into an apathy of despair; Creoles passed Spaniards on the streets with daggers sheathed and mumbled epithets, Jesuits ignored nuances of speech that might be heretical in nature and sat around moping over their rosaries, the feeling even filtered down to the slaves –cannibalism became no more than a cherished memory.

Only Don Antonio Torres was undismayed; he alone realized that the future wealth of the Indies lay, not in gold, but in sugar, cacao, tobacco, spices, dyes and hardwoods, resources either already existing in abundance on the island or easily cultivated; but the power of Spain was declining rapidly, the treasury was exhausted from the Thirty Years' War, and so the Viceroy's petition

173

begging permission to abandon the mines and commence with his plantations drew the following reply from the Duke of Olivares, and was signed by the King: "We are not interested in the base preoccupations of Englishmen and Jews. We want gold! Gold!"

Don Antonio, knowing that adherence to this policy could lead only to disaster, took it upon himself to return to Spain, beg a conference with the King, and in person attempt to persuade him of the validity of his plans. This attempt proved unsuccessful; Don Antonio Torres was accused of high treason and conspiracy and thrown into a dungeon with starved rats.

The termination of the gold on Isla Alegre, and current events in the Caribbean and in Europe coincided in such a way as to produce a situation in which not only did Spain lose interest in her colony, but her ability to protect it during wartime from the growing, now formidable naval might of England and Holland was diminishing, while during peace the rapidly augmenting forces of the buccaneers and filibusters constituted a permanent threat.

Recruited from every manner of adventurer and fortune seeker, from runaway slaves and indentured servants, from escaped prisoners and foreign settlers driven by the Spanish from their islands; the buccaneers went prize hunting alone or in small packs; but when a leader of obvious ability appeared, the pirates were often willing to cooperate in numbers large enough to attack cities.

Thus, Pierre L'Ollonois, from his practice of tearing out and devouring the hearts of captured enemies, soon inspired a following of sufficient strength to permit his sack of Maracaibo. And after Indians had put an end to L'Ollonois on the wild coast of Darien, his reputation was soon equaled and surpassed by Karel Klootzak, a Dutchman of bestial habits and perverted tastes, famous along the Main as the only pirate to murder the women and rape the men.

And it was Karel Klootzak who acted upon the generally disbelieved rumor that, the mines of Isla Alegre having failed, the rich colonists had determined to organize a convoy to transport every item of value back to Spain and leave the island to the mestizos, mulattoes, and slaves. Klootzak quickly recruited a

174

pirate armada in the then French-held buccaneer headquarters in Tortuga, and acting upon secret intelligence, he fell upon the convoy at the moment of departure.

The battle was brief and one-sided; the flaccid colonists were no match for the pirates and capitulated quickly in the hope of leniency; although many leaped over the side rather than buy their lives with their gold, an act which caused some buccaneer wag to christen the bay, Bahia de Saltaricos (The Bay of the Leaping Rich). The others attempted to ransom their liberty with their treasures and wives and daughters, but since the pirates were already in possession of both, these negotiations proved futile, and Karel Klootzak gave the order to murder the women and chain the men up for his leisurely inspection.

This order, however, proved to be a fatal tactical error on Klootzak's part. Since most of his men were of a different emotional persuasion, there was a spontaneous mutiny in which Karel Klootzak lost his life, and savage fighting broke out among the pirates as factions formed and disputed the division of the booty, and to which country, if any, they should now pledge the allegiance of their newly conquered island. Eventually the Dutch, a majority on the expedition, were acknowledged as leaders, and their Calvinist minister, Willem Lul, was elected captain.

In Holland, a medallion was struck in Karel Klootzak's honor, posthumously bestowing upon him the title: "De Groote Klootzak" (Klootzak the Great) and Isla Alegre, rechristened Blijdschaps Eiland, was lost to the Crown of Spain and became nominally a Dutch possession; although in fact it shortly developed into a booming free port for buccaneers of every nationality who, the Dutch excepted, found its new name utterly unpronounceable and called it instead, El Escondite (The Hideout).

A new and chaotic epoch in the island's history was about to begin, and soon, battles, treaties, and coups d'état would see it rapidly changing and rechanging hands between the English, French, Dutch, and various independent forces of pirates and commercial combines.

Osborne had absolutely no intention of learning seventeenth-century Dutch to decipher the existing journals and documents in that language. Jan van Gent's wife, Marja, looking for distraction anyway, helped him cheerfully: she pointed out that he had mis-read around the Klootzak medallion; it read "Klootzak de Groote" and not "De Groote Klootzak" as he had written. But he did sit down with his dictionaries, grammars, Pascal, Diderot and Voltaire and, in his own good time, began to study French in preparation for the second part of his essay.

The first part he typed up, and passed around the colony, to anyone interested in reading it. He asked Ed Robles for scholarly criticism, and was delighted when Robles pronounced it, for the most part, sound; though he quibbled with Bishop Juerga's theology in saying "The Devil, too, had a childhood" but shown proof of the quote conceded that the Bishop might have fallen into excusable ecclesiastical error in the midst of ecclesiastical rage.

A number of second-string playboys arrived; having left their Austin-Healeys behind; sailing in on their motor yachts; with the pretty transparent dispensable girls they had won with their second-rate incomes.

And Hiyo came. Hiyo: from his greeting –wide smile, hand flippered waist-high, and merry "Hi yo!": a man black enough to make the Liberals' lives a constant joy; and Pierce and the others –despite the fact that he had arrived without the usual white woman, and did not appear to be wearing the usual shoulder chip– seeing the company he kept, avoided him.

Until one night at Theodore's, Pierce –with his back to the table where Hiyo sat, with the Liberals and Orville and his crowd– heard the talk turn to a currently famous and much-extolled Negro writer. And so tuned in.

After the Liberals' predictable praise, Hiyo said, "Well, man, I tell you, I may not know so much about literature, but it seems to me he got no talent for writing books, he got a little talent for writing articles, but he the world's best genius for getting his face in the newspapers . . . Man, you don't have to tell me he's good.

Hell, I *know* he got to make it. He can't lose! He black, he ugly, and he queer!"

Pierce swiveled in his seat, caught Hiyo's eye, and made the smallest –quite sufficient– gesture of accord.

And later, after the Liberals and the others had gone, and Pierce was habitually closing out the bar with Keith Cooper and Stefan Verduin, Hiyo joined them and Pierce said bluntly, "Hey, Hiyo, you seem to have some brains; what're you always hanging around with those assholes for?"

"I can't escape, man! They the most passionate nigger-lovers I ever meet." He sighed, then smiled. "I tell you, man, it's a bad-ass world. Half the people hate me because I'm black; the other half the people love because I'm black; and none of those people understand me at all. Man, it ain't that I *like* being black; but it ain't that I *dis*like being black; I'm just *black* and all I want is for those mother fuckers to leave me alone and let me play my guitar."

Which he did: to the delight of the native musicians. And it was not long before they were embellishing their joyous jungly rhythms with doodles and flourishes acquired in Hiyo's cool school. They played far into the night; Hiyo chortling; flying and happy as loons on fine, free, Escondite weed.

"Man," he'd say, strumming, "tonight there ain't *nothing* between me and the good wood. I'm so high I'm gonna make my pad on the moon!"   ⚘

And Ole Isserstedt discovered, after twenty years of futile effort, that he was not meant to carve life into inert logs: but he also discovered that so much unrewarded work had produced a master carpenter. And since carpentry is an honorable trade he no longer needed alcohol.   ⚘

Pierce was working, Renée came from Holland –who could cope with his rages– silent, devoted, there. Pat, after a week with Craig O'Connor, just a night with Jonathan Klein-she would have liked to help but their idioms were incompatible-went to Keith Cooper, which was fine, for a while.

Children had a picnic: naked and tan, hair bleached by the sun;

the little ones played out their days on the beach; the older ones collected shells, Ed Robles's twelve-year-old son ordered a massive reference work and mounted and catalogued his four hundred species: they swam, fished, –for fun and dinner– gathered fruits, spices and coconuts, –for fun and dinner– school books were sent, and free from underpaid pedants, overgrown boy scouts, and shriveled virgins, learning was as diverting as fishing: they were taught to read what merited reading.

Jonathan Klein and Keith Cooper trapped myna birds, parrots and monkeys for them; and when they happened across a litter of Escondite hounds (–over the years some of the mastiffs brought to hunt slaves, and some of the greyhounds brought to hunt rabbits, had escaped, or been abandoned, and free for several centuries, had eventually produced a strain that bred true; strong, sleek beasts running a color range from palest lemon to deep chestnut, less spectrally thin than the greyhound, but built along greyhound lines)—: they contrived to lure the bitch away with a rabbit or pheasant, then hiding downwind they would wait for her to leave the litter, and quietly –and very quickly– they would pilfer a few pups, run for their horses and gallop away before the frightened and squealing puppies brought the mother back at their throats. Once they were too slow and Cooper had to shoot in self-defense; but it was not long before the supply of tame dogs was sufficient to meet the incessant and clamorous juvenile demand.

Pet-keeping was rife among the adult foreign population as well. Pierce had a parrot called Woman –because, when finally it got on his nerves, he would shout, "Woman! Shut up!" and it never did. Practically everyone had some sort of animal; and Marsh, of course, soon had his studio, courtyard and living quarters transformed into a seething menagerie: a dog, Claude; a tortoise, Marvin II; five cats, Abe, Sadie, Becky, Max and Morris Benjamin; and finally –knowing better– two rabbits, Anderson II, Mrs. Anderson, and nearly simultaneously, all the little Andersons. It reached the point where, as soon as Marsh sat down, the ritual was for someone to say; "No! Dammit, Alain, we don't want a rabbit!" and someone else would add; "or kittens, parrots, or monkeys!" ❦

Mal Katona finally left Rhea, and for a week, one and all were regaled with torrents of tears, tales of perfidy, and theories of Absolute Love: she didn't expect him to *marry* her, she explained; she had just wanted a permanent re*lat*ionship!

But if none of the other foreigners shared Katona's inexplicable fancy for the monumental; she enjoyed a certain esteem among the natives, who as she passed along the esplanade, her great bulk aquiver, would often stop to watch her, grin, nudge each other in the ribs, point openly, and say with evident relish, "Bobo-bobo!" an atavism surviving from the ancient Mombutu which, though having lost its original meaning, was in fact the old battle cry, and meant "Meat-meat!"

And so it was not long before even Rhea was happy: and pregnant.

Freddy Rosoff caught the island's many and tuneful moods in his bright, meticulously detailed little canvases: in nightscapes in his sky of deepest opaque blue, his stars were all five-pointed: just as they are supposed to be.

"You must have had a very happy childhood, Freddy," Ed Robles commented.

"Hell!" said Rosoff, "I was running for a bookie by the time I was eleven!" ❦

Carl Orville said: "The job of the writer today is to analyze the problems of contemporary society, and then to portray them creatively, in a way that's clear to the average reader. I don't believe these writers who say they write for themselves, or for a select audience; it's a stupid and selfish attitude to take. Because if the writer can't communicate with the reading public, what's the good of writing, even if what he has to say is worthwhile . . ." as Jonathan Klein, across the bar, moped alone over a rum, and nibbled at his cryptic mental *madeleine*, the elusive catalyst in his quest to fuse and transmute the base ore of his past into that Philosopher's Prism through which he might gaze with the (divine) disinterest essential to Freedom: perhaps it was that he did not, after all, live where he thought he lived (and therefore: sang no sweet songs)but was no more than Love's humble link-boy carrying his torch aloft through Limbo's dim back alleys: and why?— on that night years ago, when Janice had been in Europe, and after a month without so much as a card, and being with his parents at that beachside resort –gray shingles, bronzed young men, stone-coiffured divorcees developing their first wrinkles– he had swum as far out to sea as his strength permitted —:had he not gone through with it?

It was cold. So he swam back.

Janine said (with that accent); "But, Jonathan, why you are sitting so alone and triste?"

He looked up, surprised, and smiled a mirthless smile. "I'm brooding," he said, "and thinking negatively, which is a crime where I come from; they could have given me twenty years . . . (No, it wasn't amusing, or original, or honest) have a seat, Janine, and a drink. I'd buy you one if they weren't free."

"Oh! Why?"

"I'm celebrating."

"Why you are celebrating?"

"Because it's Thursday."

That was better, she liked that: and thin strong brown hands: and the way the honed and poisoned darts so often came crackling out of the gloom: and even the jagged profile that had –without his knowing– arrived at virile, if morose, tiercelity –the mirror still flung back at him a frightened gawky fledgling.

And because Jonathan alone (except Del Pierce: who was her friend) had never tried.

Nor did he as he walked her home. Although, by now (even) he saw what they all saw: barefoot now, her dress an azure patina of silk, and silken ash-blond hair silver as the moon, in moonlight (could his fragile spirit endure? the indignity of no? No!)

"Jonathan?"

180

"Yes?"

"Must you go right now home?"

"No."

"We go for a walk?"

"Sure, why not?"

And when they had gone as far along the beach as they could go, and were standing on a thin wedge of sand beneath the rugged and mustachioed cliff: since there was absolutely nothing else for him to do, he reached for her.

"*Oui!* Jonathan, *chéri!* I *will* make love with you!"

"(Annette!!)"

He nearly cried out: for the boundless idiocy and grotesque injustice of it all,

and he buried himself in Janine with the ferocity of a caveman.

Later they smoked cigarettes –the butts tossed into the night impinged their memory an instant longer with two soft pops as they died– and the sea itself sighed softly in its sleep: they swam, and the churning luminous water foamed like clouds . . .

"Ah, Jonathan, *chéri*, I should like to make love with you at the bottom of the sea!"

"Why not? Mermaids do."

"But we are not mermaids."

"Thank God for *that!*"

. . .

Janine all honey and fire "(Annette!" . . . jade, pale flowers, cool stones) her breasts tasting of salt through the night, and blond hair dank and smelled of the sea;

and by the time dawn intruded upon them in the great four-poster in her bedroom, she was, for the first time in her life, in love.

"(Annette!)"

More Tree See-ers came. Pierce had coined the nickname –as he had most: admirable not for wit but for a quality of total undetachability; once Pierce had affixed the label, there was no other way to think of Al the Schmuck, Fat Phil, Spider Ed, and Catsup Pete– for Carl Orville's growing clique, when, after reading Angus McNarr's latest book, he said, with generic scorn; "Schmucks," happy to add Jonathan's Yiddish to his vocabulary, "they live in the jungle, and what do they see? Fucking trees. Tree See-ers!"

"Why it is?" Renée asked him, strolling along the beach with Ed Robles and Katona, "that when I am with your friends everyone talks and acts different; but with Tree See-ers everyone acts the same and even looks the same?"

"Because," Pierce explained, "they're a bunch of idiots, and we're not."

Ed Robles, however, without slackening his jaunty bantam-cock stride, peripateticized. He said: "Ah! A very acute observation, Renée, and I will tell you why. You see, if you take the trouble, which it is not worth, to study a Tree See-er closely, you will find that actually one is as different from another as one genius from another, or one barrow-boy from another. But as you rightly point out, they appear alike, and this is because their moral and intellectual conformity makes their similarities more significant than their differences.

"For instance, you notice that the values and ideals by which they exist are, to all intents and purposes, identical; and almost wholly quantitative, rather than qualitative: that is to say that a chilly review, well-placed in the *Times Lit. Supp.* is deemed more valuable than a considerably warmer and shorter one obscurely placed; Carl Orville, with three books published, is rated better than Craig O'Connor with just one. Incidentally, it is an interesting sidelight that unless the Tree See-er is able to write enough trees to simulate a wood –in which case he can win the Nobel Prize, achieve veneration, his trees are not chopped down and turned into the pulp they deserve, and time at last performs the overdue termites' work . . . where was I? Oh yes, critics. It's interesting that critics, with rare exceptions, treat the young Tree See-er with consideration within a range of appreciation extending, say, from nippy to tepid; never finding anything to inspire wrath or raves; whereas in fact, the Tree See-er is the embodiment of one of the few sins worth punishing in the world of art, or any other world; mediocrity.

"At any rate, the Tree See-er's image of himself is intimately dependent upon, actually tantamount to, the image his reading public has of him; and the extent of his success, critical and financial, precisely determines the nature of the image. Artistry is not involved, because the Tree See-er really doesn't enjoy writing at all; he thinks –God knows why?– that there is something glamorous about being a Writer, capital W, and he becomes a Professional Writer, a species as odious as the Professional Virgin and Professional Do-Gooder.

"Therefore, totally lacking confidence in his own work, the Tree See-er must wait for critical acclaim before he knows what to think of himself, and meanwhile, in his need for outside support, he develops a complex built-in distortion mechanism that permits him to delude himself into believing that words such as 'promising,' 'timely,' and 'competent' are compliments, which, even if they may be so intended emphatically are not, and even 'competent' which has a sound, workman-like ring to it, is, upon examination, no more than well-groomed mediocrity, and should be judged as such. Not realizing this, of course, the Tree See-er nevertheless has no other choice but to seek out his fellow Tree See-ers, and they discuss the Plight of the Writer as they huddle over their drinks in fear, and wait for the reviews to come out.

"I've been talking about the successful Tree See-er, but there is no essential difference between, say, Angus MacNarr with his two bad published novels and atrocious biography of that wretched fascist, Clapp; and dopey Jerry Talbot with his still-worse unpublished and unpublishable book: both write out of a like desire to be Writers, both have the same total lack of inner conviction, and if you don't believe me about MacNarr, I'll give you an example. The other day he buttonholed me –actually he can't bear the sight of me because, in his eyes I'm a failure and I refuse to behave in the way he thinks a failure ought to behave; and because *he* knows that *I* know all his bravura army stories are fabrications; he was in the army, all right, but after the war –at any rate, he started complaining to me, in that ghastly glottal burr of his that Jonathan so *brilliantly* describes as innumerable bottles being emptied– that back on Fleet Street everyone regarded him as a longhair and an intellectual, and here everyone, meaning us, treats him like a square. You see, though none of us are as apparently successful as he is, except Stefan and Jan, and they're both Dutch so don't count, he can't bear the idea that we refuse to accept the public image of moderate success that he would like, but is not quite able, to maintain himself. He can on Fleet Street where everyone is as corrupt as he is, but he can't here, and his uneasiness, sensing that we see something he would rather not –which is true, we see that he's a shit– is driving him right to a breakdown.

"And since it would be suicide for them to see themselves as they really are; you'll soon see what will happen here. All of them, or almost all, have left nice comfortable jobs to come down here; and they've all spent years complaining about responsibility of a family keeping them from work, and the difficulty in producing their trash on the side. But when they finally do get here, they learn, or rather they do *not* learn, they never learn anything, but they have thrust upon them what we have known all along: that responsibility is a crutch, not a burden, and a crutch they have been leaning on for so long that without it they can barely stand, much less run, skip or dance.

"But just watch; the island will get them in the end, if not through their work, then through their private lives; through which, up to now, they have just managed to sleepwalk. You see, the success of a Tree See-er's marriage is dependent upon a job that separates them all day long; a big city that offers them diversion every night; then they go back, have one fuck, and go to sleep; and weekends are always social; so they can have been married ten years and still know nothing about each other.

"Here that doesn't work; that sort of life doesn't exist, so they have to get to know each other, they're together twenty-four hours a day. And, invariably, one discovers that he, or she sees more trees than the other, and things begin to go awry. She starts sleep-

184

ing around —mistaking that for freedom. He drinks, or philanders, or turns into the homosexual he should have been to begin with. In fact, the only hope for them is to realize what's happening before it is irreparable, decide to give it another try, go back to their jobs in advertising, publicity, television and journalism, see an analyst or –O brave New World!– a marriage counselor, take up their old way of life, and heap recriminations on Escondite for their failure to produce the masterpiece of which they are still sure they are capable . . .

"Actually, the whole Tree See-er problem would merit only pity –which is synonymous with contempt– were it not for the one small, but infuriating outrage their existence perpetuates. And that is: that because of their basic dishonesty, and their dependence upon outside approval, they are totally unaware that, with few exceptions, critics are themselves failed writers, or literary dilettantes, and their unawareness strengthens the critic still further in the unfortunate vanguard of a movement in which no one would dream of questioning the views of an atomic physicist upon science; but every Tom, Dick and Harry, because he can read, thinks he knows as much, if not more than the writer, about writing.

"And yet why shouldn't we dispute with the atomic physicist? We know how to add! We know as much about science as the average critic knows about writing: which I could demonstrably prove to be a specious comparison, though seemingly effective through a casuistic sleight known as Dispute Through Unfair Analogy . . .

"And that, my dear Renée, is why Tree See-ers all look alike; I could use a drink."

"That's what I said," said Pierce, "they're a bunch of yo-yos."

"Your hemlock, sir," Katona intoned.

Ed Robles now stopped, an erudite twinkle in his one bright blue eye. "*Doctor* Katona!" he said in mock academic shock, "Aristotle!"   ❦

And some came, not because they wanted to do anything in particular, but because, like Keith Cooper, something unintellectual-

185

ized, but intensely instinctive warned them –that no one wins a rat race– and they left. ♥

Thurston Jennet was a tall, spare, white-haired man, perennially tanned –with the sort of tan acquired only at the best beaches– given to pipes and casual suede: many women found his aura of Sobranie and old sports car irresistible.

His books had made him wealthy; but two expensive ex-wives, a five-room Greenwich Village apartment, summer house in Martha's Vineyard, winter house in Montego Bay, thirsty and demanding vintage Bentley, and hobby of collecting paintings, left little working capital.

One day, reading the village newspaper he subscribed to, he came across:

THE VILLAGE IDIOT
by Jack Thomas

I suppose some of you have seen a somewhat familiar-looking figure around these last few weeks. And I suppose some of you have noticed his somewhat Miami-looking tan, and thought, "Could that be Jack Thomas? No, that couldn't be Jack Thomas; where would he get the dough to get a tan like that in February?" Well, it was me all right. And you know what that tan cost me? Just $79.86 of which $74.86 consisted of my share of the gas and grub to drive to Mexico and back.

In the little seaport of Campeche, we then looked up a crusty local Bogart-type character called Grimes, bargained him down from $10 to $5 each, return, and in the oldest, grubbiest boat I ever saw, we were then ferried over to the forgotten Caribbean island of Escondite, and three weeks of *free* sunshine.

So you want to write the great American novel? You want to get out of the rat race? Get thee to Escondite! True, the houses are all

186

falling apart but I had a brownstone-size ruin all to myself, rent free. True, there's no electricity, or plumbing, and the way in which I took a hot shower was to take a pot, into which I put the water, then carried it over to the fire, over which I'd heat it up. But the food falls from the trees, and if I want fish for dinner, for instance, and I don't feel like fishing for it, then I gather an armful of coconuts or something, and I bring them to the little market and look for a guy who has fish but who wants coconuts or something. Simple, eh? And all for free; and that includes some pretty luscious native chicks.

Escapism? Sure it is; and I know that while I was sitting in the sun, they were lynching Carter Duncan down in Alabama, and I missed the chance to sign the petition against Richard Abraham turning Washington Square into a ten-story garage. But, hell; you can't fight 'em twenty-four hours a day.

By the way, don't look for Escondite on the map. Why not? Because it isn't there. That is, there it isn't.

But now here's the rub. I expected to find a swinging island scene, but I'm sorry to report that, aside from our old friend, Victor Veritas, the other writers and painters there don't seem very hip. In fact, if I want to describe the scene there in one word, I simply remove the first president from Washington Square. Get it?

I did meet an amusing old guy called Kurt Kummer, though, who had a play running hereabouts some years ago, and who gave me the lowdown and the gossip. And I had one interesting evening with a writer fellow called Carl Orville who's down there on a Gherkinstein, but . . .

Thurston Jennet, however, read no further. He put down the paper, picked up the telephone, and dialed his agent.

He said, "Hi, Dave, Thurston. How's tricks?"

"Not bad, not bad. Glad you called, Thurston. Had lunch with Ivan Poshlust the other day; he's wondering if you'd be interested in putting that last effort of yours into paperback."

"If the money's interesting, I'm interested . . . But look, Dave; let's go into that later; I called about a different proposition."

"I listen, all ears."

"Ever hear of a Caribbean island called Escondite?"

"Nope. What about it?"

"That's what about it. No one else has either. But you know Jack Thomas, he writes for that Village rag I get?"

"Yes?"

"Well, not that I'd take his word, but I think he's too dim to make up outright lies, and it seems there's a little island in the Caribbean, forgotten, and God knows why, but not on the map. Seems there's a little art colony there . . ."

"It sounds fine, Thurston, but I've got the mortgage to pay off and Alice's been talking new car."

"You miss my point, Dave. You see, I, too, have been making eyes at a new E-type, but the checkbook says no. So the question: what do you suppose you could extract from *Holiday* for the full treatment?"

"I see your point, Thurston. Well, it sounds promising; naturally I'd have to ring them first, but I don't see why you shouldn't expect half a Jag if you throw in some pretty pictures."

"I was hoping you would make that sort of sound, Dave. You look into it, we'll have lunch over it. On me, this time, O.K.?"

"Roger, Thurston."

"Until then, Dave."

For this urbane and cultivated gentleman had, in his own way – and single-handed– done as much to create the prevailing image of the American abroad as the State Department and the Armed Forces: he was the country's foremost author of guidebooks.

And that morning feeling? caressed from sleep, or by a breeze, buzzing still from last night's pointless drunken revel: waking to birds shrieking:— the sea gull's windblown shadow sweeps over the sand (pristine artistry of creation) and the pelican's lubberly

self-jettison? (pristine burlesque?)—:they had perhaps? an inkling, an aftertaste: just-sun-up lovemaking in the shell-strewn
deserted dunes; or in the jungle, in that choice grove of silver-blue-
boled trumpetwood; birds, birds everywhere –composers and
conductors of every morning's unfinished and unending symphony–
the daffy monkey's aerial stunts; they had some idea of what it
must have (might have?) been, to hear the prancing satyr's hoofs
ringing on Arcadian stones:

and after the rains, in a hush, dripping green; to stand on a
rattan bridge spun swaying over a gorge; to watch, spellbound,
white frothing water bounding to the sea –a rainbow in a haze of
spindrift hovers like a breath . . .   🐦

And it was Janine who discovered, after all that time, that the
baubles and trinkets the native women wore were the real thing
(of course! otherwise her old house would have yielded its jewelry
intact, along with the rest of its past.) But it was Osborne who
understood the significance of the discovery; and, although he
could not have quite explained the urgency of his mission, he
immediately called a conference of Pierce, Katona, Verduin, and
the rest of his friends, and they –grasping clearly what Osborne
meant– agreed to help him; to talk to every foreigner on the
island, and secure from each the promise not to dupe the natives
out of their treasure.

To Pierce's astonishment –and Osborne's delight– it was remarkably easy: even the Tree See-ers saw; and only Victor
Veritas offered token resistance. He said to Pierce, who approached him,

"I don't see why I should agree to anything you say, just because you think I should. I'm a free individual, and I'll do just as I
like."

"Look, you'll promise, and right now, or I'll break every bone
in your body," Pierce reasoned, "You have till three . . . one . . .
two . . ."

"O.K., O.K., man. I promise. I would have promised anyway, I
know what you mean, man. But I just don't like being told what to

do; isn't the reason we're all here to escape that sort of strong-arm police tactics. . . ?"

"Balls," said Pierce, striding away.

Meanwhile, Osborne –naïve, but not that naïve– took Theodore aside and tried to impress upon him the motives for his action. Theodore, however, had difficulty grasping the fundamental ideas, and soon Osborne found himself attempting to explain the basic principles of economics, and the preoccupation with these principles underlying the structure of every modern·society; but Theodore found this totally incomprehensible, and finally he made Osborne stop; he was laughing too hard; besides, he didn't believe it.

Nevertheless, Osborne was his friend and he trusted him, and so agreed to spread the word as he was asked.

Priceless lavalieres and pendants, tiaras and brooches were now worn with new-found childish pride:

and it was a very delicate thing, but somehow very right, to see the women walking by, aglitter.

VISIT SUN-DRENCHED ESCONDITE

IT WAS DULL AS SUNDAY.

Everyone saw everyone else every day.

Everyone had heard everyone else's stories. Too often.

Pierce's bursts of sullen drunken futile fury were embarrassing.

Jonathan Klein's mute gloom was stupid (and pointless) (he had Janine!) and catching. Or else he cracked the one-too-many wisecrack that infuriated.

And Marsh's quaquaversal babble . . . outside of painting, waiting tables in the Catskills, and Jewish delicatessen, he knew nothing whatever; and cared less; still he went on and on: and on – baseball, automobiles, home remedies, French cooking . . .

Ed Robles invented a god missing from Olympus: Onandon, the God of Ennui.

They all talked too much when they were drunk:

and evenings they were usually drunk, there was nothing else to do.

Who cared about anti-Fascism before the war?

Or the Dutch underground movement?

Or prohibition?

Osborne's relentless cheer got on everyone's nerves; it wasn't normal: or fair!

There were no new women.

And those that arrived, available, were neurotic, or unattractive, or unwashed, or all three.

The mail took ages to arrive: the Mexican post office misdirected letters. Lost them.

They were too far away; working –or not working– in limbo . . .

Chagrin, Regret, and Nostalgia reigned: torpid Furies of the Doldrums. Anything! but this: waking up to still another (goddam) sunny day . . .

The rainy season was interminable; nothing stayed dry; roofs laboriously –if ineptly– patched in plenary sunlight sprung leaks beneath the incredible rains; impossible to sit outside after dusk –mosquitoes the size of locusts; and sand fleas on the beach bit like

193

inspired scorpions; they couldn't think straight in the racket the birds made. And washing hung out to dry was retrieved spotted with droppings. An enemy gull (or flying elephant!) once opened his bomb bays directly over one of Pierce's finished pages: he wasted an entire afternoon contemplating revenge –on birddom in general, and gulls in particular (next trip in he would buy a barrel, no, two barrels of bird poison . . .)

They longed for the cities from which they had fled: noise, bustle, movies, plays, galleries, museums, Chinese restaurants, hot pastrami, taxis, store windows, a jar of Watney's Special, fog, smog, a broodje von Kootje, bars, drugstores, flaneuring through the *quartier* acquired the aura that distance bestows; and nothing relieved the identical nights . . .

Tony Vale first spotted them. He was intently, cheerfully whipping the end of a new jib sheet, whistling, when that sailor's sixth sense he had acquired bade him look up.

A bowsprit and heavy prow pushed past the promontory; clearly no member of the ocean-going yacht fraternity. A foremast was followed by a main and mizzen: one of the old bright Caribbean cargo schooners that still plied between the islands . . . that had no reason to come to Escondite. Tony Vale alerted Keith Cooper, who had volunteered to help putter that afternoon, and Cooper went below for the binoculars. Another prow filled the gap left by the first. Vale peered through the glasses, handed them to Keith Cooper. They ran off to get the others . . .

A third schooner followed; and as the ships approached, slow and stately, the crowd gathered, animated by so untoward an arrival. Katona, loafing down the beach, retraced his loaf back toward the jetty. Victor Veritas was already there. Osborne arrived, lumbering; and Pierce –who had been actually working, having left only at Vale's insistence– puffing and cursing. By the time the ships were midway across the lagoon, everyone in town waited on the beach.

In silence Tony Vale handed the binoculars around among his friends . . . powerful lenses painted the scene with tactile clarity: the decks of the schooners were jammed to the railings with people. The men all wore soiled jeans and filthy shirts –unbuttoned, but tied pirate-fashion at the waist– many were draped with bead necklaces; all wore sandals or bare feet; their beards ranged in texture and scope from the lichenous to the dendroid; each had a rucksack strapped to his back; a copse of guitar stems bristled. The women were similarly dressed and equipped, and coiffed like octopi.

Victor Veritas rocked back on his heels.

"Yeah, man," he said, "yeah, yeah, yeah."

(Jonathan!) out of all that horde who had handled her body; by night selenetropic to him, whose touch beckoned inflamed ignited until . . . "Aiee! Jonathan, *chéri-i-i-i*" at last, he exorcised her demon . . .

dallying in siesta dusk, in the great fourposter, outside spectral veiled unreal through netting:

And at high noon, in the empty dunes she saw a single sea gull wheeling, create the sky from blue; then shriek with glee, chandelle . . . chandelle: for every day was heyday.

She painted; flowers now she understood them: in the June of her life, at her window in love, in moonlight she poised (she posed!) like hot marble; he called she came; with (familiar!) fury,

and when she asked: why he alone (except Del Pierce: who was her friend) had never tried, and he (half) honestly replied, "I never thought of it" (nor would have dared) it was unpardonable: waiting for the afterwords expressive of the glow, he had never said I love you. ❧

They didn't do very much; they just hung around, a scruffy, idle, self-styled hagiocracy. Sometimes they went swimming, sometimes someone strummed a guitar; occasionally there was a lethargic verbal exchange in the cult's unintelligible Bêche-de-Mer, but mostly they just sat in the shade, in big disorderly groups, smoking the free marijuana and staring at their feet, or at nothing at all; occasionally one would stand, signal his chick, and they would slouch off together . . .

195

"Where they going, man?"

"Dunno."

"Man, they're making the sex scene."

For it wasn't love: actually, it wasn't even sex; it was just fucking.

There were not enough habitable houses remaining to shelter all these newly arrived painters and writers; some set up tents on the beach.   ❦

Kurt Kummer finished his modern version of *Candide*.

His agent wrote back:

"I like it, Kurt. It's timely, it's funny, and it's damn commercial. I like the idea of Candide as a young scriptwriter who's actually a great writer but can't get his work done because he's so irresistible to women. But just two quibbles before I send it off. Don't you think you go into just a bit too much bedroom detail in all his conquests? And sometimes I think that he's just a bit too damned irresistible to be believable. Anyway, let me know your opinion, and if you want to let it stand as is, I'll send it out as soon as I hear from you . . ."

Kurt Kummer sighed: his agent had missed all the symbolism, all the social protest. But still, he *did* find it commercial, and Kummer liked that; for he had an important message to convey, and the bigger his audience, the more people would benefit from his wisdom, and the more money he would make.

But what disturbed Kummer at this time was that work in progress –that psychological thriller involving an island, a murder, a Swedish nymphomaniac, a drunken American seaman, a disgraced diplomat, a failed professor, and a great Central European novelist– was not progressing properly.

And he knew why: the primitive cooperative system prevailing on the island was unconducive to Art. It was all right for the others to cut cane, help at the still, hunt, fish and gather fruit; they were dilettantes for the most part anyway; but he had written an anti-German play that had been successful in Germany; and if the others lacked the initiative to provide themselves with financial security before devoting their lives to Art, that was hardly his fault; besides, unprejudiced as he was, what were ignorant *Schwartzes* for, if not to make life easier for the artist, and in their own small way do their bit to further his work? It was *just* that half hour every morning, gathering oranges, lemons and limes from the trees around his house, that interrupted the inspirational flow!

Therefore, Kurt Kummer decided to do something about it; and if the others dared censure him for it, *das wurde ihn gar nichts machen,* posterity would exculpate him . . .

He chose Cavendish, the simple-minded shrimp fisherman, as the beneficiary of his scheme; and one morning, Kummer arose early, and was waiting near the jetty where Cavendish customarily beached his pirogue with the morning's catch.

The native, totally unsurprised by Kummer's presence, waved a cheery greeting, and went about his work. He unloaded the heavy, dripping box of shrimp, with one motion hoisted it to his shoulder, and set off in the direction of the market, still showing no surprise at seeing Kummer accompany him.

Kummer said, in his halt patois; "Cavendish, I would like to talk to you."

The native grinned and nodded exuberant assent. For he liked to talk, and although he talked not so well as the others, he enjoyed greatly to talk, but first he must bring his shrimp to the market.

The market, a bright, jerry-built warren of cane, thatch, and driftwood stalls and huts, was already teeming and noisy with shouts and laughter, the cries of the men herding animals to the abattoir, and the lowing, bleating and squealing of the animals themselves. Women, native and foreign, came with their fruit, spices, nuts, and vegetables, and left, having collected whatever they required for the day.

Kummer and Cavendish threaded through to the fish stalls, the shrimp box was set down, beside marble slabs aglow with extravagantly hued Caribbean fish; and Kurt Kummer fretted and fidgeted as Cavendish exchanged endless jabbering civilities with Antoinette tending the stall.

Cavendish remembered! He was going to talk! With the fat

white man. Abruptly, he cut short the chitchat; he announced proudly: he was going to talk!

Kummer led the way, Cavendish shambled along beside him, happy, humming, incurious.

In the salon, Kummer bade him sit down across a huge refectory table, and he said; "Cavendish, I am going to do something very good for you." The native beamed. "I am going to tell you how you can get what you want most in the world, how would you like that?" Cavendish nodded in supreme delight. "Now tell me what you want most in the world."

And Cavendish grinned a gain of enormous incomprehension.

"(*Scheisse! Verdammt und zugenäht!*)" he had forgotten that the native, in his ignorance, might not realize how unhappy he was.

He said: "See here, Cavendish, there are things you own. You own a hut. You own a boat. You own a shrimp net. But there are things you do not own. Things it would be of pleasure to own. Now what is there that you do not own that would be of pleasure to own?"

The retarded black scratched his woolly head. Something he did not own? Something that would be of pleasure to own? . . . Yes, once when the hairy white man came with his necklace of pigs' tusks he had wanted such a necklace; and he had thought of asking the hunters for the tusks of the wild pigs which they killed, and then he was going to make such a necklace and give it to his woman, but he had not done it in the end, for in the end it was of much more pleasure to catch shrimp.

He thought and thought. Beads of sweat formed on his brow, for if he did not think of something he did not own, something that would be of pleasure to own, perhaps the fat white man would be angry, and the fat white man was his friend . . .

Kurt Kummer lit a cigar; and the dull veil that cerebration had drawn over the native's eyes was lifted.

A fire machine! Yes! Ever since the white men had come with their fire machines, he had wanted a fire machine! But he did not know where to fish for them.

"Yes!" he said, "I do not own a fire machine; and it would be of pleasure to own such a fire machine!"

"*Ja,* good, Cavendish. Now I shall tell you how to get such a fire machine . . ." he faltered, he didn't know the patois word for work, if one existed, nor did he know one for money; painfully he paraphrased, "You must do certain things that other people ask you to do for them, and after you have done these things they will thank you, and give you some of these." Kummer spread a handful of coins over the table. "These are called money."

"Pretty!" said Cavendish, immediately arranging them into a necklace pattern.

"Now," Kummer continued, "after you have done enough things for people and you have gathered enough money, you can exchange the money for a fire machine."

"Yes, both are good. But it would be of more pleasure to own such a fire machine, for with such money I cannot set fire to my cigar."

"*Nein!* First you must gather money, *then* you can exchange them for a fire machine!"

Cavendish smiled over these abstractions; his expression describing his thought's descent from eagerness, down through perplexity, disappointment, and finally, to a stop at resignation.

"But, alas, I have no such money and therefore I cannot exchange them for a fire machine."

"*Blöde schwartze!* . . . I will tell you how you may gather the money."

Cavendish listened intently as Kurt Kummer filled in his plan in patient detail; and finally, when he had made his point as clear as possible, and sworn the native to secrecy, he concluded, ". . . so every morning, after you collect the basket of fruit and bring it to my house, I will thank you and give you three of these brown money." (He held up a penny.) "Now there are five brown money in this little silver money; and five of the little silver money in this big silver money," he took a dollar bill from his wallet, "and four big silver money . . ."

In his eagerness he had failed to notice the anger welling in the native's guileless face. So! The fat white man was making fun of him! They were always making fun of him! Because he talked not so well as the others! But even he could see there were not five brown money in one little silver money, or five little silver money in . . .

Kummer intuited his gaff; and moved to repair it. "*Ja*, Cavendish. Perhaps it does not appear that what I tell you is so; but among the white men, this is so. This is the white men's magic!"

Ho! Magic! Yes, by magic the white men could turn five brown money into one little silver money, and five little silver money into . . .

Kummer waved the dollar bill, "And there are four big silver money in one green paper money; and when you have gathered just three green paper money, you may exchange them for a fire machine!"

"It would be of much pleasure to own such a fire machine," observed Cavendish, solemnly. 🔥

Marsh was stuck. A week became two, two became three. And no new paintings came . . .

Had all his lifeblood been expended: on so few paintings? For he *had* done it. Whatever lay in store, he had reached his zenith, and if he chose to say Yea! at zenith and ignore the Nay! at nadir, that was his choice: and no new paintings came . . .

Then he knew! At zenith there was yet infinity of quality. He would paint the same painting endlessly, endlessly improving (Bonnard had done it! And Monet!) and he remembered; his favorite story. About Hokusai –when, at the age of eighty-five an admirer had paid homage to his work, and he replied, "Ah, yes. These paintings are not bad. But wait five years. Then you will see paintings!"

and once again Marsh was dancing, dancing on the high wire, and if the arena was empty, still he was dancing.

Pierce finished his book. He had been plodding along, getting too drunk for a week, more or less sobering up the next, steadily accumulating notes, scribbling illegible drafts, forcing himself to type them up, and then, for no apparent reason, one of his characters stepped overboard, and the book was done.

He decided to call it "Dragging Anchors" after all. He reread it, cut a word here, a phrase there; and for whatever it was worth, it was what he wanted to say.

The only disappointment was the feeling: he had expected elation –having set out to say something, and saying it– but he felt no more than the numb and dubious pleasure of being awarded the close split decision in a grueling ten-rounder (why did the Tree See-ers bother?)

He reread again; if not honing and polishing, at least grinding the nicks out of his broad-bladed prose. And no excuse remained, not to commence the businesslike business of getting his book into print, if possible. For he wanted the chance to say Fuck you! to the world in the only language it understood.

And he therefore sent the book first to the Orchard Press, a firm famous for its pioneering spirit:— although to earn the reputation they had done no more than import from Europe before anyone else, a number of writers of merit with already established reputations, and had dared print several books unjustly condemned by the censor. Their subsequent exploits of literary derring-do amounted to mere litigation: battling the postmaster general while, flaunting the stuff as the avant-garde of literature, they set about peddling the smutty platitudes of drugged nonentities and defiantly illiterate perverts; an enterprise bound for both critical and commercial success, since a society of diminished men cannot help but welcome the reassuring trinkets fashioned by mental dwarves.

Angus MacNarr, following the descending path accurately predicted by Ed Robles, returned to Fleet Street just in time to salvage his marriage. He resumed his job as the greatest journalist in the world, and his articles on Escondite –the first to appear in English papers– stirred up a certain interest.

On the side, he began work on his new greatest novel in the

world:— about a bunch of phonies living on an island, who conspire to drive out the one talented man among them: a young Welsh reporter and novelist. ✌

Upon arriving, Thurston Jennet had the stroke of good sense that told him to make his inquiries pseudonymously. Only Robles suspected something; but Robles was just in for supplies, and quickly back out to his plantation: to write poetry and give no more thought to the overinquisitive stranger. So as Thurston Barnet he spent a month in the sun, poking and prying everywhere; a genial, talkative gentleman of leisure, with a bent for the curious, perhaps overly addicted to photography.

Interested in paintings, he visited all the studios. Another stroke of good sense told him that Alain Marsh, that bizarre scarecrow, was nevertheless: what he was:— and Thurston Jennet postponed his E-type Jaguar on the strength of his conviction. He bought two enormous paintings for five hundred dollars each. Not cheap! considering that he proposed to show them to his friend, Sam Metzger, arrange a show, and guide Marsh from oblivion; but Marsh stubbornly refused to take less for his exit.

And he bought one of Freddy Rosoff's, since Rosoff, looking indestructible at sixty-four, seemed a fair gamble to attain eighty, perhaps ninety, and who could tell? a hundred –and everyone knows the value of a centenarian primitive.

And he bought one of Janine's, a good one at that, but from motives dissimilar. Yet despite Kurt Kummer's assurance that Jonathan Klein was homosexual, and Janine nymphomaniacal, Jennet's aura of Sobranie and old sports car failed signally; the one flaw in an otherwise wholly enjoyable month.

On the day of his departure, he collected his paintings, paid for them with checks; and it was not until the following day, when Alain Marsh extracted his from his wallet –to admire it– that anyone noticed the name –surnames on Escondite had a way of being forgotten upon introduction . . .

Jennet? Thurston Jennet?

He bumped into Mal Katona on his way to town for dinner and

drinks, and asked if Thurston Jennet meant anything to him.

"Sure. He writes the guidebooks."

"Well, that's who bought my paintings. The guy who left yesterday."

"That was Thurston *Barnet*."

"Not on my check!" Marsh stopped; he struck his forehead. "No! The fink! It's a bum check! I gave away two good paintings for nothing!"

Katona examined the check; considered.

"No. I think the check's real but the Barnet wasn't." His philosopher's face wrinkled in thought; he cocked one stoic eyebrow.

"Well, Alain; we've had it," he said.

"All I can say," Marsh replied, "is that the check better be good."   ❦

The Orchard Press held Pierce's book for six months before returning it. When they returned it, the following printed form rejection slip was enclosed:

Thank you very much for sending us your manuscript for consideration by The Orchard Press. After due consideration however, we regret to inform you that we do not find it suitable within the scope and framework of our current program of publication and we will not therefore be able to undertake the venture of its final publication.

We regret that we are not able to comment more fully on the reasons for your manuscript's rejection and that it is made unfortunately necessary, by the large number of unsolicited manuscripts we receive, to return your manuscript to you with this form letter. However, we hasten to assure you that your work has been thoroughly read and evaluated by the members of our editorial staff and that our concluding decision has been reached upon the basis of that evaluation.

We wish you luck in placing your manuscript.

The rejection itself meant nothing to Pierce –in his own drunk way he was an artist– but he gagged on that mouthful of mealy euphemism and pappy periphrasis.

He said, " 'Framework of our current program of publication'! Why can't those morons just say, No. Six goddam months of waiting and what do they send me? Bullshit!"

There was, however, this consoling note: the rejection slip proved, whatever its faults, his book had not been turned down because of his use or misuse of the English language; for The Orchard Press was ignorant of the matter.

But it also proved, if he cherished the wistful and romantic desire to be treated by publishers with some vestige of consideration, that he had better find himself a literary agent.

Robles knew nothing of the American situation; but could assure him, although his own personal experience with hillbillies was limited, dealings with publishers had convinced him that the prevailing extent and rate of literacy among the two groups must be comparable, and therefore searching out a literate literary agent amounted to pure luxury. So Pierce, knowing Carl Orville dealt with Brace and Auger, an outfit with a knack for launching successful Tree See-ers, approached him and asked for the address.

Orville said, "Sure, Del, but in all honesty I can't recommend it to them without reading it first. You understand, don't you?"

With smoldering tranquillity Pierce reminded him: he had asked only for the address.

"I know, Del. I realize that. But what I meant was that I'd be glad to read it, and if I like it and can honestly recommend it, it can't do you any harm. I don't make a million, but I do carry some weight with them."

(Blackmail by best intention!) he submitted, and two days later was amazed when Orville said; "Del, not only will I recommend it, I'll recommend it highly. It's a damn promising first novel! (Maybe it wasn't such a good book.) I have some technical suggestions if you're interested in hearing them; and I feel the theme is too pessimistic for it to reach much of an audience, but as soon as you retype it I'll be happy to put in my two cents."

"Retype it?"

"Of course. You can't send it in looking like that!"

"Why not? What are they interested in, the words, or the typing?"

"It's not that, Del. You don't understand. You see, an editor gets a manuscript in that condition, he thinks you have no respect for him or his firm."

"Damn right, too! Fuck them! If they like my words, they can print them. I'm not spending a month typing for anyone in the world."

Carl Orville laughed. "O.K., Del, have it your way. But you're starting out with one strike against you; two more and you're out."

"Yeah, but I'm starting out with two balls in my favor; two more and I'm on first."

Again, Carl Orville laughed, and handing back the thick folder, he said, "Oh, and Del, I think I owe you an apology; I really never thought you did anything but drink. I was wrong. I see you're one of us."

If there were two things he hated, they were humility and inaccuracy!

Nevertheless, his slovenly, ring-stained manuscript went off to Brace and Auger lauded by Carl Orville: whose praise created among the Tree See-ers, especially the unsuccessful, a certain esteem for him; which made him squirm. For they pressed their own stuff on him; they wanted him to read their trees. 🐾

Cavendish's fire machine was a success. Because he had a fire machine he was able to take Bonsoir's fat woman away from Bonsoir. And he chased his thin woman out of his hut, and moved in Bonsoir's fat woman. He had never enjoyed his thin woman. He had always enjoyed Bonsoir's woman, who was fat. 🐾

And rarely, some windfall word or phrase fell . . .

For instance, one evening Ed Robles was in town; they had all gathered at Theodore's and were, as usual, making noise; when

Eli Rapp and Betty joined them. The Liberals followed shortly and sat down at the overlapping perimeter of an adjacent Tree See-er table, but slowly losing interest, or unable to insert their own opinion into the discussion –the relative merits of Nathanael West and Thomas Wolfe– their chairs came about into, if not more bracing, at least gustier winds; which they ignored; and were soon arguing with Eli Rapp.

Beginning with current civil rights procedures; in which they tried, and failed, to interest Hiyo; the Liberals complained of the incumbent government's failure in achieving certain reforms promised in its platform; while Eli Rapp, resolutely sinistral, held that any measure attempted by a government erected upon the foundations of capitalism, however liberal and well-intentioned, had, *a priori*, to finish in fiasco . . .

Words flew; with increasing velocity, opacity, and specific gravity; eventually impeding the unravel of a tangled Robles comedy involving Steve Seley, Paris before the war, the poet Eluard, Germans and spies . . .

Interrupted in mid-parabasis, Ed Robles listened; to words he could have repeated by rote before the Spanish Civil War (when they had seemed –even now did– justified; at any rate, justifiable.) He waited for a lull: then, knowing full well the futility of explaining moonbeams to the blind, he said precisely what he meant.

"Look, the only really important question facing modern society is this: Can science continue to furnish the new Thingolatry with an unending and ever-changing supply of unbreakable plastic icons? If it can, the iconoclast is doomed. If it can't, who knows? Perhaps there will be a new Renaissance:— not like the old Renaissance: after all, the old Renaissance man thought the sun revolved around the earth; but some sort of resurgence of the spirit: and if that happens, human beings will be born again."

Rosoff, in a loud aside to Katona, said, "Hey! What language's he talking?"

"As a poet," said Eli Rapp, "you naturally place spiritual values before mundane problems; and I admit that what you say is not without a certain validity; but it's narrow-minded and egotistic to simply ignore the basic crisis of a world in which the prevailing tension arises from nothing more complicated than a fundamentally unjust distribution of economic resources and opportunities . . ."

Pierce set his glass down, with all the noise disgust can generate.

"The 'basic crisis' of the world," he said, "is that there are too many fucking *people* in it; that's the 'basic crisis' of the world." The vernacular permitting him to describe the problem, pinpoint its origin, and offer a commentary upon it, simultaneously. "Stupid bastards have nothing better to do than sit around and *breed!* They ought to tax the dumb yo-yo's, that's what! First kid free; ten thousands bucks for the second, fifty thousand for the third. That'd solve the 'basic crisis' of the world!"

. . .

A baby tax!

Though Ed Robles, of course, knew it was not original; there had, in fact, been a baby tax levied in England in 1694, to help finance the war with France; but then burials, bachelors, and widowers were taxed as well, and the tax, in those days, was hardly designed to solve problems of excess population; so he said nothing and let the idea pass as Pierce's.

A baby tax! It provided that spark! The idea was picked up, tossed about, spun, volleyed, juggled:— the Liberals and Eli Rapp, serious souls, uninterested in games of any kind, and especially those intellectual, took spectator seats.

The baby tax! . . . Immediately it was evident that Pierce's original scheme lacked finesse, and was an unfair and objectionable excise that would affect only the lower and middle classes, and serve to populate the world with the vacant and smug progeny of the rich. No, the tax had to be as just as it was effective . . .

It would be pro rata: first baby free; second, say, five year's income –for the rich an equivalent chunk out of capital as well– and the third baby would be taxed an exorbitant and unthinkable amount. Thus within two short generations, allowing for mistakes and cheating, the world's population would be reduced to around a third of its present size; and meanwhile urgent reform would be in progress . . .

At first glance, the Great Population Contraction appeared to create a concomitant and catastrophic economic depression; but examination indicated just the contrary. For the myriad workers currently involved in tasteless construction would simply divert their energies to useful destruction; and back to construction as parks, pleasances, promenades and gardens replaced housing developments and shopping centers. Sculptors and marble cutters would flourish; as would architects:— turning from steel and glass pyramids in which the century buries its live, to pavilions, gazebos and cafés for living.

Meanwhile, the government –they never stopped to figure out exactly who would run it (anyone! but not themselves!)– attempting to be just, if undemocratic, would have to impose certain measures to ensure the progress of the general welfare: the automobile, almost solely responsible for the condition of modern cities, would be discouraged, but not outlawed, through a tax similar to the baby tax –pro rata and exorbitant– and the return of the horse and carriage would be actively sponsored, not only by propaganda, but with offers of free fodder from grain surpluses already accumulated.

The return of the horse and carriage would accomplish any number of direct and ancillary objectives: first, it would provide employment for workers unemployed by the decline of the automobile; secondly, and more important, laborers would become artisans –and artisans are contented with their lot– for the government would prevent the automobile combines from simply switching to carriage production by the elemental expedient of forbidding the production of more than one hundred identical carriages per year by any one firm –automatically re-creating the small businessman and entrepreneur– and to hinder hedging through merely altering a few bits of trim, carriages would be subject to the scrutiny and approval of the Carriage Commissioner –a man specially chosen for total blindness in one eye, and 50 per cent vision in the other– who would have to discern a difference between one year's model and the next, at a distance of one hundred yards, at dusk.

Commercial airlines would be summarily abolished, extirpating the tourist and reinstituting traveling –again worthwhile since distinctions between people and places would be likely to re-develop. Railroads would regain their former favor, and perhaps splendor, providing work for the dispossessed airline people; and while old clipper ships would be promoted, steamships would be allowed to remain (they sort of liked steamships).

Over the course of the evening, other problems were dealt with which at first appeared not only unsolvable, but unavoidable.

For instance, the Government –benevolent, but when need be, autocratic– would bluntly obliterate advertising, television, public relations, the yellow press and all their kindred growths, as affronts to the new human dignity. Now the problem: what honest trades were there in which all the people involved might exercise their peculiar talents?

Jonathan Klein provided the obvious answer. The return of the horse and carriage would naturally re-create a demand for lackeys and flunkeys: account executives, time and space buyers, all the managerial personnel of the defunct shams, men patently born to these arts, would flock to fill in the newly established positions.

Furthermore, the return of the horse, while it replaced the disquieting snarl of the combustion engine, with the soothing and integral sound of clopping hoofs, would be inescapably conjunct to an unpleasant befouling of streets and highways: copywriters, scriptwriters, TV directors, reporters, all the idle creative minds, experts at handling this material in a synthetic form, would certainly welcome a unique opportunity to deal with the real article . . .

And the military. That was difficult . . . Clearly, an enlightened society rejected war as a solution to anything; obviating all armed might. But it was equally clear that, outside of the police force – itself of diminishing necessity– there were almost no jobs uncomplicated and menial enough to allow this vast multitude to utilize its training.

Naturally, the government could continue to subsidize the

demobilized men; in doing so finally drop all pretense, label their wages accurately "Relief" and by eliminating spurious distinctions between the ranks, save . . .

Ed Robles said: "Brass bands!"

Of course! Everyone loves brass bands! At the sound of a brass band children shout and strut; old men's hearts quicken. The military would remain intact, retaining all its hierarchical hocus-pocus. They would all have to learn to play an instrument –those too dense or tone-deaf would pretend and, if nothing more, serve to swell the ranks– and every city over a specified size would be granted its own brass band, satisfying one and all.

For the first time in history, the military would serve a useful function! And more important: they would be content; for if denied the hope of murder, rape and plunder, still any soldier will admit there is little kick left in modern warfare, and this way, at any rate, no limit existed to the degree of extravagance to which their uniforms might aspire . . .

Politicians, lawyers, merchants and bankers had always existed in one form or another, and, no doubt, would always.

Scientists? Well, if they still had the adolescent urge to fly to the moon, let them go there; stay there if they cared to . . .

And now, as a world rendered unsafe for animals and unfit for people again became habitable; and life assumed the meaning inherent in the heartbeat; other salutary developments would follow quite naturally: priests, rabbis and ministers would at last become totally superfluous:— but they would not go idle: deprived of their vestments and ritual paraphernalia they would continue to function happily enough as businessmen. And analysts would languish as knifeless lobotomy fell into disfavor. Their futures were less certain, however. Those few among them not actually psychotic but merely misled might perhaps rediscover the works of their forefathers, and turn from the depraved and comic attempt to explain man in terms of beast to the inefficient –but at least honorable– quest for the Philosopher's Stone. The others would carry their researches further along their present lines:— into haruspicy, oneiromancy and voodoo: since even this model and improved society was bound to produce some few

deluded souls to whom these, and related sciences, were attractive
. . .

There was silence at the big round table: it was obvious: they had done it! With perhaps some few easily rectified oversights and miscalculations, they had solved all the world's problems through Pierce's baby tax. There was just one fatal, irremediable catch:— and they all knew it . . .

"Nah!" said Pierce, "it's too damn sensible. Who'd do it? There has to be another way."

Mal Katona said; "International Suicide Week!" the profound efficacy and practicability of which provided the evening with an inspired second wind . . .

International Suicide Week! It had to work . . . as, government sponsored and promoted, Big Business utilized the tremendous machinery of opinion-manufacturing mass media industries in the battle for the profits . . .

MAKE MONDAY GUNDAY!
The Suicidal Sportsman Does it With a Smith and Wesson .38!

Verduin's imperfect English allowed him the rope combine's counter:

MAKE TUESDAY NOOSEDAY!
TRY "THE TYBURN"!
Dunbar presents the home gibbet with the old London air.
Preferred by the man of extinction

SHOW HER YOU CARE
Barricini's Borgia Bonbon Assortment:
Deliciously! delectably lethal!

PERISH THE PATRICIAN WAY!
Gillette's handy new wrist-slitter uses ordinary blue blades!

SIP PHILOSOPHER'S FINISH
genuine old-fashioned hemlock! just $3.95 the gallon!

. . . distilleries would advertise the obvious, while Pierce suggested that the brothel syndicate might covertly propose a method which, to many, would appear not undiverting . . .

DIE WITH YOUR *FLORSHEIM* BOOTS ON!

SATURDAY IS SPLATTERDAY!
Whatever your income, go like a millionaire!
Leap from fashionable FINANCIER'S LEAP atop posh 40 Wall Street!

WHEN YOU SMASH THAT CAR TO SMITHEREENS
MAKE SURE YOU SMASH A
NASH!

Exhibitionists would go cheerfully in public; on a television program called "This Is Your Death": excursion boats, with a banner proclaiming, "Go Jump in a Lake!" would flourish, as would an ingenious Los Angeles firm, provisionally named Suicide, Inc. Catering to those with dreams of grandeur, this enterprising operation would construct any number of historic stage sets; then, for an appropriate sum, a costume would be rented to the customer, a toga, say, and walking into a mock forum, mock senators would stab him. For women with visions of sanctity, there would be pyres and jeering mock soldiers . . .

IF IT'S SUICIDE, IT'S GOT TO BE GOOD!

They had passed another evening.   🎋

"Fi' cen'!" said Thomasina, smiling, swinging a glistening, still-wriggling string of fish.   🎋

". . . but, Adele, honey; there aren't any hotels. It says there aren't."
   "I know there aren't dear; but wouldn't it be a *fun* place to see?"
   "We've only got two weeks, you know that."

"Let's ask Billy. The Krazy Kupples Klub could charter a plane!"

"There's no airfield."

"You're always so *prac*tical, Georgie . . . we could charter a *sea* plane!"

For Thurston Jennet's article had aroused nationwide interest in the forgotten island of Escondite; *The Saturday Evening Post* hastily summoned best-selling novelist Rupert C. Roach and offered him five thousand dollars to write an article on it for them; inquiries poured into travel agencies everywhere, but even these were unaware of the *Zapata*, the cargo schooner a Campeche firm had fitted out with crude passenger accommodations, which now made a regular weekly run to the island and back; so for the present, inaccessibility and the lack of hotels kept all but the most adventurous tourists away.

However, upon reading the article, Simon J. Grockle, founder and president of booming Grockle Line, sent his son, Simon Jr. as scout: to see if the island was worth adding to the list of cruise stops on the popular twenty-one-day "Explorer's Cruise" that offered visits to lesser-known ports of call as a lure to travelers jaded with Jamaica, Trinidad and Puerto Rico.

Simon Jr. returned enthusiastic. The town was "quaint," the natives "friendly," the art colony "picturesque," the beach "sandy." He pointed out the impossibility of docking the big cruise ship and the need for a landing launch. And he bemoaned the fact that there was almost nothing to buy there –which meant the firm would have to forego the kickback it usually received from factories and shops it recommended to its passengers.

And Simon Sr. chuckled as his son concluded, "So you see, Dad, the place is wide open and waiting; an absolutely golden opportunity, and nobody has any sense there. O.K., they may not have the capital to start big-scale construction, but if anyone had any brains there the least they could do is to teach those niggers some native crafts; they could clean up!"

No, Simon Sr.'s fears were unfounded: Harvard Business

School hadn't made any mealy-mouthed, New Deal Do-gooder out of his son; the kid was a chip off the old block after all. ❦

Eddie Davidson's play about Janine was not going well; nor was the novel Craig O'Connor was writing about her.

"The next yo-yo that says 'Say, Del, any word on the book?' is going to get a fist in his face," fumed Pierce. "Who do those pricks think they are, anyway? Three goddam months and no letter! Either they like the goddam book or they don't! They've got no goddam consideration, that's what! What do they think I'm supposed to be doing all this time; sitting around on my ass?"

"Well . . . *ac*tually . . ." said Jonathan . . .

And shortly afterward he heard from his agents. The book had been first submitted to Gibbon, Mandrill and Barbary, who had rejected it after "serious" consideration –therefore the delay. Quoted from the publishers' letter was, ". . . much as we admire Mr. Pierce's storytelling ability and the blunt power of his style, we regret to say that the editors feel that too many novels have recently appeared about merchant seamen to justify the publication of 'Dragging Anchors.' "

Pierce snorted and slugged back his gin.

"Dumb fucks!" he said;

his book –about men at sea– had nothing to do with merchant seamen, other than that that happened to be the calling his characters practiced. ❦

". . . no, I don't mean those; I mean real writers; writers who make a lot of money," said Rupert C. Roach.

(Could he be serious?) Osborne hesitated, unwilling to be the butt of a joke: since he suspected prolonged life on Escondite might have turned his natural naïveté into yokeldom . . . real writers? who make a lot of money? . . . yet had he not read, just the other week, an interview with a respected, successful lady author of domestic comedies; in which she considered "serious" any writer who makes over $20,000 a year; a criterion conferring solemnity upon her own work, and relegating Marcel Proust to the ranks of the frivolous . . . yes, Roach meant it.

If only –for the moment– he had been Jonathan, or Ed Robles, or even Del Pierce: he could hear Pierce;

("Real writers! Who make a lot of money! Up yours, Jack! Who the hell are you? An eighth-rate hack who couldn't write an honest line if your life depended on it! Who cares about your money? Stick it up your ass! Go back where you came from. No one needs you around here!")

But Osborne couldn't say that;

He said; "I guess not, not by those standards, anyway."

(What was wrong with those standards? What other standards were there?) he had worked long and hard for success, he was entitled to be proud of it. Nor did he flaunt his literary achievement; if he was America's richest writer, he never claimed to be the best (second best, maybe), and, in fact, he knew he would not write the first Great American Novel since Ernest Hemingway had already done it in *To Have and Have Not*.

So it was with humility that Rupert C. Roach had set out –in the master's stylistic footsteps– an awed, but not a blind disciple, dedicated to supplying those errors of omission that marred even the best of his mentor's work:— scenes of violence glossed over, leaving something to the reader's imagination; important contortions omitted from bedroom scenes; the themes, virile as they were, could have been still more hirsute and brutal; his heroes occasionally displayed human failings and therefore fell short of the level of perfection the reading public demanded and deserved.

With these flaws in mind, Rupert C. Roach devoted his life to carrying on the great tradition. Centering his story about a colorful and significant protagonist, such as a big-game hunter or a war correspondent, (Roach, had he ever heard of it, would have violently disagreed with Steve Seley's premise: that the dramatic events in one's life are precisely those not worth writing about –and he would have had his millions behind him to seal the argument): he proceeded to outdo the master to such an extent:

215

his hero shot so many lions; had –and generally beat up– so many women, all of them beautiful; won so many fist fights; endured such physical hardships and excruciating tortures; and all in such vivid and exhaustive detail: that the advent of a new novel had top Hollywood producers battling, book clubs vied, his publishers let out a truly stentorian gardyloo, and amid tumult and clamor, thousands and thousands of copies rained down upon the heads of eager readers everywhere.

It should have been enough: it was not (could there be other standards?). For despite his wealth and fame, despite his own conviction that history would see him in the same light as his master, still it affected him deeply that contemporary men of letters, other writers, even critics, with few exceptions, refused to admit that he had ever written anything of value . . .　　🦃

"Ten cen'! Dime!" said Mardi, grinning; pointing to the heavy bunch of bananas balanced on his head.

Jack Thomas, Sue Pinely, Sal Cohn and Mort Goodman drove down in Thomas's Pontiac. Thomas had been granted a year's leave of absence. To write the book he had always wanted to write: about an honest young liberal columnist who is –almost– corrupted by working for a dishonest reactionary news magazine.

Once in Campeche, they decided to ship the car across on the *Zapata*; there were practically no passable roads on the island, but it would be useful about town. At low tide they could load up with the hip and the groovy, and drive out over the packed sand to some spot conducive to making the swinging party scene.

The car entranced the natives. It was the biggest, shiniest armadillo they had ever seen: and it rolled! They wanted to know how many fire machines cost such a rolling armadillo.　　🦃

The jetty had been repaired. As quaint an introduction as it would have been, Simon Grockle, Jr. could not risk a client's taking a false step, falling into the water, and then suing the company.

216

The old, blanched, broken-keyboard planking had been removed, and new planks laid; new concrete pilings had been sunk.

All details had been seen to with care: a typical meal had been arranged for the tourists, and an exhibition of typical music and dancing to go with it. With some difficulty a guide had been hired from among the foreign population. Simon Jr. had approached Alain Marsh with a proposition for bringing the tourists up to his studio, to watch a real artist at work, and had been repulsed with what he considered totally unbusinesslike and unwarranted rudeness.

Kurt Kummer found him a tamer and more tractable –if less picturesque– painter; and Kummer agreed to become the official representative for the Grockle Line –it only involved a day or so out of the month, the pay was good, there would be ample time to write, and rich widows and divorcées went on cruises, *nicht wahr?*

One of the swinging chicks had once run a hip shop on MacDougal Street, and she now convinced the natives that to earn more fire machines they must stop making the chaste, white, straw sun hats they had always made; and instead weave hats in more imaginative shapes and dyed in bright colors. She taught them to embellish their work with designs, little funny animals, flowers, and the legend, SOUVENIR OF ESCONDITE.

The natives were excited by the new game. They competed to make the most fanciful shape in the wildest colors; until it was feared that the hats would become so improbable that even the tourists would refuse to buy them. But on the maiden arrival of the S.S. *Simon J. Grockle* it was discovered the most lurid, inutile, and expensive creations were, in fact, the first to go.

The main Grockle Line office in New York mentioned these typical hats as one of the attractions of Escondite.

Theodore's bar was now far too small to handle the evening trade. Freddy Rosoff once, in a rage, when he was unable to find a free chair for himself, almost swung a beer bottle at a table full of perfectly innocent people. His friends managed to restrain him and calm him, finally. But help was on the way in any case. Victor

Veritas's new bar and coffee house, The Protest, was nearing completion, and as soon as it opened he would, naturally, draw off the unsquare trade to listen to poetry readings. And the retired English eagerly awaited the inauguaration of a replica pub that an ex-naval commander was having built.

Carl Orville's father-in-law sent him a portable television set as an anniversary present. The natives had never seen such a magic midget box, and they now split into two camps; those that still saved for a rolling armadillo, and a new faction saving for a magic midget box. ✧

It was a disconsolate Mantis Mortmain who, in 1934, paused by the bulletin board of the Kansas City Rotary Club and read:

> GOD: The Businessman's Friend
> An Informal Chat at 8:30 tonite
> With the Rev. Elmer Vincent Beagle

But it was a light-hearted Mantis Mortmain who emerged from that lecture. For Dr. Beagle had successfully convinced him that the image he had always worshiped as God was, in fact, an erroneous one. God was not, as he had always thought, an awesome Someone Special, a haughty and inscrutable Master. No, on the contrary, God was the Celestial Chum, the Omnipotent Pal, and the Greatest Business Partner of Them All . . .

A historic friendship had begun; between the then impoverished hotelman and the obscure backwoods preacher. The latter – pouring moral mercurochrome over the scratched American soul in volume after inspirational volume– would shortly become rich and famous as the nation's leading dispenser of spiritual first aid; while Mantis Mortmain –in 1934 only solvent by the grace of a string of economy hotels the source of whose profits remained a mystery to unimaginative competitors– acting upon new-found knowledge, would rocket into prominence, famous as Mantis Mortmain, the Praying Millionaire, the world's richest hotelier . . .

With God on his side, Mantis Mortmain began acquiring hotels.

218

Rival businessmen learned to quail before the invincible merger of Mortmain and God, nor did Mortmain make any secret of the reason for his success. But if competitors tried to beat him at his own game, all were doomed to failure. As a ruined former partner put it, with grudging respect, "You can't expect to outpray Mantis. Mantis just prays *bigger* than anyone else."

Naturally, his ascent was not without problems. By the late thirties he found himself too preoccupied to divide his time fairly between God and Hotels, and his wife and family. Mantis Mortmain prayed for guidance. And was informed that his wife, by comforting him through the dark years and pawning her jewelry when he needed ready cash, had contributed to a design transcending mortal grandeur. But before divorce proceedings had been instituted to terminate the purely tellurian liaison, divine providence intervened on behalf of Mantis Mortmain:— a jury of Texas psychiatrists judged his wife insane and she was committed for life to a local state asylum.

At the end of the war, Mortmain emerged as the richest hotelman in America, eager to expand operations in both personal and economic areas. He decided to become an art lover: he began collecting old masterpieces and was soon so expert in this field that he was able to place full-page advertisements in prominent newspapers extolling Rembrandt and condemning modern art.

On the economic side, he ventured into international development. Within a decade there was scarcely a European capital without its gleaming Mortmain hotel —welcome refuge for Americans chary of unsanitary architecture and foreign management. And as new hotels opened, Mortmain took on a new role as unofficial ambassador and promoter of good will. For instance, at the inauguration of the Madrid Mortmain he spoke at length —and in fluent Spanish— warmly praising the Spanish liberator as the only European head of state to maintain his country entirely free of the taint of Communism. The Spanish audience cheered, impressed by this remarkable American, who, brought up in a tiny town on the Mexico-Arizona border, was able to address them in their strange and difficult tongue.

Yet the restless nature of Mantis Mortmain forbade him to stop building. "Even when I'm dancing with a beautiful girl, I'm still thinking hotel," he once confided to a friend.

Upon reading Rupert C. Roach's article, he phoned Miami to get the yacht ready. The following morning, leaving church, he put the idea to his advisers –a tolerant man, Mortmain did not care which religion his associates observed, as long as they attended early-morning services. "As far as I'm concerned," he declared in his authorized biography, "hiring men who don't pray, don't pay." Adding with a twinkle, "Excuse my grammar."

"Well, boys," he said, "that's the situation as I see it. My opinion is that we skedaddle right on down to that little old island, and if it looks right, why then we put up a great big new Mortmain, eh? I'd like your candid opinion, boys . . . Clay?"

"I think it's a great idea, Mantis," said Clay Fess.

"Joe?"

"I'm all for it, Mantis," said Joe Gules. "Get there firstest with the mostest!"

"Harry?"

"It's a brilliant stroke, Mantis," said Harry Pheon. "You can count on me."

"Dex?"

"It sounds lke a winner, Mantis," said Dexter Chief. "Providing that article isn't a phony."

"Jerry?"

Jerry Shield imitated the whine of a bullet. "Peeow! Bull's-eye, Mantis!"

. . . Indian summer of the island of Escondite:

they could still sit serenely at the edge of the new impersonal jetty, but gaze out over the moon-besotted bay; by night tiny fish still scribbled silver Persian script on the surface of the sea; lovers still trysted in the dark, in the dunes, alone . . .

Certain developments were undeniably improvements. Dr. Chaim Sulzberger arrived; a tiny, bald, Austrian Jew with an incessant smile, a fussy Old-World manner, and a trunkful of horrid Teutonic kitsch-craft. In a parody of an accent, Dr. Chaim would introduce himself to strangers formally, saying, "My name is Dr. Chaim Sulzberger; I have come here because I enjoy the company of artists and writers, and because I love the sun."

He was welcome. Until then, illness had been the one major disadvantage of island life. Several native women were accomplished herbalists; the tradition of midwifery bequeathed them by former masters had been upheld —a few foreign women insisted upon modern attention, but others realized that childbirth had preceded gynecology, and entrusted themselves to the local midwife with perfectly satisfactory results. Severe illness was something else. There had been no remedy when it struck suddenly —old Ned Gifford might have lived had proper care been available— but Dr. Chaim Sulzberger solved this problem. Attending complaints with a sideshow of grimaces, clucks, tsks, and hmms, asking no fee from those unable to pay, and driving them all to (tolerant) distraction with his interminable, superannuated, and hopelessly romantic notions about art and the artist.

It was Indian summer; and there were those who remained optimistic: a luxury hotel or two, a few modest pensions like the one Kurt Kummer had a piece of, a couple of millionaires erecting flashy barbarities in the hills, a chic yacht club, a few new bars and restaurants, several cruise lines adding the island to the itinerary, prices would go up somewhat, but everyone would mind his own business, with a bit of extra trouble they would keep gardens and forage for themselves in the jungle, life would go on pleasantly enough . . .

The majority, however, felt otherwise. As Ed Robles put it, "No, it can't last. Progress, like the pox, strikes hardest at the point of least resistance."

And among these realists talk turned to possible new retreats (Morocco? Turkey?); almost nothing remained within their means. The prudent and those with families began to look ahead: Robles wrote his agent in quest of further hack work, Stefan Verduin and Jan van Gent wrote to Dutch TV producers and editors, Tony Vale and the yachtsmen figured on charters and fishing excursions to buy the freedom of the off-season, others schemed to cash in on the boom, Katona? . . . well, Katona "would see"; and Pierce checked if he had lost his seniority in the union, and wondered if there were any alternatives to shipping out. There were not. Unless, of course, the book sold.

It did. Ulladge and Lees accepted it; called it "powerful" and "highly promising" –although, they, too, thought it was about merchant seamen– and asked politely if Pierce would consider deleting the obscenity, since leaving it would quash any hope of book-club sales. Pierce answered, equally politely –he thought. He said:

Dear Mr. Poshlust:
I'm glad you like *Dragging Anchors* and will publish it.
I'm sorry you object to the profanity, but when one of my characters says "fuck" he means "fuck." I didn't write the book with book clubs in mind so as long as it's printable, please print it the way I wrote it.

Sincerely,
Delaney Pierce

"Do you like this island?"
  "I'm not sure."
  "I like this island. It's so typical."   ☙

It was Indian summer: and by day the sun performed –and this it always would– its blazing hyperbole; artifacts of the old tranquillity remained:— the ancient Negroes still dozed in the shade, their backs to the wall of Theodore's bar, at peace with their simple memories . . .

although various religious organizations, made aware of the forgotten island, sent missionaries to teach the natives to fear God; and a militant Negro society dispatched an agent to see if they understood the importance of being black.   ☙

Keith Cooper pointed in derision. "Ha!" he said. "Look at them! They're grockles, that's what they are. Grockles!"

222

Which they were: grockles.

Milling about the funny hat kiosk; tall ones, short ones, fat ones, thin ones; red-faced, perspiring, clad in garish cruise garb, harnessed in cameras; they were passing the funny hats around, trying them on, taking snapshots of one another, and emitting little squeals of delight and astonishment: they were grockles.

"Do you think that's one, Lucy?"

"I don't know."

"He looks like one, doesn't he?"

"I think so. That's how they're supposed to look."

"Should we ask him?"

"I don't know. You ask him."

"*You* ask him."

"I don't know if I should. I don't know what to say."

"Oh, Lucy, you're silly. I'll ask him then . . . Excuse me, but my friend and I were just wondering, are you a contemporary painter?"

"No," said Marsh, "I'm an old master."

It wasn't their fault: still; they were grockles.

And once, as Hiyo sauntered down the beach, astride his drowsy burro, humming beneath his floppy sun hat, and silhouetted against a lavish sunset; one of them materialized in his path, simultaneously grinning, making abundant hand signals for Hiyo to halt, jabbing significantly at his camera, and attempting vainly to organize a welter of arcane mechanisms dispersed about his person.

Hiyo nodded genteelly. But plodded right on.

The complexity of silent communication was accelerated, exaggerated; the dimmest aborigine could not have failed to comprehend the gesture that meant "Halt!" Hiyo plodded on.

The man jumped awkwardly out of his path, and as Hiyo passed, he smiled, leaned over, and said, "Man, you got me all wrong. You see, I ain't included in the itinerary."

Back aboard ship, the outraged would-be photographer complained to the purser. The company propaganda explicitly described the natives of Escondite as friendly, but this was a lie; the events of the afternoon constituted proof apodictic: the natives of Escondite weren't friendly at all; they were unfriendly; the company was gypping its clients.

Grockles! There was magic to the word. It was, in some intangible way, onomatopoeic. That's what they were: ineluctably: grockles . . .

And they were off! On a merry morphological jaunt: grockles, living in a state of grockledom, ruled by a grocklocracy; happiest in captivity, kept snug and warm in grocklecoops; timid when away from home, wary in strange lands, but easily lured with grockle bait –toy Eiffel Towers, wooden shoes, Toledo-ware– the branch of Ecology concerning them, Grocklology; the specialist, a grocklologist –or better yet, euphonically– grocklogian.   ₩

Osborne's history continued:

This era was the point at which an intrinsic change took place in the nature of European civilization.

In France, the civil war of the Fronde appears, to later ages, as a last confused and abortive attempt of the French nobility to retrieve the feudal power it had gradually lost over the past four centuries.

In England, the principles and ideals of the Puritan movement fused for the first time in the one man capable of using them, Oliver Cromwell; and at the time when they could be applied. And although, almost universally regarded as a hypocrite and a fanatic for the century and a half following his death, Victorian historians, from the vantage point of elapsed time, could look back and see him –admitting, and if not condoning, at least justifying, his excesses– as the herald of their own age, embodying in his person the altering character of English life and of the English people. In his *Origins of Progress*, Watney Whitbread-Charrington sums up Cromwell's contribution to the future in the following manner:

"To you who would defame, insult this name Oliver with opprobrious cries; who cant of past, insalubrious days of our forefathers, and see not the ameliorative influences of these, our present days: ranting Romantics, stilted stylists, carping critics, to you, in unvarnished prose, yes, common sense, we reply; these: it is just that most transcendentally memorable of English heroes, Lord Protector, Oliver; Oliver who first steered stately ship, England, upon her noble course, unwavering course; yes, Oliver, none but he, finally and forever, who exscinded, expunged and extirpated from the English heart yet lingering traces of mediaeval and maleficent honour; Oliver, yes, none but he, first who invoked, inculcated and instilled therein righteous God-fearing morality; respect for duty, for thrift, simple fare supplanting disgustive, esurient, time-consuming gluttony of our ancestors, these: lofty principles, celestial principles, Oliver's: working then in unenlightenment, tenebrous error, to make a today England: least frivolous of nations! most industrious therefore, England bestfitted, most zealous in acquisition and administration of Empire: these principles, Oliver's. Praise Oliver who taught, first he, Lord Protector, when menaced by scoundrelly, by Romish foe: 'Shield thine intentions behind the Book, execute them with the blade!' "

Added to spiritual and moral developments was a considerably altered balance of power. Under Cromwell, England had quickly become the most dreaded and formidable military power in Europe –although this ascendancy would soon be lost by Charles II. France, momentarily embroiled in civil war, would soon be guided by Louis XIV, ably assisted by Colbert and Louvois, to domination in Europe and challenge overseas. Spain had sunk into virtual military impotence. Nations no longer allied to wage war against Spain, rather Spain sought, through complicated dynastic successions and marriages, to ally herself with other powers in such a way as to prevent the further dismemberment of her empire.

Widespread religious controversy everywhere ensured a steady incidence of violence; and only in Holland, despite fierce contention between Arminians and Calvinists, was bloodshed avoided, though this precarious state was very nearly disrupted when, in

1651, the Dutch poet and pamphleteer, Frans Vogelsang, published a pamphlet condemning slavery and the slave trade –a principal source of Dutch income– as immoral and unethical. Eminent men of letters, painters, and musicians took up the cause; the wrangle grew in scope and intensity, interrupting the bustle and prosperity of Amsterdam, until, finally, prominent churchmen of the land convened, and from this gathering emerged the theory that not only was slavery justifiable, but distinctly praiseworthy, since without slavery, innumerable Negroes were doomed to pagan ignorance in Africa, while due to slavery, thousands were now in the position to seek grace and enjoy the benefits of Christianity –a line of theological thought that cost the opposition most of its support, and enabled the slave traders to carry on their thriving businesses with unblemished consciences and a crusading spirit as well.

In the Caribbean, the particular situation of each European power, dictated its constantly changing, but individual type of Colonial policy.

France, with something of a head start, tried to fill the coffers of her treasury –emptied by the civil war and a conflict with Spain now twenty years old– by colonizing and planting extensively. Except for Cuba, Hispaniola, and Escondite, most of the islands claimed by Spain were settled sparsely, if at all; and enterprising French charter companies had little trouble organizing settling parties; they would then squat illegally on one island or another, nourish it to prosperity, and wait for Spain to lose a war to make the French claim official in the treaty.

Holland, although she tried to colonize Brazil, and fiercely defended her monopoly of the East Indian spice islands, in the Caribbean was interested, not so much in colonization, as in the establishment of secure ports from which her trading fleets might safely operate.

In England, Cromwell, knowing his rule depended upon the support of the military, had overextended the forces of both army and navy, while at the same time, radical elements within these forces were themselves threatening his power and safety; and he therefore employed his troops in the Caribbean for the manifold purpose of keeping them occupied and at a distance, letting them earn their own keep, expanding English colonial power, avenging the Spanish massacres of the English on St. Kitts (1629), Tortuga (1639), and Santa Cruz (1650) and of course, spreading the Puritan faith.

Escondite –Blijdschaps Eiland– however, was for the moment safely in Dutch hands; canals were under construction, slaves were being taught the art of carving wooden shoes, and the harbor bristled with incoming and outgoing ships.

The first Dutch Governor-General was Berend Bartelsz Botterick, the hero of the Sack of Copaverde, but by this time, Botterick had become too fond of the genever cask to administer efficiently, and he happily left these matters to his factor, Jaap Katz –the same Dutch Jew who, twenty years before, had successfully cleared out the ant plague.

After his bankruptcy at the hands of the Inquisition, Katz had led an adventurous and spectacular life. His experiences taught him that Catholicism was, for him, an unprofitable religion. Switching to Calvinism he then looked about for some way to employ what little remained of his capital, and he shrewdly foresaw the sharply increased demand for slaves.

Beginning with a few aged and infirm Negroes whom he purchased for a pittance –from masters about to manumit them in lieu of continuing to feed them– Katz coaxed them back to health, taught them some simple trade to make them again useful, built up their morale, and eventually sold them for a profit which, skillfully parleyed, soon saw Katz the owner of his own slaver.

From this point his rise was meteoric. As original and far-seeing as he was wily and dedicated, Katz's ventures made him into a figure of international renown. He conceived and organized the world-wide *Katz Neem Een Huur-slaef* (Katz Rent-a-Slave) combine; he was perhaps one of the earliest coiners of sales slogans, and signs of his far-flung offices urged;

Waarom Een Moriaen Te Coopen
Als Gy Hem In Huur Kunt Laeten Loopen?
(Why buy the black,
When you can hire his back?)

His hard-sell attitude, coupled to a crude form of vertical integration of his enterprises made his name a byword in the hinterlands of Africa –tribal mothers brought errant children into line by threatening to sell them to Katz; and while English slavers prided themselves upon the quality of their wares, Katz's African agents were instructed: *"Is hy swart? Wy veylen hem!"* (Is he black? We can sell him!) and millions of guilders poured in as Katz agents rounded up thousands of slaves, processed them through Katz "factories" on the Gold Coast, shipped them to the Indies on Katz slavers, and sold them on Katz auction blocks.

With his fortune made, Katz reverted to Judaism and attempted ɔ retire, but he found that the sybaritic life of the rich Amsterdam burgher ill-suited him. His pleasure lay, not in spending money, but in making it. And seeking diversion he therefore turned to founding and financing a religious movement called *"Ashkenazy Weg!"* (German Jews, Go Home!) which acquired an enthusiastic following among Sephardic Jews. But Katz was unable to convince the Gentile authorities of the validity of the cause, interest waned, and in any case, Katz, after years of plying the tropics, found the chill and damp of Holland unappealing. The lucrative and sunny sinecure of factor to newly conquered Blijdschaps Eiland offered itself, and Katz seized it.

Left to his own devices by the gin-preoccupied Governor-General, Katz determined to follow the example of La Vasseur of Tortuga, and create a haven for pirates regardless of nationality –excepting the English, the Navigation Act having touched off the First Dutch War.

In return for safe harboring, shipyard facilities, rum, women, arms and ammunition, Katz demanded, and received, a 10 per cent cut of the booty. Under Katz's skillful management the island enjoyed several riotous and orgiastic years. It was pirate custom never to set sail with money on them, but to spend everything on shore, so to the pirates the island was the famous "El Escondite" (The Hideout) while to the prospering tavern keepers and tradesmen, it was, indeed, Blijdschaps (Happy) Eiland.

How long matters might have continued in this fashion is open to conjecture, but in 1658 two events provoked the departure of the capable but erratic factor.

The first was that his son announced his intention of marrying a gentile girl. The second was the death of Oliver Cromwell. For while furious with his son who remained adamant, Katz foresaw Richard Cromwell's inability to keep his father's unpopular Commonwealth together, and therefore the restoration of Charles II upon the throne; and counting upon Charles to continue Cromwell's policy of permitting Jews to enter England, Katz, after disinheriting his son, set sail for Holland, determined to gain an audience with the English king at his court-in-exile at Breda, and, if possible, buy himself one of the many peerages then being distributed on a barely disguised commercial basis.

Presumably the ship went down, for no further record exists of Jaap Katz, and deprived of its factor, Escondite life became more disorderly than ever. But Dutch rule, nominal as it was, was not to prove long in duration. Though the First Dutch War ended in what England claimed was victory, and Holland insisted was not defeat, France demanded English support –as a reward for her biased neutrality– in her claim against Holland for Blijdschaps and Manhattan islands. Holland successfully defended her right to the latter, but considered the cession of the troublesome nest of outlaws an easy method of reparations. Blijdschaps Eiland became a French colony, L'Île de Joie.

Colbert had not yet formed the French West India Company, and, at this time, French policy was a nearly hypothetical arrangement, whereby charter companies, in theory responsible to the Crown, settled the colonies through governors, in theory responsible to the companies. But in practice, the governors, once installed on the distant islands, were virtually their own masters. The powerful French navy was still twenty years in the future, there was no way of forcing the governors to turn over to the company profits rightfully belonging to it, and matters actually reached the stage where de Poincy, the renegade emperor of fourteen Caribbean islands, felt strong enough to jail the company representative dispatched to remonstrate with him.

The first French governor of L'Île de Joie, Aristide Bidet, was no exception to this rule. Only he grew rich, while the debauched younger sons and ruined gentlemen who had come to settle, faced by the combination of heavy jungle, refractory Protestant and convict "engagés," inferior slaves supplied by the English and Dutch, the tropical climate, efficient stills, and the legacy of comely and willing mulatto women bequeathed them by the Spanish, soon dropped any pretense of seriousness, and, as one ailing nobleman wrote: "Yes, we die quickly, alas, too quickly here in the tropics; but we die as Frenchmen like to die."

By 1663 the company was bankrupt. The island was put up for public auction, and Bidet, grown rich by this time, tried to buy it back for himself, but the company refused to deal with him. Bidet's brother, Gaston, using an assumed name, then bid successfully, but after signing the deed refused to return the island outright, demanding a half share for himself. Aristide refused, in a duel the brothers killed each other and the island automatically ceded to the French Crown.

The foundation of the French West India Company now turned French colonization into an organized process; planting on L'Île de Joie, as well as on other islands, went apace despite increased pirate activity –Morgan raided in 1666 but spared the town after collecting ransom, Heyn landed on the southern extremity in 1668 and burned several plantations– and almost ceaseless war in Europe had the seas seething with battles. England, Holland and Sweden signed the Grand Alliance to curb growing French aggrandizement; an English fleet under Admiral Bing (grandfather of the famous Admiral Byng, executed a century later for failing to relieve Mahon) fell upon the French fleet of de Bongue and destroyed it; although shortly afterward, Charles II, secretly a Catholic, and bribed by Louis, would renege upon the Alliance, and aid France in the Third Dutch War; the De Witt brothers were emasculated and beheaded in The Hague, and Danish efforts to trade St. Croix for Brazil ended in failure.

But as events in the Caribbean reflected those current in Europe, so life in the colonies tended to become, so far as was possible, a tropical version of life in the mother country; and on L'Île de Joie, Governor Pierre Poubelle was taking measures to produce an island society approximating that most salient feature of the France of that era, the court of Louis XIV.

Brought up in the strife of the Fronde, Louis had realized that to wield power as a monarch, it was of paramount importance to keep the resentful and disgruntled nobility both disunited and pre occupied, and this he brilliantly achieved by creating a court at which constant attendance was a requisite toward the obtaining of favors, and the most important signs of royal pleasure were made manifest through the assigning or denying, now to this duke, now to that prince, the seemingly most trifling tasks and duties in the elaborate and intricate protocol of palace life. Thus holding the candle for Louis as he said his prayers was construed as a sign of particular favor, while the man selected to button the king's boots in the morning could be certain that whatever petition he had in the balance, be it an embassy or a generalship, was being weighed by the king in a benign frame of mind.

On L'Île de Joie, Pierre Poubelle seized upon these tactics and embellished them with enthusiasm and imagination. Perhaps the most important of the posts he created in his miniature court was *Le Grand Souffleur de la Soupe* (the noble chosen to blow on the soup) and other important titles were *Premier Gardien de Coffre de Tabac à Priser* (Keeper of the Snuff Box), *L'illustre Collectionneur de Bouchons de Champagne* (Champagne Cork Collector), and *L'honorable Verificateur de la Température de L'eau du Bain* (Bath Water Tester).

Few significant events mark the fifteen-year tenure of the autocratic but efficient Poubelle, although, briefly, in 1671 the island became a focal point of Caribbean interest.

Henry Morgan had spectacularly succeeded in sacking Panama

City. However, his march across the isthmus had given the citizens of the town warning, the chief articles of value –priceless church statuary, trunks of jewelry, precious gems and bullion– were loaded aboard a ship called *La Trinidad*, and before Morgan arrived to plunder and subsequently destroy the city, the ship had sailed from the harbor and eluded him.

But *La Trinidad* never reached whatever port she was destined for; in fact, no further news of her was ever heard. Rumor, however, had it that an independent band of French corsairs had captured her, and that the hoard had been buried on L'Île de Joie. Poubelle denied the rumor, but closed the port to foreign treasure hunters. Meanwhile, work on the plantations ceased as planters directed gangs of slaves in digging operations. But several months devoted to such work uncovered nothing, interest waned, and gradually island life returned to normal, although rumors persisted over the centuries, and now and then a new band of hopefuls arrived furnished with a supposedly authentic map.

Strangely enough, it was Poubelle's own talent, linked to his pride and indiscretion which eventually caused his downfall.

In France at that time, Louis XIV had himself invented a game that became the rage throughout Europe. Although customarily comporting himself with a regal dignity that overawed his subjects, as well as his court, and deeply impressed his fellow monarchs, one evening, after cards, chatting with his mistress, Mme. de Montespan, he allowed himself the luxury of relaxation and was diverting himself with her, laying wagers on who could spit olive stones the furthest. The Duc du Maine, Louis' bastard son, observed them, and decided to take advantage of this evidently permissible but rare frivolity, and when no remonstrance checked him, the heir-apparent, Monseigneur, followed suit. Before long the entire court was engaged in this activity, encouraged and prodded by Louis himself, who delighted in the apparent fact that none could spit the stone further than he.

Though late at night, the English, Swedish and Austrian ambassadors were summoned to court and challenged. None could outdistance Louis, and Saint-Simon reports that the king, upon emerging victorious, had laughed, and flushed with triumph, after spitting another stone mightily, had shouted, *"Voilà! Regarde! Celui-ci! La gloire de France!"* (Aha! Look! That! The glory of France!) And the game becoming known as La Gloire de France, it soon displaced cards, gaming, bear-baiting and dueling, and for several years reigned as Europe's chief diversion; pursued by rich and poor alike, and with such intensity that so great a French general as de Gueulasse, having thrashed the Dutch under Bosneukerszn at the Battle of Bierenbroodspot, but losing to him later at La Gloire, could admit, *"Hélas! Il aurait mieux valu perdre la bataille, mais gagner La Gloire."* (Better to lose the battle, but win at La Gloire.)

The game, however, created serious problems on a political and diplomatic level. Louis was then, circa 1680, at the height of his power, and though ringed by enemies, provoking him unnecessarily was, from a political point of view, a distinctly undesirable maneuver. Yet it was one of Louis' most glaring defects, as a man and as a monarch, that he was incapable of distinguishing between flattery, even of the most servile sort, and genuine praise. His pride in his mastery of La Gloire was inordinate; naturally, in his own court none dared surpass him; foreign ministers and ambassadors knew that wars had been fought for less grievous insults and diplomatically lost. But the extent and efficiency of Louis' international network of secret agents, spies and informers was common knowledge, and adept La Gloirists, in their cups, often forgot themselves and overreached the royal record. In London, in Vienna, in Madrid the courts met with barely concealed anxiety, waiting to learn what would follow after Louis discovered as he must, that others existed more proficient than himself at his favorite game.

But in the interests of world peace, it was perhaps fortunate that it was a French subject who eventually suffered the effects of kingly wrath. Pierre Poubelle, thousands of miles away on L'Île de Joie, feeling himself secure from the scrutiny of Versailles, not only soundly topped Louis' records, but had the temerity to boast about it.

One moonless night, an armed guard removed Poubelle from his palace, put him on board a ship, and sailed into the darkness. Poubelle was never heard of, or from, again, and although certain historians believe that the masked and mysterious prisoner who lay thirty years in the Bastille, in solitary confinement, and whose identity was never ascertained, may have been Poubelle, the truth lies still in the realms of conjecture.

Meanwhile, colonization proceeded, and though any number of islands changed hands several times, L'Île de Joie remained French –except for several months of Swedish control during the brief War of the Hungarian Electorate, 1688–1690 (the so-called "Goulash Conspiracy").

Lovely French baroque plantation houses went up on the newly cleared land, but except for infrequent periods, and for a variety of reasons, the island never showed a profit.

To begin with, so determined was Colbert to enrich the Company, rather than the individual, that the complexity of rules and regulations, checks and balances imposed by him, denied to the planters the commercial latitude they in fact required in order to keep out of debt. Secondly, the French tended to settle more thickly than the English and Dutch, dispersing the profits, and events such as Louis' revocation of the Edict of Nantes (1685) sent thousands of Huguenots fleeing for the New World, to colonies already struggling against bankruptcy. And thirdly, though the French were capable of individual acts of almost unprecedented barbarity –Leon Fauve of Sorayaba who used to throw aged and ailing slaves into a pool full of piranha fish– in general the French treatment of the slaves was the least harsh of the colonial powers, and in 1667, laws had even been passed defining certain Negro rights. As the English political arithmetician, Noah Jones, pointed out in 1780, ". . . thus, by good-hearted but sentimental French ladies allowing their slaves to live out to their ends the lengths of their natural lives, their plantations must support the surcharges coevally incurred by the maintenance of these unproductive properties, and further, by allowing this labour to repose and to observe the multitudinous Holy days and feast days proclaimed by the Catholick religion, the French do inescapably forswear those additional profits that in other colonies accrue in the account books of the wiser and thriftier merchants of the English and Netherlandish nations."

And when, finally, the Company relaxed its monopoly and private merchants were permitted to trade in the colonies, again they were less effective than their English and Dutch competitors, aggravating matters perilous at the onset, by cutthroat price wars, or else holding out proudly for exorbitant and unrealistic profits. The French priest, Père Labat, touring the Caribbean in the early 1700's analyzes this situation: "The English and Dutch are wiser, for although they are no less greedy than ourselves, they have not tried to compete with each other, and have therefore maintained the price of their commodities."

L'Île de Joie, naturally, fell prey to most of these defects of character and policy, and as the century drew to its close, island life was summed up by Governor Pompier in these words: "*Beauté, pauvreté! et des orges!*" (Beauty, poverty, orgies!)

The eighteenth century arrived, European civilization now exhibited a number of new characteristics and among them, perhaps the most remarkable was, that although religious intolerance still seethed in the hearts of the masses, statesmen no longer employed religious differences as either the real, or pretended excuse for opening hostilities. The Age of Reason had dawned, during which occurred the following conflicts:

1700–1702 – The War of the Savoyard Uprisings
1702–1713 – The War of the Spanish Succession
1713–1717 – The War of the Hapsburg Confederacy
1717–1723 – The War of the Camelias
1723–1730 – The War without a Reason
1731–1735 – The War of the Transylvanian Principalities
1735–1739 – The War of Houel's Breach of Promise
1739–1748 – The War of Jenkin's Ear (The War of the Austrian
      Succession)

1748 The Peace of Aix-la-Chapelle
1748–1756 – The War of the Peace of Aix-la-Chapelle
1756–1763 – The Seven Years' War
1763–1770 – Princess Heloise's War
1770–1776 – The Six Years' War
1776–1781 – The Five Years' War (The American War of Independence)
1781–1785 – The Four Years' War
1785–1788 – The Three Years' War
1788–1790 – The Two Years' War
1790–1791 – The One Year War (The Short War)
1791–1815 – The Napoleonic Wars

The Caribbean now entered into the most turbulent period of its history. Islands changed hands with bewildering rapidity, and L'Île de Joie was finally wrested from France during the War of the Hapsburg Confederacy. The victorious general, Abernethy, sent the French planters packing and took immediate measures to anglicise the island: the cafés were turned into clubs, the slaves were set to work planting hedgerows and building fences and stiles, a shipload of foxes was ordered from England.

However, these activities ceased with the Peace of Zwijnshoop, signed in Flanders by George I, Philip V, the Regent, Duc d'Orleans, and Wenceslas IV of Beroslavia who happened to be visiting. L'Île de Joie was ceded back to France in return for fur-trading concessions in Canada, while Dutch and Russian negotiations to trade Saba for the Behring Sea ended in mutual recriminations and a deadlock.

But under a succession of bungling governors, L'Île de Joie languished. And plain bad luck played a part. Sugar was planted just as sugar prices fell, and tobacco just as the tobacco market was about to plunge. French attempts to sell the island to Frederick William of Prussia, and later, to the Knights of Jerusalem were unsuccessful, and L'Île de Joie remained what it had always more or less been, a home and refuge for the inept, the criminal and the disgraced.

. . . "(Annette)"

and plunged: to her golden core; where a Jordan of honey flowed . . .

To elicit:

"Aiee! Jonathan! *Chéri-i-i-i!*" (though he had never said, I love you.)

When by (votive?) candlelight beside her, he smoked in silence. And despair who is mother to insight (at last) bore this:

that he would never replace the Sonata Sopra Sancta Maria: not with Adam's simple garden song; he smoked in silence.

And Janine, her body still racing and delirious, could bear not one more such bout of ecstasy (too proud to ask; she *would* not ask)

"Jonathan, *chéri?*" she asked,

"Yes?" (How very commonplace.) (And how inexpressibly hopeless.)

"Do you love me?"

If only she had asked the day before: he would have answered yes, since it would have been more true than no:— if degrees in love existed.

He took her hand in both of his, and kissed it with whatever reverence he knew.

"No," he said (and ruined it all). "I'm sorry."   ❦

For others though, Indian summer . . . of a sort: Theodore called it the wettest rainy season in his memory, and they huddled in bars, or around stoves, in their sodden dripping mansions. Dr. Chaim administered pills and elixirs against an onslaught of colds; everyone griped and grumbled, but reflecting upon the situation revived a collective sense of humor. There wasn't much (even of this) time left; and meanwhile, better to live like ruined aristocrats:— they could afford to eschew comfort, the bourgeois' conception of luxury.

At the far end of the beach, before the charred hulk of a burned-out French plantation house, Mantis Mortmain jammed a gold-tipped cane into the sand; he gestured grandly, expansively, directing the gaze of his associates out over the virgin coastline, to where, at near-horizon, the town glittered in the blade-bright air. He swept his arm prophetically and proffered them the sea . . .

He smiled.

"Well, boys," he said. "This is the real McCoy. The way I see it is this. An island like this deserves, not just a Mortmain Hotel, but *the* Mortmain Hotel, the Mortmain to end all Mortmain's . . . But first, boys, I'd like your candid opinion . . . Clay?"

"I think it's a great idea, Mantis," said Clay Fess . . .

"Joe?"

"I'm all for it, Mantis," said Joe Gules. "Get there firstest with the mostest!"

"Harry?"

"It's a brilliant stroke, Mantis," said Harry Pheon. "You can count on me."

"Dex?"

"It sounds like a winner, Mantis," said Dexter Chief. "Providing we don't hit any building snags."

"Jerry?"

Jerry Shield imitated the whine of a bullet. "Peeow! Bull's-eye, Mantis!"

"Quatah!" cried Marie-Louise, grinning and coquetting with her pannier of citrus fruits.

Still, Indian summer . . . Delia bore Osborne yet another burbling, toast-colored version of himself, and they gave a huge feast. There was no rush to leave the island: Osborne, at least, had plenty of money, and doled it out freely to those friends caught short.

They managed to amuse themselves, each in his or her own fashion; and one afternoon, Ed Robles, sitting in his study, with no particular poems to write, was musing upon a situation that put him in the privileged position of being the world's first grock-logian so to style himself. There was something comforting about it: knowing what he was and having a word for it. And he sat

238

wondering, thinking about earlier fellow grocklogians, his spiritual ancestors. Would it have made them any different? happier? knowing they had a name, and a respectable one,

Flaubert? The arch-grocklogian,

and Diderot, Voltaire, Molière, Pascal; Baudelaire, Büchner, Byron, Bierce ...

He had never considered before. History teemed with grocklogians. Offhand he conjured up:

Aristophanes, Lucian, Petronius, Rabelais; Villon, Tacitus, Langland, Hobbes;

Ibn Khaldun!

Shakespeare? A grocklogian? No ... Shakespeare had no need for grocklology, but Cervantes, yes; and Dante. La Rochefoucald.

And Gibbon, Gogol, Giordano Bruno; Skelton, Marvell, Swift, Ben Jonson. Sam Butler –both Sam Butlers– Bunyan, of all people! For *Mr. Badman*; grocklogians turned up in the oddest places: Karl Marx –didn't they?– in the *18th Brumaire of Napoleon Bonaparte.*

And Goethe? Certainly no grocklogian. Not even a grocklophobe; but not *quite* a grocklophile ... the hell! he was a grockle! ... horrible thought: der Ubergrockle!

Dostoievski? ... no. Turgenev? ... no. Proust? ... no. Joyce? ... no. It was not that an interest in grocklology was a requisite for quality, some were grocklogians, others weren't.

Quevedo? for the *Epístola Satirica y Censoria* to Conde de Olivares? ... on the whole, yes.

But Gongora? for *Answers to the Inquisition?* Actually, not. This was rather fun, being an erudite had its moments.

Grocklogians Tu En, Po Chu-i, T'as Ch'ien –in a sense every Chinese poet;

and Schopenhauer, Nietzsche, Corvo, Wilde; Pushkin, Nabokov, Gombrowicz, Pound.

Kafka? ... Ah, poor Kafka; the frailest titan! A grocklophobe, certainly, but he had let them get at him, and succumbed ... still, yes! a grocklogian.

Pascal? No, he already had Pascal, but Blake.

Mencken, Sinclair Lewis? Yes, even though he wrote so poorly. Traven . . . Trelawny! He almost forgot Trelawny! There was a grocklogian for you!

And Beddoes in his letters; De Coster, Stendhal in *Telegraph*; and there was *Simplicissimus*. Who the devil wrote *Simplicissimus?*

Grocklogians Hašek and Jarry; Ibsen, Strindberg, Frank Norris, Nathanael West . . .

and debatables Thoreau, Boccaccio, Fielding in *Jonathan Wild?*

but Rochester definitely; Veblen, Erasmus, in his *Colloquies:* Gissing, and Juan Ruiz, Arcipreste de Hita, to name a few. It wasn't bad company to keep:— this Royal Society of Grocklogians: and Grimmelhausen! Grimmelhausen wrote *Simplicissimus!* . . .

It was Indian summer.   ✿

Alain Marsh had long since given up hope of Thurston Jennet's fulfilling his promise: to show the paintings to Metzger –not that he cared, work was going far too well. Just that his stake had been practically exhausted –besides he could borrow money for materials from Osborne, and something *had* to happen sometime . . .

It was unimportant –Vasari took it for granted that painters painted for fame, but then of course the most famous painter was likely to be the best. No, it was pointless –and undignified– to covet fame. Now that it was synonymous to, and interchangeable with: notoriety.

. . . but still . . . but still; to read the art magazines, to see the reproductions, to know they wielded lesser spoons, those who scooped up all the caviar.

To hell with it!–what he really wanted: would she appear? in good old (blue-moon) time, that one woman who spoke his language?

When, suddenly, salvation! Jennet wrote –he had been away, extensively touring, preparing a guidebook to South and Central America– Metzger had seen the paintings, pronounced them "electrifying" "overwhelming" (better yet) "salable", Metzger offered a show; wanted a contract . . .

It was (goddam well) about (good goddam) time! (those finks!) . . .

and that night he regaled his friends, with the best food Greenbaum's had to offer –all the sturgeon they could eat, lox and cream cheese, pastrami, cole slaw, pickles, cheese cake, the lot– and later, the drinks were on Marsh as well.

But in his elation he drank too much and too fast. Jonathan and Del Pierce were improvising –to the general hilarity of the company– a skit involving two fictitious imbeciles at the coming vernissage who, in the end, do *not* buy a painting . . . Marsh, however, realized that another swallow would mean relinquishing Greenbaum's splendid sturgeon.

He fought down his rising gorge, allowed a minute for recuperation, tried to get up from his seat, fell back into it, tried again, fell again, succeeded on a third attempt, and swaying ominously, bade his adieus.

Haughtily refusing aid –talk stopped, breaths were held– Marsh windmilled (successfully, ha!) up the stairs and out the door. Mal Katona and Tony Vale followed to see if he kept on his feet. He had; and they both laughed as they watched him. Marsh lurched along into the night, singing a dirty song.

Meanwhile, at The Protest, Mort Goodman had been toying at seducing Sue Pinely. He thought she was a groovy chick; he had always had eyes for her; there was something special about her: she swung. Furthermore, it was a chance to get back at Jack Thomas. For Thomas, whom he had always considered hip, had proven himself, to the contrary, square. Thomas had laid the bread on for Goodman's hot-dog stand, but now Thomas already, unreasonably, was demanding his bread back.

Goodman was, of course, playing it cool; for he had the whole evening at his disposal, since Thomas was in bed sleeping off an overdose of estramonian tea –at this period, all the nonconformists were getting their kicks from estramonian tea. But something was going wrong; he wasn't reaching her, and The Protest, just then, wasn't the easiest place in the world to operate: there was always some cat reading poetry aloud; and Hiyo's combo made conversation difficult –Hiyo played The Protest weekends

and whenever the grockle boats landed– The Protest was listed in
all the grockle brochures as "a typical artists' cabaret":— he
made enough to live; and if he preferred to play for friends, he
was still perfectly willing to play to anyone, hangers-on, grockles,
stones; as long as he could play.

Finally, outside, Mort Goodman put it to her bluntly.

"What do you say baby? How about it?"

"How about what?"

"You and me?"

"You and me what?"

"Making the sex scene, chick. What do you think?"

"Oh, Mort! Not now!"

"Why not, baby, don't you dig me?"

"That's all men want!" she cried. "To fuck! I'm tired of fucking; that's all I've done the last five years: fuck. I'm sick of it,
man. I'm just not going to fuck any more! And that's all!"

Mort Goodman shrugged. "O.K., baby, if that's the way you
want it." He took her by the shoulders and after a pause said,
"But I got eyes for you . . . really."

Sue Pinely ceased resisting his grasp. "You mean it?"

"Sure I mean it . . . feel."

She made a sound, half coquetry, half approval.

"Gee, Mort," she said, "you have a nice prick."

"It's yours for the asking, baby. So, what d'you say?"

Sue Pinely considered the proposal.

"Crazy," she said. "But Mort. . . ?"

"Yeah?"

"First I have to get my jelly."

"The hell with the jelly, baby. Let's split."

But Sue Pinely stamped her foot. "Oh no! I'm sorry! But I
won't! Not without my jelly!"

"O.K., baby, let's get it then. You got the wheels."

Mort Goodman jumped into the driver's seat of Jack Thomas's
Pontiac, started it, and pressed the accelerator to the floor. But
rounding the statue of Francesca, at the end of the esplanade, he
misjudged the lack of adhesion of cobblestones still wet from the

afternoon rain. The car slid, out of control, to the shoulder of the road, and ran over Alain Marsh, who had not made it after all, but had sat down, intending to rest until he recovered the strength to continue. ⟨symbol⟩

The following week Pierce's book was lost.

Osborne was standing behind him in the queue –at the American Express branch where they now picked up the mail– when he received the news . . .

"Anything good?" Osborne asked –prematurely– as Pierce tore open the envelope.

"Don't know. My yo-yo publishers." He scanned the long letter quickly, and by the time Osborne had collected his own mail, was standing, staring straight ahead, smiling a set, grim –but at the same time, incredulous– smile. Wordlessly, he handed the letter to Osborne . . .

Profusely apologetic, and in great detail, Ivan Poshlust explained: at the last minute the editors had decided to include *Dragging Anchors* in their fall list, and since time was of the essence, had entrusted the manuscript –along with several others, he stressed– to a bonded messenger from the firm they habitually dealt with. This particular messenger, although known to be a heavy drinker, had nevertheless always proven trustworthy in the past.

But for reasons still a total mystery, the man had never arrived at the printers with the envelopes, had never returned to his employer's office; had apparently –at least for the present– vanished from the face of the earth. The police were investigating the case, but meanwhile, and in the event of the messenger and the manuscripts not turning up, Ivan Poshlust asked –apologizing again for the inevitable delay, and for putting Pierce to unnecessary trouble– if a duplicate manuscript could be forwarded to New York at the earliest possible date.

Osborne snorted. "Well, that's a rotten break! But it's not all *that* . . ."

He paused, noticing that Pierce had not yet made any comment

243

WE TURNED
JUNGLE
INTO A

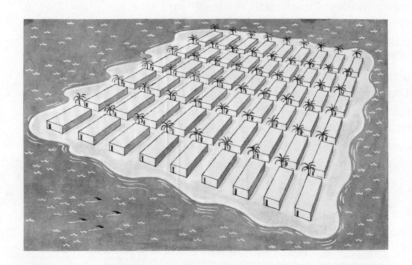

BUNGALOW
EDEN

244

Bask in sun-drenched Old-World Tranquillity with every modern comfort at your disposal. Own your own fun-galow on primitive undiscovered Escondite! Two exhilarating styles to choose from

---

AUTHENTIC SPLIT-LEVEL
CARIBBEAN BAROQUE!
SPACIOUS RANCH-TYPE
HAWAIIAN ROCOCO!
TWO BATHROOMS
THREE BEDROOMS!
GIANT 14 × 17 SALON-BANQUET ROOM!
TASTEFUL INTERIORS BY TAPETTE AND
SCHWÜLLE!

Two shopping centers; group movies; bonded baby sitters;
planned activities; round-the-clock police protection!

AND MORE! Caribbean Cabins offers a new exciting dimension in community living. All applicants are carefully screened by our staff of professional psychologists—undesirables are
weeded out . . .

And *you* move into your fun-in-the-sun-galow assured of
guaranteed friendly neighbors.

So don't wait, don't worry! Buy on the easy pay-as-you-play plan. Call! Write! Visit! Caribbean Cabins, 640 Fifth Ave., New York.

whatsoever: was still smiling his grim, set smile: and understood.

"*No!*" said Osborne.

"Yes," said Pierce.   ♛

Faced by the unmistakable, retired pensioners, otherwise-social-
square-pegs, painters with no paintings to paint, and writers lacking for words had moved –out of petty avarice, boredom, or
necessity– to take advantage of the inevitable: big homes had
been converted into resort rooming houses; little shops and kiosks
had sprung up, purveying wares to satisfy the grockle appetite for
typical souvenirs; little bars and cafés had opened, each with its
imposed motif:— The Fisherman's Hangout– nets, glass floats,
mounted barracuda, pirogue paddle; The Pirate's Den –iron-
bound chest, rum cask, rusty cutlass, candlelight; The Bistro
–checkered tablecloths, copper pots; each designed to titillate the
grockle yen for the exotic, and inspire them to relinquish holiday
dollars for elaborate, iced-rum concoctions touted as "Typical
Caribbean Punches."

But Indian summer was over . . .   ♛

Osborne finished his history.

The most striking political feature of the eighteenth century, the
conquest and expansion of the British Empire, was everywhere in
evidence. By the end of the Seven Years' War (1763) England
had conquered more territory than she could efficiently administer, but attempts to force L'Île de Joie –again won in the War of
Houel's Breach of Promise– back on France without provoking
fresh hostilities were unsuccessful, and the English resigned themselves to ownership of the notoriously unprofitable island, though
its utility as a safe deposit for excess convicts, debtors, prostitutes,
and even gentlemen of good family who, for one reason or another
had made themselves undesirable as resident citizens, provided a
measure of consolation.

Such a gentleman was Randolph Pigford, the first governor of

Escondite –now renamed Happy Island. As a public figure, over the course of thirty years, Pigford had managed to incur the dislike and derision of most of the prominent men of his age. William Pitt, Earl of Chatham, called him "A poltroon and a bungler." Johnson, working on his dictionary, considered simply entering, as a joke, "mild Pigfordism" as his definition of "Oafdom"; Goldsmith, descending to the obvious, quipped, "Better to live like a pig than a Pigford," while no less a devoted libertine and wit than John Wilkes admitted that Randolph Pigford was, "The first man to practice Vice in a manner making Virtue attractive," and he was further quoted saying, "My only fear of Hell is the certain prospect of encountering Randy Pigford there." A popular and scurrilous tavern song called "The Hag's Hosannah," ridiculing Pigford's lack of discretion in choosing his mistresses, terminates with these lines:

> If thou be one he hath not kissed yet,
> Fear not, for one too ugly ne'er existed.

Yet, oddly enough, during the brief period in which he sat in the House of Commons as member for Soughborough, the one speech he made has gone down in history.

This happened in 1739, when trade restrictions imposed upon each other by the various continental powers were causing increasing irritation that would shortly lead to war.

In the Commons, Walpole, recognizing this, and determined to avoid war if possible, was making an eloquent plea for moderation, when the young Pigford rose, and, in the opinion of the French historian, Duprés, shouted: "*Ces quelques mots; clairs, honnêtes, impolitiques, resonnant parmi la confusion et la chicanerie, et que donnerent à la politique étrangère d'Angleterre, sa définition précise et éternelle, Hélas! 'Tout pour nous! Rien pour eux! Vive le roi!'*" (These few words, clear, honest, impolitic; ringing out from the midst of subterfuge and confusion, which first gave to English Foreign Policy, its precise and eternal definition, alas! "Everything for us! Nothing for them! God save the King!")

Pigford, however, remained but a short time in politics. Having gambled away his inheritance, to escape his creditors, he fled to Ireland where he lived several years on a stipend allotted him by an elder brother. But caught cheating at cards, he was forced to flee Ireland, and sought refuge in the château of the Duc de Pigford, a distant relative in France. His attempts to seduce his hosts's thirteen-year-old daughter became public and terminated his welcome there; and several years later a scandal of a homosexual nature drove him up north again, under his brother's protection.

Exasperated, but ever loyal, his elder brother tried to justify him, pointing out that Randolph was, in fact, no worse than the majority of English gentlemen of his day, he simply had the bad luck to be always caught out in his peccadilloes.

But one day, Randolph's sister-in-law, Lady Pigford, heard a commotion about the trout stream running through manor's land, and investigating, she came upon Randolph battering a kitten to death with a rock. Profoundly embarrassed, he explained that he had tired of the kitten's forever following him about, and had resolved to drown it. But having tied the sack insecurely, the animal had escaped, and as it swam to shore, without stopping to consider, he had seized it and dispatched it in the manner witnessed by her.

This, however, was the final straw for Lady Pigford. She spoke to her husband, and when the opportunity arose to buy the governorship of Happy Island, it was taken, and Randolph sent to the New World, provided with an income as long as he stayed away from England.

Perhaps fortunately, Randolph Pigford exercised direct control over the island for only a short period. Soon after arriving he contracted a rare and agonizing venereal disease that swelled his genitals to the size of melons, incapacitating him, and keeping him bedridden and in constant pain, though it was not this malady which, at the age of sixty-eight, finally carried him off. According to the archives, he died, ". . . of a surfeit of pork, consumed while rejoicing at the demise of his brother."

Under Pigford's lieutenant, and now new governor, Marsden Udge, Happy Island experienced a measure of prosperity, although achieved, like every colony of every nation, in spite of –not because of– the policies of the mother country. And like every other colony, Happy Island had to support its garrison of soldiers, and had to contend with bewildering and intransigent restrictions, taxes and tariffs, and lists of enumerated and nonenumerated goods.

But under Udge, a severe martinet, a certain order developed. For the slaves, the relative holiday enjoyed as French property came abruptly to an end. "If they cannot be worked into shape," declared Udge, "then let them be whipped into shape." And a system was initiated whereby regularly every Sunday, after compulsory religious services, the slaves were flogged by the soldiers and the soldiers by the slaves. A rapport was soon reached by the two groups, however, and it was discovered that by surreptitiously running the lash through a palm reddened with red ocher, and simulating a hard blow, a realistic welt appeared without inflicting severe pain. But this subterfuge was discovered by Udge who requested from England, and was granted, a contingent of Prussian mercenaries to whom the performance of such duties could be safely entrusted.

However, Udge, while recognizing the value of regular corrective punishment, deplored the common and wasteful practice of beating slaves to death in fits of anger, or under the influence of alcohol. And to break the planters of this habit, he instituted a new law whereby murdering a slave was punishable by a fine of fifty pounds, a delicate point of law soon to be aired in the Admiralty and Probate Court in London.

In 1771, Nathaniel Hawley, a slaver, put into Happy Island with his ship, *Lily of the Valley*, and a cargo of prime slaves. Faced by Udge's unreasonable and exorbitant mooring fee, Hawley refused to pay. A man of rigid principle, and therefore obstinate, he would listen neither to the entreaties of planters eager to bid for the slaves –who offered him premiums sufficient to more than compensate for the mooring fee– nor to Udge's threats. By the end of the week, no agreement had been reached and meanwhile the slaves had all suffocated in the airless holds of the slaver.

Udge leveled his fine of fifty pounds per head for the willful destruction of property. Hawley refused to pay, claiming Udge's bylaw ran counter to age-old, time-tested English laws permitting the individual to dispose of his property as he saw fit. The case was brought to London where, after considerable controversy, Blackstone's comment, "Property is property, but without slaves there can be no trade, and trade is the soul of England," swung legal thinking toward Udge and decided the case against Hawley. In English colonies, at any rate, it was no longer permissible to murder one's own slaves, a measure applauded by economists everywhere, and by churchmen of various dissenting puritan sects who voiced the growing anti-slavery sentiments of their congregations. Wesley called the new law, "An important step forward in the cause of Humanity; verily, a triumph over Rome."

Meanwhile, European life was at another point of significant change. The Industrial Revolution drew near; and in England, the middle classes had been developing over a century, as a succession of enclosure laws drove the yeomanry from their freeholds, into the cities and towns where they became the basis of both a new landless proletariat, and a distinct lower middle class, intensely puritanical in spirit, and finding religious expression not only in a number of new sects such as the Quakers, Baptists, but by 1775, most dramatically by Methodism, finally organized by Wesley upon a misinterpretation of such men as William Law, Jeremy Taylor, Arminius, Richard Hooker and St. Augustine.

In France, the comparable movement had been the Jansenist attempt to provide something akin to this essentially Protestant spirit within the framework of Catholicism. But this movement, attacked violently by the Jesuits, condemned by the Pope, and persecuted by the government, provoked the equally violent Atheism of Voltaire and the Encyclopaedists, among the many irreconcilable conflicts that would finally explode in the form of the French Revolution.

At any rate, though the rise of Methodism affected most stratas of English life, the effect in the colonies was generally less remarkable and severe. Colonial society was predominantly comprised of the rich few –who regarded the new sects as forms of lunacy– and slaves; and Methodist thinking and behavior was, for many years, confined to a limited number of minor officials, shopkeepers and tradesmen.

By 1785, however, the movement had acquired impetus, and with it strong missionary proclivities. Methodist clergymen now followed in the footsteps of the Jesuits two centuries earlier, preaching dogma of a far different nature, but with a crusading spirit and sense of righteousness of equal intensity.

To Happy Island, to found a church, came Lemuel Mudd; a young divine recognized by the aging Wesley as possessed of all the qualities required by a preacher dedicated to living and spreading the gospel, the son of the man who, hearing Whitfield preach in praise of Frederick the Great during the Seven Years' War, had written in his diary, "The Lord stirred up the King of Prussia and his soldiers to pray. They kept three fast days, and spent about an hour praying and singing psalms before they engaged the enemy. O! how good it is to pray and fight!" a sentiment described by Macaulay as "exquisitely ludicrous."

Like his father, a conscientious diarist, Mudd's journals provide a detailed account of island life, both temporal and spiritual, during his stay there, and are especially interesting for the account they provide of Irrisibilism, the sect founded by Lemuel Mudd upon Happy Island, and which dominated the island during the concluding years of the century.

For old John Wesley, while approving the ardor of the young preacher, could have no inkling of the streak of doctrinal originality that would eventually lead his disciple to refine and develop his theories to such an extent that he would eventually turn upon his old mentor, and dismiss the founder of orthodox Methodism as "well-meaning but frivolous."

However, upon arriving at Happy Island, the inspiration for Irrisibilism was several years in the offing, and the task of constructing a chapel, and acquiring a congregation while strictly adhering to the rigorous daily routine of a devout Methodist life, kept Mudd too busy for original theological pursuits. He describes a characteristic day:

"I rose at four o'clock in the morning, and fell to my knees and praised God for granting this sinner yet another day in which to devote himself to His glory, and to do good. O! sinners who lie late abed, beware! Do ye not know that repose·is Evil in the eyes of the Lord! For the time ye waste in carnal slumber should be spent in singing aloud the praises of Him who made all things! How can ye think virtuous thoughts when ye lie insensible as gorged dogs? How?

"Until five o'clock I sang aloud psalms to Him, though I was interrupted in these devotions by blasphemous shouts and remonstrances from my Neighbour, N. . . . I replied to him in a gentle manner. I told him that in the ears of Jesus Christ, our Lord, it mattered not that a voice be tuneful, as long as it be lifted in His praise, and I bade N. . . . enter and fall to his knees beside me, and join me in songs of praise, but he would not do so. O Lord, have mercy upon this sinner!

"At five o'clock several serious people gathered and I led them in reading from the Bible until seven o'clock whereupon we breakfasted upon black bread and unsweetened tea. I recited: 'Whether we eat or drink, or whatsoever we do, we must do all to the glory of God.' Cor. x. 31.

"From the quarter past seven until nine o'clock there were public prayers and we beseeched God to improve us and to cast down upon us the effulgence of His light that we might see new ways to do good.

"The subject of my nine o'clock devotions was humility.

"From nine o'clock until noon I studied pious literature and I prepared my sermon for this Sunday. The subject of my sermon this Sunday will be: 'What must I do to be saved?' The collection last week was disappointing for the third successive week.

"At noon several serious people gathered, our devotions were upon the subject of Intercession, and we rejoiced upon the exceeding love which Christians bear for one another, and we discussed what good had been done since yesterday's meeting, and at one o'clock we dined upon cold mutton and boiled potatoes and bread. Praise to Him, the Provider! O! God, Thou art Good!

"At the quarter past one went to see Governor Udge to see if he had yet decided to embark upon the meritorious plan I am urging to deny to the slaves the customary rest hour after the noon meal which they idle and slumber away, and to let this time be profitably spent by virtuous people instructing them in religion, but Governor Udge still does not consider this proposal with unmitigated gladness. He said that without their rest the slaves would not be able to perform their duties with dispatch and industry, but I said that once they had true religion they would gladly work all the harder. Governor Udge promised to further consider this matter, he is a serious man, and devout, but I do not think he is a man entirely given over to God.

"Accompanied by several devout ladies, I then went to visit the poor wretches in prison, where we distributed Bibles and exhorted and encouraged them to penitence. I spoke on: 'What must I do to be saved?' but it was not well received. O! Jesus Christ, in Thy infinite mercy shed light upon these miserable and abandoned sinners.

"The subject of our three o'clock devotions was resignation to Divine pleasure.

"We then paid a call upon Miss Sharp who was dying of a consumption. She asked me what sins she had committed that God should use her so cruelly but I prayed away this spirit. I replied that we are all of us sinners and that she suffered because it was God's will that she suffer. This gave her great comfort and she died with the praise of Jesus Christ, our Lord, upon her lips. But her friend, Miss Thwaite, being present, did lament and weep most bitterly until I bade her cease, and told her that such tears were not merited for theirs had been but a merely human friendship, not founded upon religious considerations, or supported by a course of mutual prayer. But never have I seen a more comely corpse.

"At four o'clock we prayed together, after which I catechized the children taken in charge. Today was the day for instructing the female children. I expounded against the sins of the flesh and I exhorted them to relinquish wasting their time on vain prettifying and such conceits and frivolities when they should be forming little societies devoted to poverty, virginity and devotion, and though they seemed to hark my words, as soon as they departed and the door closed behind them, through the keyhole I espied them break out into laughter of an unbecoming nature, and I cried, 'O! God, in Thy good world there is yet much room for Improvement!'

"I spent from five o'clock to six o'clock on my knees in private prayer. I beseeched God to show mercy to all sinners everywhere and to grant them all salvation, each and every one be he never so lost, including my Neighbour, N. . . . who is an egregious sinner. And I prayed that this Sunday my sermon be well received. Last week the collection was disappointing.

"At six o'clock the Bible Society gathered and we were glad and praised God. We dined upon gruel and bread, and we then went to visit and comfort the poor people and to encourage them in Virtue. I told them that even if they had nothing to pay, God would forgive them. I preached on the benefits of poverty, and I told them that God must love them most prodigiously in making them so poor. The subject of my speech was: 'It is easier for a camel to go through the eye of a needle, than for a rich man to enter the kingdom of God.' Matthew 19: 22 which was well received.

"At eight o'clock we gathered again and we prayed for each other, and thus instructed and exhorted each other until ten o'clock whereupon we dispersed.

"I prayed my bedtime prayers to God on high, and as is proper for the moments before sleep I turned my thoughts upon thoughts of Death, I reflected upon its terribleness and its nearness, and I prayed that I should always be conscious of it, though I was disturbed in these devotions by shrill female laughter and drunken shouting emanating from the house of my neighbour, N. . . . a

254

most hardened sinner, and I prayed to God in his infinite mercy to shower His light down upon his soul."

For several years Mudd toiled on, enjoying a certain amount of success with the English, but his efforts on behalf of the slaves were consistently dissatisfying; though forbidden to practice the pagan form of Catholicism they had developed under the French and Spanish, they remained unenthusiastic about Mudd's substitute gospel.

Meanwhile, in his journal, Mudd dutifully recorded his triumphs, as well as his defeats, his personal struggle to improve himself, and, by 1796, the first signs of the spiritual labor pains that so often precede the birth of a new sect were beginning to manifest themselves. Mudd found himself beset by doubts, fears, and worst of all, temptations of the flesh.

"Last night, O! Lord, was that one set aside by myself and Mrs. Mudd to beget another sinner to glorify Thy name. Thou hast willed it, Most High, and we obey! But, Lord, while we were thus engaged I did feel, not lust, Lord, no, not lust, but sensations superfluous to the performance of this duty, and afterwards, O! God! I inquired of Mrs. Mudd and asked her if she had experienced such sensations and she replied to the contrary, she had experienced no sensations whatever, except the disgust natural to these occasions which she had been endeavouring to diminish by reciting psalms to herself. O! Lord, is not woman, according to wise Tertullian, but, 'a temple built over a sewer,' and yet, Lord, Thou hast made this woman, my wife, holier than I, thy devoted servant! Lord! Thou hast created me to do good on earth, canst Thou not make me be good as well?"

Everything, in Mudd's mind, seemed to conspire against him. At one point he felt compelled to keep a week of fast days after falling to his knees for his seven o'clock confessional prayers, and finding himself unable to think of any sins to confess. But from the distance, it now becomes clear that this was preparatory to, and perhaps necessary for the moment of revelation that would result in Irrisibilism.

One day, looking for solace in the correspondence he had carried on, as a young man, with John Wesley, he came across these words of advice: ". . . labour after continual seriousness, not willingly indulging yourself in any the least levity of behaviour, no, not for a moment."

Something in the passage arrested Mudd's eye. He reread it. The moment of vision had come. In his journal this amounts to some forty pages of mingled exclamatory material and complex theological argument, but its essence is this: that since man is created only to serve and to praise God, and since a devout life requires man's attention to be directed unwaveringly upon Christ upon the Cross for every moment of his wakeful existence, not only levity, but still more serious, levity's aftermath, laughter, no matter how innocent, must logically be construed as blasphemous, and a mockery of God. Lemuel Mudd had discovered a new sin.

Tried out first upon his followers on Happy Island, Mudd's revelation struck as an obvious and heaven-inspired truth. He soon organized his thinking into a treatise which, sent to leading Methodist preachers in England, created an immediate and controversial sensation. Muddianism was the talk of the town. (The name Irrisibilism was given the movement as a joke by the philologist, John Horne Tooke. After circulating through London, it eventually got back to Mudd who, thinking the word meant an inability to be provoked into laughter, adopted it for his movement, much to the delight of the fashionable circles of England.) At any rate, the Irrisibilists ardently faced up to the task of expiating a lifetime of ex-post-facto sin. Mudd counseled, "In your prayers beseech God to grant you Divine knowledge and permit you to remember each and every instance wherein the Devil possessed your soul and you did laugh, and repent thereof most solemnly." He advised, "When you find yourself in company engaged in making mirth, you should first gently reprove them and remonstrate with them, and explain to them the grave sin they are committing, and urge them to cease and repent forthwith, but if they cease not and continue sinning, then you should remove your-self from their company and retire to some private place where you should pray for their souls."

Mudd, practicing what he preached, dutifully recalled, de-scribed, and did penance for –in the form of prayers and fast days– every remembered lapse into the new sin. But to his chagrin, on rare occasions, he found himself still prey to temptation. "O! Lord, Almighty who knoweth all, cast down Thy light upon this most depraved and miserable of sinners. Today I laughed. I went out into the schoolyard to see if the boys were instructing each other in religion as they had been ordered to do, but they were not doing so. O! Lord, they are incorrigible and pernicious young pagans, and they were hurling taunts at Solomon, the humpbacked Jew peddler, and, Lord, unprepared as I was for the sight of such merry pranks, I laughed. I flogged the boys and proscribed for them one fast day, for myself, two. Lord, I beg Thee: make me strong!"

Finally, however, his ceaseless efforts met with success. "Lord, long have I prayed and earnestly, and now I believe, yes, I believe that Thou hast favoured me and turned upon me the Divine radi-ance of Thy countenance. For today, Lord, as I set out to visit the poor wretches in prison, I encountered Miss Emily, the daughter of the Colonel, along the way, and the Devil was in her, Lord, she would tempt me from holy gravity, and as her slave walking be-side her carried a basket of eggs, so Miss Emily took to removing these eggs and commenced in breaking them over the head of the aforesaid slave, and, Lord, though in my former sin and error I do declare this would have provoked my mirth, so fortified Thou me in righteousness that I did not laugh, no, nor even smile, for the smile is to laughter as the lewd thought to fornication. Lord, Thou hast made me Irrisible!"

And total irrisibility finally put an end to the last vestiges of lingering doubts and fears. "Last night, merciful God, was one devoted to the begetting of another sinner to raise his name in praise of Thee, and while carrying out Thy will, Mrs. Mudd and I chanted in unison the Angel's Hymn and we terminated our duty with perfect dispassion, Lord, feeling nothing but tremendous love for Thee."

Unshakable in his faith, Lemuel Mudd now exercised growing influence over life on Happy Island. He converted the new governor, George Grout, to Irrisibilism, and so dominated him, that the governor took his advice on all temporal matters in order to further those spiritual. The taverns now closed on Sunday, and at eleven o'clock in the evenings on weekdays, and if prohibitive taxes levied upon alcohol and tobacco made little difference to the rich planters, they became formidably expensive sins when practiced by the lower classes. The bordellos closed, as did the theaters, ballroom, cockpits and other diversions. "O! Lord, why hast Thou forsaken me? My endeavours to show the true light to my neighbour, N. . . . have come to naught. For he would not share in the augmenting godliness and piety of this community, and yesterday he left, heaping imprecations upon my head, and though I fell to my knees and prayed for him, I fear he will yet burn in the deepest regions of Hell, for he is the most hardened, unregenerate, abandoned and miserable sinner that ever I have seen."

With the slaves, however, Mudd's efforts continued to be unsatisfactory, and in his enthusiasm to reform and convert, he failed to take notice of a rapidly changing situation.

Though the Napoleonic wars preoccupied most of Europe at this time, apart from the fighting, a humanitarian anti-slavery, or at least, anti-slave trade movement was gaining considerable ground, particularly championed in England where it had been discovered that importing voluntary labor from India at a penny a day was cheaper than maintaining slaves.

Meanwhile, among the slaves themselves, resentment was building. And coupled to the knowledge that with Europe embroiled in war, troops could be ill-spared for the suppression of uprisings, the slaves began to make demands and drive them to some sort of favorable conclusion. In 1797, the Maroons had revolted in Jamaica, and defended themselves so successfully in the mountainous and inaccessible jungles that the English were forced to grant them autonomy. In Haiti, hostility was mounting as replies from the new revolutionary democratic government to slave requests for freedom revealed to them that they were considered ineligible for *"Liberté, Égalité, Fraternité."* And on Happy Island the slaves endured religious instruction during rest periods, and exorbitant liquor and tobacco taxes with growing impatience, until at last Lemuel Mudd took a step which, if not directly inciting rebellion, at least created the state of mind conducive to it.

Mudd's efforts to make the slaves practice chastity except for the strict purpose of reproduction were perhaps the least fruitful of his reforms, and he therefore convinced the governor that, since the practice of this basic tenet of Irrisibilism was a prerequisite to salvation, should the slaves remain adamant, in their own interests, they should be compelled to conform, and the men and women locked up separately at night.

Not long after this unpopular measure went into effect, Mudd, as was his custom, was attending the regular Sunday floggings. "Myself and several of the serious ladies were exhorting and encouraging the slaves, and I was preaching to them from the Wisdom of Solomon: 'The souls of the righteous are in the hands of God, and there shall no torment touch them.' 3:1. And also I told them: 'Having been a little chastised, they shall be greatly rewarded.' *ibid*:3:5, when without provocation the slave, most assuredly a gross sinner, did turn and himself seize the lash and began applying it with great vigour upon the person of the unfortunate German who had been doing his duty with praiseworthy diligence and industry. Perceiving this I cried, 'Cease, villain! Hast thou forgotten the teaching of the devout Law? Dost thou not know, "A slave can only live unto God in one particular way, that is by religious patience and submission in his state of slavery."' But upon hearing these remonstrances, and not dissuaded from his error, the slave relented from the German and began berating myself in a grievous fashion, whereupon other slaves undergoing chastisement and those awaiting it, perceiving these events taking place, did similarly turn upon their masters and raised a great hue and cry. In vain were the entreaties of myself and other Chris-

259

tians; the rebellious blackamoors listened not, nay, scoffed when we told them that this disturbance was sinful in the eyes of great and glorious God, and that if they did not soon repent and do penance they would be denied entrance into the blessed Kingdom of Heaven.

"O! Lord, Thou hast not this day chosen to favour Happy Island with the radiance of Thy countenance! The unruly disorder spread like a daemon steed lashed on by the Devil himslf. The planters and gentry being surprised while engaged in idleness or debauch were seized and apprehended and all of us bound like common felons and clapped in gaol, and by nightfall the traitors were everywhere victorious and many lay slain and drenched in gore upon the ground, sinners and devout people alike. O! fateful day! O! day most unpleasant!

"In gaol I made a speech to hearten and cheer us in our pitiful condition. The subject of my speech was: 'The Lord gave, and the Lord hath taken away; blessed be the name of the Lord.' Job: 1:21.

"Meanwhile, outside, our oppressors rioted in drunkenness and debauch and committed sins upon the persons of the wives and daughters of the English. Sins, O! too horrible to depict! Although I must confess that even while engaged in excesses the slaves did still maintain such traces of religion and fear of Hell as not to defile the good ladies of the Bible society. These poor souls were flung pell-mell into gaol intermingled with the men despite their earnest entreaties to be placed in a separate cell commensurable to the preservation of modesty.

"All night we sang psalms in praise and glory of all-merciful God, and we prayed for deliverance, and in the morning, the Lord in his infinite goodness saw fit to answer our prayers, for he softened the hearts of the blackguards and sinners who had so ill-treated us and made them repent of their deeds, for they did not put us to torture and death as we feared and anticipated. No, albeit it with abundant kicks and curses, we were led into three slave schooners which happened then to be lying at anchor. O! foul and stinking vessels they were, unfit to transport Christians!

And our women were returned to us although steeped in great carnality, and we were suffered to depart for England or wheresoever we chose, although leaving all our possessions behind.

"As we set sail, I stood on the deck and replied to the jeers and taunts of the victors with an earnest speech, exhorting them to repent and to mend their evil ways. The subject of my speech was: 'What must I do to be saved?' "

The journey to England and Lemuel Mudd's subsequent adventures are perhaps of interest, but irrelevant to the history of Escondite. It is sufficient to record that he lived until 1864, having seen Irrisibilism triumph in most of England and America, and much of Europe as well, and he died at the age of one hundred and three, according to a witness, ". . . in full possession of his faculties, in a rapture of gravity, chanting the Song of Solomon."

The return of the refugees to England caused considerable consternation. If a few slaves on a territory as tiny and insignificant as Happy Island were able to successfully rebel, the future of larger and more valuable possessions was in grave jeopardy as well. The Treaty of Amiens had provided but a brief respite in the long war; Napoleon was marching through Europe; England was the only power capable of raising an army qualified to oppose him, and no troops were available to avenge the Caribbean defeat. The previous uprising on Jamaica and the explosive situation in Haiti made the entire colonial situation an ominous one, and Parliament, although in session, could come to no decision since the month being February, most of the members were scattered about the land fox hunting.

Eventually, however, an ingenious solution –originally credited to a jest of Samuel Rogers, but never verified– was decided upon. But to operate successfully this measure required the cooperation of other colonial powers and accordingly, couriers sped to Holland, Spain and France. The former two gave immediate assent; the latter pondered, weighing the satisfaction of English humiliation against the strong probability of inciting trouble in her own colonies. Finally the prospect of security won out; France accepted the English proposal, and in an unprecedented fit of unan-

261

imous international pique, Isla Alegre, Blijdschaps Eiland, El Escondite, L'Île de Joie, Happy Island was stricken from the maps.

Though obliterated from official thought, the memory of the island naturally lingered on, as did the persistent rumor that Henry Morgan's lost treasure lay buried there. But the few adventurers seeking to land were beaten off by the determined ex-slaves; and Jean Lafitte, searching for a Caribbean stronghold in 1808 was equally unsuccessful. By the end of the Napoleonic Wars in 1815, the island was virtually forgotten, and whatever few individuals may have toyed with the idea of reclaiming it, their plans must have been abandoned in view of the expense and arduousness of recovering a bit of land that only for short periods and at rare intervals had ever shown a profit.

Just one passing incident marks the otherwise-undisturbed tranquillity of Escondite.

Throughout the 1850's a soldier of fortune named William Walker played an active part in Central American and Caribbean history. An American who foresaw the passing of abolition laws, it was Walker's scheme to seize power in one or several Central American countries, set them up as slave states, and after the inevitable occurred, sit back and reap the profits.

Initially supported by money donated by Cornelius Vanderbilt –interested not so much in Walker's plans, as in finding an easy and cheap method of transporting his passengers from Atlantic to Pacific en route to California for the Gold Rush– Walker and his band of fellow adventurers succeeded in 1858, in conquering Nicaragua. But sickness, dissension among the ranks and lack of popular support lost the country to him within a year.

Undismayed, Walker went north to gather fresh recruits and backing; but while in power, his refusal to take orders and his high-handed manner of dealing with Vanderbilt had not only lost his support from this quarter, but gained him the enmity of the railroad magnate who used his considerable influence and soon had the United States Navy alerted and searching for Walker with a warrant for his arrest.

Walker succeeded in eluding the navy for the time being, but with a force insufficient to carry out his grander scheme, he was forced to seek a compromise.

Traveling through Mexico he had been made aware of the forgotten Escondite. And he now determined to visit the island, conquer it if possible and perhaps by filing a legal claim under the protection of his friend, Lorenzo Pardo, dictator of the island Republic of San Sabado, be able to set up in miniature a working version of his original enterprise.

Accordingly a small ship was fitted out. And heavily armed, the force set out for Escondite. Expecting sharp resistance, they were agreeably surprised to encounter a curious but not unfriendly welcome. Two generations had passed since the slave revolt, only a few ancient men remembered firsthand the former injustices they had suffered, and to the majority their old servitude was an item of folklore and legend.

Recognizing his advantageous position, Walker gave orders for his men not to disabuse the hospitality. Under the incredulous eyes of the natives, they spent a week ostensibly digging for treasure, but actually canvassing the defenses of the Island, taking stock of its potential as a slave state.

Lorenzo Pardo approved of the scheme. A claim to the island was prepared, duplicate to the one Walker had left behind in the trunk with his notebooks and belongings, and Walker, with his crew, prepared to sail back to Escondite, intending to land as the advance party, and later give the secret and prearranged signal for the propitious moment of attack.

However, a few miles from the San Sabado shore, the United States Navy finally caught up with Walker, captured him, and jailed him. He died in jail soon after.

Lorenzo Pardo, fearing the opprobrium of the United States and the action which might result should his alliance with Walker be disclosed, refrained from pursuing on his own, the joint plan they had worked out, leaving the island of Escondite in peace for a century, the principle events of which are common knowledge.

His *History of the Island of Escondite* complete, Osborne went to Ed Robles for erudite counsel.

Robles had several comments. He first asked Osborne what he thought of Watney Whitbread-Charrington, and when Osborne replied that the man was obviously a lunatic, Robles informed him of the well-known fact that Thomas Carlyle often referred to Whitbread-Charrington as the second-greatest mind and stylist of his age. But apart from style he pointed out that Watney Whitbread-Charrington erred blatantly calling Cromwell the harbinger of the characteristic insipidity and paucity of English cuisine: the Lord Protector had been a hearty eater, if the Puritans had one outstanding vice it was gluttony, "They weren't impious enough to make it tasty," Robles said, "but they sure ate with both feet in the trough."

Secondly, he felt Osborne had given a rather skimpy picture of island life during the first half of the eighteenth century, and to Osborne's explanation –that nothing much interesting happened– he replied that as far as scholars were concerned, this did not constitute an excuse.

Thirdly, admitting its irrelevance, he wondered why Osborne hadn't at least touched upon the peculiarly squalid scandal in the court of Frederick William that had touched off the War of Houel's Breach of Promise.

"Christ, Ed, I'm no prig," Osborne told him, "but I couldn't put *that* in."

Robles considered. "No, I guess you couldn't," he agreed: and he congratulated Osborne for having produced a lucid, and to the layman at any rate, perhaps instructive account of this quite unremarkable, but hitherto neglected bit of Western history. ҉

Big business now moved in; displacing, overwhelming and overshadowing the small-fry enterprises. And the boom, once underway, received additional impetus when steam shovels excavating for the foundations of the Buccaneer-Mortmain unearthed the lost treasure trove of *La Trinidad* –the ship, laden with the richest prizes of the city, that had eluded Henry Morgan at the sack of Panama, and subsequently vanished without a trace– and the island of Escondite splashed across the pages of the international press. 🐦

At daybreak now, the broken and docile esplanade lay silent; myna birds now argued their endless sophistries in the dwindling jungles of the sierra; though occasionally a lone parrot might pass, alight on the tin roof of SOUVENIRS   NATIVE ARTWORK, or ORANGE PUNCH   COOL DRINKS, cackle briefly at one of its own jokes, and vanish in a whirr of green; and there was a lull now between night and day . . .

Few were aware: Osborne knew –who had once so much enjoyed the smooth transition of night sounds into day sounds. But now, after the dance bands had packed in their instruments, and the canned calypso stopped, a city silence fell upon the town, punctuated perhaps by a drunken grockle's laugh, or the squish and rumble of an automobile over the cobbles, and hotels hummed monotonous air-conditioned hums.

Still, it was silence; and Osborne rose early:— out of habit, for there were no fish left to catch in the dredged-out bay, and the game had long since been hunted from the hills . . .

Sometimes he just wandered, past the town limits, out along Billion Dollar Beach:— "The adventure goes on and on," wrote Roscoe Drekberg in the *Times*, "and the horizon is not yet in sight." Past Murrain and Mandible's twin projects; the completed luxury Murrain Internationale –where he might be rewarded, now and then, with the whistle and shriek of some bird whose name he had never learned, gay and anomalous from the eunuch shrubbery of the hotel garden– and the rising, economy-budgeted Mandible Arms; past the penny arcade, and the Waffle-orama, the jai alai courts, the dog track, the miniature golf course, and the incipient amusement park; out to where construction was merely implied upon huge billboards promising this or that hotel or cooperative apartment; sometimes he even went as far as the spot that he knew had served Jonathan and Janine for so much high-noon trysting. A new beach restaurant stood there now. And before. It a sign stuck in the sand said:

NO
Dogs
Fires
Picknicking
Spearfishing
Changing Clothes
Unseemly Behavior
Transistor Jammers

In the distance, the glass towers of the colossal Buccaneer Mortmain pierced the horizon . . .

Or his amble might take him inland, tracking the gaudy anabasis of Caribbean Cabins . . .

But at other times, a morbid teratological interest made him first stop before the store front of The Island Improvement Committee, to see what the latest plans were; and on these mornings he just sat in one of the shanty cafés, that had mushroomed out of orange crates amid the equipment sheds, travel agencies, and souvenir stands on the periphery of the newly finished harbor. Here he might enjoy an hour of solitude, and –beyond the drab cement-and-steel-laden freighters, the gleaming grockle liners, and the rakish hydrofoil ferries that now whisked passengers from the mainland in two hours– watch the sun slip out of the east and shake sequins over the blue stippled sea . . . but soon the construction workers came: loose-jointed Jamaicans talking their lilting argot; Puerto Ricans firing machine-gun Spanish at each other; all of them imported for the boom. There would be a raucous half hour, an unhurried exodus, a short silence.

Whistles blew. Big cranes and Caterpillars farted and snorted awake. Jackhammers and riveting guns vied, overwhelming all but the loudest of foremen, awakening, briefly, the grockles from their all-included sleep: morning began on Escondite. ☙

"This isn't cream, this is milk," said Mrs. Ella Weinberg. "I ordered coffee with cream and you brought me milk."

The bellboy made a practiced servile gesture. "I am sorry, m'om. The hotel is out of cream for the moment."

"Well, I won't drink my coffee with milk," said Mrs. Ella Weinberg. "Not at fifty dollars a day, I think they have some nerve. Serving coffee with milk at fifty dollars a day."

"But m'om," the bellboy explained. "It is not the fault of the hotel. It is the island that is out of cream. Until the next boat."

Mrs. Ella Weinberg drew tight her pink silk dressing gown –over her pink silk peignoir. (He had been *look*ing at her. Of course they all did.)

"Well," she said, "all I can say is that you can take that coffee right back. I won't drink my coffee with milk."

"Yes, m'om."

"And you can tell them," she said, at the starched departing back, "that maybe their other people will drink coffee with milk, but that Mrs. Weinberg will not. Not at fifty dollars a day."

The door tocked shut with the comfortable tock of a luxury door, and Mrs. Ella Weinberg turned on her husband. "Can you imagine that," she said. "They wouldn't dare serve you coffee with milk at the Fountainebleau, or the Eden Roc."

Saul Weinberg looked up from the stock market quotations of three days ago. "But, dear, if it's the island that's out of cream . . ."

"Then all I can say is that it's no way to run an island. I think I'll complain to the tourist bureau, that's what I think I'll do. There must be someone around here who's responsible." Mrs. Ella Weinberg reached for the telephone. Outside a brace of jackhammers erupted into noise. "And I can't stand that racket," she said, slamming it back in its cradle. "You pay fifty dollars a day for some peace and quiet and it's worse than New York."

But Saul Weinberg, leaning back, blew contemplative smoke at the ceiling –from the morning's first Monte Cristo. "You know," he said, "I could have had a piece of this place two years ago. Dirt cheap."

"Luxury hotel!" said Mrs. Ella Weinberg. "All I can say is that you practically kill yourself every time you go into the bathroom at night and have to find the light switch."

"And if you ask me," she said, "I think that bellboy was extremely rude."

Steve Seley, after all this time, finally wrote Ed Robles. He had finished his book (comprehensible, perhaps, to five hundred people in the world), he had borrowed some money, he was coming to Escondite to write the next one . . .

Robles cabled back: DONT COME ISLAND SHOT DETAILS FOLLOW as:

nouveau-riche garment czars with auriverous wives; glossy lawyers with sleek dim blondes; epicene dentists and henpecked chiropodists; indistinct factory managers, branch chiefs, personnel men; inarticulate majors and their drink-fuddled squaws; whooping Moose and Rotarians from states known only to geography students; bumptious lairds of boondock shoe stores; rock-jawed male models and their reedy catamites; intense, nubile Jewesses burning to give their hymens to a Negro; rasping viragos from fashion magazines; simpering newlyweds, popinjay collegians; martini-addled account executives and their Kodachrome families; monolithic club-women tasseted in Lastex; copywriters a.w.o.l. from their analysts; bleached Bronx trulls in plastic shoes; Iowa schoolteachers with peeling arms; huge, red, bovine engineers; waddling ministers grown fat as their flocks; scientists, doctors, bankers, accountants:— armed with cameras, flashing credit cards, blazing trails with crumpled, lipstick-smeared balls of Kleenex —:the janizaries of The American Way of Life descended upon Escondite.

It was no longer safe for children and dogs to play in streets.

And Germans came.

OSBORNE'S ARMY!

WHEN, ON THE DAY BEFORE HE PLANNED TO LEAVE, AMOS OS-borne conceived the idea for his army, it seemed remarkable chiefly because it had not occurred –to him or to anyone else– much earlier.

There had been any number of precise and palpable moments that could have (and should have!) inspired such an idea. But they had not: not when Victor Veritas's crowd arrived, not when Kurt Kummer introduced money, not when the S.S. *Simon J. Grockle* first anchored outside the bay, not when the bars and restaurants began opening, nor when the boom began in earnest, not even when his mother had been crushed to death in the debacle at the opening of the supermarket . . .

She had insisted upon going, above Osborne's objections. "Well, I *know* it's silly, Amos," she had argued, "but I just want to see. And besides, they're giving orchids away, and we haven't had orchids since they cut the jungle down." So she had gone.

But in the architect's office, someone had made one of those inexplicable blunders that elude detection up to the last moment: the ingenious labyrinth of inflow and outflow aisles –calculated to shepherd shoppers past the maximum possible percentage of enticing merchandise– had gone awry on the drawing boards, one of the inflow aisles failed to make contact with its necessary outflow counterpart, a cul-de-sac resulted, that went unnoticed in the rush to open for the season; and at the inauguration of the immense store, as increasing numbers of people thronged in, egress from this exit-less aisle became increasingly difficult, and finally, impossible. Before the management could realize that the augmenting noise and confusion was incited, not, as they thought, by happy customers venting aloud their enthusiasm for the store, but by a fatal architectural flaw, the pinned and breathless shoppers panicked, their screams touched off store-wide pandemonium, and in the ensuing stampede, four women were trampled to death, Mrs. Osborne among them.

. . . no, reflecting: in his grief and rage, the idea for the army could hardly have been expected to occur. But provoked, as it was, by Jonathan Klein's chance and irrelevant wisecrack, it seemed particularly remarkable that the idea hadn't struck some one of them, some other time or another in the past . . .

They had been picking their way along the packed beach –himself, Delia, Jonathan, with little Albert cavorting ahead– when Jonathan suddenly stopped, pointed –at a group of grockles lying on the sand, bright red and bellies sunward– and cracked gloomily, "See, Darwin had it wrong; what he meant was 'Survival of the Fattest.' "

And in that instant, not only the concept of his army formed, but its structure, strategy, and tactics.

. . . although he still believed that each man had the right, and perhaps the duty, to run or ruin his life to suit himself; although he still believed that each man had the right, and perhaps the duty, to think his own thoughts; he still believed in that Great Auk: Human Dignity . . . and said:

"Why don't we boot these grockles off our island?"

"Sure! What-ho! Four billion of them . . ." Jonathan retorted, assuming –adeptly– Colonel Blimp accent, "against four of us!"

Which was true: only the two of them, Ed Robles and Mal Katona, out of their old colony, remained . . .

When the Island Improvement Committee had been formed:— by the joint efforts of leading businessmen who had had to learn by experience that the internecine boundary disputes and incessant quarrels over precedence on the tax-free and restrictionless island, resulted in advantage to no one, and were actually impeding them all in the quest for profit—: Ed Robles had taken rare (for him!) wise measures. Recognizing the autocratic commercial authority with which the Committee would invest itself, and wield, Robles –before the bulldozers of Caribbean Cabins had razed the jungle to his front door– had filed a territorial claim, subsequently approved on the condition that one day a week, the doors of his typical old plantation house be thrown open to the public. Though the Committee members were unable to understand Robles's refusal to serve as guide in his own house –and collect the tips as well– the revenue from this weekly visit, combined with money made selling surplus fruits, vegetables and poultry produced by his little farm, enabled him to remain; to complete the book of poetry, real poetry, that had occupied him since his arrival.

And Katona? Katona. managed . . .

But the others –excepting those with a gimmick or an angle– had gone; the few genuine artists, the Tree See-ers, Victor's crowd, the English pensioners, the homosexuals and lesbians, the second-rate playboys, and those who knew that no one wins a rat race: one by one, all those who had been unwilling, or unable, to join –and who, therefore, had been beaten– had gone: (to the disappointment of the Island Improvement Committee). They had not cherished this new role of living grockle bait; and they had gone . . .

But now, not yet too late! Osborne conceived of his army. He ignored Jonathan's rejoinder, and speaking slowly, outlined the plan that had come to him, pristine in its simplicity: and infallible.

He required two dozen men, no more, perhaps less, and for that he needed only time: to summon those whom he knew he could trust. They would come –and quickly: for they had gone, disgusted and disheartened; having to carry their Escondite within them wherever they went. Yet, oddly enough, solvent . . .

Alain Marsh's posthumous exposition had been an unprecedented success. The recognition –that he would have basked in, but had been too proud to seek– had come. Within months museums had bid the price of his biggest canvases up to twenty thousand dollars. Magazines now reproduced in color those joyous out-size prodigies proclaiming: Yea, at zenith. Marsh had hit the big time . . .

And on Escondite, over the years, that flood tide of paint had overflowed: drawings, aquarelles, gouaches, collages, small oils, even big ones, covered the walls of his friends' houses. They sold as many as they had to –Marsh, they knew, would have been sorry to see it, but would (of all people *he* would) have understood –and they had gone.

Ed Robles's single bright blue eye blazed. Even Mal Katona slipped off his mask of invincible sang-froid, though the thought that first struck Osborne now struck them: Why hadn't anyone thought of it before? Could it be? that anarchic and unique as each one considered himself, they had all, nevertheless, reached the shameful stage where they not only accepted, but expected to be kicked around by the brummagem society they disavowed and derided?

. . . no matter: there was time, ample time, for that sort of self-scrutiny.

But not now:

now was the time to summon Osborne's army;

to call home from the diaspora those few butt-ends of the Renaissance; to rally to arms this one last little band of *les enfants perdus*; and to fight this one possible last-ditch rear-guard action, in defense of a routed and dissolving civilization that had, in fact, never existed –outside the minds of some few chosen men: greater no doubt, but still, something akin to themselves.　　**W**

Not one failed to respond.

One by one Osborne's army arrived, eager to get under way, and chortling for having used enemy facilities to get there in a hurry: Del Pierce, then Keith Cooper, Stefan Verduin, Jan van Gent, Tony Vale, Ole Isserstedt, Dr. Chaim Sulzberger –looking ridiculous holding a pistol, but who said, tossing both palms congenitally outward, "When I pull the trigger, poff! so silly I no longer look!"– Hiyo, Janine, and finally Freddy Rosoff, who waddled off the ferry beaming, and winking an (under)wordly eye at Osborne, asked: "You got guns?"

Osborne had. Though his scheme, if successful, would proceed without bloodshed, a show of arms was imperative. While waiting for his troops, he and Robles had gone to Campeche. Grimes asked no questions, supplied them with pistols, half a dozen old 30–40 Craigs and 303 Springfields, and a few grease guns, B.A.R.'s, and 30-caliber machine guns just in case, and tried to sell them planes. He could get his hands on Martin Marauders, a steal at fifteen grand each. But they had no need for planes.

In crates plainly labeled ELECTRIC TOOTHBRUSHES FRAGILE the arms and ammunition were loaded in broad daylight.

"You sure you don't need no planes?" Grimes asked, as they cast loose.

"No planes, sorry Grimes."

"O.K., then. Good luck. See you." 🐾

They took target practice:— just in case, at sea to avoid detection. Pierce sobered up and started doing push-ups. Just in case. And they were ready. 🐾

Early in the morning, on Grockle Day at Ed Robles's plantation house, they lay armed and concealed in the stand of jungle before it. The grocklebus arrived . . . Ed Robles, hushed but annoyed, said, "Damn it to hell!" He had just remembered: that he had forgotten to write to Steve Seley: to ask him to obey this one single draft that did not deserve dodging . . . through the foliage they watched grockles debouch, and led by Eli Rapp, file into the house.

Five minutes later they followed. With weapons drawn, they encountered the group in the ballroom.

Eli Rapp said, "Hey, Amos! What's the idea?"

Grockles emitted involuntary cries of outrage and astonishment.

Osborne shouted: "Quiet!" and leveled his revolver.

He said: "This is a revolution. No one will be hurt if orders are obeyed. All tourists are to leave this island, this group here will serve as hostages until transportation can be arranged . . ."

A fresh burst of indignation drowned him out. He fired a shot into the ceiling. A shower of dust and plaster fell –in silence– over the grockles.

"This is not a joke," continued Osborne, "but I promise you that if orders are obeyed, no one will be harmed in any way. You will be treated well, and you will leave the island with your money and possessions intact. But you will leave it. You will now, please, follow me. No questions will be answered so there is no need to ask any . . ."

But Mrs. Doris Bonhom was pointing; her one crimson-tipped moral finger aquiver: "Jonathan!" she cried. "Jonathan Klein!"

"Well, I'll be damned!"

Osborne's army paused . . .

"So! That's what's become of you! You're a revolutionary! That's what I always told Janice; I always told her you were unstable! Well, I can tell you one thing; I won't *stand* for this!"

Jonathan Klein smiled one of the very few genuine smiles of his life. Slowly he raised his pistol until it was aimed directly at her navel.

"Mrs. Bonhom," he said, "Shut. Up."

Events now proceeded with the swiftness and smoothness Osborne had envisioned. The hostages were driven to the Murrain Internationale, the situation was explained to the hotel management, the hotel commandeered, and the hostages placed under guard in the dining room. The hotel detectives and private policemen caught unawares, surrendered their weapons. And it remained merely to communicate the news of the revolution about the island.

The hotel's public address system now stopped piping Christmas carols out to bathers on the beach, and informed them of their change of status. Stefan Verduin, Jan van Gent, Theodore and the two Horaces appeared, fully armed, to convince them that it was, indeed, no practical joke. The sound truck employed by the Island Improvement Committee to bruit about beauty contests, fashion shows, and bingo nights, now toured proclaiming the revolution, instructing motorists and pedestrians to return at once to their hotels and houses and prepare to leave. The mimeograph machine formerly devoted to a weekly sheet called "Island Fun" turned out posters listing the steps that must be taken to ensure safe and speedy departure.

Keeping order was their chief concern. Dispersed about the

island as the army was, its limited size had to remain conjecture. They were armed and the enemy was not. But a riot would have resulted inescapably in violence, and Osborne –despite the knowledge that whatever might be the political future of the island, it, in no way, depended upon either the presence or the absence of bloodshed– nevertheless hoped to avoid it (some of the others wouldn't have minded mowing down a few grockles though).

Travel agencies wired the news to shipping lines. Ships sped to Escondite to evacuate the population. Construction workers received a week's advance pay, and carried out the task of transporting and loading the luggage, household effects, shop inventories, the machinery from the amusement park, everything movable of value. Except: construction equipment . . .   ▓

The coup made news:

¡Guerra en el paràìso!

ISLAND IN REVOLT!

Coup militaire rompt
la paix du paradis touristique

Kapitän Osborne:
Alle Feriengänger 'raus!

MORE CARIBBEAN
HEADACHES
FOR UNCLE SAM

OSBORNE'S ULTIMATUM

LOT VAN GIJZELAARS BLIJFT
ONZEKER TOT
VERTREK TOERISTEN

but Osborne's policy provoked an immediate journalistic outcry:

NEWSMEN NIX ON ESCONDITE!

OSBORNE REFUSE D'EXPLIQUER SES MOTIFS

NO ARBITRATION: HOSTAGES HELD UNTIL ISLAND EMPTIED

Schicksal Escondites Gefangene (7 Deutsche und 51 Menschen) noch in der Wage

¡OSBORNE NO QUIERE TESTIGOS!

OFFICIAL SPOKESMAN: SITUATION "UNCLEAR"

Meanwhile, in the evenings, initiates in a new Fehmic Court –dedicated to at least some of the principles of the old– sat at tribunal: to preserve the public peace; and to try, and mete out justice, to those found guilty of –not treason: heresy. Kurt Kummer . . . went:

Playwright opposes one-party Osborne govt.: exiled!

BANISHED PLAYWRIGHT ONE OF ISLAND'S EARLIEST RESIDENTS

OSBORNE LUTTE CONTRE L'INTELLECTUALISME

¡NO! A LA INTELIGENCIA

Hvorfor forvise en stakkers forfatter

Victor Veritas . . . went. Tom Barry: with a ninety-foot yacht in the harbor, his instigation of Caribbean Cabins was unjustified and unnecessary: heresy . . . went. The Liberals: the discount appliance-store chain owned by Liberal Don's father provided them with an income; with which he wrote, she painted; the island branch opened by them was: heresy . . . went:

Ex-ban-the-bomber banned

Un miembro del club de los amigos de la paz mundial expulsado

NEWSMEN STILL DENIED ENTRY

Eli Rapp: short of returning to Grocklization, grockle-herding in some form or another was his only means of livelihood . . . stayed. Eddie Davidson: if he was willing to operate a rooming house to remain –to write plays upon such topics as capital punishment (con) and racial integration (pro)– it was perhaps misguided, not heretical . . . stayed. Rhea Hammacher: there was no objection to her position as Madam; having chosen the profession she had no other choice:— in the huge bloom of her youth she had been hard put to bestow her favors; she could hardly be expected,

at a fissured and mountainous forty, to profitably peddle them
—:but the wham-bam-thankyou-ma'am establishment she ran
was an insult to honest lust; the price of drinks soared in season;
clients too addled to notice were short-changed; and those who, in
the old days –out of pity– had treated her civilly received no
preferential treatment . . . after considerable controversy: heresy
. . . went. And so forth:

La Professeur Bannie:
Osborne monstre misogyne!

Vigilante Law on Escondite

EX-TEACHER EXILED

LA PROFESORA HAMMACHER,
CATÓLICA, EXPULSADA

PRIME MINISTER:
OSBORNE'S LEGAL
SYSTEM UNDEMOCRATIC

Gesetzloser
Militärgerichtsterror
auf Escondite

The natives posed another problem. Theodore, the two Horaces, a few others, were on the army's side. There were several who began to weary of working eight hours a day in the NATIVE VILLAGE, at typical trades they had never before practiced; but the majority were still enchanted by the Age of the Magic Midget Box. And it *was* their island . . . "and America belongs to the Indians," observed Mal Katona.

A compromise was reached: since a visit to America was their most cherished dream; they would ask –and undoubtedly be granted– asylum, they would be given the opportunity to realize their dreams . . . "and when they wake up they can all come back!" said Jonathan Klein:

OSBORNE SEEN
WHITE SUPREMACIST!

LES INDIGENES
ANTI-OSBORNISTES
BANNIS

ESCONDITE HOU
VAN SWARTES NIE,
SEL BAJE STRENG
APARTHEIT KRIJ

GEORGIA'S LEE OPPOSES NATIVE ASYLUM

Manuel Zonda:
Sin sangre, no hay revolución

MALERISCHE EINGEBORENE
AUS IHRER HEIMAT GESTOSSEN

INGEN PLATS FÖR FARGADE:
ESCONDITE EN ANNAN ALABAMA?

РАСОВАЯ ДИСКРИМИНАЦИЯ В ИМПЕРИАЛИСТИУЕСКОМ ПРАЗДНИУНОМ РАЕ: РОДНЫЕ НАСИЛЬСТВЕННО ВЫТЕСНЯННЫЕ

The S.S. *Simon J. Grockle* now sailed from the harbor on her final
shuttle, carrying the last of her eponyms:

COUP SUCCESS: ISLAND EMPTY

QUESTION MYSTERIEUSE:
POURQUOI PERMET-ON
AUX OUVRIERS DE
CONSTRUCTION DE
RESTER A ESCONDITE?

the last of the shopkeepers, hotel personnel, and parking-lot attendants:

HUNDREDS JOBLESS!

Construction workers stay: why?

LUXUSHOTEL BETRIEBSFÜHRERARBEIT FRÜCHTE VERLOREN

the last of the gigolos, balloon vendors, and travel agents:

MORTMAIN ITALIAN DANCE ESCORTS GO!

Tanz-Partner
unerwünscht
erklart worden

Osborne: Barbare ou Puritain?
Jeunes hommes
de compagnie
chassés
d'Escondite

287

the last of the natives off to see the land of the rolling armadillos; the freed hostages; and the last of those upon whom fehmic justice had descended:

AT LAST! OSBORNE TO MEET PRESS

Die Schleier des Geheimnises aufgehoben: Osborne empfängt die Presse

HOSTAGES CHARGE CRUELTY: OSBORNE REFUSED CHRISTMAS CARD DELIVERY

ELAINE SCHWARTZ, ISLAND HOSTAGE: OSBORNE "CUTE"

EL CAPITAN OSBORNI TRIUNF

288

The news came out. The Western press reacted in the anticipated fashion:

Rebels to Destroy Island

KOLONEL OSBORNE PRIVATUNTERNEHMUNGSFREIHEITSFEIND

OSBORNE FREE ENTERPRISE FOE!

Osborne to spend personal $\frac{1}{2}$ million to raze $\frac{1}{2}$ billion

but how long would it be? Before the destruction workers could blow up, tear down, carry away, and dispose of the hotels and apartment houses; the cabarets, jai alai courts, cinemas, and equipment sheds. . . ?

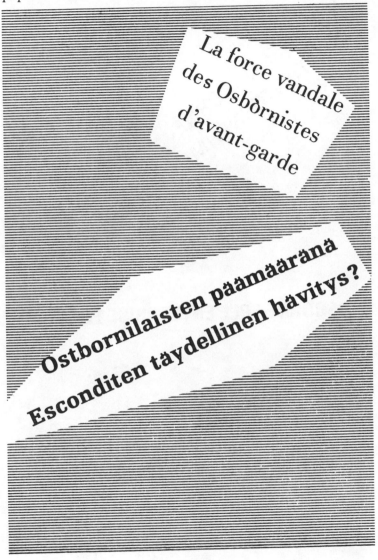

before the latanier palm and ceiba tree again grew on the site of
the Waffle-orama and the U-Needa-Hotdog. . . ?

OSBORNES OPSTAND:
NOZEMS TEGEN
BESCHAVING

BEAGLE HITS REVOLT:
"ILLEGAL, IMMORAL,
INHUMAN"

before the charred rectangular mementoes of Caribbean Cabins
grew green again and vanished. . . ?

ISLAND UPRISING DEEMED
OUTRAGE BY LONDON FINANCIERS

before the fraternal and benevolent sea silted over with sand the debris-filled harbor, and coral again grew and fish swam in their rightful dominion. . . ?

LA CAMARILLÁ
DE OSBORNE
DESTRUYERA
TREINTA MIL MILLIONES
DE PTS.

**Svensk finans
inte inblandat!**

how long before savanna covered over the demolished airstrip, and the wild horses again stood, rippling in the morning light, in cool, high, dew-heavy verdure. . . ?

BEATNIKS
TO SACK
ISLAND

PARADISE

However, the Western world now had to contend –as had been anticipated– with Communist interference:

ОСЪОРН
ПРИТЕСНЯННЫЙ
КАПИТАЛИСТИУЕС-
КИМИ ЪЮРОК-
РАТАМИ; ИЩЕТ
ПОМОЩЬ   С С С Р

Reds offer tanks,
aid for missile-tracking station

OSBORNE FEARED
KREMLIN-CONTROLLED

MESSAGE DE
M. LE PRÉSIDENT
À WASHINGTON:
"N'IRRITEZ PAS MOSCOU!"

ROBLES, SEQUAZ DE OSBORNE, ERA COMUNISTA

Official spokesman:
situation "BECOMING ALARMING"

¿ESCONDITE EIN ZWEITES BERLIN?

Meanwhile, in exile, the Island Improvement Committee concluded that the motives behind the coup were not political, but commercial:

I.I.C. offers Penthouse, Yacht, Cadillac, 50 G's: Island Ransom

Offer made to buy out Rebels

Offre Refusee!

unable to believe that a price for the island did not exist, the ante was raised:

Deux belles vedettes amèliorent le compensation de l'I.I.C.: elles s'offrent elles-memes!

CHURCHMEN DEPLORE LATEST ISLAND OFFER

VALE, FATHER OF OSBORNE ADMIRAL, CUTS HIM FROM WILL

295

higher and higher:

I.I.C. Angebot:

eine Million D.M.

until Osborne, at last, was goaded into an impolitic communiqué:

OSBORNE WORLD LAUGHINGSTOCK:
REJECTS OFFER   SAYS
"WHAT'S ALL THE FUSS ABOUT?
IT'S JUST MONEY."

OSBORNE REFUSE
L'ARGENT :
"MAIS CE NE SONT
QUE DES DOLLARS!"

TERWIJL FINANCIELE WERELD WANKELT DRIJFT
OSBORNE SPOT MET GELD

OSBORNILLA EI
RAHANTARVETTA!

Norske
Finanseksperter
forstor ingenting
mer!

OSBORNE EIN
HALBSTARKER
GELDVERNEINER!

SHOOTING TOO
GOOD FOR REBELS:
MORTMAIN
SPOKESMAN

OSBORNE
CALLED "NAIVE"
IN HOUSE OF COMMONS

But the main objective was to force a deadlock between East and West:

OSBORNE PONDERS RED OFFER

L'INFLUENCE COMMUNISTE GAGNE A ESCONDITE

REBELS DEMAND U.S. RECOGNITION: PRICE TO SPURN RED AID

GANGSTERS OSBORNISTAS AMIGOS DE RUSIA

Moose oppose recognition

ISRAEL CENSURES KLEIN, OSBORNE AIDE: "DISGRACE TO JEWRY"

OFFICIAL SPOKESMAN: SITUATION "GRAVE"

though Ed Robles, inadvertently, almost gave the game away. He had been discussing the latest developments with Mal Katona; so intently that he failed to notice one of the wire service reporters take a seat to his blind side; and before Katona could signal him, he had blurted it out.

"For the time being, we've got the island out of the hands of the lunatics," he said, "now, how the devil do we keep it from falling *in*to the hands of the barbarians . . ."

"Can I quote you on that, Mr. Robles?"

Ed Robles started, then turned with –he had not spent years becoming disillusioned, for nothing– perfect composure.

"I beg your pardon?"

"You called the Commies "barbarians." Can I quote that?"

"Me?" said Robles, incredulously. "Me? Call the Communists barbarians?"

"You said you didn't want the island falling into the hands of red barbarians."

"Ba*v*arians, I said! I said our policy was to be anti-Bavarian! Strongly anti-Bavarian! Certainly you can quote me."

"You think we want the place full of huns?" Katona chimed in.

"I don't get it."

"Look," said Robles, his voice rising unnaturally, "I lost this eye fighting fascism, you understand? And do you know who the worst of all the fascists were? The Ba*v*arians! I said we've got to keep this island out of the hands of the Bavarians! At all costs."

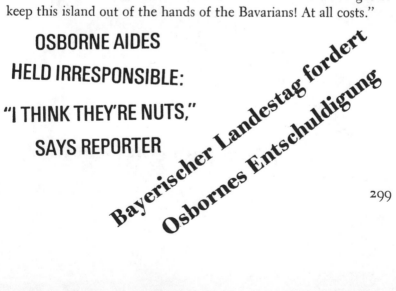

OSBORNE AIDES
HELD IRRESPONSIBLE:
"I THINK THEY'RE NUTS,"
SAYS REPORTER

Bayerischer Landestag fordert
Osbornes Entschuldigung

Though world governments grew impatient as Osborne remained on the fence:

LORD GOOSEBERRY: OSBORNE CONFOUNDED TROUBLEMAKER

Sen. McEwen: Osborne "Pink Anarchist"

Ou restent les sympathies politiques Osbornières?

Vad än Osborne ar Sverige holler sig neutral

Welchem Ismus gehört Feldmarshal Osborne an?

¿Qué pasa con Osborne?

300

Osborne, in fact, would not have satisfied them, had he been willing: he didn't know the name of his system, if it had one. Finally he asked Robles, who told him: "Actually, we're a timocracy:— in the Platonic sense. But there's no point in trying to explain *that* to them."

BLACK BUDDHISTS CALL

"HIYO" DANBY, OSBORNE HENCHMAN:

"UNCLE TOM-IST"

100 G'S TNT TO ESCONDITE

Hotel boom-boom planned

Osborne Adamant

Official spokesman: situation "CRUCIAL"

And, presents failing:

I.I.C. DEMANDS FORCE

GEWALT SOLL JETZT DEM
VANDALISMUS ANTWORTEN!

**U.S. POLL SHOWS
AVERAGE CITIZEN
IN FAVOR OF
INTERVENTION**

MARINES ALERTED

however:

FINNS DET INGA ANDRA·MÖJLIGHETER?

SMALL NATIONS PROTEST INTERVENTION

Washington fears stepped up Asian red activity

LOS E.E.U.U. NO PODRÁN SALVAR ESCONDITE SIN LA AIRADA PROTESTA DE LOS PAISES COMUNISTICOS

State Dept. weighs voiding rebel passports

Rebels Blacklisted from Hilton Hotels

Washington decides:
reprisal, no!—but no recognition

REDS FOLLOW U.S. LEAD— WASH HANDS OF ESCONDITE

HET!

Island to remain No-Man's Land

The stalemate had been accomplished. Though, from the one quarter where sympathy, extending as far as recognition, had been hoped for:

Grossherzogtum Luxemburg kämpft gegen Anerkennung Escondite

LUXEMBOURG DEFEND SON DROIT DE MINISCULITÉ

KLEINSTE BENELUX-PARTNER IN VERZET TEGEN ERKENNING ESCONDITE

Monaco demands à être reconnu en precedence d'Escondite.

LUXEMBOURG ANTAA VASTALAUSEENSA

Lilla Luxembourg börjar kampen

LUXEMBURGO TEME EL RECONOCIMIENTO MUNDIAL DE ESCONDITE

Luxembourg opposes Escondite recognition

In an impassioned address before the General Assembly, the Luxembourg delegate charged that by recognizing upstart Escondite, the United Nations would deprive its law-abiding, long-time member, Luxembourg, of its *raison d'être*. He pictured eloquently the prospect of an entire populace dejected and dispirited by no longer being members of the world's smallest country. Other small nations concurred, each unwilling to be set one notch back in the order of minuteness . . .

But they had long since become accustomed to going unrecognized . . . ⟡

No one ever found out who did it –Kurt Kummer was odds-on favorite, but any one of them might have (would have) done it, had the thought occurred. Someone remembered that century-old claim, made by the adventurer, William Walker, in conjunction with Lorenzo Pardo –then dictator of the Republic of San Sabado– in order to make the island of Escondite a slave state; and duly recorded in his *History of the Island of Escondite* by Amos Osborne.

Whoever it was that remembered –for all had read the History– informed Mantis Mortmain, Mantis Mortmain informed his friend, Alfonso Pie de Cerdo, present dictator of the Republic of San Sabado. The San Sabado archives produced a duplicate claim, and Mantis Mortmain had no need to urge his friend into taking steps requisite to winning over to their side those desirable nine-tenths of the law . . .

Osborne offers to draw straws, but dissent is unanimous: it is his privilege, his alone.

Grinning he turns a thumb up.

The army shouts: "No!"

Grinning he turns a thumb down.

The army shouts: "Yes!!"

He pushes home the plunger, a thousand pocks of fire flare in the night sky, explosion booms leisurely behind . . . there is a seismic jolt . . . a transfixed pause . . . and slowly, symmetrically, hyperbolically –like a ham actor playing Caesar– the Buccaneer Mortmain thunders to the ground.

The party lasts almost till dawn; and dawn is breaking by the time Pierce reels up the maze of ramps and stairways leading to his house –he had passed out momentarily at "Rosoff's Rest," the ledge that had offered them, in the old days (and would in the new!) respite, as tipsily aiding, guiding and impeding each other, they performed the nightly stumble home from Theodore's.

Leaning out to close the shutters he shakes his head –gin clouds refuse to disperse– he rubs already bloodshot eyes (pink elephants, O.K.; hobgoblins, giant bugs, Hamlet's father's ghost, O.K.: but just what: in the fuck: is this?).

Silhouetted against the glaucous overture to a perfect Caribbean day, a line of destroyers blockades the bay, troop transports loom behind, and blue water is churning white: the landing craft are already halfway to shore.

Del Pierce chuckles to himself; "One if by land, and two if by sea. One if by land, and two if by . . ."

He is sober.

He thuds (not that sober) heavily against the door. Rosoff's house closest. But out of the way.

Jonathan's! And Jonathan runs like a whippet.

Crashing into walls, he lumbers down the tortuous route to town: bursts into Jonathan's, pounds on the bedroom door, shouting: "Jonathan! Get the fuck up! Invasion! Wake the others! I'm going to Theodore's!" repeats it, and is off.

(Even *he* has never been in such a hurry to get to a bar!)

The guns and ammunition are cached there; the landing boats a hundred yards from shore as he makes it (where the hell are the rest of those finks?).

Jonathan Klein bolts awake, reaches . . . (Oh NO!!) He broke his glasses at the party. He had waited, in agony, for the moment: "Will you come back to me, Janine?"

"Oh, *oui!* Jonathan, *chéri!*" she said, and her kiss dislodged his

306

glasses. Jan van Gent trampled them underfoot dancing by . . .

He pushes her out of bed. "You wake Mal's side of town, I'll wake Jan's!"

(What should she wear?) she slips last night's jubilee dress over nothing; zipping his fly he aims at the blurred and shifting doorway: is out (bare-eyed!) in spinning morning: she at his heels . . .

To Jan van Gent's! sprinting: over queasy and transitory cobbles, phantom buildings loom undulate recede: running, looking through refracting planes of air (gap of light means street) . . . there! hooks left, legs churning, fights for balance (pavement pitching) almost runs into glass window of (yes, must be) supermarket. Wrong street, Jan's on other side (of what used to be Plaza Real –shops and alleys now. Retrace? No. Find cooperative alley!) sprints right, alley halts so does he: doesn't recognize: nose to shopwindow . . . behind glass dim clothes slowly pavan: high above his head (can –just– read big E in) LENNIE BERNKOPF THE HOLIDAY HABERDASHER (brother of Bernkopf button man?) not-even-alley-but-slice-between-buildings turns left, turns right, angles right (toward esplanade? away?) backsides of shops restaurants (slice *must* intersect bigger alley, street) dodging crates: enchanted garbage cans sprout: slice bends left, narrows, barely shoulder width: stops: at big red door: locked . . .

(What the hell was taking them so long?) soldiers leap from the landing barges into waist-deep water, advance to shore under protective fire, Pierce fumbles with a belt of 30-caliber bullets.

Invaders fan over the beach, advancing steadily, shooting (where the *fuck* were they?).

Retraces along slice (has to get his licks in! a métier at last? *Sancta Maria.*) in direction of gunfire (beach must be that way.)

In hotel rooms, construction workers dive beneath their beds.

(Don't fire until you see the whites of their eyes, Grrrrrr!) rifle bullets thud into the thick walls of Theodore's bar: through the open door, past him (!) concealed behind: the mirror goes in back . . .

zeroed in, some of them, flanks defile into town: he'll get a few though: gentleman only fights for lost causes (who said that? wished he had but he hadn't: 'd have to ask Ed Robles,) right in the sight now one he *knows!* Impossible! He could swear he knows him . . . Pedro! Little Pedro behind Fénix bar in Valparaiso, could be his brother: peers through the sight again, spit and image of Pedro.

He says aloud, "Ah, the hell with it." He turns his back on the advancing enemy, goes behind the bar, and pours himself (Borges. Borges said a gentleman only fights for lost causes: what good was a dead gentleman? he could think of better ways) his first big tumbler full of morning gin.

Gunfire closer: if he can backtrack, go the other way, if he doesn't get lost again: somehow get to the B.A.R. . . .

he turns the corner and they are there: he throws up his hands and lets the enemy come to him:— gray, woolly, faceless creatures, indeterminate in number, approaching –that much he can see– but from a distance impossible to ascertain. (*Ora pro nobis!*)

One by one, Osborne's army is apprehended and captured, as, befogged and hungover, they make the belated attempt to reach the arsenal. Dr. Chaim Sulzberger, puffing around a blank wall, runs smack into a squad of them, is gunned down by a startled sergeant who has been taught: think later. And Amos Osborne, roused from deep cucumber sleep, encounters the enemy at his front door. Like the others, unarmed and defenseless, he has no choice but surrender.

EXEQUIES

THE WORLD

ESCONDITE

Blotch of World Trouble

Broke, this sun-drenched December morning, by machine-gun fire and the crackle of snipers' bullets, was the silence of rebel-held tourist-haven Escondite (rhymes with S. Cohen, he say). Up the beach, under non-smoking, teetotaling General Pie de Cerdo, stormed San Sabado freedom-fighters, expecting hot resistance from solidly entrenched defenders.

But caught napping was Amos Osborne*'s rebel army. After a night of vandalism and debauchery (in ruins sprawled $30,000,000 luxury Buccaneer Mortmain Hotel) abed lay the exhausted troops. And almost bloodlessly (only casualty: shot resisting arrest, rebel sawbones Sulzberger) this strife-torn blotch of world trouble passed back into the responsible hands of Democracy.

Shining Example. Not long ago, this tiny (pop. approx. 460) drowsy tropical island lay forgotten, a backwater in the march of progress. Illiteracy rate was 100%, and potbellied kids squatted in the overgrown streets and alleyways. Natives fleeing Osborne's one-party rule report that three years ago per capita income was $35 a

ment Committee) hotels mushroomed magically on long, (11 mi.) sandy Billion Dollar Beach, and jobless natives now discovered an eager market for their handicrafts. Justly beamed I.I.C.'s brown-haired, fun-loving Irving Mandible: "We have created another Miami. The committee is a shining example of how individual business interests can all pull together in a pinch and get the ball rolling. The Commies would like to build their own Escondite, all right, but it's pretty obvious to the world that they haven't done it yet."

Rabble Without a Cause. Determined to take over and destroy this peaceful, prosperous tourist Mecca was beetling, (6' 2½") burly, (227 lbs.) bearded, (brown, curly) Amos Osborne and his ragged band of followers; but uncertain as yet are his motives. Insists he: "We wanted to make the place fit to live in." But this cuts little ice; a cold look at the stark facts reveals another picture.

U.S. State Department officials probe into Osborne's past for Red affiliations, but Moscow flatly denies them. Claims *Izvestia*: Osborne is the ploy in a Western conspiracy to discredit Communism. Peking styles Osborne, "another megalomaniac Caribbean dictator;" while, voicing African sentiment, towering (6' 10") left-leaning Vrumian chief, M'gu, calls Osborne a White-supremacist Capitalist Imperialist.

But certain it is that the rebels' cock's crow of victory ends in the death rattle of defeat; and tropical paradise Escondite returns to normal, and again beckons the overworked businessman to fun-and-sun it ($30 per day for two, average hotel bite) and give a well-deserved rest to his work-weary bones.

SAN FULANO

Glimmer of Hope

Cheered through the streets of tidy, progressive-minded San Fulano, in triumph rode barrel-chested pro-U.S. President, Manuel Zonda. At last, for this diminutive, (22,560 sq. mi.) rich but coup-conscious country there shone a glimmer of hope. The statistics revealed the heartwarming news. A burgeoning economy increases at 15% to 20% a year; a growing wave of tourists last year shelled out $50,000,000 on San Fulano serapes and sombreros; exports rose 40% to $73,000,000; the nimio stood firm at 48 to the dollar, as bank assets, under the watchful eye of youthful, Harvard-degreed (Ph.D.'s in Metafinance, Theo-Economy) Eduardo Marrano, doubled over his three-year tenure.

year: before that, lower still.

A thriving art colony improved conditions, but not until prestigious Simon J. Grockle line tacked Escondite onto its cruise itinerary, were the full benefits of the twentieth century felt. Under the benevolent eye of the I.I.C. (Island Improve-

* No kin to Akron Steel's Fred Osborne.

Which of these descriptions fits? No one knows as yet. But the truth, undoubtedly, lies somewhere in between.

Legal Pundits Ponder. Meanwhile, in grim San Sabado prison, awaiting the hand of justice, lies ex-USIA underling Osborne and his henchmen, among them: left-hand man, ex-Red Robles; draft-dodgers Pierce and Klein; turncoat chieftain Theodore; beatniks Cooper and Katona and –for that little something sextra– slim, trim, (34-21-35) camp-follower Janine Lindeman.

But who will try Osborne? Legal pundits ponder, as, in anguished conferences, U.S. and San Sabado officials dispute the right to call the tune. Says U.S. spokesman Mellikan (rhymes with pelican): U.S. citizen Osborne must face charges, ranging from entering a foreign armed service (maximum penalty: deportation, loss of voting rights) to willful disregard of the public interest, and disturbance of the peace. Strongman Pie de Cerdo disagrees, says Osborne is guilty of high treason, should stand before San Sabado firing squad.

Interviewed by on-the-spot reporter Hrucicz, jolly, pear-shaped (246 lbs.) Jack Mellikan looked stern. Admitted he: "It's a rankling problem. We're groping toward a middle-road solution, but one thing is certain; whoever gets him is going to take a tough line. It's been a little bit too much to swallow, and no one's going to take it sitting down."

All's Well That Ends Well. What lies in store for Osborne's army? Only time will tell. The final chapter has yet to be written.

Confident Expectations. U.S. State Department officials confidently expect family-man Zonda to keep his promises. Firmly in power four years after his military uprising unseated inept, hard-drinking Luis Borracho, Zonda now promises free elections in the coming year, or, if that proves im-

A Note About the Author

John Anthony West was born in New York City in 1932. He received his B.S. degree in Economics from Lehigh University. For the past nine years he has lived mostly on the island of Ibiza, and has now moved to London. He is the author of *Call Out the Malicia*, a collection of short stories published by Dutton in 1963.